LARA PRODAN

THE THIN THREAD OF DESTINY

Novel

Lara Prodan
Novel: **The Thin Thread of Destiny**
Accent Graphics Communications, Montreal, 2014.

ISBN : 978-1-77192-057-5
320 c.
© 2014 Lara Prodan

Chapter 1

The morning of Saturday, 7th September 2005, seemed to be a bad omen. The low heavy clouds were about to come forth with rain. The yellow leaves whirled in the air around the trees as the wind picked up speed. The past few days were quite chilly, but today was so cold and dank that you had to wear coats and jackets, for which it was still pretty early. Alex appeared in the yard, dressed in his tracksuit, ready for his daily workout. For the past twenty years, Alex always started his day with a physical workout. Not only did it cheer him up, but he also sincerely believed that it would help him escape the oncoming senility. He not only feared it because it was in human nature, he was mainly afraid of not fulfilling the promises he had made a long, long time ago – twenty years ago.

The other day, Alex turned fifty-five – an indicative age for a man. At this age, many begin to sum up their personal and creative life, re-examine their actions, and plan the next 40-50 years of their lives. But many are convinced that they have been, and are still leading a proper life. These are usually the average workers, average husbands, and average lovers, who think that the whole world revolves around them. They believe that everyone owes them something: the employers must provide them with a good salary, their wives and children must be implicitly obedient, and their lovers must kiss them just because they have them. Generally, men that fall into this category don't think about their future and only concern themselves with the present.

Alex falls into the first category. His whole life he aimed to be honest with himself, as well as the world around him, which is a quality that he inherited. Alex was the great grandson of one of the Ukhtomsky Dukes. His father told him that his great grandfather had been forced to move his family out of Russia in 1918 as he feared that the Bolsheviks, the new Russian power, would pursue and arrest him. Two of his brothers refused to leave. He never knew what happened to them in the far away Russia. In the early 1940'"s, Alex's great grandfather, and later on, his grandfather, tried to find out the fate of their relatives, through the Embassy of the Soviet Union, but they never got a reply. Honesty, adherence to principles and, at the same time, marvelous generosity, were Alex's distinctive character traits. He was quite a tall and lean man for his age. And he had the right facial characteristics. His blue eyes were always openly and sincerely directed at the person he was talking to. His high forehead, with slightly high temples, indicated that his mind was strong and sharp. His dark blonde hair already bore the stamp of old age, it was white at the temples, and one could notice a few white strands amongst the thick hair at the crown of his head. Amazingly, he had plump cherry red lips, like a young woman, which his wife, Melinda, really liked.

Alex was born and raised here, in the North-West of the United States. He always considered his beautiful and cozy city of Everett to be the best place on Earth. He was born here, he was raised here, and this was where he returned after getting a degree at Harvard. He became a lawyer and got married to his Melinda. Unlike Alex, Melinda wasn't tall, and she was a bit chubby for her age; she was fifty. Her eyes were grey with a slight shade of bluish-green, the so-called "chameleon eyes". They always changed color, depending on the color of clothes she was wearing. Her hair was light and shortly cut, which made her look like a boy. Regardless of her chubbiness, Melinda looked like a swift and active young woman. Her smile almost never left her face. This smile, which seemed to light up everything around her, is what Alex, in his time, fell in love with her for.

The minute Alex entered his house after his morning run, he heard his wife's troubled scream. She was screaming their daughter's name, as if she had lost her.

"Darya! Darya! Oh my god! Darya!!!" she screamed.

Alex ran, almost sprinting, to his daughter's bedroom, which was on the second floor. His wife, with her arms crossed at her chest and tears in her eyes, stood in the middle of the room and stared at the bed. Darya's bed was empty and, as always, carefully done. There was no sign that Darya had spent the night home.

The clouds finally came forth with a heavy, sharp rain. He felt heaviness in his chest. Alex had a grating sensation around his heart, and had a feeling he was about to fall. No, nothing bad should happen to his precious daughter. Darya was twenty, and she was a self-reliant, reasonable and serious girl. She never took any hasty decisions, without having thoroughly thought them through. She inherited this from her father. Suddenly Alex remembered that, five years ago, when Darya was fifteen, she had fallen in love with her classmate. In order to grab his attention, Darya ran away from home and went missing for a few days. As it was later discovered, she had gone to live with her auntie, Melinda's sister, in Belleview. The boy still paid no attention to her, and didn't even notice she was gone. The parents raised a commotion and alerted the police along with the school teachers. After that incident, Darya promised she would never leave home, without warning her parents first. And now...

"Maybe I should call Roger. Perhaps he knows something," thought Alex, as he walked towards the phone.

Roger was Alex's closest friend. They were friends ever since they were in diapers. Their mothers were friends and, practically, gave birth to their sons at the same time. Roger's son was almost the same age as Darya. Michael and she were friends, and it was likely that he knew where Darya was. But Alex never reached the phone. The entrance door was suddenly opened wide, and three happy young people, all wet to the skin, walked in.

"Dad, dad, daddy I am so sorry that I never warned you. Where is mum? Mum, my beloved mummy, please don't be mad at your stupid daughter!" shouted, or more like – sang, Darya.

She was shining with youth, mindlessness and happiness. It was impossible to be mad at her or be offended by her. She was a tall lean girl, with big blue eyes on her pale mat skin, slightly snub nose and her fine delineated cherry red lips. Her blonde hair was tied up in a ponytail and her high forehead was framed by her grown-out fringe. It felt like she had a warm and trusting relationship with her parents, which should, basically, exist between people who love and respect each other.

"Well, Darya, honey, thank God you are okay," Alex uttered quietly. His heart still ached. The young men still stood at the door. They were the same age as Darya. One of them was Roger's son, Michael. The other one was unknown to Alex, but judging from the way he was talking to Michael while Darya was talking to her parents, it seemed that they all knew each other well.

"Mum, dad, meet Vladimir Zlotov. He is Michael's friend. They are both undergoing training at Microsoft," Darya introduced the young man. His heart still ached. Alex looked at the young man, and shrugged. He lowered his eyes and observed him more thoroughly. His heart ached even more.

"Impossible! No, it can't be!" Alex thought to himself, as he slowly turned his head toward Melinda.

Melinda stood at a distance from the guys; her gaze was directed at Vladimir. Her face was frozen with horror, and, at the same time, the bitterness of loss. She quickly came to and slowly looked at her daughter, inviting them to have breakfast altogether. The young people didn't notice anything. They walked into the dining room where the breakfast table was already set.

Alex walked up to Melinda, held her hands, lovingly looked into her eyes, and asked, "did you also think that the young man looked like…" he never finished his sentence.

His daughter walked up to them, holding Vladimir's hand.

"Mum, dad, why you are standing here? We're waiting for you in the dining room. We're so hungry!" said Darya cheerfully.

"Alex, Melinda, I am so happy to be in your house. Darya and Michael told me so much about you. I am sorry that I came here uninvited…" Vladimir's voice was slow and ambient. It was obvious that he was nervous and wanted to make a good impression…

It was impossible for someone not to like him. His body was tall and well-built, which people normally describe as "broad as a barrel". He had thick ash grey hair with a neat parting at the side, a high prominent forehead, wide open eyes, and lips that seemed to be carefully delineated with a sharp pencil. There is no way that a young man like that couldn't grab attention and arouse aesthetic admiration. Alex and Melinda shifted their gazes from Darya to Vladimir, from Vladimir to Darya. Their eyes reflected their sense of alarm, as well as love. Melinda was the first one to come back to.

"Indeed, I'm so hungry. Let's go sit at the table," and they disappeared behind the dining room doors.

The breakfast went unconstrained and easy. Alex and Melinda tried to listen rather than talk. To be honest, they couldn't really talk. They were both worried after meeting their daughter's new friend. At least Darya wouldn't stop talking. Her voice rang like a bell. She sat in between the two guys, and it was obvious that she was nervous too. After the breakfast was finished, everyone stood up from the table. The rain had finished and the tree leaves began to play around with their fresh red-yellow-green colors. The grass freshened up, returning its bright green color. The roads and pavements became cleaner, as if the cleaning brigade had passed by. Freshness was in the air. Darya saw her friends to the door and returned to the living room, where her parents had some questions for her to answer.

"Mum, dad, it's so good to be home! Oh, how I love having breakfast and dinner all together! Please don't be mad at me. I called you last night to tell you that I was going to spend the night at Michael's. Uncle Roger called you too, dad. But no one answered the phone," jabbered Darya, looking at her parents with love, realizing how much they were worried.

Alex remembered that the day before, Melinda's headaches came back. She suffered from migraines most of her life. None of the medical institutions could explain what caused the migraines. They couldn't cure them either. Gradually, Melinda got used to the headaches and even learned to ignore them. But the night before, she couldn't handle it and so she asked Alex to turn off any electrical appliances that rumbled, hissed and rang. As a result, the mobile and home phones were turned off, too. They went to bed early, without waiting for their daughter to get back from university.

"Okay, Darya. But tell us, why did you spend the night at Michael's? And why at Michael's per se? Spending the night at young man's place, even if he is your best friend, is considered inappropriate. Or am I just old-fashioned, Darya?" Alex's voice gradually lost its softness and turned hard as steel.

Whenever Alex was worried or alarmed, he became cold and tense deep inside. On the outside, this could be seen through his extremely upright posture, and his voice, which change from soft to hard and cold. Darya knew this distinctive part of her father's character and instantly realized that he was alarmed.

"Mum also seems kind of lost," Darya thought to herself.

"Mum, dad, it's not like something bad happened. I'm alright. Dad, you know that Michael is like a brother to me, we grew up together. Uncle Roger and Aunt Rosie were home too. Honestly, we were calling all night and we wanted to tell you, but no one answered the phones," uttered Darya, worried.

She felt sorry for her parents. Suddenly, she clearly understood their pain and concern for her. Apart for the five year old incident, when she had been stupid enough to run away to her auntie in Belleview, she spent every single night in her bed. She valued the hours she spent with her parents in the evenings. The three of them loved to gather in the cozy living room and discuss the events of the day. They had no secrets from each other. Suddenly, she heard her father's voice, which staggered her. He asked a simple, almost trivial, question.

"Darya, tell us, who is this young man, your new friend, Vladimir?"

But he asked the question in a voice which was hard as steel, yet delicate as a thing string of silk, and it seemed like that string would tear any second now. She sensed her father's fear and terror. She was shocked by this.

"He probably didn't like Vladimir. Dad was pretty cold when he talked with him at breakfast. And mum was so quiet, yet she always loves to talk to my friends," thought Darya.

Alex and Melinda were looking at their daughter, nervous and concerned, awaiting a response.

"Vladimir is Michael's new friend," Darya began to explain. "He is from Russia, Saint Petersburg, I think. He came here for training at Microsoft. By the way, dad, he got an invitation from the company's management. Vladimir sent them his new development for the enhancement of some program, or something like that. It was considered to be the best one they were offered. You didn't like him, did you?" Darya's voice sounded offended. "He is the best guy I ever met," Darya uttered quietly.

Alex and Melinda exchanged looks. They loved their daughter more than anything, and they valued and trusted her opinions. They knew that now, more than ever, they had to be very careful with her. At her age, any resistance might be greeted with stubbornness, and a friend can easily turn into foe. And anyway, it is mere guesswork and they might be completely wrong about Vladimir.

"Everything is okay, Darya, honey. We really liked Vladimir; he is an interesting young man. He and Michael have something in common," Melinda responded with a soft, yet deep, voice.

This voice was so full of love and care that Darya calmed down and told them about how she had spent the previous day. After university, she met up with Michael and Vladimir. They decided to show Vladimir how Seattle looks at night. Then, all together, they went to Michael's place to watch a movie which Vladimir had brought with him. It was a movie about his motherland, Russia. The movie was long, so Michael's parents offered Vladimir and Darya to spend the night at their place. And today, Darya promised Vladimir to meet up at five o'clock.

"And what about Michael?" asked Melinda. "Are you going to meet up all together? Michael is your best friend and he introduced you to Vladimir. Moreover, you know he is attracted to you. Roget says that Michael writes poems for you at night, and burns them in the morning. So romantic!" She smiled and her eyes sparkled. "You have to respect his feelings. You will never find a more devoted friend. Also, I think that it's inappropriate for a young girl to go on a date with a young man she met the day before. Your father and I," here, Melinda gave a significant look at Alex, "think it's best that you invite Michael tonight as well," she went silent for a moment and then asked, "So, honey, will you invite Michael?"

Darya stood, undecided. Her mother sounded convincing. Yes, Michael was the best, most attentive and most devoted friend in the world. They'd known each other since they were in diapers, but she never saw him as her potential boyfriend. Moreover, she always considered him her brother and she trusted him with her deepest secrets.

"I think mum is wrong about Michael. We are friends, really close friends, and we are like brother and sister. That's it. Inviting him on a date with Vladimir? Hmmm..." Darya thought to herself.

"Okay, mum. Maybe you're right," said Darya out loud. "I will call Michael and tell him where to meet us. I'll also ask him to find out how Vladimir feels about me. I really liked Vladimir, but he is a bit shy, I think. I felt he was a bit uncomfortable here today, and he was quite tense. And you, dad, you weren't very welcoming when you talked with him in the morning. You were looking at him as if you feared something.

Concerned, Alex looked at Melinda. After a moment of silence, he told their daughter that he and Melinda were simply upset due to Darya's disappearance at night.

"What if Michael picks you up, and takes you to Seattle, where Vladimir will be waiting for you?" Melinda said out loud, signaling an end to the unpleasant conversation. "I think Michael will only be happy to accept your invitation. And your father and I will be calm as well," Melinda added quietly.

"Okay, mum," agreed Darya, so as not to upset her parents. Then she thought to herself, "Perhaps, I really should go with Michael. We could talk about Vladimir on the way there. I wonder if Vladimir said anything about me to Michael."

When Darya went to her room, Alex and Melinda sighed with relief, looked in each other's eyes, smiled, and decided not to take any action yet. Let everything run its normal course. Time will sort everything.

Chapter 2

A whole month passed. It was now October. Almost all the leaves had fallen off the trees, and lay curled up in a brownish yellow pile on the ground. The sky was now covered in low, gray clouds more often, and it rained almost daily.

As always, Alex went on his morning runs, had breakfast with Melinda and Darya, and left to work. Alex was a co-owner of a major legal firm based in Everett. He loved his job. Moreover, he was considered the most experienced and qualified lawyer in the city. He consulted people from all over the state. Melinda was very proud of him and almost considered him a legal god, thus leading Alex into a bashful state. Melinda, herself, hadn't worked for the past ten years due to the never-ending headaches that made her suffer. Ten years ago, when the ambulance took Melinda to the hospital from her workplace, it was decided at a family council that Melinda should quit work. The amazing thing was that even though the headaches never stopped, they became rarer. Melinda would wake up early in the morning and go to the backyard. There, she carried out her "ritual", which she believed gave her strength for the rest of the day. Alex and Darya were afraid to ask what this "ritual" consisted of, and they never watched her do it.

"If it helps her, let her do it. We won't bother her," they decided.

Having gained her strength and energy, Melinda cooked breakfast. Usually it consisted of a fruit salad for her and an egg-scramble with bacon for Alex. Darya preferred coffee and a sandwich. Following Alex, Darya went to university. Darya was a student of the business school at the University of Washington. She followed her mother's steps and dreamed of becoming the best financial analyst in her home state of Washington, if not the best in the world. She loved studying. Darya wasn't only beautiful, but also inquisitively smart, and she had an active life. One could see her at conferences and student clubs where urgent economical and financial problems were discussed. It's not surprising that Darya grabbed the attention of many young people. Most of the guys at the university tried flirting with her, but she was haughty and always joked that she was waiting for "her prince in shining armor". She was only friends with Michael.

"This is my bro-friend, Michael. I beg you to be kind and gracious to him!" This is how she always introduced him to her course-mates. She was convinced that he treated her like a sister. When they met, he often said, "Hey, little sister."

Michael always told her about his periodical girlfriends. She knew he liked natural blondes with blue eyes and long, long legs. According to him, they had to be "extremely sexy". Although, it was hard to explain what exactly Michael meant by that. He said that you have to feel it inside, below the heart, and he always laughed at that. When Darya asked him if he found her sexy, he always joked.

"No, little sister. You are more like a stuffy girl. However, I can't exactly call you a blue-stocking. But I wouldn't say you're sexy. Sorry, but you are the result of your parents" upbringing, whom I, by the way, love and respect."

Michael was undergoing training at Microsoft after getting a degree in Computer Science at the University of Washington. His father, Roger, was extremely proud of him. Firstly, Michael was following in his father's footsteps, and Roger was already dreaming of the Wellington dynasty of computer programmers; Wellington was their surname. Secondly, Michael was raising everyone's hopes as a specialist and had a good reputation.

"They are very satisfied with him, Roger," Rob once told him. "The company management is ready to make him a member of staff."

Roger had no reason not to believe his friend.

Michael had the reputation of a computer genius. This was why, when Vladimir was introduced to him as a computer genius from Russia, at first, Michael was struck dumb. He became cold and felt an unpleasant lump in his throat. But then, he was sincerely interested in the big, as Michael saw him, young man. In fact, Vladimir was only a tiny bit taller than Michael and had broader shoulders. Michael's first thought was, *So that is what a Russian bear looks like – strong, massive, yet smart. We'll see what happens.*

Michael liked Vladimir straight away. Indeed, Michael had a pretty interesting appearance. He was a young man with eyes so dark they bordered on black, which he inherited from his Indian great-grandmother. His black curly hair was shortly cut. All this perfectly contrasted with his marble skin, which is characteristic of an Englishman. Michael had a big straight nose, a prominent chin and an average-sized mouth framed with pale cherry lips. This mixture of an Indian-English appearance made an indelible impression on Vladimir. Moreover, Michael had an uncanny ability to grab attention. Vladimir didn't even realize why he was so interested in Michael. Actually, that wasn't the time for Vladimir to analyze his feelings.

It had only been a week since he arrived in Seattle and was in desperate need of friends. Vladimir and Michael had a lot in common. They were both twenty-five, they were both in love with computers and they both dreamed of creating the ultimate programs. As it was later discovered, they both loved football; although Michael loved American football while Vladimir preferred English football, which the Americans call "soccer". They even had the same taste in women. Vladimir also preferred sexy blondes with long legs.

The company's management offered Michael and Vladimir to produce a creative tandem to solve an important task, which a number of computer developments depended on. They were given one working week for the project. Michael and Vladimir decided to break down the tasks in order of their priority and interdependency. Every day, from morning until night, they spent their time at work. So as not to waste time on travelling, Michael often spent his nights at Vladimir's, who was renting a flat in Redmond. Redmond was much closer to Seattle that Everett, where Michael lived with his parents. Having worked too many late night hours, Michael and Vladimir were sleeping so soundly they almost didn't hear the beep of an incoming call on Michael's phone. Michael glanced at his watch. It was half past twelve in the afternoon.

"Oh my God, I completely forgot. I promised Darya that I would pick her up after her lessons," exclaimed Michael.

"Who is Darya?" asked Vladimir, half-awake. "Is she Russian?"

"Why Russian? She's the daughter of our family friends, my best friend and the best girl in the world," said Michael in a soft voice.

"I wonder why she has a Russian name. We have a girl's name – Dasha, or Darya," said Vladimir as he gave Michael a questioning look and got out of bed.

"I never actually thought about why Darya is called Darya. For me, she is just Darya. No one ever called her Dasha. I don't think there is a better name for a girl than Darya," Michael added quietly. "By the way, Vladimir, you still haven't seen much of Seattle, and you've been living here for almost two weeks now. Would you like to go somewhere with us? I'll call Darya and apologize, and then I will ask her to wait for us at the park by the university. There, we'll decide what to do next. Deal?"

Vladimir didn't take long to respond. He had nothing planned for the day. His only plans were to lie in bed for some time and then loiter around the city where he lived. He liked the sound of Michael's offer, and so he agreed with pleasure. Besides, he really wanted to meet the girl with the Russian name Darya.

Darya was sitting on a bench next to a beautiful branchy oak, waiting for the boys. She loved that bench. For some reason, it was on this particular bench that Darya always came up with unexpected solutions to her problems. It was an ordinary bench, last painted a long time ago, with a few eroded parts on the back. It was just like any other bench in the cozy park by the university. But this one perched right underneath the crown of the oak. And the oak, itself, was magnificent. It seemed to radiate strength, calmness and conciliation. Darya was reading a book when she heard Michael's voice.

"Hey, little sister. Meet Vladimir. He is my comrade from Russia."

Darya tore herself away from the book. Having said hello to Michael, she slowly turned her eyes to Vladimir. He gazed at the girl with wide eyes, in which he failed to hide his interest and amazement.

Darya's appearance made a strange impression on a young man. There was something imperceptibly familiar in her face. He was definitely sure that he had already seen her snub nose and high forehead framed by a fringe. But where?

"Hello, Darya," the stranger greeted her. "Pleased to meet you. My name is Vladimir. Michael assured me that there is no better girl in the world than you."

"He's over-exaggerating," she blushed.

Vladimir gazed at Darya, making her feel uncomfortable. But she liked the tall, well-built guy with charming blue eyes, and felt an attraction to him.

Sensing that Darya was confused, Michael came to her aid. "Well, little sister, let's show the nighttime Seattle to my new friend. Let him fall in love with it like we did," said Michael.

And they did. They roamed the streets until Darya begged for mercy. "I can't. My legs are killing me. Let's sit and rest somewhere. Then you can take me home," she suggested.

"I have another suggestion. Why don't we go to my place?" exclaimed Michael, who didn't want to leave neither of them. "Especially seeing as my parents are nagging me all the time, asking when I will finally introduce Vladimir to them. Darya and I were practically raised the same. We have no secrets from our parents. I told them so much about you. My father is especially interested because he, like you and I, is an IT guy, and a very talented one at that."

A whole month passed after that night. Darya spent almost every night somewhere with Michael and Vladimir. Michael tried not to leave Darya alone with Vladimir. He sensed their mutual attraction and often caught himself feeling upset when Vladimir would sneakily take Darya's hand and bring it towards his lips to kiss it. And Darya— *his* Darya — whom he was afraid to even breathe upon, from whom he concealed his feelings and whom he called his "little sister" so that she would never suspect his love, trembled at Vladimir's every touch. Michael saw it all. He saw how Darya looked at Vladimir with admiration and unspoken love. He saw how Vladimir changed every time he saw Darya; he became taller and his eyes sparkled, and he desired to see, listen to, and breathe everything Darya. Vladimir wanted to be with her, and Michael did not like that.

Michael's inner voice whispered, *just pull them apart and confess to Darya the love you have concealed for years.*

But he was afraid to insult his love, and he was afraid to insult his friendship. He was terrified to lose the two people he valued most. This was why Michael was silent and only persistently and humbly followed Darya and Vladimir everywhere they went. He understood that he was the third wheel amongst them, but there was nothing he could do. Like a magnet—a huge, powerful magnet—he was attracted to both of them. And Darya and Vladimir always calmly responded to Michael's company. It was natural, since Michael was their best friend.

But lovers act as lovers; they kissed sneakily, cuddled in secret, laughed out of place, and their happy yet shy smiles never left their faces. It hurt Michael, a lot, but he never showed it. Sometimes he would simply turn away, or squat, pretending to tie his shoelaces, or run off for a few minutes to get an ice cream for Darya. His soul suffered, but his face was masked by amity. How long this could last for, Michael couldn't say for sure.

Chapter 3

Alex and Melinda were calm as long as Michael accompanied Darya and Vladimir. At the same time, they knew that Michael couldn't always be the inconspicuous third wheel. They saw his torment. Alex and Melinda suffered, too, because they had no idea who Vladimir really was. Every time they wanted to talk with him, learn more about his family, they always ended up postponing the conversation. They feared it, though they knew the faster they talked, the faster they would calm down and be able to look their daughter and her lover in the eyes.

Christmas was nearing. The expectation for something unusual, magical and exciting was in the air. The shops already began their advent sales. Neighbors were decorating their homes, making them resemble magical towers. Alex and Melinda's house was also being prepped for the most long-awaited and joyful holiday of the year. They spent this day with Roger, Rosie and Michael each year. Melinda's older sister, Kelly, came from Belleview, and Andrew, Alex's brother, came with Pam and Jenny, his wife and daughter. This Christmas, Darya asked her parents if she could invite Vladimir.

"Mum, dad, can Vladimir come over for Christmas? He is all alone here. His family is so far away and he has nowhere to go. I really want you to get to know him better. He is so wonderful," Darya said quietly, yet confidently.

Alex looked at Melinda and noticed how pale she was. Her eyes blinked helplessly and her mouth was open. She gasped for air. He held his wife's elbow and caressed her back, calming her.

"Don't worry, honey. Everything will be okay," he said quietly. Then, loudly but softly, he told Darya, "Of course, Darya, sweetie, you can invite your friend. We would love to talk with him."

When Darya cheerfully ran out of the living room, Melinda asked her husband anxiously, "Are you sure? Are you sure we are doing the right thing, approving their relationship? What if it gets serious and we won't be able to control the situation anymore?"

"Honey, look," Alex sounded calm and thoughtful, "until we learn more about Vladimir, it is too early to come to conclusions. Perhaps we're wrong. There are so many people that look alike, but not all of them are related."

Christmas arrived. Alex and Melinda were greeting their guests. The preparations for the holiday began about a month ago. Every year, Alex and Melinda, with the help of Darya, due to the many arguments, were choosing the theme of the decorations outside the house. They tried not to repeat themselves. This year, they decided that the theme would be "The Snow Queen". In front of the house, on the left, they placed a small sled decorated with garlands from thin silver paper, glass icicles lit from the inside, and decorative snowflakes for different sizes. Inside the sled on a silver pillow was the figure of the evil Snow Queen, which was made out of metal wires and clothed in a white dress with a long silver veil. The queen's head was slightly lowered, and her wide-brimmed hat was covered by white tulle, as if protecting her from the snowy wind. There, behind the queen, sat a wire figure of Kai dressed in black trousers and a black coat. The improvised head was covered in a warm striped scarf. The figure looked so pitiful that the passers-by stopped by it to give alms. On the right side of the house, was the wire figure of Gerda in a fustian cherry-colored dress. Over that dress was an old overcoat from rough grey fur, and she wore red mittens and a knit red hat. Her face was covered by a mitten, which represented her hand. Gerda's figure was bent in such a way that it looked like she couldn't straighten her back due to the strong northerly wind. Both Gerda's sled and figure stood on artificial snow, which was heaped densely in front of the house. Garlands with lights of every color, iridescent icicles and snowflakes, were lit up everywhere. It was Darya who thought of the whole idea. The story of "The Snow Queen" had always been her favorite.

Melinda was responsible for decorating the interior. She had a collection of Santa Claus figurines; she had over a hundred. They were of different heights, thickness, colors, and trimmed with different types of fur coats, hats, and even canes. The figurines were arranged according to size. The biggest were placed by the Christmas tree, while the smallest were put on the shelf over the fireplace, by the Christmas stockings. The others were placed in clusters all around the living room. Upon entering the living room, it felt like you were on a meeting of Santa Clauses from all over the world, and they were actively discussing international problems. Colorful balloons, small lanterns, and snowflakes added to the room's décor.

On the morning before Christmas, Alex's brother, Andrew, arrived with his family from California. Andrew was three years older than Alex, and was the head of a real estate agency in San Diego. The brothers had a lot in common and were like best friends. Andrew knew all the twists and turns in Alex's life, and often gave him valuable advice. Alex was impatiently waiting for his brother. He wanted to take the weight off his shoulders and tell his brother that, for the past four months, ever since Vladimir came into their lives, he was always anxious. He felt sorry for Melinda. During the past few months, her headaches had become stronger and she practically lived on medication. Her daily meditation only helped so much, but the sense of alarm haunted her. Alex was worried not only for her physical state, but also psychologically. Even he felt a piercing pain in his heart.

"I need to talk to you. Let's go to my study and…" Alex whispered to Andrew the minute he entered the house.

Pam, Andrew's wife, approached them smiling. Alex never really liked Pam. From a sweet and pleasant girl whom Andrew fell in love with twenty-six years ago, she turned into an annoying, boring, dreary woman. Pam loved to butt into others" affairs and give relevant and irrelevant advice. She loved to gossip about others and savored it. This was why Alex decided to change the conversation, and, quickly trying to be as pleasant as possible, greeted Pam.

"Pam, honey, hello. I am so happy to see you. You look great." Having spouted these standard phrases, he turned to his brother. "Andrew, I really hope you will be staying for a few days. This way, we will have time to talk." Hoping to avoid any questions from Pam, he quickly headed towards the doors.

Kelly, Melinda's sister, was coming in. Unlike Melinda, Kelly was a tall and lean woman. She was fifty-seven and lived alone, as her personal life didn't work out. Kelly had been married three times. None of her husbands could stand her quarrelsome and scornful character. Her longest marriage was the last one, and it lasted five years. Due to gynecological problems, she couldn't get pregnant. At first, Kelly cried a lot and suffered from this, but she eventually got over it. Gradually, she learned to live alone, think only about herself and care only about herself. Kelly worked as an accountant for an insurance company, and spent most of her time in the office. Solitude turned a joyful woman into a closed-up, dull, sarcastic person. But Melinda loved her only sister and needed her.

Having said hello to Alex, Kelly walked into the kitchen where Melinda was working magic on the turkey. The two sisters weren't particularly as close as the two brothers; the age difference of seven years didn't exactly bring them closer together. But they were always attentive to each other. Kelly didn't like Melinda's exhausted look. Her tired eyes, grayish skin and the lack of a smile on her face all pointed to the sleepless nights and deep torment.

"Oh my God, Melinda, what happened to you? Is it the headaches again? Have you seen the doctor?" Kelly began questioning.

"Everything is alright, "Melinda replied. "Don't worry. I'm just really tired these days."

She decided not to tell Kelly about her problems, or that she was tensely waiting for that day's meeting with Vladimir, hoping to resolve their worries. Kelly was never really interested in Melinda's personal life, and Melinda didn't like to tell everyone about her problems. To be honest, Kelly didn't wait for Melinda's explanations. She quickly turned and walked into the living room.

At the same time, Roger entered the house with his family. All three of them were unusually and extremely excited. As always, Roger and Rosie were arguing over some nonsense. They were always arguing about something. Alex could never understand what it was that connected these two completely different people. Nevertheless, Roger and Rosie have lived together for over twenty-five years, and they somehow got on with each other. Roger always said that Rosie, with her quarrelsome character, never let him stay in one place for long. According to the famous saying, "Thought thrives on conflict", Rosie, without even realizing it, often pushed her husband onto interesting solutions. As far as the manner of the argument was concerned, it was always a high tone, slowly turning into screams. And Roger learned to ignore it. He, as an intelligent person, was more interested in the nature of the argument rather than its tone.

"Roger, my friend, I am so happy to see you," Alex greeted his friend. "Rosie, Michael, come inside. Almost everyone has gathered. Michael, could you be a dear and entertain the girls? They are on the second floor in the recreation room."

"Are you waiting for someone else?" Michael asked with interest.

"Darya invited Vladimir to celebrate Christmas with us. I thought you knew," Alex replied, slightly nervous.

"What? Vladimir? Again, Vladimir?" said Michael angrily. "He didn't tell me he was coming over. Maybe he changed his mind," Michael said in a hopeful voice.

But then came a polite knock on the door. In a few seconds, Vladimir walked in. He was dressed in a magnificent blue suit, pale blue shirt, which amazingly matched his eyes, and black shoes with a thin sole. His appearance was distinctly different to that of all the other men. Alex, Roger, Michael and Andrew were all dressed in a typical American manner – jeans and shirt.

"I didn't know that the dress-code was casual. In Russia, everyone dresses formally for celebrations. I am sorry for my pretentious look," Vladimir was somewhat embarrassed.

"It's alright, Vladimir," uttered Melinda quietly as she came out of the kitchen. "You look perfect. Christmas is a great celebration and it must be celebrated in fine and stylish clothes. You are dressed just right for the occasion. I hope you will feel at home," Melinda cheered him up and then excused herself to her room for a moment.

Melinda sat on her bed, wrapped her head with her arms, and pressed hard, hoping that her headache would go away. All she could see in front of her was Vladimir. She feverishly flipped through her mental images of him and tried to compare his facial features with the image of the person she forgot about a long, long time ago.

Alex quietly entered the room. "How are you feeling? Is everything alright? I don't like the way you look," he anxiously commented. "All the guests have gathered, and you should come down. Everything will be alright, I promise. I will speak to Andrew and ask him to pay extra attention to Vladimir. A third opinion would be helpful. Is that okay with you?" Alex asked with love.

Darya and Jane were cheerfully talking about something in the recreation room on the second floor when the young men came upstairs. Michael walked in first. He knew Darya's cousin really well. Jane greeted Michael with a joyful scream and began asking him about his life. She was particularly interested if he had a girlfriend. Michael slightly blushed, slowly looking at Darya with eyes tormented from love.

"I think the girl who shall one day win my heart hasn't been born yet," Michael said calmly.

Darya felt so much pain and hopelessness in his voice that she felt sorry for him. She came up to him, gently kissed his cheek and said, "Don't worry. There are so many nice and beautiful girls out there. Just open up your heart and they will definitely love you."

Vladimir, who quietly walked into the room without being noticed, observed what was going on. He hadn't heard what Darya said to Michael, but he definitely saw how tenderly she kissed him while whispering something into his year. He felt uneasy. For the past few months, he grew to love Michael as a brother and, at the same time, had deep feelings for Darya. Vladimir suddenly understood why Michael was always with them. He stood in place, as if rooted to the ground, unable to do anything. Jane came up to him.

"Hello there, beautiful. My name is Jane. I guess you're Vladimir. Darya can't stop talking about you. I never thought you'd be so interesting," said Jane.

Jane had beautiful facial characteristics. She had bright blue eyes, a small nose, and expressive, sensual lips, on which she put natural colored lipstick. She was twenty-five and, after graduating from the Faculty of Architecture at the University of California, she was working with her father. She was a glib girl who knew her worth. Jane was the complete opposite of Darya. She loved loud parties, discos and night clubs. All the guys were attracted to her, and she was determined to win the heart of Vladimir, whom she liked at once.

Vladimir didn't like Jane's familiar and over-free tone, although her physical appearance particularly enchanted him. Jane didn't only have a pretty face, but also a well-built body. He politely said hello and quickly joined Darya, who was looking at him with an unconcealed smile.

"Vladimir, this is my cousin, Jane. Jane, this is Vladimir. He is from Russia, and he is undergoing training at Microsoft. He is Michael's friend and my—" Darya began introducing Vladimir to Jane, but she was interrupted.

"I know, I know. He's your boyfriend, whom you are absolutely in love with. He's cute. More like from Playgirl, to be honest," Jane interrupted rudely.

Michael was disgusted by what Jane said. At the same time, he realized that if Jane would flirt and try to win Vladimir over, Darya would be free. This was why he said nothing and walked up to the window. Darya was shocked by her cousin's behavior. She hadn't seen her since last year's Christmas. Jane had changed a lot. Darya did not expect so much overdue familiarity and pragmatism from her.

"Darya, the design of your house is excellent. The story of "The Snow Queen" is my favorite. When I was small, I asked my mum to read it to me every night," Vladimir said gently, trying to relieve the tension in the atmosphere. "Back in Russia, no one decorates their houses like this. It's so beautiful. Did you think of it by yourself?"

Darya calmed down. She was pleased that Vladimir appraised her efforts. She was grateful for his tactfulness.

"I am so glad you liked it. Let's go downstairs. Everyone is probably sitting at the table already," Darya replied, and having overcome the unpleasant feelings, invited Jane and Michael to the living room.

The room was noisy. Roger and Andrew were playing chess and let out screams of satisfaction after every successful move. Pam and Kelly were actively discussing new fashion trends for the upcoming year. Darya joined in to their conversation. Vladimir and Michael were discussing the new project that they were working on. At the same time, neither of them took their eyes off their beloved girl. Darya felt their gazes, which made her feel happy and uncomfortable at the same time.

Jane came up to Vladimir. She noticed his loving gaze directed at Darya and didn't like it. Jane decided to draw the attention of her new friend on herself.

"Vladimir, you said that "The Snow Queen" was your favorite story and that your mum used to read it to you every night. I wonder what your mother is like. Where is she? I would love to learn everything about you," said Jane in a slow, flirty tone.

Silence fell in the living room. Everyone looked closely at the young man with interest. He turned pale and his eyes watered. His face became miserable and sorrowful. Finally, coping with himself, Vladimir said, "My mum… My mum lives in Saint Petersburg. I call her every day… I'm sorry. I can't talk now. It's so hard… It was so unexpected. We still can't believe it happened."

Melinda and Alex, who were standing by Darya's side, instinctively interlaced their hands in a tight knot and tensely, without blinking, gazed at the young man. Their eyes reflected their deep astonishment and sense of alarm. Both of them were puzzled by the same questions: "What could have possibly happened to the young man's mother that he doesn't want to talk about it? What happened with this family?" But neither of them dared ask Vladimir.

At least, not now. First, I must consult with Andrew and Roger, thought Alex.

Vladimir quickly came to his senses, apologized for his moment of weakness and closed up. His face instantly became impenetrable, cold and unpleasant. This change staggered everyone, but nobody said anything. Michael, who was standing nearby, watching Vladimir, was just as shocked as everybody else. He understood that Vladimir wasn't as simple as he may have seemed a few minutes ago. Michael glanced at Darya. The girl was looking at Vladimir, her eyes full of tears. It seemed that she could only see Vladimir and nothing else. She was watching his sorrowful turned stern grieving eyes. Darya slowly walked up to the young man, held his hand, and asked the first question that sprang in her mind.

"Would you like to look through our family photo album?" she asked.

"Darya, sweetie, the Christmas dinner is getting cold," Melinda said quietly. Then, in a louder voice, she invited everyone into the spacious dining room where the huge round table was already set.

After dinner, everyone spread around the house. Alex, Roger, and Andrew all went into Alex's spacious study, which was furnished with the owner's style and taste. They sat on the big armchairs around the small coffee table. Quietly, Melinda came in and put wine glasses for cognac and brandy on the table. Alex opened a bottle of an expensive French cognac, Hine Mariage. He knew that Andrew was a connoisseur of cognac, and so he bought this expensive rare bottle especially for him. For Roger, Alex bought a bottle of a perfect Peruvian brandy, Pisco Peruvian, produced by Capel.

"Ah, Alex, you know exactly how to please me," Andrew said with admiration, as he examined the exquisite bottle. "I'll have to admit that it's been ages since I've last drank it! As far as I remember, this label has a distinct fragrance and a strong taste."

With pleasure, Andrew took a sip of the cognac from his glass. Roger tasted his brandy, which his friend helpfully poured into his glass. Alex preferred Californian wine, a glass of which he walked into his study with, rather than the strong drinks. Silence fell in the cabinet for a few minutes, during which each one of the men enjoyed his drink.

"So, brother, tell us, what's bothering you?" Andrew suddenly asked quite loudly. "I have been watching you and Melinda all evening long. You don't look your usual selves. It's like something is eating you from the inside. Melinda's eyes are always joyful and sparkly, but today they were dim and dull. How is she feeling? Is it something to do with her migraines?"

Alex took a long time to answer. He couldn't find the right words to explain everything that was going on. He suddenly thought that he shouldn't ask his brother and his best friend to judge his doubts and concerns about Vladimir. At least, not on that day. He didn't want to upset his friends and ramble on about his problems on this beautiful Christmas day. So, after taking a while to think, Alex said in a calm, measured voice, "My friends, I am so happy to see you in my home once again. You are my closest friends. I would like to propose a toast for this occasion. Let us always be happy together…"

Suddenly, without warning or knocking, Darya ran into the study. Her face was flaming and her eyes were glowing with an unusual inner light. In her hands, she held a photo. It depicted a young woman in her twenties wearing an elegant ball dress from Jeanne Paquin, a well-known French fashion designer in the early 20th Century. The woman had a gorgeously difficult hairstyle, and she wore an antique emerald necklace. Darya's lips were trembling and hundreds of questions were ready to burst forth. Darya ran up to her father, and with a vibrating anxious voice asked, "Dad, dad, who is this girl?"

"Darya, honey, where did you find this photo?"

"It's not me who is interested. It's Vladimir. I was showing him our family photo album," Darya replied. "He assured me that he knows this woman. Vladimir is convinced that it's his mother's neighbor, except she is strangely dressed."

"It's impossible, honey. This photo is over ninety years old. Ninety-five, to be precise. It is a photo of your great grandfather's sister, Princess Elisabeth Ukhtomsky. In 1912, Lisa married Prince Vikhulev Igor Dmitrievich and went to live in his manor. It just so happened that nobody ever heard anything about her ever again. So it's highly unlikely that Vladimir ever saw her, or even knew her. My great grandfather took it from Russia in 1918. He valued it a lot, and said that it contains the history of our kin."

Darya was astonished by what she heard. She looked lost, and her eyes were a mixture of amazement and curiosity. She wasn't sure how to react to her father's confession. Darya was wrestled by questions: Why has her father never told her about their family, and why has she never wondered about her family roots? In the evenings when their family would gather together, they discussed everything: Work, university, plans for the weekend and for the holidays, books, movies, concerts and so on, but her father never said anything about their family. Darya never met Alex's parents, as they passed away long before she was born. She never met her mother's parents, either. Darya grew up without grandparents and it was natural for her. Her parents didn't like to go through old photo albums, and she never expressed any desire to look at them.

Andrew, who was highly interested in the conversation between his niece and brother, walked up to Alex. "Tell me, did you ever tell Darya about our family? Does she know that we are Russian, even though we were born in America? Does she know that we are descendants of the Old Russian princely kin of Ukhtomsky, which started from the kin of Rurikovich?" Andrew's voice was stern, yet proud. "My Jane knows that she has Russian blood flowing through her veins. She speaks Russian quite well, although she reads and writes with difficulty. Unfortunately, I didn't manage to teach her the written Russian language. But we have always spoken with her in Russian ever since she was a little girl. Jane is proud of her Russian roots. I don't understand you, Alex. I don't even understand Melinda. She is a smart, delicate and psychologically subtle woman. How was it possible to forget to teach her about her family name?"

Alex listened to his brother quietly, hanging his head, completely understanding his rightness. He remembered that, when Darya was born, he and Melinda decided to never talk about Russia. It was a sore point for them. At the same time, the couple knew that sooner or later, they would have to tell Darya everything. They feared that moment and so they found every excuse to postpone this conversation.

Then, there was a gentle knock on the door, and after being invited it, Vladimir, Michael and Jane filed in. Jane was holding the family photo album.

"Dad," she said to Andrew, "Look at this photo."

The photo depicted three young men standing behind chairs, on which sat two young women. They were dressed according to the fashion of the 20th Century. The photograph was dated 1912.

"Dad," continued Jane, "Is the photo of the Ukhtomsky princes with their wives? I recognize grandpa, and the other men look like him. We don't have a photo like this."

"Yes, my darling, you're right. These are, indeed, the Ukhtomsky princes. This photograph was taken at the wedding of their only sister, Lisa," uttered Andrew. "Jane, I always thought you looked like your great-great grandmother. Look here, she is sitting on the left."

"Indeed, they do have a lot in common," Vladimir joined in to the conversation. "I noticed it at once and told Jane. She speaks Russian perfectly. It's such a pleasure. But Darya doesn't look like her grandmother, although she does have something in common with Jane, appearance-wise. I think she looks more like the woman on the photo she is holding.

Chapter 4

Russia, October 1918.

The family manor of the Ukhtomsky princes, just outside of Petrograd, is practically destroyed. Only three rooms remained habitable. Those were the rooms which the families of the Ukhtomsky princes settled into. In one of the rooms—the biggest and most spacious one—behind the once exquisite and expensive oval table, sat the representatives of the Ukhtomsky princely kin. The oldest prince, Alexander, is just over forty years old. He was a tall, well-built man, and officer of the Tsar's army. His uniform, even though it was without any shoulder boards or other distinctive elements, suited him. The cut and the material of the suit pointed to its owner's high rank. Prince Alexander was, indeed, the army's colonel. After graduating the Pavel Military School, he was sent to serve as a second lieutenant in the Life Guards of the Finnish Regiment. He served there up until February 1917. The February Revolution of 1917, leading to the Emperor's abdication, gave rise to chaos inside Alexander. The prince couldn't get over what was going on in Russia. He remained loyal to the Emperor when the Provisional Government gained power over the country, and when the Bolsheviks gained power through the October Revolution. Alexander didn't take part in any of the military conflicts during the past few years. The chaos in his soul slowly transformed into the fixed idea, which seemed to be the only right solution, to flee from

Russia—the Russia he loved so much but couldn't understand or accept.

"You have to understand me! We can't just stay here! Look at what is going on! Destruction and starvation aren't the worst part. Sooner or later, all that was destroyed will be rebuilt," said Prince Alexander, over and over again, with an excess of hotheadedness, which was not inherent in this calm and confident person. "There is something worse than that. No revolution takes place without the annihilation of the dissidents, and I think that there are plenty of those in Russia. It's not just the people from our society, but also the sensible, intelligent people, and even the prosperous peasants—all those who *have* something to lose. Oh my God, ladies and gentlemen, you have no idea what will happen to us!" Alexander was walking nervously up and down the room. However, he suddenly became silent as he walked to the window and gazed at the street. The room was tensely silent. The wind outside whirled the yellow leaves fell off the trees. The puffy clouds were about to pour down with rain onto the wounded ground, which yearned for care. It was dark and uneasy. In the distance, an obscure noise swelled and quieted down. Suddenly, Alexander turned around abruptly. His face was distorted with horror and indecision.

In a slow steel-hard voice, Alexander addressed his brothers, "I want you to know. I swore an oath to His Majesty Nicholas II and I do not intend to betray him. But the Emperor doesn't exist anymore. The Russia I served for and defended doesn't exist anymore. I don't intend to swear a new oath to anyone."

In the absolute silence of the room, his clear, well-placed voice sounded like a hammer striking an anvil. The hearts and souls of the present of those present were the anvils. Prince Alexander's wife, Princess Helen, looked at him with love. She always supported him. Their son, George, turned sixteen a month ago. Helen was worried about his future. Moreover, she didn't see a future for him in this new, hostile Russia.

"I have decided to leave Russia. Forever," uttered Alexander, clearly pronouncing every word. "My brothers, I suggest that you join us, and we will leave altogether. We must decide this tonight. Tomorrow might already be too late." His light-blue eyes suddenly darkened and, in the depths of blue, everyone could read such firm confidence in his decision that his brothers couldn't find anything to say. Deep silence fell.

The middle brother, Leon, stood up from his chair, where he sat the whole time without moving, his head hanging, and walked up to the window. It was already dark outside, and the wind was still strong. The boring autumn rain was starting. It grew stronger and stronger, and began angrily beating down the window panes. The room was just as dark. Olga, Prince Leon's wife, lit three candles, and put them on the table. In the flickering dim light from the candles, the faces of those sitting at the table looked exhausted and tormented. Their eyes looked lackluster and expressed their suffering. The oppressive silence was interrupted by Leon" quiet voice as he walked up to the table.

"I understand you, Sasha. You always keep your word and you always follow your principles. You don't want to go against them, even now. Yes, I understand that it's hard to imagine yourself in this new Russia. But leaving the country, to go God knows where, as you are suggesting, is stupid. It's highly stupid."

Leon came up close to his older brother and looked him right in the eyes. Alexander also looked Leon in his eyes. It felt like the staring-war would never finish. Alexander's blue eyes, which looked like two deep lakes, and Leon's deep brown eyes were staring at each other, as if communicating, arguing, and trying to find answers for the crucial questions: What to do next, where to live, how to live, what to believe in.

"No, Leon. Perhaps you don't fully understand what the new Russia is like and who is making history in it now," Alexander broke the prolonged silence. "According to the anthem of the Bolsheviks, you and I, and everyone like us, are like a pack of dogs and executioners and, according to their beliefs, our whole class should be destroyed. He who was someone must become no one, and he who was no one must become someone. Do these words mean anything to you? It is their new action program with respect to us and those like us. I will not allow my family to be destroyed due to some idiotic idea about equality."

The prince's voice was becoming stronger, and his last words were uttered with a stern, severe voice. His long thin nose with flared nostrils, his handsome high forehead, streaked with barely noticeable wrinkles, was covered with perspiration, his pale skin became slightly pinker, and his lean figure became tense. Both Alex's face and figure pointed to the firmness of his decision.

Prince Leon didn't expect such pressure from his older brother. Regardless of an age difference of five years, they were very friendly with each other. Quite often, in childish arguments, it was Leon who would win. Moreover, Alexander often lent his ear to his younger brother's opinions. On the one hand, Leon could understand Alexander. Alexander dedicated his whole life to military science. Even as a little boy, he dreamed of military accomplishments. He had two idols, and both were named Alexander – Alexander Nevsky and Alexander Suvorov. He was also an Alexander and was getting ready to defend his fatherland from conquerors. He wanted to be remembered as a skilful General on the battlefield. But he couldn't be at war with his own people, the Russian people, even if they wanted to destroy him and his family. Leon completely understood his older brother's reasoning. However, he couldn't agree that fleeing Russia was the only solution.

"No, Sasha. You… You are very cruel to yourself and your family," said Leon, his voice trembling with agitation and the overwhelming sense of alarm. "Do you even realize what doom you are bringing upon yourself, Helen and your son? Where are you planning to live? How are you going to earn money? What are you going to do? Sasha, did you think about any of that?" Leon's voice sounded like an alarm bell, alarming and appealing. He then addressed the youngest brother, "Why are you so silent, Aleksey?"

Prince Aleksey stood by the window, gazing at the streets, where the wind was at its strongest, ripping off whatever yellow leaves were left on the trees, breaking the dry branches, whirling up the withered blanket of flowers and leaves off the ground. The rain was beating down on the window panes for a good seven minutes, failing to properly wet the ground, providing more work for the wind. The room became chilly and uncomfortable. All the present women put warm woolen shawls over their shoulders. Princess Olga approached the sofa by one of the walls where her three-year-old daughter, Lida, was fast asleep, and covered her with a duvet. Shivering from the cold, Aleksey walked up to the fireplace and lit up the fire. The slightly damp birch logs arduously absorbed the energy of the warmed up dry chips, doubling the warmth for the present people. The room gradually became warmer. Prince Alexander walked up to his wife, and gently offered her to sit closer to the fireplace. Princess Olga followed her example. Alexander and Leon remained at the table. The candles were almost burnt out. They decided not to light new ones. The light from the burning logs illuminated almost half of the room. It was just enough to see everyone's face.

Prince Aleksey sat on the chair by his oldest brother. They had a huge difference in age. Last week, Aleksey turned twenty-seven. Their parents died in 1895, during a fire in the neighboring manor, which belonged to Prince Golovin Victor Alekseevich. The fire happened during the Christmas celebration due to the carelessness of one of the owner's servants. The only survivor, who was severely burnt, was the prince's son, Golovin Gregory. He spent a long time abroad with doctors, and then decided to stay somewhere in Italy. The three brothers were left under their uncle's care, their mother's brother. Alexander was eighteen and was getting ready to go to the military school. Even though he was far from home, he visited quite often. These short leaves from the army were a celebration for the brothers, especially the youngest, Aleksey.

Aleksey tried to be like Alexander, who was an asset for him in everything. Nevertheless, Aleksey chose a different route in life. From a young age, he dreamed of learning about the earth's riches, finding deposits, and he was especially interested in the geological exploration of oil pools. Aleksey graduated from the Saint Petersburg Mining Institute and became a mining engineer. He wasn't married and wasn't planning to be entangled in Hymen's meshes with anyone until at least the age of thirty. Science took up the first spot in his life. He was a cheerful young man full of hopes. But today, he realized what it was they were deciding. His, his brothers", their wives" and children's futures depended on their decision. Just like Leon, Aleksey could understand his oldest brother. But, at the same time, he also agreed with the middle brother. Aleksey couldn't imagine how it was possible to leave his home country at the time when it needed them the most.

Suddenly, he stood up and walked up to the fireplace. In the gleam of the burning logs, the prince's face looked pale and nervous. He gritted his teeth. Standing by the fireplace for a few moments, he uttered the phrases which he was thinking about all night, "Alexander, you know I love you. I respect you as the oldest member of the family. You practically replaced our father for me. But I can't support your decision right now." He took a deep breath, and continued. "Russia is our motherland. We were born here, we grew up here. Our parents and ancestors are buried here. The history of our kin, the Ukhtomsky princely kin, lies here. Yes, we served the Emperor Nicholas II and all the tsars before him. We served them faithfully and loyally. The time has come and Nicholas II was overthrown. Now the Bolsheviks are in power. But they were also born and raised in Russia, and I think they love it just as much as we do. The Bolsheviks are trying to build a new government where there will be no class division, no poor and rich. I don't know, but perhaps someday they will accomplish it. I don't know. All I know is that amongst them and their supporters are many intelligent, sensible, educated people. They won't let them destroy the Russia that we love," Alex said, and then fell silent. His voice gradually quieted down, lost its loudness and became coarse. Alex poured himself some water from a carafe into a small crystal glass, drinking in big sips. Everyone in the room watched him silently. The young prince abruptly turned towards his brother and said, with a relaxed and, once again, loud voice, "Sasha, the motherland doesn't become worse just because the rulers change. The motherland is where we were born and raised, where we have a family and a home. Think about it before you make a final decision. Remember, once you leave Russia forever, you will lose the powers of Antaeous, and it's extremely hard to live without them."

At this point, Alexander, feeling highly proud for his younger brother, hugged Aleksey, and then looked him in his blue eyes, just like his own. He looked at them for a long time, as if he wanted to leave something in them, or take something for himself.

"Oh my God, I haven't even realized how much you grew. You became a real man, an intelligent, fully-fledged man. I am so proud of you," said Alexander in a tender voice. "You are absolutely right, Aleksey, when you talk about Russia as a motherland. Yes, I was born and raised here, I was educated here, and I served for my fatherland. But the fatherland I served for doesn't exist anymore. Russia is not the same, and I don't feel my complicity in the future of the new Russia. It's foreign to me. Aleksey, Leon, you have to understand, the motherland isn't only the place where a person was born and where his ancestors and relatives are buried, no. The motherland is a place where a person feels at home. I am afraid of the new Russia and I am afraid of the people who are now in power. I thought this through and I asked myself whether I can accept the new Russia and whether I can serve for her. And I always came up with the same answer: No."

Alexander went silent. His eyes watered, his lips trembled, and his cheeks blushed nervously. After a moment of silence, which gave him time to calm down, the prince continued in a quiet, yet stern, voice, "Well, I understand you and your reluctance to leave Russia with me. In three hours, my family and I will meet my comrades from the Finnish regiment. They will help us get across to Sweden, and then to England. From there, we will most likely head for America if we are lucky enough to survive."

Alexander stopped talking. His mouth went dry from the stress and nervousness. He reached for his glass of water. Everyone in the room was so silent that they could hear the mice rustling next door. Having taken a few gulps of water, the prince continued, "I think this is our last night together. I don't know what our destiny is. I would like us to always remember each other. Perhaps, one day, our descendants" paths will cross…" Alexander's voice trembled with anxiety, and his eyes watered. He walked up to his wife, rested his hand on her shoulder and quietly said, "It's time to go. George is waiting for us outside. The carriage and the horses are ready. We don't have much time."

The prince brusquely turned towards the others. His brothers and Princess Olga were standing and waiting to bid their goodbyes to

Alexander and his wife. Everyone was depressed, in tears, and silent because they couldn't talk anymore, not that anybody wanted to. They were overwhelmed with emotions. The brothers hugged and, after a few minutes, made a quiet promise.

"We will always remember each other!"

The brothers couldn't let go of each other's hands. Now, more than ever, they felt like one whole.

Princess Helen walked up to the brothers.

"Leon, Aleksey, I'm afraid we have to go now. Soon it will be dawn, and it will be very hard to leave. Moreover, we risk letting our friends down," she said to the brothers. She then turned to Olga, hugging and kissing her tenderly on the cheek. "Goodbye, Olga. I don't know if we will ever see each other again. Take care of Leon, Aleksey and Lida."

At the doors, Alexander and Helen bowed to their family and quickly left the house.

Chapter 5

The morning after Christmas, everyone woke up late. The previous night, everyone had found it hard to fall asleep after the heavy conversation brought about by the old family album. Alex and Melinda felt guilty in front of their daughter.

"Andrew was absolutely right," realized Alex as soon as he woke up.

He had nightmares all night long; he dreamt that Vladimir and Darya were walking away from his house, holding hands. No matter how much he begged them to come back, screaming until his voice was coarse; Vladimir and Darya didn't even look back. They just continued walking further and further away, until they disappeared in the dark blue shadows. In his dream, Alex couldn't understand why they were walking away, and he strained to see the place they disappeared into. But no matter how hard he tried, the dark-blue hole swallowed them both. Alex was horrified. He tried to scream but couldn't make a single sound. He tried to run but his legs wouldn't listen. There was no one by his side, not even Melinda. He stood, solitary, in a lifeless void.

Alex woke up in cold sweat. He instinctively held his head and tried to squeeze the gnawing pain out of his head. He was afraid of losing his daughter. Melinda wasn't in bed. She had woken up an hour earlier to cook breakfast for the family and relatives that stayed the night. Alex put on his robe and walked into the bathroom. In the mirror, he saw a man with a washed-out face and sore eyes. He freshened up his face with cold water and, without drying it, walked towards his daughter's room and peeked through the door. Darya was peacefully asleep. Her blissful hair covered her pillow, her face was serene, and her lips were slightly apart, smiling. Having admired his daughter, Alex calmed down and went downstairs, where his wife was bustling about the kitchen.

"How are you feeling?" Melinda asked. "You were moaning, and tossing and turning all night long. Were you in pain? You don't look too good."

Melinda lovingly kissed Alex.

"Mindy... Mindy..." Alex didn't know what to say. "Mindy... I don't feel well. I really don't feel well. But it's not by body that's tormented. I can't forgive myself for forbidding you to ever mention our past in the conversations with our daughter... You were right; sooner or later we would have still ended up telling Darya everything. It's best that *we* tell her, rather than someone else." Alex found it hard to mention every word.

The images from his nightmare haunted Alex. They felt so real that he involuntarily made deterring hand movements. Melinda carefully observed her husband and listened to his trembling voice. Their gazes met, and both of them read what they saw in each other's eyes. Alex felt a silent agreement in Melinda's eyes. Melinda, on the other hand, saw fear and helplessness before the future in Alex's eyes. She felt sorry for him. Melinda hugged her husband and whispered, "Everything will be just fine. We will correct our mistake."

For the twenty or so years that they were married, Melinda's fortitude preceded Alex's. He was often amazed by how his wife could control his mood and emotions.

"Good morning, my dear parents!" their daughter said in a loud, energetic voice. "Mum, you already cooked breakfast? You are so caring!"

"Thank you, honey. Did you sleep alright?" Melinda asked Darya with an amiable smile on her face. "What did you dream about? They say that dreams before or after Christmas are prophetic."

Alex shrugged from Melinda's words and stood up abruptly. His eyes blinked helplessly and his eyelashes sparkled with involuntary tears. It took a lot of effort to suppress his unpleasant feelings. Alex walked up to his daughter with a radiant smile on his face.

"Good morning, my beloved daughter," he addressed Darya with affection. "Go and wake Jane up. I will go check up on Pam and Andrew. I hope they are already awake. It's breakfast time. Your mum prepared the most delicious festive breakfast."

In about twenty minutes, everyone was sitting at the table. As always, Melinda displayed her culinary skills. She managed to take everyone's taste into account. Aside from the fruits, yoghurt and cottage cheese, there were carefully arranged ham and cheese sandwiches, porridge, which had a pleasant subtle smell, pancakes with syrup, toast bread, cereal and milk – everything was neatly placed on serving platters. And, of course, there was coffee prepared in an electric coffeemaker. There were also jars with orange and tomato juices.

"Wow!" exclaimed Jane as she sat down at the table. "Mum, you should learn something from Aunt Mindy. Look how nice and delicious everything looks! All *you* can make is egg scramble and toast."

"What are you saying, Jane, honey?" asked Pam, embarrassed. She blushed and shivered. "I try so hard. I do everything for you. And you…you…shameless nit!" Pam's voice gradually became stronger, and she finished her sentenced in a hysterical tone.

"Yeah, I already know I am a nit for you. Poor dad, I wonder how he handles you!" Jane avenged.

Andrew remained silent. The hostile relations between his wife and daughter strained him, and so he learned to ignore their wrangles. It all began two years ago when Jane brought a young man home and announced that they were getting married. Pam, who was used to making all the decisions, kicked the young man out of the house. He never came back. Jane also wanted to leave, but Pam stood in her way. She told Jane that if she left, she would get no money from the family. So Jane stayed. She was only a student at the university at the time, and she was dependent on her family's financial support. But ever since that day, Pam and Jane became cold to each other. Jane found every excuse to talk back rudely to her mother, thus showing her contempt. Pam was really worried and, within two years, she became a shrew, constantly guilty woman. She became old and lost her good looks.

Jane was harsh and arrogant. She loved to have the last word in conversations. And so, after brusquely rising from the table, she thanked Melinda and Alex for the breakfast and last night's party.

"My dear parents, I won't be back home until late, so don't wait for me. Vladimir and I are going to a night club," said Jane to her parents.

There was an awkward silence. Everyone looked at Darya. The poor girl froze with a sandwich in her left hand and a cup of coffee in her right hand. Her eyes blinked involuntarily and helplessly, while her face was covered with red patches. Darya couldn't find anything to say. When she had said goodbye to Michael and Vladimir last night, they made no plans about going to a nightclub today. Vladimir promised to call her back after lunch. The last thing she expected was that Vladimir would be interested in Jane.

Darya caught her mother's worried gaze and Jane's insolent glare. She jumped out of her seat and rushed headlong to her bedroom, refusing to cry in front of everyone. Only when she slammed her door could she finally let her emotions take over her. She didn't cry, no. She was merely angry. She dashed around the room, from her window to her door, from her door to the window, running into her bed and hitting the corner of her chest drawers. A nasty chaos, which was tearing her apart, raged inside her head. Her temples ached, and her thoughts were all tangled. She couldn't think straight. She was extremely exhausted and fell on the bed. She wanted to cuddle up under her duvet and forget about everything. She wanted to forget about everything, and everyone to forget about her.

There was a knock on her door. Darya had no strength or desire to talk with anyone. Whoever it was, waited by the door for a moment and left.

Thoughts rushed through Darya's head. *What shall I do? What is this? Did Vladimir betray me? Or maybe Jane said she would meet with Vladimir just to anger me?* Darya had so many questions, yet she had no answers. All her thoughts were about Vladimir. They knew each other for four months and Darya was used to the fact that Vladimir was always with her. Even though he never actually told her he loved her, she was sure that he did. His attitude towards her was more expressive and eloquent than words. Maybe she was wrong…. Darya squeezed on her temples with all her might.

Why am I suffering in ignorance? I have to call Vladimir and maybe that will resolve everything, Darya decided.

She feverishly dialed Vladimir's number and waited. Darya waited for about three minutes while the phone was beeping, until an electronic voice offered her to leave a message or call again later. Darya sat on her bed and closed her eyes. She then jumped up and decided to call Michael. She dialed his number and waited. In about fifteen seconds, she heard Michael's sleepy voice.

"Hello there. Sorry, I just woke up, and still haven't got out of bed. Is something wrong?" asked Michael, his voice gentle and calm as always. Darya said hello. Her voice trembled and she wasn't pleased. She hated when people felt pity for her, whether it was her parents or her best friend, Michael. She was silent for a moment, sorting out her thoughts and emotions. Then, in a calm, firm voice, she asked Michael if he was meeting with Vladimir later on.

"Nope, I'm spending the day with my parents," said Michael, his voice still sleepy. "We're going to have dinner together in an Italian restaurant not far from our house. It's called "Graci". You can join us, if you want."

"I'll think about it and call you back," Darya's voice lost its firmness and sounded more concerned.

Michael instantly caught his beloved girl's changed of tone and realized what this was about.

"If you want," he said gently, "I can come over."

Darya was silent. She didn't want anything at the moment.

"No, there's no need, Michael. Thanks," Darya said quietly after a few minutes. "I'll stay home and spend some time with Mum and Dad. I have barely spent time with them during the past few months."

Having said goodbye to Michael, Darya slowly put her phone down, lay down on her bed and closed her eyes. She wanted to try and call Vladimir again, but she was afraid that the only response she would get would be from the nasty electronic voice. Darya was a proud girl but, at the same time, she was shy. Vladimir was the first young man she had such deep feelings for.

No, I won't call him. Let him call me. After all, he promised to call me after lunch, so I'll simply wait. It's about one o'clock now, so he should call soon, decided Darya as she walked down to the living room.

In the spacious, cozy living room, Melinda, Alex, Pam and Andrew were sitting on the sofa in front of the T.V. No one was watching the program that was on. Instead, everyone was deeply immersed in a conversation that seemed important for each one of them. Darya only managed to catch a few words from her father's last phrase.

"…and what shall we do about it?"

When everyone noticed Darya, they looked at her, their eyes full of interest.

"So, Darya, my darling, are you feeling any better?" Melinda inquired.

"Mum, did Jane leave?" Darya asked anxiously. "Did she say anything? Did she say where she was going? What time she will be back?"

"Darya, you know Jane," Andrew joined into the conversation. "She never tells anyone how she spends her time. She is very insolent and thinks she has every right to do whatever she pleases with her life."

"Unfortunately, she never listens to us," Pam added, sorrowfully.

"Perhaps she won't be meeting with your friend. She may have simply said that just to play with your emotions," Andrew supposed.

Darya walked away into the kitchen without responding. Whenever she is anxious or in low spirits, she gets a ravenous appetite. She had a splendid idea.

"Mum, Dad, why don't I make dinner tonight and set it up, here, in the living room? I want to make a nice surprise for you and my dear uncle and auntie. But you have to promise not to bother me or help me!" Darya shouted from the kitchen.

"Perfect!" Melinda shouted back. "I can have a small break from cooking. Seeing as you know what lies where, go on, conjure something for us!" she finished her sentence joyfully.

Darya loved to cook, and she had a talent at that. So, with pleasure, she began to plan the menu for tonight. Moreover, she knew that cooking would distract her from the bad and nasty thoughts. By seven in the evening, the table in the dining room was set up for dinner. Darya did wonderfully well. The table was crammed with a variety of dishes. There was lamb in its own juice, young boiled corncobs, and vegetable stew with brown rice, asparagus stewed in cream sauce, Caesar salad, tomatoes with Mozzarella cheese and basil (seasoned with olive oil, muffins, and garlic bread).

"I would like to invite everyone to the dining room and taste what God has sent us," said Darya with a sad voice and yet a playful tone.

She continued to glance at her phone every few minutes, but it still hadn't rung. Cooking dinner slightly distracted her from it, but in the end, she was absolutely worn-out. She was too proud to call Vladimir, and she felt too disgusted to call her cousin. This unawareness was tearing Darya apart. Her constantly sparkling eyes were now dim. Dinner went by quietly in peace. Nobody asked Darya any questions, and the general topic of conversation was the plans for the upcoming year. They were discussing the possibility of going on holiday to California altogether. After dinner, not knowing how to distract Darya from her gloomy thoughts, Melinda suggested the first thing that came to her mind.

"Why don't we all play a game of Lotto? Darya, darling, do you remember how we often played this entertaining game in the evenings? I will go get the game. Could you, in the meantime, prepare some drinks for everyone?"

Darya gratefully looked at her mother and accepted her conditions. In ten minutes, everybody sat down at the table in the living room.

The game had only just started when the main door opened and Jane showed up at the entrance with Vladimir. They both looked excited. Vladimir walked inside and calmly, politely said hello to everybody and apologized for visiting them at such a late hour. Jane, on the other hand, without acknowledging anyone, mumbled something about being tired and wanting to sleep. When Jane went upstairs and disappeared in her room, Vladimir walked up to Darya.

"I am so sorry. Jane called me in the morning and asked to meet up. I thought that we'd meet up only for a short time. I know I promised to call you after lunch. It's not that I didn't want to call you. I really did, I swear," the young man was worried.

"And what happened?" Darya interrupted him, her voice trembling. "Why didn't you call? What's your excuse? You forgot to charge your phone? Or did you forget it at home? Or, worse, you lost it?" Darya's voice was quiet, but her every single word was clearly heard. Irritation replaced the trembling in her voice. "What I value most in people is honesty and integrity, Vladimir. But today, you were dishonest and showed no integrity. You simply lied to me. Like an idiot, I was sitting all day long and waiting for you to call me, like you promised. And all this time, you were with Jane, my extravagant and thoughtless cousin."

Darya went silent. Hey eyes watered and all she wanted to do was to run away and be alone. But Vladimir grasped her hand.

"Darya, yes, I'm guilty and I know it. I apologized... Alright, if you think that I disappointed you so much that you can't forgive me, I can leave so as not to irritate you anymore," Vladimir spoke slowly, weighing every single word while looking Darya straight in the eyes. In a few minutes, during which they were both silent, Vladimir continued, without waiting for Darya's response any longer, "I'll come over tomorrow and we'll talk, alright?"

Vladimir then turned towards Darya's parents and their guests, who, during this whole time, sat quietly at the table. They stopped playing, refusing to continue, afraid they would bother the young people.

Vladimir turned to Alex. "Alex, I am sorry, perhaps this is none of my business but... I can't forget your family photo album which we were going through last night. There are two photos in particular that I can't forget. I am of the impression, a firm impression, that I've already seen them before – the one with the young woman, and the one with the Ukhtomsky princes. Moreover, I know that I have seen the woman from the picture somewhere, although I can't remember where."

"No, Vladimir. No. This is impossible. You couldn't have seen these photos," Alex said anxiously. "These are very old photos and it was a miracle that they remained in our family album. Even Andrew doesn't have these photos. Am I right, Andrew?" Alex asked his brother.

They young man looked at Darya intently. His eyes reflected his amazement, and then confidence in what he said.

"Then why is Darya's face so familiar? It's like I've seen it somewhere else, long before I met her. I've seen it so many times, although I do admit it was a long time ago. It's hard to remember, but I promise that I will," Vladimir blurted out. "I'm leaving to Russia in two days. There, hopefully, I'll have an opportunity to remember where I know these photos from. Darya, all I'm asking of you is to meet with me tomorrow. This is very important. Please don't refuse.

Darya shrugged her shoulders, silently nodded to Vladimir and went upstairs without uttering a single word.

All night long, Darya couldn't sleep. Only in the morning did she manage to obliviously fall asleep for about three hours. But by seven o'clock, she was already up and about. She took a cold shower to freshen up, and got dressed. By eight o'clock, she was already downstairs in the living room. Melinda was already bustling about the kitchen, and Alex was sitting on the sofa, going through the mail. When he saw his daughter, Alex stood up, kissed her, and said that Vladimir was already on his way.

"Darya, darling, please hear Vladimir out. Something happened between him and Jane. Didn't you notice Jane's strange behavior after she came back? She didn't look at anyone, didn't say anything, and just ran into her room like she was stung by a bee. Evidently, something went wrong on their *date*."

"Okay, dad, I'll try," Darya replied quietly.

In about twenty minutes, Pam and Andrew came downstairs, about five minutes after Jane. They were ready to go home. Unlike her parents, Jane was crestfallen. She didn't greet anyone and didn't even look at Darya. She just sat in the armchair and stared into empty space. This behavior was not characteristic of Jane and shocked Darya.

"Jane, what's wrong? Are you feeling okay?" asked Darya.

"Leave me alone, and don't bug me with your questions. I feel just fine," Jane said, glaring at her cousin. "What does he even see in you? There is no fire in you, just some smoldering firebrand. You're so proper, it disgusts me!" Jane sounded vexed and angry.

"Who are you talking about, Jane?" Darya inquired, calmly. "Oh, right, I get it. Dad was right, Vladimir didn't respond to your claims. I feel sorry for you, Jane. You just can't understand that insolence and licentiousness don't suit a girl."

"What do I know?" replied Jane rudely in a fit of temper.

Melinda interrupted the verbal wrangle between the two cousins by inviting everyone to have breakfast. The meal passed quickly and silently. Andrew's family was in a hurry. They had to be at the airport in two hours. They stumbled into Vladimir practically in the doorway. The moment Jane saw him come in, she jumped up, surprised. She mumbled "hello" and quickly ran outside. Having greeted the owners of the house and, at the same time, bid farewell to the guests, Vladimir ran up to Darya. He was holding a beautiful bouquet of white roses. Darya quietly accepted the flowers.

"Darya, I'm leaving to Russia tomorrow. I'll be gone for three months. I really want us to make up before I go," Vladimir anxiously said to his beloved girl.

For a moment, Darya was silent.

"Vladimir, thank you so much for the flowers. They're so beautiful. … I'm not offended by you, don't worry. Jane's behavior said a lot about the outcome of your date," she said gently.

Vladimir impatiently interrupted Darya, "Yes, yes. When I agreed to meet with Jane, I was sure that it would be for a short time. Moreover, I only wanted one thing from her. I was of the impression that she knew her genealogy; at least it seemed that way when we were looking at the old photos in your family photo album. I'm still prostrated. Don't you just hate the feeling when you know, saw and met a person, but can't remember when and where it was? It makes me feel awful. I was only trying to make the picture clearer."

"And did it become any clearer?" Darya interrupted.

"No, not really," Vladimir replied as he observed Darya, trying to understand what mood she was in. Darya was acting calmly, and spoke quietly and emotionlessly.

"Much to my distress, Jane only repeated what was said earlier. Then we took a walk at the quayside, visited the aquarium, sat in some café…and that's it! She was trying to convince me to go to a night club, but I rejected her offer," Vladimir went silent. Darya didn't say anything, either. In a minute, Vladimir continued, "Even though Jane is a bright girl, I am not attracted to her. You see, she lacks the warmth, the sincerity and the purity which I value in girls. You, you are completely different…"

Darya remained silent, staring at a spot on the carpet.

"Don't worry, Vladimir, I already told you I'm not offended," she finally said. "You know, you made me want to find out more about my family's past. I honestly don't know anything about any of my ancestors. I was so blissfully ignorant."

Darya smiled with her adorable shy smile, and hugged Vladimir.

Alex walked up to his daughter and the young man. He witnessed their conversation and didn't know how to react to what he saw and heard. He wanted to be happy for Darya. She loved Vladimir, and Vladimir loved her. But he was sick at heart. Alex was worried about Vladimir, who resembled the woman he tried so hard to forget, and almost had. For the past twenty or so years, nobody had heard from her. Alex was also worried about one more thing.

The photos… Our old family photos… Could Vladimir really have seen them? Alex thought. *No, I doubt that's possible.*

Alex remembered his father's words when he passed down the family album with the photos of the Ukhtomsky princes. His father made him promise he would keep it safe.

"This album contains the history of our kin, my son. Keep it safe. We are the last of the Ukhtomsky family."

Thoughts were flashing through Alex's mind, confusing him. But one thought was distinct and persistent. "I should agree with Vladimir. Perhaps he is right. Perhaps, the descendants of my great grandfather's brothers are alive somewhere. We have to find them." This thought was so persistent and strong, that Alex didn't realize that he voiced it to Vladimir.

Vladimir left Alex and Melinda's house long after midnight. The whole family saw him to the door. Darya's parents hugged him, said goodbye, and left him with Darya. Darya saw Vladimir to the car. She didn't kiss him, but she squeezed his hand, hugged him, and wished him a safe journey. She brusquely turned around and walked back to the door. Vladimir waited for Darya to disappear behind the door and only then did he sit in his car. Alex and Melinda, who were watching their daughter from inside the house, were surprised and, at the same time, pleased by their beloved daughter's behavior. They glanced at each other, smiled and hugged each other as they walked into the living room.

Chapter 6

It had been almost a month since Vladimir returned to his hometown. Nothing had changed in his house during his absence. Only, his mother was feeling much worse. She barely got out of bed. Vladimir's mother was fifty-seven years old, but her face preserved traces of her former beauty. Her wavy hair, styled in a bob cut, was rather grayer than ash blonde. Her big blue eyes looked like a dying campfire. They periodically lit up and sparkled joyfully due to her son's return, and at times they dimmed due to her constant fatigue. Her body, which had once been lean, grew plump because she barely moved. Her once snub nose grew fatter, and was now bulbous. Her naturally bright red lips wonderfully stood out from her face. She didn't use make-up anymore because she didn't need to. Alexandra, Vladimir's mother, had been suffering from severe arthritis for ten years, and she was now bedridden for over a year.

"Mum, do you remember our neighbor from upstairs? I think her name was Anastasia," Vladimir asked his mother as he served her dinner.

Alexandra strained to remember her. She often remembered her neighbor whom she was friends with ever since she moved into this old house, which had survived the revolutions. Anastasia was only friends with Alexandra and no one else in this big house on Izmailovskiy Prospekt. She was an interesting woman, and Alexandra respected her ever since they had first met on the stair landing, the day the Zlotov family moved in. Anastasia had something in her that attracted everyone. Her face was incredibly unusual. Her bright blue eyes were like fathomless lakes, framed by think black eyelashes. Her thin black eyebrows accented her marble white skin. Her big open forehead pointed to her great intellect. Her small nose adorned her face, while her soft cheekbones and perfect, slightly cherub pink lips absolutely did not suit her big salient chin that pointed to her stubborn, tough and proud character. Anastasia was quite tall and always had a proper upright posture. In the older times, people would say that she was "as stiff as a poker". She was only slightly older than Alexandra, but, in her thirties, Alexandra was married and had three children, while Anastasia was all alone.

Her first husband couldn't stand her tough and arrogant personality, and so he divorced her after five years. They didn't even have children. Her second husband was no gift, either. He hid his alcohol addiction well before their marriage, and became an even heavier drinker about a month after becoming Anastasia's lawful husband. When Alexandra met her, Anastasia was in a horrible mental state. Not a single day went by without her husband coming back home absolutely wasted after a night with the same old soaks like him. Sometimes he even beat his wife. She suffered for about a year before throwing all his belongings from her balcony, screaming "Don't you ever dare set foot here again".

Ever since that day, Anastasia's life was dead calm. She suddenly decided that she was too old to seek a new relationship, or even another marriage. After her disastrous personal life, Anastasia immersed herself into work, defended her Candidate's dissertation, and even got a Doctor's degree. She often went on expeditions, from which she came back exhausted, yet creatively energized. In her free time, she observed the specimens she brought back, with a magnifying glass, and then compared and analyzed her discoveries. Anastasia's results were presented at conferences and published in science journals. She had the reputation of the most meticulous researcher among her colleagues. Many asked her for advice, hoping to develop a future relationship. But she was closed for any sort of relationship and refused to let anyone into her world.

Alexandra, on the other hand, was a very open person. She and her husband, Valery, loved having guests. And their guests loved them. Their home was practically always open. Children's voices, and, in the evenings, music and songs from their guests were always coming from their apartment. Alexandra often invited Anastasia over, but she always said she was busy.

"Why are you asking, my dear Vladimir? Why did you remember Anastasia all of a sudden?" Alexandra asked quietly.

"Mum, remember how you were looking through her things and noticed an old photograph of some family? You even noted that it must have been a noble family," Vladimir watched his mother closely. Her head rested on the pillow, her eyes closed, and her lips trembled. "Mum, what's wrong? Does something hurt?" he asked, concerned.

"No, honey, it's the same old stuff. It's just that I remembered the year when it happened to Anastasia. I don't have any of her things or documents. I don't need them. Nadya has them. After all, she is Anastasia's niece. Why are you so interested in the photograph?" Alexandra asked, with a hint of concern in her voice.

Vladimir told her that he saw the same photograph in the album of an American family that had Russian roots. He didn't tell her about Darya. He didn't want to worry his mother. Vladimir had no doubts about his beloved girl. He loved her and wanted to spend the rest of his life with her. But Darya's coldness on their last night upset him. Vladimir had no idea why Darya had behaved like that, and he planned to find that out upon his return to America.

"Interesting. Very interesting. Yes, I remember that photo clearly. When I saw it, I couldn't tear my eyes away from the people in it. They looked so proper and noble. It was an old photograph," Alexandra's voice was a mixture of sorrow and respect.

"Did Anastasia say anything about the photograph? Where did she get it? Are those her relatives?" Vladimir attacked his mother with questions.

Alexandra pondered. She saw the image of Anastasia looking at the photo with a remote look, but her eyes were glowing with an inner strength.

"They have such beautiful faces," Anastasia said to Alexandra. "Every time I look at this photo, I am amazed, and I can't stop admiring them."

But, for some reason, Anastasia always avoided Alexandra's questions concerning the history of the photograph and the people in it.

"Why do you need to know?" Anastasia was getting cross. "I can't tell you who these people are. It's not my story."

"Mum… Mum? So will you tell me what you know about this photograph?" Vladimir interrupted his mother's memories.

"No, my dear son, I won't. Anastasia never told me anything about it. She preferred to keep quiet. You know what, why don't you call Alena? She's friends with Nadya, so she should know how to get in touch with her. As I already said, Nadya has all of Anastasia's photos, documents and belongings. I hope she knows something."

Having fed his mother, Vladimir sat down by the phone and dialed Alena.

"By the way, Mum, why don't we invite everyone for dinner?" he suddenly offered. "We'll invite Alena with her husband, and Tatiana. I still haven't seen my lovely sisters. We only talked over the phone. It's just that as I was dialing Alena's number, I realized how much I miss her and Tania. Nobody's answering the phone. So, Mum, shall we invite them all?"

Vladimir glanced at his mother, who was lying in bed and smiling with joy.

"Of course, my dear, I'd be so happy. Tania visited recently, but I haven't seen Alena in quite some time."

In a few minutes, Vladimir called Alena again. This time, he heard an exhausted young female voice on the other side of the line.

"Hello."

It was Vladimir's older sister, Alena. They agreed to meet in an hour, and Vladimir also invited them over on the following Saturday. Alena was thirty-four. She was a mother of two lovely little girls, a wife of a man who was in love with her ever since her first year at university, and a marvelous journalist. She was highly valued at work, and her colleagues were amazed by her ability to get hold of essential, and often secret, information. Alena used up all her energy and strength at work, and so, by the end of the day, she felt like a squeezed lemon. When Vladimir called her, she only just managed to sit down on her sofa and stretch out her overworked legs. Alena loved her only brother and was impatient to see him. In about fifteen minutes, the small round table in the living room, covered by a white embroidered tablecloth, was set for dinner. There was the Olivier salad which everyone loved: Fresh sliced tomatoes, cucumbers, and bell peppers; herring under onion marinade, and boiled potatoes. Alena took out a bottle of red dry wine, wine glasses, three utensils and plates, sat down in her armchair, and called her husband.

"Sergey, could you please buy some grilled chicken?" she asked her husband, who was on his way home. "I got so exhausted at work today, that I have absolutely no energy to cook. Thank god we still have leftovers from the Olivier salad and some other dishes from last night. Did you pick the girls up from their nursery? Perfect, I'm waiting for you."

Vladimir arrived about forty minutes later. Alena's whole family met him by the door. After all the delightful hugs and kisses, everyone walked into the living room. The adults sat at the table and the kids went into their room to play with their toys. Sergey and Alena made a toast for Vladimir's arrival, and they all sat down to eating.

"Vova, is something wrong?" Alena finally asked her brother. "You're sitting as if on pins and needles. I know you have a habit of fiddling on your chair when you're interested in something."

Vladimir smiled. He loved it when his sister called him "Vova".

"You're right, Alena. Do you remember Anastasia, our neighbor from upstairs?"

"Of course, and I feel so sorry for her. She had such an unhappy life. But in the end, she was so lucky. She found a real gentleman, and even got pregnant. Everything seemed to go so well in her life. And then... poor woman," Alena went silent.

"Mum said that Nadya has all of Anastasia's belongings. Do you know her?" Vladimir's voice sounded concerned.

"Do I know her? She's my best friend. We studied together at university. Why do you want meet her? She's a bit too old for you, dear brother," Alena smiled. "I'll call her and ask her to come over. We don't need to go to work tomorrow, so we can sit all night long if we want. Oh my God, I missed you so much. I hope you'll stay the night."

The next day, while waiting for Nadya, all three of them were sitting on the sofa, looking through the photos that Alena had taken out from the cupboard.

"These are our latest photos. This photo is from Nadya's birthday, and this over here is Nadya."

The girl on the photo was a tiny bit younger than Alena. Her beautiful dark blonde hair was styled like a chaplet around her head. Her big blue eyes sparkled mischievously, while her small, straight nose and thin red lips accented her outstanding looks. Vladimir looked at the photograph more closely and noticed a faintly familiar necklace on Nadya's chest.

The doorbell rang, and Vladimir's sister let Nadya in.

"Vladimir, meet Nadya. Nadya, this is my brother Vladimir. He would like to talk to you," Alena introduced her guests to each other.

The girl looked so much different to what he expected. With her simple hair and hardly any make-up, Nadya didn't look as bright and stylish as she did in the photo. Nevertheless, Alena's friend was like a magnet. She had something in her that attracted people to her, even without her external entourage. Vladimir briefly told Nadya and Lena about the family he had met back in America and the photographs from their family album.

"Which photo, exactly, are you interested in?" Nadya asked in a low voice. "My auntie passed down a whole photo album and some of her valuable belongings to me. I think it's best if you come over to my place. If you want, we can even go now. I don't live far, just a few blocks and it's only a twenty minute walk from here."

"I don't know if it's appropriate. I mean, it *is* quite late..." Vladimir tarried slightly and glanced at his sister.

Alena rolled her eyes and walked away, showing that Nadya was not interested in *that*. After a few minutes of deep thought, Vladimir rejected Nadya's invite, using the excuse that it was too late.

"Oh well, then, it's not worth crying for the moon. It's getting late and I should get going," Nadya said as she slowly got up from the sofa.

"That's some chore you gave me, Vladimir. I'll spend the morning going through my aunt's things which I put in an old chest, which I also inherited from her. Anyway, I'll wait for all three of you at my place at around three o'clock. I'll make something for lunch, and then we'll go through my inheritance. Okeydokey?"

It was decided.

Vladimir woke up by eight and called his mother first thing in the morning. He asked how she was feeling and if Lyuba had come yet. Lyuba had been his mother's caretaker for the past seven months, ever since Valery had passed away. Alexandra's husband died suddenly and unexpectedly - his kidneys shut down. After his death, Alexandra's health became worse, and now she almost couldn't move. That was when her children decided to hire a caretaker, who also took care of the housework. Vladimir was assured that his mother was alright and that the caretaker was there. He warned his mother that he would come home late, so she wouldn't wait for him.

Alena was already bustling about her kitchen, making breakfast, and Sergey was taking a shower, while the kids were still asleep. Alena smiled when she saw her brother.

"Morning. So, are we going for lunch at Nadya's? But watch out, don't swallow her bait. She has a honey tongue, but a heart of gall," Alena teased her brother.

"Oh, Alena, Alena, you always treat me like a little child. I'm a grown up, already. Look, I'm almost a head taller than you," Vladimir said, smiling. "But seriously, I am not interested in her in that way. I already met the one and only girl for me. But don't ask me who she is and where she's from."

"You didn't even tell Mum? You didn't tell her about your new girlfriend? I thought you had no secrets from her!" Alena was surprised.

"Yes, can you imagine that? I didn't tell Mum because I didn't want to upset her. You know her attitude towards Americans and America in general. Remember how she was screaming that she wouldn't let me go, no matter what, and that that country is taking away all the people she cares about?" Vladimir asked Alena.

"Yeah, I do. I still can't make sense of what she said. Okay, you left, but only for a short period of time, and she perfectly knew that. I still don't understand why she said "people", in plural, and why she sounded so hopeless. What did she mean when she said that America was "taking away" her loved ones?" his sister said quietly, but clearly.

In the afternoon, at about three, Nadya heard the doorbell in her apartment. Alena's family and Vladimir were waiting at the door, fiddling about. A good three minutes passed before Nadya finally opened the door.

"What took you so long? We're so hungry. And the smell… Oh, the smell. What are you preparing?" Alena jabbered.

The table in the living room was already set, ready for the guests. The only thing missing was the dish with the lamb breast baked in dough. Nadya was taking it out of the oven when her guests rang the doorbell.

"Ah, the Russian women know how to set the table like this and cook such dishes so delicious that you'll lick your lips on them," Vladimir noted, satisfied, as he finished his lunch. "Thank you so much, Nadya. By the way, did you find the photos and the other things your Aunt Anastasia left behind?" he asked impatiently.

"Maybe we should have tea and coffee first. I bought wonderful éclairs. I didn't have time to make dessert myself," Nadya continued to play the role of a good housewife.

"Nadya, I honestly didn't think you would be such a zealous housekeeper today. It's not like you. You hate cooking. Or is there something you're not telling me?" Alena whispered in her friend's ear.

Nadya simply nodded and went into the kitchen to make tea.

In about twenty minutes, everyone was sitting on the comfortable sofa around a small coffee table. The massive old photo album and an old ivory casket were already on it.

"This is the main inheritance I got from my aunt," Nadya said sorrowfully, as she rested her one hand on the casket, and the other on the album. "Anastasia kept these relics safe, and said that this was all her mother had left her."

With awe, Vladimir picked up the antique album with the leather binding. He wanted to quickly open it, but, at the same time, he was afraid to be an involuntary witness of the strangers" lives which were imprinted in the photos.

It took Vladimir a long minute to open the album. The photograph he was so interested in happened to be the first one. Glued underneath it was an old piece of yellowed notebook paper with barely legible writing. He took a long close look at the purple ink, which had faded over the years, and finally made out the words "Lisa's wedding, 1912". Vladimir stared at this familiar, yet, previously unknown photograph with eyes wide open.

"So, Anastasia, Andrew and Alex are relatives!" Vladimir concluded in his mind. "No, wait, don't rush," he said to himself, remembering that his mother said Anastasia never mentioned anything about the people on the photographs.

"Nadya, you said that Anastasia was your auntie, right?" Vladimir asked their hostess.

"Well, my Mum was friends with Anastasia her whole life. They had a very warm and sincere relationship. I don't recall them every fighting with each other. I think they were more than sisters. They were the closest people to each other. I always considered her my auntie," said Nadya, looking at the photo.

The following pages of the album were filled with photos of strangers. But one photo depicted a young woman dressed in a white blouse and a black sarafan, which was fashionable in the 1970s. Vladimir couldn't tear his eyes away from it. The woman seemed so familiar.

"Who is this?" Vladimir asked Nadya, his voice trembling.

Nadya took the photo and examined it closely. She checked behind the photo, but there were no notes.

"I think this is Anastasia," she finally said, unsure.

"What was her surname?" Vladimir asked impatiently.

"She had a strange surname. It was either Khulev, or Kholev."

"Interesting! Do you know if that was her maiden name or her husband's?" Vladimir was excited.

Alena interfered, "Stop cowing poor Nadya with your questions. Does it really matter what her surname was? I can't even understand why you began this investigation. Who's it for? Your Americans? If they haven't tried to learn about the history of their family for so many years, it means they don't care. Why do *you* care?"

Vladimir got up from the sofa, walked across the room, and stopped in front of his sister. He looked into her eyes, as if trying to transfer his thoughts to her.

"Alena, how well do you know your husband's family?" he suddenly asked his sister.

"Well, well, well… What will you say to that?" Sergey asked his wife as he walked up to her.

"That's a stupid question. Of course I know my husband, his brothers and their parents very well. I know what they do and even what they dream about. I have a good relationship with his relatives," she looked at Sergey with love and winked.

"See? Then why should I be ignorant about the family of my future wife? I also want to know everything about them, up until their seventh generation," Vladimir smiled.

"Alright then, let's start with your girlfriend's surname," Alena offered, slyly glancing at her brother. "We shall uncover the secrets of your hearty obsession, my brother."

"Darya's surname is Tommy. She is one of the descendants of the well-known princely Ukhtomsky kin," Vladimir said, feeling proud deep inside. "I promised her father that I would try to find something out about his great grandfather's brothers, who stayed behind in the revolutionary Russia. I also promised to try and find any of their descendants, if there are any. I always keep my word. And, I would like to ask you, Alena and Nadya, to help me out. You are journalists and you could use your professional abilities to get some documents from archives and other sources. Will you help me?" Vladimir looked at his sister and her friend, his eyes full of hope.

In about ten days, Vladimir woke up to the loud ringing of his phone. His worried sister said that she would come over in about forty minutes.

"Could you please make me a cup of coffee, Vova? In return, I'll feed you some interesting information. Ask Mum… Actually, no, ask Lyuba if I should get anything at the store while I am on my way."

Alena came in an hour, loaded with plastic bags filled with food. On her was a heavy black bag in which she often carried her laptop. But today, instead of her laptop, it held two thick folders with documents.

"Here you go, Vova. These are the documents Nadya and I were lucky enough to get hold of. We had to commit a little occupational crime, but I think I could use them to write an article about fates, broken and destroyed by the Bolshevist regime," said Alena as she handed the folders to Vladimir.

"Let's talk in the kitchen while Mum is sleeping," Vladimir offered.

He poured his sister some fresh coffee and asked her impatiently, "So, what did you find?"

Alena looked closely at her brother for a few minutes. Finally, in a quiet and trembling voice, she said, "I took a quick look through these papers… Horrible fate. It's almost like the Ukhtomsky family was doomed. According to these documents, there are no living descendants. They were either executed by shooting, or died for various reasons…"

Alena went silent. Vladimir said nothing either. He didn't know what to say.

"I think you should take a close look at the documents," his sister finally broke the silence. "Maybe you'll find something I missed. Perhaps someone survived. I don't understand; it was a massive, happy family, and then it was gone. Everyone died. It's horrible…"

"Thank you so much, Alena. Tell Nadya how grateful I am for her help," said Vladimir quietly, in a dull toneless voice. "I'll go through the papers tonight. Now, it's not just a matter of keeping my promise, but something more. Understanding the past means seeing the future."

When Alena left, Vladimir made sure that his mother didn't need any help, and then sat down to analyses the documents. He took the first folder, on which Alena wrote "Aleksey Nikolayevich Ukhtomsky". He glanced at the second folder, which read "Leonid Nikolayevich Ukhtomsky", written in Alena's neat handwriting.

Here lie recorded the lives of at least two families, he thought to himself. *It's horrible. I am horrified to even open them, never mind reading these lifeless letters, forming lifeless words, behind which stand the fates of the members of the once strong and powerful family.*

Vladimir didn't even realize how he immersed himself into reading the official words on the carefully arranged sheets. There were copies of interrogation papers; accounts from neighbors, comrades, colleagues and friends; references from work, residence and places of confinement. While reading these documents, Vladimir often reached for a cigarette, brought it towards his lips, but then scrunched it and chucked it away without smoking it. A few times, he stood up from his chair and walked fast around his room, squeezing his head. He then sat back down and continued to read. It was far beyond midnight, when his head was cracking from the horrors he read, and his eyes were watering either from exhaustion or from compassion for the once happy, living, loving and loved people who were grinded to death mercilessly by the ruthless machine of the Stalin repression. Vladimir closed the first folder. He sat, without moving, without opening his eyes. His hands were in tight fists and his body was tense. It seemed like he was about to fight someone. But whom? Whom could he possibly file a claim to concerning the vanished family of Aleksey Ukhtomsky?

Vladimir walked up to the window. The fluffy snowflakes whirled smoothly behind the glass. The stars began to fade in the thinning dark, surrendering to the coming morning. He watched as a new day in January 2006 was born.

"I wonder," he said to himself, "if the Ukhtomsky princes were rehabilitated. None of the documents mentioned it. Wait a minute... this could be a clue." Thoughts were rushing feverishly through his head, one after the other. "I need to make a plan, rather than cling on to my wild ideas. For now, I'll have some sleep. I will dedicate the whole day tomorrow to the analysis of the documents from the second folder. Then, depending on what I'll learn from them, I will plan my next moves. I have to check the addresses mentioned in the folders. Perhaps, there is still someone who remembers the surname. And I should probably make an inquiry to the Russian Gentry Assembly. Perhaps someone filed a claim for the membership of the Ukhtomsky family."

Chapter 7

The train was slowly approaching Leningrad. A man in light canvas trousers and a short-sleeved shirt of the same color was sitting in the train's coupe carriage. He was just under the age of forty. He was silently staring outside the window, interested. The coupe of the train, heading from Moscow to Leningrad, was stuffy and the windows didn't open. The summer of 1925 happened to be exceptionally hot and dry. After some time, Aleksey, the passenger, turned his gaze at the two young girls sitting opposite him. One of them was twice as old as the other. They joined him in his coupe on the previous stop.

"My dear ladies, shall we introduce ourselves?" Aleksey broke the silence. "My name is Aleksey Nikolayevich Ukhtomsky, but you can call me Aleksey. What about you?" he asked the older girl.

The girl lit up and threw back her dark blonde hair, twisted in a tight braid.

"My name is Polina Khuleva, and my sister is called Sophia," she said.

Aleksey looked closely at the girls. He really liked the older one. She exuded inner strength and confidence in her own self. She wasn't the prettiest girl around, but he found her high forehead, her thick dark blonde chaplet wrapped around her head, her slightly aquiline nose and her plump pink lips attractive. Sophia, Polina's sister, was only a little girl, around the age of 11-13. She was sitting quietly, but her big blue eyes were continuously watching Aleksey. He thought he saw something familiar in Sophia. He wasn't sure why, but he suddenly remembered his sister, Lisa, whom Aleksey hadn't seen since the day of her wedding.

"I wonder where she is. I wonder if she's still alive," he thought to himself. His eyes dimmed, and he immersed himself into deep thought. It seemed that he lost interest in his fellow travelers.

The girls watched the man sitting in front of them with genuine interest. Polina was already twenty-five, but for a girl who still didn't get to know what love is, the growing feeling of voluptuous sensuality mixed with respect for the mature man sitting opposite her was new and unexpected. She couldn't do anything with herself. She couldn't find the strength to tear her eyes away from Aleksey's virile face, his fathomless blue eyes, and his beautiful sensual lips. She wanted to bury her hand in the stranger's thick ash blonde hair, which had become grayer with age, and press his head against her.

Aleksey felt her passionate stare. He quickly shook his head to try and free his mind from the rushing thoughts. He looked at Polina with all seriousness and attention. The invisible strings of sympathy connected them. It seemed like nobody else existed for them anymore, only the two of them. They couldn't tear their eyes away from each other. Their gazes were more eloquent than words.

Sophia broke the prolonged silence. She was sitting quietly, watching a new love being born. At the same time, she was feeling somewhat conflicting emotions. Sophia knew what Polina felt, and was happy for her. However, her outer childishness concealed her inner passionate nature. Sophia noticed Aleksey's well-built figure and noble appearance the moment she had entered the coupe. She watched Aleksey with wide open eyes, hoping he would notice her. But he didn't. Aleksey and Polina were absorbed by each other's gazes. Sophia didn't exist for them, and this offended her. She broke the silence by saying the first thing that came to her mind.

"Polina, I'm hungry. Can we eat something?" Sophia said loudly and clearly, as she expressively pulled on Polina's sleeve.

"Yes, Sophia, my dear, of course. I bought some bread before we left. It's in my bag. You can take some," Polina said, feeling guilty. She felt uncomfortable for revealing her emotions. She apologized to Aleksey, and reached for a little package with a few slices of bread inside.

"Ladies, don't worry and don't fuss about. I'm a provident person," Aleksey interfered as he took out a bundle with cooked chicken, bread, tomatoes and cucumbers, and set them on the table. "Please, help yourselves. Don't be shy."

Polina mumbled words of apology and gratitude at the same time. She blushed from shyness and inconvenience due to Aleksey's attention. She was glad, but it felt so unusual. Polina didn't know how to react but Sophia came to the rescue. Without ceremony, she took a piece of chicken, put it on a slice of bread, and then a slice of tomato and cucumber on top of it all, thus creating her own original sandwich. The girls hadn't eaten all day long, so Sophia decided that hunger was, indeed, a stiff task-master and it wouldn't wait.

"This is delicious food!" Sophia noted, satisfied. "Polina, eat something or you'll faint like you did two days ago."

Aleksey carefully looked at Polina, afraid to offend her pride, and asked her why they were going to Leningrad and if they had a place to stay. He was shocked by what he heard. The sisters were going to Leningrad on the off-chance. They had no friends, no relatives, and no accommodation there. Polina decided to go to Leningrad, hoping to find work. This was pretty much all that Aleksey managed to get out of her. The sisters weren't very communicative. He was of the impression that they were afraid of something, that they were keeping something back. Nevertheless, the way Aleksey formed his sentences and expressed his thoughts helped him win the girls" trust. Besides, he really didn't want to part with Polina, so, when the train arrived to Leningrad, he invited the girls to stay with him.

"I am not burdened with a family. My apartment is small, but there's enough space for all of us. You two can live in one room and I can live in the other. Besides, I'm almost never at home. I only come home to sleep," said Aleksey, hoping that the girls would agree.

Sophia smiled happily and begged Polina to accept the invitation. The older sister was perplexed. She thought it was inappropriate to stop at a stranger's house, but he was so attractive, Polina didn't take long to answer.

"Thank you so much, Aleksey, it's like you were sent to us by God. It's true what they say – the world is not without good people. However, you don't know us at all, and we can't afford to pay you rent. I am unemployed, and Sophia has to study. We don't even have any savings, we spent all the money we had on train tickets and some snacks," Polina said gratefully and politely, looking at her virtue.

"That won't be a problem. I would never take money from you. I don't make a profit from other people's miseries. My origins and views on life wouldn't allow me to do that. And, about the fact that I don't know you well enough... Sometimes, you can live with a person for years and still not know him. There is some rottenness in that person, that isn't evident at first, but it gradually reveals itself, and shocks and disappoints you every time. You, on the other hand, are like an open book, and I liked what I read. Sorry for the platitude, Polina. And I won't take "no" for an answer. I will go find a carrier, and then we'll go to my place on Izmailov Prospekt."

The days ensued. Aleksey was almost never home. He was a professor at the Mining Institute, and was researching the polymetallic ores of the Altai Mountains. His work took up all his time. If he wasn't on an academic trip, then he would sit in his laboratory until the dead of night. Polina and Sophia were living with him. They turned his bachelor's den into a cozy home where one could feel the presence of not just a woman, but a lover. Indeed, the love and respect for Aleksey that had sparked in the train was growing into an incredibly powerful fire inside Polina. Every night, she impatiently waited for her beloved man to come back from work. Her heart was longing for Aleksey, but her mind always reminded her about their difference in age, their difference in social status, and that Aleksey probably pitied her rather than loved her. Polina had nobody to share her feelings with and nobody to ask for advice from. She didn't know what to do. Polina felt that Sophia was too young, and didn't want to let her in on her deepest secrets.

She often remembered her mother, who had passed away when Polina was only ten years old. She remembered how, a few days before that, she had said, "Polina, my darling, I'm going to die soon. I can feel it. But remember, if you're ever in trouble, ask the prince for help. He will help you. He has to."

That was when her mother began to cough out blood, her face went pale and, as she helplessly gasped for air, lost consciousness. The poor woman was like this for two days until she quietly passed away. With her last breath, she only managed to say, "He... he..."

Polina grew up without a father. Her mother came from an impoverished princely kin and lived in the prince's manor on the rights of a distant relative. For as long as Polina could remember, they always lived in the distant room of the manor. Her mother helped the prince with the housekeeping. Even though Polina didn't have a father, it didn't bother her. The prince wasn't married for a long time, but he loved children. He looked after Polina as she grew up. He even hired tutors for her, and she was home-schooled quite well. After the death of her mother, Polina continued to live in the two rooms of the massive manor, where she used to reside with her mother.

"Oh mother... Oh how I wish I could talk to you, and ask you for your advice and guidance," Polina whispered quietly as she gazed with her sad eyes at the small photo of her mother, which rested on her bedside table.

It was late. Aleksey was supposed to come back from his trip to Altai. Sophia was already seeing her umpteenth dream of the night. Polina loved to admire her sleeping little sister. Even now, Polina was sitting on the corner of Sophia's sofa, caressing her hand.

"It's okay, everything will be just fine. We have been through so much together that God won't let us perish in this cruel world. It was no coincidence that we met Aleksey. He is our reward for all the challenges that we have faced," Polina mumbled as she continued to caress her sister's hand. Involuntary tears trickled down her cheeks in thin streams. "Aleksey, Aleksey," she repeated the name of her new love.

"What should I do? I am in such torment. I can see that he's not indifferent to me. I can see the fire in his eyes when he looks at me. I can feel his desire to be with me. He is so kind to me and Sophia. We would perish in this city without him. Aleksey doesn't only provide us with a roof over our heads; he also shares his bread with us, which he worked for, himself. We are so grateful... But it can't go on like this anymore. I have to tell him everything." Polina's muttered words were interrupted by a knock on the door.

It was a conventional knock that Aleksey and the sisters agreed upon. Polina automatically fixed her simple hairstyle, straightened out her clean knitted dress, which she had obtained by chance from an old lady about a year before, and walked up to the door. Before opening it, she looked at herself in the oval mirror, which hung in the hallway, and smiled. Aleksey entered the apartment carrying a small brown leather suitcase. In his left hand, he held a small bouquet of chamomiles. Before taking off his coat, he said hello to Polina, gifted her the simple bouquet, and, having grown bolder, he squeezed Polina in his embrace. She didn't resist.

"I missed you so much, my darling," Aleksey's voice was quiet and gentle.

Polina wasn't expecting Aleksey to express his feelings so suddenly. She was shy and even jumped back slightly, even though she longed to be held in his arms. Aleksey looked at her, puzzled, but then felt her hands tenderly hug his head, as her warm damp lips covered his face with kisses.

"My dear, my darling, my love, my sweetheart, I've been waiting for you so long. I never dared to speak of my love for you..." she whispered tenderly.

They spent the rest of the night together. It was fantastic. Polina bathed in love. Her timidity, shyness, and natural fear of her first night with a man were overcome by Aleksey's love and tenderness. They felt good together. Their lips, when they weren't busy with passionate kisses, were whispering words of love to each other. Their arms embraced and caressed each other's flaming passionate bodies. In their passionate expressions of love, they didn't notice how the dawn of the new day replaced the night.

"Tomorrow... No, today, I will introduce you to my brother and his family. I love you, and I would love to offer you my hand and heart. Will you marry me?" Aleksey asked Polina, his voice serious, eyes hopeful.

Polina covered her face with her hands, her shoulders trembled, and she quietly cried.

"What is it? Is it something I said? Why are you crying?" he hugged Polina, and, in a burst of tenderness and passion, began kissing her eyes, wet from her tears, and her trembling lips. "Polina, my darling, what's wrong? Did I offend you?"

"My God, Aleksey, you have no idea what your words mean to me. I loved you from the moment I first saw you. With every day, my love became stronger and deeper. Today, I realized that I can't live without you. I was eating my heart out, waiting for you to come back. And you read my feelings, you understood them. And now, I am sure, more than ever before, that we aren't just made for each other... we are one whole. Yes, I want to always be by your side, breathe the same air as you, be your wife, lover and friend," Polina said the words on a single breath, unable look away from his face.

Aleksey couldn't tear his eyes from Polina's magnificent eyes and her face, flushed with anxiety. He hugged her with tenderness and passion. She didn't resist. Their love-filled night continued through the break of dawn.

Polina suddenly exclaimed, as if she remembered something, "Aleksey, what about Sophia? She's going to live with us, right?"

"Polina, don't be silly. Of course, she'll live with us. Sophia is your sister, and she'll become my sister, too."

Aleksey went silent and his face became gloomy. He stood up from his bed and walked up to the table, without saying a word. He picked up a cigarette, wanting to light it, but then put it back and walked up to the window. The sun's rays adorned the windows of the house opposite his. A new day was beginning. The neighbors in the house opposite were beginning to wake up. The yardmen were working in full swing with their brooms, clearing the paths from the fallen leaves. The early autumn was about to replace the late summer. The trees were decorated by an attire of colorful leaves, which slowly left their haven on the trees and whirled onto the still warm ground. Aleksey's gaze stopped on one such yellow-red leaf, helpless and solitary. He remembered his sister, Lisa, whom he hadn't heard from for the past 10 years. She didn't write him any letters. Even if she had, they wouldn't have reached him. Their address changed, and according to what Aleksey heard, their manor was robbed and burnt to the ground. Aleksey's eyes were thoughtful, and his face was twisted with torment.

"Aleksey, my dear, is something wrong?" Polina's voice sounded distant in Aleksey's head.

He turned away from the window, walked up to Polina and hugged her.

"It's nothing, my darling. Everything will be just fine." He kissed her hard and gently at the same time, and offered her to have breakfast. "We should check up on Sophia, as well. Did she sleep alright without you?"

Sophia slept curled up on her sofa in the girls' room. Polina decided not to wake her up. At around nine, when Polina and Aleksey had already finished their simple breakfast consisting of an omelet and some bread, drank their hot tea, and were about to get up from the table, the kitchen door opened and Sophia's shaggy head appeared in the doorway.

"Good morning, Aleksey. You're back already? I'm so happy. I mean, *we* are happy," she corrected herself, and, ashamed, glanced at Polina. Sophia noticed that her older sister was glowing with an inner light. "Polina, what's going on with you? You're so much different to what you were yesterday. What happened?"

"Everything changed, my dear Sophia. Everything will be different now, right, Aleksey?" Polina uttered quietly as she looked at her beloved man, her voice full of hope.

Sophia quickly realized that something happened between Aleksey and her sister, which brought them closer together, and made them one whole. She smiled and her eyes sparkled with hint a mischief.

"Aleksey and Polina, sitting in a tree, K – I – S – S – I – N - G. First comes the love, then comes the marriage, then comes a baby in the carriage," chanted Sophia.

"Stop it, stop being so childish!" shouted Polina as her face flushed with embarrassment.

But Sophia didn't hear her. She brusquely turned around and rushed headlong into her room. In a minute, Polina and Aleksey heard noises coming from her room, as if she was moving the furniture around, and then things falling on the floor. The lovers ran into Sophia's room.

Sophia was standing in the middle of the room holding a slim volume of Pushkin's poems, observing it. Chairs were lying all around her, the bed and the sofa were displaced, the table was about to fall over, and books were scattered all over the floor. Sophia didn't move, and her frozen eyes were turned at the book filled with Pushkin's poems. But she didn't see it. Her cheeks flared up, her arms trembled and she had a nervous tremor. Polina ran up to her little sister and hugged her to calm her down. But Sophia pushed her away and looked at her with tormented eyes.

"Go away! Go away! I don't want to see you!" she screamed. She fell on to her sofa, buried her face in the pillow, and began to cry.

"Sophia, my sweet little sister, what's wrong with you? I've never seen you like this. What happened? Talk to me..."

Sophia didn't say anything. She simply lay on the sofa, facing its back, ignoring everyone. Polina and Aleksey sat down on the chairs that they picked up. In a few minutes, Sophia turned to the lovers and smiled, although her smile was crooked. But her anger and misery had faded away. She apologized to the two people she cared about most and asked for breakfast.

"Of course, of course, honey. Your breakfast is already on the kitchen table. And please, don't take too long like you normally do. We'll all be going to Aleksey's brother in about an hour and a half," Polina spoke quietly, slowly and calmly, afraid to trigger Sophia's strange emotions.

Surprisingly, Sophia reacted calmly to her sister's news. She quickly ate her breakfast, drank some warm water from the kettle, and ran into her room to get dressed. In five minutes, she was ready to go.

"I'm ready!" Sophia exclaimed, sounding unnaturally happy.

Around midday, the three of them were already walking up the stairs in a house on Nevsky Prospect. Aleksey rang the doorbell on the right side of the hall. The door opened in a minute, and Aleksey's brother appeared in the doorway of the big cozy apartment.

"Hi, Leonid, these are my lovely neighbors. Meet..." Aleksey began to introduce the girls to his brother, but Leonid interrupted him.

"Aleksey, who in the world introduces themselves in the doorway? Come inside, lovely ladies. I am Leonid Nikolayevich, Aleksey's brother. Olga, Lida, come and meet our guests. You are Polina, right?" Leonid carefully looked at the beautiful young blushed lady.

"Aleksey told me so much about you. You must be Sophia," he turned to Polina's sister.

Leonid saw something distantly familiar and dear in Sophia. He gazed at Sophia for some time, making her feel uncomfortable.

"Leonid, let us finally meet our guests," he heard his wife's voice. Olga hugged the two sisters and invited them to the table, which was set in the big room. Lida, Leonid's daughter, was around the same age as Sophia, and so they had a lot in common. The two girls sat at the table for some time, and then excused themselves and disappeared in Lida's room.

Lunch went by pleasantly and quickly. They were discussing the problems that the two brothers had at work and about the situation in the "poor" Russia, as Leonid called it. At the same time, Leonid could barely keep himself from asking Polina about her relatives and Sophia, for whom he felt a sudden affection. But Polina was so radiant and blissful that he felt these questions inappropriate for now.

"I'll find it all out later," Leonid thought to himself. "Anyway, Polina is a humble girl with dignity, and this says a lot about her."

"I think Aleksey will finally be happy," he shared his impressions with Olga when their guests left. "By the way, Olga, what did you think of Sophia, Polina's sister?"

"Well, she's a nice girl with beautiful lively eyes and a pretty face. I can tell she'll be more beautiful when she grows up. However, she's a bit too impetuous. I think the fact that her mother wasn't around is beginning to show. After all, she was raised by young Polina ever since she was seven. I can't even begin to imagine what they've been through!"

"Olga, did you notice anything familiar in Sophia?"

Leonid's wife pondered. She strained to remember Sophia's face. Olga shrugged her shoulders.

"No, not really. She doesn't remind me of anyone. Why, who does she remind you of?" she asked her husband.

"I don't know... I really miss my dear Lisa. We haven't seen her in over ten years. Maybe I'm just too sensitive. Every time I see a woman or a girl in the street, I look for her... Lisa is our only sister. She was a delicate flower among us, her brothers, the spiky burdocks," Leonid sighed. "Anyway, my darling let me help you clean up. Ten years ago, who would have thought that we would be cooking, cleaning and washing up all by ourselves?"

Chapter 8

A week had passed since the day Alena had given Vladimir the two bulky folders with the documents on the Ukhtomsky family. In addition, Alena and her expert friend Nadya put together one more folder. Alena had no idea where Nadya coaxed it out from, but the third folder had considerably more information on the princes. The documents weren't arranged in chronological order, some of them were frayed and although some of the writing had faded, it was still legible. Once again, Vladimir immersed himself into reading the new stack of papers. With every new document, his face became gloomier, more shocked and twitched furiously. The face of the young man—who hadn't yet experienced the worst of life—was loaded with emotions.

"My God, did this really happen? These families went through so much torment and suffering, and for what?!?" he practically yelled involuntarily.

For a long time, Vladimir was sitting with his head on the table, his arms wrapped around the back of his head. It was getting late. The street lights were already on. Vladimir refused to turn his lamp on. He felt gloomy, uneasy, and anxious.

"Vladimir, is everything alright? Why are you sitting in the dark?" asked Vladimir's mother.

It took some time for Vladimir to come to. He rubbed his temples.

"Do you need anything, Mum?" he finally asked.

"No, honey, everything is alright. I'm worried about you. Why haven't you turned the lights on? Your eyes are red and they look inflamed. Were you crying?"

"What are you talking about? Of course I wasn't. Although after what I read, I wouldn't be surprised if I did. The times were so rough! How did the people survive it all? Whole families were wiped out, and for what?" Vladimir's voice trembled from indignity and his nervous tremor.

Alexandra gazed at her son without hiding her interest. She was impressed by how much her son had changed. It seemed only yesterday, he was running around the streets and partying, not caring about the past or the future. And now he was seriously interested in the history of a family which he met by chance, as fate would have it. She knew that big things start with a little desire.

"Come on, go make us some tea, and then we'll talk," she calmly asked her son.

In less the ten minutes, Vladimir set the little table by Alexandra's sofa for tea. He poured the tea in big faience cups and brought a small vase with sweets and cookies. Alexandra was lying on her sofa, covered in her checkered furry blanket.

"Tell me, my dear son, what impressed you so much. Why are you so upset that you can barely hide your manly tears?"

Vladimir sat down in the armchair by his mother's sofa. His temples and head ached, and he tried to rub his forehead with his fingers, hoping that the pain would leave. He glanced at his mother, who was looking at him with great interest.

"Mum, I really need to get this off my chest, and talk about what I read in these horrible documents. Mum, you cannot imagine how shocked I am by what I read."

Vladimir sat comfortably in the chair and, in a slow, soft voice, he began describing the twists and turns of the Ukhtomsky brothers" lives. He described the picture that formed in his head after reading the documents in the folders…

Leonid Ukhtomsky couldn't wait until the evening. He only had one thing on his mind, and it couldn't let him concentrate on work. He still couldn't believe that in a month, he could be in America. And there, he could try and find a way to contact, or find some information about his brother Alexander and his family. It had been ten years since he left Russia. During all this time, Leonid only heard from Alexander once. The former member of the Nobility Association, and now a worker for the Commissariat of Foreign and Domestic Trade, gave Leonid a short letter from Alexander, where he wrote that he was going to be moving to America with his family. Life in Austria, where they were currently living, was getting harder and harder, but Alexander refused to even consider moving back to Russia. His last words in the letter were:

We will probably never see each other again. Take care of yourselves. May God be with you.

Leonid received this letter five years ago.

He was very excited after talking to the institute's director. Nikolai Andreevich told him that they are planning to send a group of specialists with an important mission to the USA, and that he, Leonid Ukhtomsky, was to be part of the group. Leonid practically flew home on his wings of joy. He couldn't wait to tell his wife about this.

"Olga, my love, you will never guess what happened!" Leonid shouted the moment he walked into his apartment. Olga came out of the living room to meet her husband. His shining eyes and cheerful face amazed her.

"Leonid, it's been a long time since I last saw you this handsome. You are shining with joy. What happened?"

Leonid ran up to Olga and twirled her in a small dance. She laughed, hugged her beloved husband, and kissed him.

"So, tell me. I'm all ears."

It was late at night, long after the couple finished their dinner and had their tea. They were sitting and hugging on their sofa in the twilight.

"Okay, Leonid. Let's assume that you'll go to the States with your colleagues," Olga uttered anxiously. "But how are you planning to find something out about Alexander? You have to know where to go and whom to speak with."

"You're right, Olga. I have to think this through. Perhaps, I should talk to my old friend from university, Andrey Gerasimovsky. Do you remember him? Surely, he can advise me and give me a few suggestions," Leonid said as he gently kissed his wife.

Olga shrugged her shoulders.

"I don't know. I don't really like the idea of talking to Andrey. He is dishonest with his friends. There was even a time when he proved it."

"Don't worry. It will be just fine. You'll see. Let's go to bed, my dear. It's quite late. As they say, morning is wiser than the evening."

The following day, he agreed to meet with his old friend after work at Leonid's apartment. But first, Leonid decided to talk with Aleksey. He went to Izmailov Prospekt. He rang the doorbell, and Sophia opened the door. She wasn't the same playful little girl she had been the first time they met three years ago. The two brothers didn't meet often. They both had a lot of work, and Aleksey was often away on academic trips. It was natural that Leonid didn't notice how she was growing up, changing from a clumsy little girl into a charming young lady. Her wavy ash blonde hair was tied up in a tight ponytail, her eyes, blue as the smooth surface of a lake, sparkled, and her small snub nose gave her face a mischievous look. Sophia wasn't tall, but her body was well built, and she looked noble.

Leonid didn't expect to see her so grown up and so beautiful. Second of all, he was still amazed by his inexplicable feeling of compassion for her and complicity in her fate, which he also felt when they first met three years ago.

"Hello, Sophia, is my brother at home?" Leonid asked, smiling at the young girl.

"Yes, of course, come on in, Leonid Nikolayevich," quickly replied Sophia, closed the door behind Leonid, and disappeared into her room.

Aleksey was in the kitchen, working magic on a small saucepan on the stove. Unlike his older brother, the youngest Ukhtomsky brother loved cooking.

"Come on in, Leonid. Take a seat. Dinner will be ready in a minute," said Aleksey the moment he saw his brother.

"Good evening, Leonid Nikolayevich," Polina still couldn't allow herself to call him by his first name. She respected Leonid, and not only because he was much older than her. Polina grew up without a father, and she felt that Leonid replaced the father figure for Aleksey, as well as for her. She continued, "We're so happy to see you! Why don't you stay for dinner?"

Polina took out a fresh starched tablecloth and began to set the table for dinner.

"Aleksey, I need you to give me some advice," Leonid stated anxiously.

Aleksey carefully looked at his brother. Something in Leonid's voice made him alert. He felt that Leonid didn't just visit because he missed his brother. It seemed that this visit was very important for Leonid.

"Leonid, I can see that this is going to be a serious conversation. Let's have dinner first. It will be hard to make any decision on an empty stomach. Besides, its rumbling would constantly disturb us," Aleksey smiled at his brother and invited him to the table.

When everyone was sitting at the table, Leonid looked at everyone and smiled. He was pleased to be in this house. He felt good and free. Love and mutual understanding were in the air. Little by little, Leonid glanced at the people he loved, and was happy for his dear brother. Aleksey had a gentle, caring and loving wife. But Leonid still couldn't fully understand Sophia. She was tender and courteous, but only towards Aleksey. When it came to Polina, Leonid noticed Sophia was tense with her. It wasn't obvious, though. Sophia always smiled when she talked to her sister, but her smile was insincere and unnatural, and her eyes had a tiny spark of jealousy and hatred. And Leonid couldn't understand this.

I need to give this some more thought, and observe Sophia some more, decided the older Ukhtomsky brother. *I hope she doesn't do anything stupid.*

After dinner, the brothers disappeared into the big room, which served as the couple's bedroom and living room.

"So, Leonid, tell me what happened. I'm all ears."

"I'm going to the States," said Leonid, quickly. Aleksey was taken aback by this news. Leonid gave Aleksey a moment to digest it and continued, "You know how the Bolsheviks decided to develop the country's industry? They're right, Russia needs this now. And I support this particular decision of the Bolshevist Party," Leonid smiled at this remark. "Perhaps, this is the first time I support any of their decisions. But I still don't support the Bolsheviks themselves. They did everything they could to destroy the old Russia – the Russia in which I was born and raised. However, I am serving my country, and I'll do anything to make sure that it can firmly stand on its feet, be powerful, and develop faster and better than any other country."

Leonid went silent. His face was flushed and his eyes were burning. Aleksey didn't say anything, either. He agreed with his brother and was interested in hearing more. After a short pause, Leonid continued.

"I was introduced into a group of specialists. In a month, we are going to the States to get training at the Albert Kahn Inc. bureau. Can you imagine what this means?"

"You…" Aleksey said as he looked at his brother anxiously. "You're hoping to find Alexander? But how? Through who? No, this is absurd. Moreover, it's dangerous. It's dangerous for everyone, especially for you. And you know this." Aleksey's voice was getting quieter and quieter, and Leonid could barely hear his last words.

"Yes, I know that I still have a lot of undecided questions. But the very idea, that we can finally find our brother and his family overwhelms me. Ever since I found out that I will be going to the States, I'm always excited. Just tell me one thing, Aleksey; do you think that there is the slightest chance that we can find Alexander? Do you agree with me and my desire?"

Leonid gazed at his brother, waiting for a response. Aleksey pondered. He was in a dilemma. On the one hand, he really wanted to find his brother and he thought that Leonid's newfound opportunity was fate's gift. On the other hand, Aleksey knew the dangers, and he was worried for Leonid and his family. Aleksey knew that the Council of People's Commissars had a Main Political Administration (MPA), whose duty was to reveal and annihilate anyone opposing the Soviet regime. This wasn't just a rumor. A few days ago, they had arrested one of the most authoritative specialists in their university, who was researching metal ore deposits. Professor Vernikov was only arrested because, at the Institute Council Debate, he fallaciously reflected upon the methods of mining gold from the deposits in the Bodaybinsky District, and noted that USSR was well behind most countries in this field. Aleksey also knew that the MPA had their spies in practically every organization.

"Leonid, did you tell anyone that you are planning to look for our brother in the States?" Aleksey didn't hide his concern from his brother. "I'm just curious."

"I was thinking of discussing it with my old friend from university. I invited him over for dinner tomorrow. I think you may remember him. He used to visit us often. It's Andrey Gerasimovsky."

"Andrey? You still keep in touch with him after what he did on your birthday in 1916?" Aleksey's voice was indignant.

"Well, yes. He's working at the Council of Peoples Commissars now. If you remember, he was the one who gave me Alexander's letter. I have no reason not to trust him. Besides, he often travels abroad, so he should know where I should go for advice on how to look for relatives. I know that many people have this problem, and I don't recall anyone being arrested or imprisoned for trying to find their missing relatives."

"You're being presumptuous, Leonid. I would never trust Gerasimovsky."

"I think you're wrong, Aleksey. Just like us, Gerasimovsky was from a noble family and used to be an earl a long time ago. I'm sure he wouldn't want to sully his name by betraying his own kind," Leonid stopped for a moment, weighing his thoughts, and continued, "As far as his idiotic prank is concerned, he apologized to me many times after that. He said he had no idea what came over him. He was jealous of me, but now there is nothing to be jealous of. No, I think I'll go and ask him for help. If you want, you can come over for dinner with Polina and Sophia, as well. Olga and I will only be happy."

The following evening, Leonid and Olga were awaiting their guests. It was obvious how nervous they were. Leonid couldn't forget what Aleksey said about Gerasimovsky. Deep inside, he agreed with his brother. Gerasimovsky wasn't the brightest man, and he was indeed quite despicable. Andrey's prank on Leonid's birthday of 1916 proved it. Leonid remembered that day. He, a cheerful and hopeful husband and father, was greeting his guests. Gerasimovsky, a dandy, a friend from university and Gentry Assembly, was one of the guests.

Regardless of his bright appearance, none of the women liked him. Perhaps they could sense his foulness inside. The men, on the other hand, not being as scrupulous and perspicacious as the women, endured Gerasimovsky. They welcomed him into their homes, talked to him in clubs, and were even friends with him. Gerasimovsky was unmarried, but he was desperate for a wife. He was well over the age of thirty, yet there was still no contender for his hand and heart or even his earldom. This made Andrey suffer. He was jealous of all his married friends. He hated Leonid on the sly. He hated him for his successful career of a civil engineer. But mostly, he hated Leonid for marrying Olga, whom Gerasimovsky was in love with from his student years.

When Gerasimovsky entered the house of the Ukhtomsky brothers in 1916, he immediately saw Olga. She was joyfully radiant, which is inherent in women that are in love. He couldn"t tear his eyes away from her beautiful face. Olga was busy with her guests and she didn't notice how Gerasimovsky walked into the living room. He stopped by the door and admired the woman that didn't belong to him, the woman that he dreamed of all these years. His head was dizzy and he could hardly breathe. He could feel a lump of hatred and anger in his throat. It was hatred and anger towards everyone who surrounded Olga, especially Leonid—her husband and the father of her daughter. Gerasimovsky listened to his inner voice and walked into the second living room where he could be alone. He had to cool down and clear his thoughts. But a small demon, sitting deep inside him, was dictating his will to Gerasimovsky. Andrey couldn't resist it. Calm on the outside but highly strung-up on the inside, he walked up to Olga, said hello, and asked her to talk with him in the garden. Olga excused herself from her guests, whom she was talking to at the moment, and went outside. He led her to a summerhouse deep within the garden. Olga followed him, not suspecting anything.

The end of September 1916 was still warm from the summer. Surprisingly, there was very little rain. The summerhouse was warm and cozy. It was entwined with wild vines and ivy, forming a live hedge. It was isolated from the rest of the garden. When Olga walked in, she felt fiery male hands roughly and shamelessly grope her waist and chest from behind. Olga was disgusted and horrified. She fell into a stupor. She brusquely tore his repulsive arms away from her and jumped forwards. She quickly turned around. Gerasimovsky stood in front of her. His eyes burned with desire, his cheeks flared, and he looked like he was about to leap onto Olga. The princess glanced at him, her eyes filled with rage.

"Earl, are you in your right mind? How dare you? Leave our house, NOW! You may forget we even know each other!" said Olga quietly, yet firmly.

Gerasimovsky stood in one place, as if rooted to the ground. He couldn't believe that the woman he was in love with for so many years was kicking him out of her house. Olga looked at him with a hateful stare. His eyes flushed. His temples ached with a piercing pain. He was growing more hateful and dissatisfied.

"You'll pay for this, princess. My day will come, and then you should beware," said Gerasimovsky in his coarse voice. After a short pause, he continued, in a different voice with a hint of mocking respect, "And now, princess, allow me to take my leave. I am sorry for the troubles and my tactlessness. I just couldn't resist. You *are* one of my greatest desires."

The count bowed. He briskly turned around and left. The princess gave herself a few moments to calm down and returned to her guests. But she couldn't conceal her irritability from her husband's loving and careful eyes.

"What happened?" Leonid asked his wife, when she came up to him after seeing their last guest to the door. "You look white as a sheet. Is something wrong? Everyone seemed to enjoy the night and they were all grateful that we invited them."

"Yes, the night has indeed been successful," said the princess, and paused. After a moment, she continued, "I can't even find the right words to say this. Did you notice that Earl Gerasimovsky left and didn't even talk to any of our guests?"

Surprised, Leonid glanced at his wife.

"He was here tonight? He never came up to me, and I didn't even see him anywhere. Yes, I did invite him, but I assumed that he couldn't come. So he *was* here… So why he leave so quickly?" The prince was so perplexed that Olga felt sorry for him.

She knew that her husband was studying with Gerasimovsky and that they were friends. She panicked and wasn't sure if she should tell her husband about the terrible incident. But, at the same time, she knew that Gerasimovsky didn't only disrespect her, but also her husband. She took a moment to think. Olga decided it was best that she would be the one to tell Leonid about what happened, hence foreseeing another dirty trick from Gerasimovsky. Leonid carefully listened to Olga's account. He was silent. Only his gritting teeth gave out his growing rage and inner tension. Ever since that September day in 1916, Gerasimovsky was dead to the Ukhtomsky family. The earl himself tried not to see them, either. And he succeeded. Their paths didn't meet. Until March 1923, when Gerasimovsky found Leonid in order to hand him Alexander's letter. The earl simply walked up to the man he once despised, and held out the letter.

"Prince, let's forget our past. A lot has happened ever since. I think it put everything into its places. I believe we shouldn't fight anymore, and we should support each other, instead. Please, forgive my attitude towards your family in the past. I've changed. I hope you will forgive me," he told Leonid.

The earl's face expressed so much remorse that Leonid believed him. Everything that happened before the October Revolution of 1917, which changed the lived of many generations in Russia and other countries, seemed like a distant memory from a past life. It was impossible to return anything. All that was left to do was remember and revere. With time, the bitterness and joy of the old times had faded. They knew that they have to live here and now. Leonid decided to leave the unpleasant memories of his former friend, Gerasimovsky, in the depth of his mind, and not bring them up to the surface. He was grateful that Andrey brought him news about Alexander. But that was all. He did not intend to be friends with the earl anymore. But, a bad peace is better than a good quarrel. Leonid remembered this popular wisdom and tried to live by it. He parted with Gerasimovsky in 1923 on a friendly not, promising to remember each other and try to keep in touch. And now, Leonid had a good excuse to meet with Andrey again.

Gerasimovsky came late for dinner at Leonid's house. He wore his finest clothes, as always. His sturdy suit, made from woolen covert, fitted him like a glove. His blue tie with thin stripes perfectly matched his suit and his light blue shirt. However, no matter how good the suit was, it couldn't overcome the unpleasant feeling the Ukhtomsky couple had when they looked at Andrey. Time had no mercy on him. His forehead was furrowed with wrinkles, and the deep folds around his mouth pointed to stomach problems. His once big and sparkly eyes became small slits, barely seen under the heavy upper eyelids, while his bottom eyelids were scarred by hernia. But that was not all. Olga and Leonid were staggered by the haughty and arrogant look on Audrey's face. When Gerasimovsky saw Olga, he smiled, walked up to her, and kissed her hand.

"Princess Olga, I am so glad to see you. You haven't changed a bit. You still look just as beautiful. But let's forget the past. I still curse myself for my expansiveness. Let's remain good friends," he said as he smiled at Olga.

"Andrey, don't worry. I've forgotten all about it. Please, come in. Dinner is almost ready. You know all of us, apart from Polina, Aleksey's wife," Olga blurted out, and quickly turned away. She walked into the kitchen and looked outside the window. Her face was burning with hatred and indignation.

I still find him unpleasant, Olga thought to herself. *But what can I do? I'll just play the role of a hospitable housewife… for the sake of my family.*

Olga picked up the tray with the serving plates and walked into the living room.

After dinner, the two men sat on the sofa to talk.

"Andrey, do you still work at the Council of People's Commissars? I mean, the Supreme Soviet of the National Economy?" Leonid was slightly nervous when he started the conversation he was so interested in.

"Yes, Leonid. But now, I'm not just an ordinary worker. I am now the head of the administration of mechanical engineering and metal-working. The Bolsheviks trust me. It took me a lot of time and effort to work in this field and prove myself to them. I think that I was successful. The Bolsheviks even offered me to join their Party! Can you imagine?" Gerasimovsky was brimming with pride and self-admiration. "Even though I may not have a family… Yes, I still don't have a family. I still can't find the woman of my dreams. But I will fulfill myself as a valuable specialist. Fortunately, this country doesn't have enough specialists in this new structure, as the Bolsheviks call it. I am in their good graces, and I like it." Gerasimovsky threw an arrogant glance at Leonid. "I'm sorry, you said you wanted to ask me something."

Leonid was silent. He couldn't bring himself to have the candid conversation with his old friend. A part of him didn't want to talk to Gerasimovsky about his sacred problem. Something in his tirade put him on his guard. Leonid didn't trust him.

"Oh, that. No, I just wanted to see you again. We used to be friends, and we have so much in common. We've been through so much in the old times," Leonid uttered calmly, with a hint of nostalgia in his voice.

It was well past midnight when Gerasimovsky left the Ukhtomsky apartment. Leonid closed the door after him.

"You and Aleksey were right. I shouldn't have invited Andrey. Time taught him nothing," Leonid admitted to his wife.

"Yes, Leonid. He's a very unpleasant man. I feel uneasy after his presence in our home."

Chapter 9

It has been almost a month since Vladimir went back to his home country. Darya spent her free time from university researching the Ukhtomsky family on the internet. Alex told her daughter everything his father and grandfather had told him. They both studied the photographs with the Ukhtomsky princes.

"Dad, which one of the princes do you think I resemble most?" Darya asked, anxiously awaiting her father's response. She began to examine her nose in her pocket mirror, comparing it to the photographs. "Do you think my nose looks like your great grandmother's nose? And my ears… I've got your great grandfather's ears." She then held her father's face in her hands and began to thoroughly examine it, comparing it to the pre-revolutionary photos of the Ukhtomsky princes, Alex's grandfather, his father and her face.

"I can't tell whom I look like. You, Dad, are an exact copy of your grandfather. But…my separate characteristics look like my ancestors, but as whole, I don't resemble anyone. I don't look like you or Mum. I do look a bit like your great grandfather's sister. Or maybe I just really want to look like her. Princess Elisabeth was so beautiful and noble.

Darya was glowing as she was analyzing the photographs and coming to conclusions.

"You know, Dad, I don't get it. Why didn't you ever tell me about your family? Why did you never show me these photos? I am so happy to have met my ancestors, even if it's only through these photos. At least, now I know who they were and what they looked like. I even feel different now. I feel richer, and somehow more protected."

After talking with Darya, Alex asked his wife, "Melinda, do you remember when we got Darya twenty years ago and you suggested that we should hide the box with the documents that my father left us?"

"Of course I do. It was a small box wrapped in blue paper. I even wrapped it in oilcloth so that nothing would get lost or wet. It's on the top shelf in the garage. Why do you need it, anyway?"

In fifteen minutes, Alex appeared in the living room with the sought-for box.

"I think it's time to read these documents and tell Darya everything," he said.

"Alex, don't!" Melinda's voice was loud and anxious. "I thought we agreed. You were never interested in your family's past, you never really cared that you have Russian roots, and you barely know the language. Why do you need to do this *now*?"

"I don't want to lie to our daughter. She needs to know the truth."

"Why? Tell me, why does she need to know the truth?" Melinda was going out of her mind. She was outraged and irritated by her husband. Her voice became harder and more adamant. "Get a hold of yourself. We risk losing our daughter. She will never forgive us if she finds out the truth."

"No, Mindy, I think you're wrong. You have to understand, no relationship should be based on a lie. Sooner or later, the truth will come to the surface. You know what they say—nothing is secret that shall not be made manifest. It is best she finds out the truth from us than from anyone else. We have to tell her now, before she immerses herself too deep into the history of the Ukhtomsky family and disappears in her unreal dreams.

Melinda looked into Alex's eyes, her gaze as firm and decisive as that of a warrior before a battle. She spoke to him in her low and quiet voice, which always had a sobering effect on him.

"Well, then, honey, why did you keep this a secret from your daughter for the past twenty years? And don't you dare blame this on me. I did suggest that you hide those documents and not tell Darya anything. I even suggested that you forget you have Russian roots. But *you* are the one who agreed. We both thought that we were doing the right thing. And I still think it is."

Melinda suddenly felt sorry for Alex. He stood in front of her, his head low. His eyes were frightened and tormented. She looked at her husband with pain and sadness.

"Look, I'm sorry. But I honestly think that now is not the best time to tell Darya about her origins. Do you know what she told me last night? She said that now she finally feels complete, and she's finally happy. Do you really want to destroy her illusions? I don't think Darya would be happy with you for this. In our case, I think a sweet lie is better than the bitter truth. Honey, let's just let fate take its course for now."

Alex remained silent. He was perplexed.

Once again, Melinda happens to be right, Alex thought.

It was already dark outside. Another boring cold rain, typical for this season, was beginning. Here, in the North-West of the country, the winters aren't cold and snowy. The Pacific Ocean has its effect. But the sky is always covered in heavy clouds, and the never-ending drizzle is in reign. Darya still hadn't get back from university. Recently, Alex began feeling nervous around his daughter. He constantly felt guilty for lying to her, and so he was burdened by her presence. His desire to get rid of this nasty feeling was pushing him to tell Darya the truth.

The raindrops were falling onto the wet ground, sometimes lazy, sometimes fast and powerful. As Alex watched them drop from the sky, he thought about Melinda's words. He remembered his daughter's joyful eyes, her anxious and excited voice when she was discussing who resembled who. He remembered the day, twenty years ago, when they got Darya. They were so happy. Finally, after so many years of being married, they became parents. Those were the unforgettable minutes, hours, days, and years of joy.

Could Melinda actually be right? Will Darya not understand us if we tell her the truth? Even when a person loves and trusts someone so much, the slightest element of lying can easily kill that love and trust, Alex thought to himself. He couldn't afford to lose his daughter's trust.

Darya and Michael spent all their evenings at the computer, trying to find any information they could on the Ukhtomsky princes. Somehow, Michael managed to get permission to study the database of Familytree.com. This website has the information on all the immigrants that ever moved to America. For two weeks now, the two of them were meticulously studying the information from the previous century. The evening of February 15th was slowly turning into night. The clock struck half past ten. Michael jumped up from his chair, and joyfully exclaimed, "I found something! Darya, here, read this."

There were only a few lines of text. It said that on May 15th 1928, a citizen of Soviet Russia called Ukhtomsky Leonid Nikolayevich made an unusual request to the Immigration Office in Detroit. He was asking them for any information on his older brother, Alexander Nikolayevich Ukhtomsky, his wife Helen, and their son George. The response of the Immigration Office was short and abrupt:

In response to your request, we inform you that Ukhtomsky Alexander Nikolayevich, with his wife Helen and his son George did not pass through Detroit's migration borders.

Then there was an advice to file a request to the country's immigration office. That was all the information that Darya and Michael found.

"Darya, I think I'll be going home now. It's getting late," said Michael in a sad voice. "Don't give up. I'll think of something."

Michael stood up against his will and walked up to Darya.

"Do you miss Vladimir?" he asked.

Darya blushed. She did not expect this question.

"Michael, I think this is none of your business."

"Why not? I myself miss him a lot. We're friends."

Darya gratefully glanced at Michael then turned away.

"You should get going. Thanks Michael, you're very tactful. I'll call you tomorrow, alright?" her voice sounded a bit constrained.

"Of course! Good night, Darya."

Michael went outside where the rain was drizzling.

The following morning was clear and sunny. For the first time in many days, the sky was cloudless. It was a simple blue dome. Darya woke up in a cheerful mood. It was a Sunday and so she didn't have to go to university. She could stay home, bask in her bed, and dream. On her bedside table was a small photograph of Vladimir. It was taken on a ship when he went on sightseeing tour around the ocean gulf by Seattle. Vladimir's face was looking at Darya with sparkling eyes and a bright smile. Suddenly, a crazy idea hit her.

"What if I go to Russia, to Saint Petersburg, to see Vladimir? Oh my God, I miss him so much!"

She imagined Vladimir's strong, gentle arms embracing her firm body, and his passionate lips kissing her. A warm bliss passed through her body. Darya didn't want to move. She closed her eyes in an attempt to prolong the sweet feeling of an unreal intimacy. She lapsed into oblivion. But this oblivion was neither a dream, nor reality. What she experienced didn't feel like either. Her body was weightless. It hovered, rising higher and higher with every moment. Darya couldn't hear, see or touch anything. At the same time, she could feel a light cover made out of invisible and incredibly soft, warm strings over her. It's like she was flying on a magic carpet over the forests, field, cities, villages and the boundless ocean. Suddenly, she trembled and felt dizzy. With her inner vision, she saw a small room lit by a table lamp. Vladimir was sitting at the desk. His head was in his arms, which rested on the desk. His eyes were closed, and it looked as if he was asleep. By the lamp lay a couple of thick folders with documents. Vladimir's hands rested on a few sheets, covered with faded purple ink. Darya screamed. He raised his head, looked at her and mumbled in Melinda's voice.

"Darya, honey, get up. Breakfast is already on the table."

Darya slowly opened her eyes. She couldn't believe she was in her room. She looked around.

"Mum, I just saw Vladimir. I saw him as clearly as I can see you now. Can you believe it?"

Melinda looked at her daughter with sad eyes, but smiled.

"It's not surprising. You and Vladimir are far away from each other. And distance can prove to be fire and wind at the same time. The wind blows, and the fire flares up. Come on, get up, wash yourself, and come down for breakfast, my darling. I made your favorite bilberry muffins." Melinda kissed her daughter and walked out of her room.

Darya lay in bed for another five minutes, stretched, and finally got out of bed. One persistent thought, which suddenly hit her, refused to leave her mind.

While Darya was having breakfast, Jane phoned her, sounding excited.

"Hey Darya, how are you? What are you doing?" the standard questions sounded dry in Jane's voice.

"What do you want, Jane?"

Even though a long time had passed since Christmas, Darya still couldn't be at peace with her cousin. She always expected some sort of nasty trick from Jane.

Jane was silent for a moment, and then continued, "Darya, please don't hold a grudge. It's so silly of you. You know the Russian saying? Holding on to resentment hurts no one but you."

Darya laughed, "What? It doesn't exactly hurt me?"

"First of all, it hurts those who are offended for no reason. Second of all, it's just a saying. You resent me for no apparent reason. It was only a momentary crush. You know, I haven't even thought about Vladimir during the past few months. Well, no. I did think about him, but for a completely different reason. He sparked a desire in me to learn about the history of our family."

"Okay and your point is…"

"Darya, I recently had an idea, and I've been thinking a lot about it. Why don't you and I go to Russia? We can stay with Vladimir. I hope so, at least."

Darya jumped up from her chair when Jane said this.

"And how exactly do you picture me doing this? Hi, Vladimir, meet your guests, we're here? Is *that* it? I'm not that close with him yet. I can't just appear at his doorstep any time I want. What would his mother think of me?"

"Well, if you don't want to go, don't. I'll go alone. I'll check up on him, see who he spends his time with, and report it to you over the phone. You don't mind, do you?" Jane's voice was disgustingly sweet and derisively ironic.

"I need to think about it, my dear cousin. Such decisions shouldn't be made at once. I'll call you later."

"Okay, I'll be waiting. Say hi to Aunt Mindy and Uncle Alex for me," said Jane before hanging up.

"Are you still upset with Jane, honey?" Melinda asked.

"I don't know, Mum. She threw me off. By the way, she says hi."

"Thanks. Why did she call, anyway? I'm honestly quite surprised. Jane never keeps in touch with you, or us. And now she calls?"

"She has an idea. She wants to go to Russia, and she'd like to take me with her."

"And what did you say?" Melinda's voice trembled. She involuntarily closed her eyes and turned away.

"Mum, what's wrong? Are you afraid I'll leave? Of course I'd love to go and visit Vladimir, see where he lives. I really miss him. We're so far away from each other, and I'm afraid that Vladimir will lose interest in me."

"Darya, remember what I'm about to tell you, and make your own conclusions. If people part then it's their fate to do so. People who are destined to be together will never part. And no distance and no barriers will keep them from being together."

There was a short pause. Melinda hugged Darya and asked in a barely audible voice, "Darling, does Vladimir really mean that much to you?"

"Of course, Mum. I constantly think about him. Sometimes, I even catch myself mentally asking him for advice, and I compare my opinions with his opinions, as I assume they'd be. I don't know, but perhaps I'm in love."

"Time will tell. And what about Michael? You've been spending so much time with him lately. Do you not care about him at all?"

"Mum, of course I do. I really care about Michael. He is my only friend, and I know I can always count on him. I know that he will never let me down, and he'd never betray me. That's important. I trust him with my deepest secrets and most sacred thoughts."

"Oh, really now? And what does he think of your relationship with Vladimir?" Melinda asked, failing to hide her curiosity.

"I don't know. He seems to be calm about everything in this world. By the way, he's the one who often provokes the conversations about my sore points. And he does it so subtly that I only realize it when I analyze the day right before I fall asleep."

"Interesting, and how exactly does he provoke you?" Melinda laughed.

"Well, for example, do you remember a few days ago when I came back sad and melancholic from university? I didn't want to see or talk to anyone. All I wanted to do was lock myself in my room and kiss Vladimir's photograph. Then Michael came over and said only one thing. "Are you feeling sad? I read something by Caroline Holland. It said that grief can take care of itself, but to get the full value of a joy you must have somebody to divide it with. So come on, tell me why you are so sad." And I talked to him for about an hour, telling him about how much I miss Vladimir."

"And he just sat there and listened to it all? Oh, poor fellow! You can't just taunt your friend like this," said Melinda and kissed her daughter. "I'll remind you that Michael *is* in love with you. And you are so harsh with him, to put it mildly."

"I know that, Mum. I can see his grieving eyes follow me around. Not that it upsets me. A part of me actually likes it. I feel warm when he looks at me. But Michael is just a friend. By the way, when he was trying to make me talk about Vladimir again last night, I didn't tell him anything. In fact, I politely interrupted him. Was I right?"

"You should know. It's hard to give any advice in this. His Majesty, the Heart, is in control of this. No one else is."

Chapter 10

It was a warm June day. The morning drizzle had already passed. The new leaves on the trees absorbed the lively rainwater. The streets smelled of wet asphalt, mixed with the blooming lilacs in the yard on Nevsky Prospect. Dinner was being served in Leonid Ukhtomsky's apartment. Olga was running around the table arranging the plates, utensils, dishes, and jars with drinks. She was nervous. Lida and Sophia were helping her. They brought a small basket with buns and slices of bread.

"Those were the last touches. That's it, everything's ready for dinner," said Lida cheerfully and glanced at her mum. "Mum, why are you crying? Everything's alright. Dad will be here soon. I missed him so much! How long was he away for?"

"About four months, darling," replied Olga as she dried her eyes with her batiste handkerchief, hugging Lida.

Polina and Aleksey were standing by the window, looking outside.

"He's coming! He's here!" they suddenly exclaimed.

Everyone dashed to the doors. In a few minutes, Leonid walked through the doors, to be greeted by the smiles of his loved ones. Olga and Lida rushed to him. He hugged his wife and daughter, and walked into the living room.

"It's so good to be home! I'm so tired. I missed you all so much!" Leonid said, his arms still embracing Olga and Lida.

Aleksey and Polina stood by the living room door, smiling, waiting for their turn to greet and hug Leonid. Finally, Leonid turned around and smiled as he saw his brother and Polina.

"Aleksey, my brother! Polina! Hi! I am so happy that you're here," Leonid was ecstatic. They could see he was extremely happy to have finally come back home.

"Leonid, Aleksey, Polina, please, let's go eat dinner. Lida, where is Sophia? Call her and join us at the table," Olga's voice was ringing with joy.

When everyone was finally sitting at the table, there was a new wave of joy and excitement.

After dinner, they all sat on the sofa and the armchairs, waiting to hear the details of Leonid's trip.

"Come on, Leonid, don't keep us in suspense. Tell us about your trip," Aleksey demanded.

"I don't even know where to begin. I had so many good impressions, as well as bad ones. The journey was long and exhausting," Leonid went silent. In his mind, he was going through the events of the past four months. Nobody rushed him. Everyone's eyes were burning with curiosity, carefully watching Leonid. His face was a mixture of emotions.

The Soviet Russian delegation arrived to Detroit early in the morning. The representatives of the Albert Kahn Bureau greeted them at the port. After passing through the Customs, the group sat in the bus which took them to Bureau. Everyone was silent all the way. Only the representative of the Bureau, who spoke good Russian, was telling the guests about Detroit's history about the places they passed, and about the history of Bureau. It seemed that nobody was listening to him. They were all looking outside the windows. Someone uttered a meaningful "whoa" and sighed.

The bus passed by a construction, which resembled a hut. It was built in a slapdash manner from some planks and sticks, and was covered with rugs. In front of the hut was an iron oven, which looked like a cast-iron moveable wood stove, along with some dirty domestic utensils. A girl, around the age of five, and a younger boy were hugging a man, who was probably their father. He was talking to a woman standing in front of him. Both bore marks of despair, misery and sorrow. About a kilometer away was a log cabin with broken windows and a wide, open door. It was lifeless.

"Who are they? Why do they live in a hut?" someone asked in the front. The person's voice echoed.

The guide calmly looked out the window.

"It's a farmer's family. They were forced to leave their house and lands behind. They owe a lot of money to the bank," he responded quietly.

This image made everyone give the guide a questioning look. Their guide was a young Russian immigrant around the age of thirty. His parents fled Russia with him just after the revolution. He spoke perfect Russian, but there was nothing Russian in his physical appearance. George, as the guide was called, was staring out the window with apathy, and glanced at the Russian guests in the bus just as apathetically. He lowered his gaze, apologized, and sat back in his seat at the front of the bus. There were about twenty minutes left until they would reach Detroit, and George didn't utter a single word until then.

Detroit's architecture amazed its Soviet guests. The unusual, exquisite, monumental buildings and the numerous cars in the streets were impressive. The silence in the bus was broken by George's voice.

"Welcome to "Paris of the West", as our city is often called."

The bus suddenly stopped. The road was blocked by a lengthy queue of people with bowls in their hands. The queue began by a tall building where a van with flaps was standing. Under the guidance of a well-dressed man in a hat and a summer dust coat, two men dressed in grey overalls were carrying a massive cooking pot out of the van. The queue was agitated. There were anxious screams. Someone in the back pushed the people in front, creating a jam. People were falling. They tried to get back up, but were knocked back down by others falling. A middle-aged man, whose face was twisted from pain and torment, waved his metal bowl at the old man by his side, almost swiping him off his feet.

The queue stretched out along the brick building, which had a massive sturdy poster across the whole wall. At the top of the poster, it had *"World's Highest Standard of Living"* written in big letters. The poster depicted a nice passenger car. The finely dressed father and the charming fashionable mother with a wide open smile were sitting in the front seats of the car while their child, who was glowing with joy and the concentrated babysitter were sitting at the back, along with a well-groomed dog, whose head was sticking out of the window. Across the whole poster, it said *"There's no way like the American Way"*.

"Now that's an advertisement," said the man sitting next to Leonid. "It's graphic, simple, compact and modest. But, at the same time, it's hypocritical."

George glanced at the passengers from Soviet Russia. He only said one phrase. And it described the whole image in front of them. "It's the crisis. And it's only the beginning."

"Leonid, it's getting late. You can tell us about America later, and we can even gather at my place for that. But now, tell us what you managed to find out about Alexander," Aleksey asked his brother impatiently. His voice was anxious.

"Nothing, Aleksey, I found nothing. First, I asked at the Immigration Office of Detroit. It was the first place we went to. They suggested that I file a request to the Federal Immigration Office. I filed an official request there, but there was still no response. Maybe they will never respond. I'm beginning to think this was a bad idea altogether," Leonid sounded flat, sorrowful, and depressed.

The room went silent.

"Why do you think so, Leonid?" Aleksey wondered.

"You see, I talked to a few immigrants from Russia. There were so many of them. They all fled from Russia right after the revolution, just like Alexander. And many of them changed their surnames. Some lengthened or shortened them, and some changed them altogether. I think Alexander may have done the same thing, and entered the States under a completely different surname. And if that's the case, we will never find him."

Chapter 11

"And here comes the end of summer. Look, Aleksey, the leaves on the trees almost lost their green freshness. Now they're slowly turning yellow, red…" Polina said sadly, as she was looked outside the window. "It's Sunday. I love Sundays. It's the only day that we get to spend together. Let's go for a walk in the forest while it's still warm. Do you remember how we almost got lost last year, not far from a village? It had such a beautiful name…. Ah, yes, I remembered. It was called Otrada. We were wandering around for about six hours, until we came across the forester's house."

Polina joyfully glanced at her husband as if she was waiting for something. For the past week, Aleksey would come back home from work sorrowful and preoccupied with thoughts. Polina noticed the fear and confusion in his eyes, especially when he didn't know she was watching. Even now, Aleksey didn't react to her words. He just sat there, silently eating his breakfast.

"Aleksey, are you even listening to me?" his wife was troubled. "What happened? Is there a problem at work?"

Aleksey didn't say a word. It took him twenty minutes to finally raise his head and smile at Polina. But it was a forced, unnatural, unhappy, dim smile. Aleksey stood up from his chair and pushed it towards the kitchen table. He brusquely turned around, hugged Polina's shoulders, pressed her head to his chest, and gently kissed her.

"Everything is alright, my dear Polina, everything is alright. Everything will be alright," he uttered. But his troubled voice contradicted his thoughts.

Aleksey gently pushed his wife away and left the room. Polina ran after him.

"Aleksey, are you ever planning to talk to me? What is going on with you? Answer me!"

Aleksey stopped by the window. His unseeing gaze skimmed the windows of the neighboring house, the pedestrians, the trees… It was raining. People in the streets quickened their steps, trying to escape the raindrops. Aleksey gave his head a quick shake in an attempt to get rid of his tormenting thoughts and turned to his wife.

"Yes, why don't we go for a walk in the forest? Come on, go make some snacks. We will decide where to go later. Where is Sophia? We'll take her with us."

"Aleksey, you're scaring me. Did you forget that Sophia is in summer camp? She's been working as an instructor there for over a month now."

Aleksey walked up to Polina, looked her in the eyes, and hugged her.

"I'm so sorry, my darling. Please, take a seat. We need to have a serious talk. I don't know what to do."

Polina sat on the sofa while Aleksey nervously paced the living room.

"Leonid came to see me while I was at work today. He changed. He lost a lot of weight. His cheeks are sunken. He became high-strung and easily irritated. We went to talk in the small park opposite my workplace. Leonid was panicking. He said that people from his institute are being arrested. Everyone who went to the States for that academic trip three years ago were arrested for supposedly contacting the imperialist agents. Leonid is afraid that he will be arrested any minute…" Leonid's voice was becoming more and more agitated with every sentence.

Polina was silently sitting on the couch. Her face was pale, her forehead was covered in perspiration, her palms were sweaty, and her temples ached. She felt weak, as if she was about to faint. But Polina didn't give in to the weakness. Fear kept her alert. She feared for the fate of the people she loved so much. She knew that they had to do something to save Leonid, his family, and perhaps even Aleksey, Sophia, and herself. She stood up, held her husband's hand, and seated him on the chair by the table. She sat by his side, trying to assure him.

"We have to hide, Leonid. We have no time to spare. My colleague's husband was arrested two weeks ago. They came to their house at night and practically dragged him out with no explanations. She still hasn't heard any news from him."

The sound of the doorbell forced the two of them to quiver. They weren't expecting any guests that day. The Sundays belonged to just the two of them. They never invited anyone, and never accepted any invitations on that day.

"Who could that be? Sophia shouldn't be back for another week," Polina's voice trembled. "Aleksey, go look out the window and check if anything looks suspicious. You know what I mean."

Aleksey carefully skimmed the street from the window. He stood behind the curtain, trying to be as unnoticeable as possible. The streets were clear. The doorbell continued to ring. There was a loud knock on the door, and a male voice shouted, "Aleksey, open the door!"

The voice sounded familiar. The couple exchanged glances and slowly walked up to the door. The person kept knocking.

"Come on, open the door already. Aleksey!" the voice sounded persistent.

Gerasimovsky stood on the other side. Without being invited, he ran into the apartment and practically dragged Aleksey into the kitchen.

"I'll be brief. They will come for Leonid tonight. You have to warn him."

"How do you know this?" Aleksey's voice trembled with indignation. "And why do you suddenly care so much about my brother's fate? You were probably the one who wrote the report on him, and you are now trying to cover it up by warning us."

Andrey gave the youngest Ukhtomsky brother a reproachful glance.

"You don't understand, Aleksey," his voice was flat, toneless and feeble. "I'm tired. I'm so tired. Do you think that I, an earl, am so pleased to serve these plebeians? Did you honestly believe that I support the Bolsheviks and that I'm on their side now? Do you think that I, the descendant of a well-known Gerasimovsky kin, can forgive the Bolsheviks for what they did to my family, for what they did to my Motherland?"

His eyes were burning with hated. His face was twisted with torment.

"You don't know me, Aleksey. Do you know..." said Andrey, his voice almost a whisper, and sounded conspiratorial. "Do you know..." The earl carefully looked at Aleksey. He thought for a second, and continued. "Do you know the eastern saying? "Fear the one who doesn't fear the Lord". I fear and hate the soviet power. Yes, I serve it, but only for cover, and because I don't have much choice."

He brusquely grasped Aleksey's shoulders and shook him.

"You have to understand. Leonid is innocent. He didn't do anything. He's simply a smart, honest, respectable, intelligent person. I've always treated him like a friend. Yes, we did have our misunderstandings, to put it mildly. But it's only because of Olga. I love her too much to hurt Leonid. Aleksey, we can't waste time. You have to warn your brother *right now*."

Polina interrupted, "Don't believe him, Aleksey." She carefully observed Gerasimovsky. "He's lying. Tell us, Andrey, when did you ever speak the truth? Before, you were showing off, bragging about how much you are valued at work, that you are an irreplaceable employee, and that you are in their good graces. Did I remember that right? I clearly remember your face when you were saying it. You were glowing from your own superiority, and, at the same time, pity for others, especially those sitting by your side. Or have you decided to say the truth *now*, showing a different attitude to your current hosts?"

Andrey stared at Polina, shocked. He didn't understand her, and he felt sorry for her. He had only seen Polina twice. This young woman made no impression on him, and he barely noticed her.

When Gerasimovsky first came to Leonid's apartment, where the whole Ukhtomsky family had gathered, Andrey simply noted that Aleksey was now married to a young pretty woman. That was it. And now he realized that Polina has her own opinions, and she is trying to impose them onto her husband! Amazed, Gerasimovsky couldn't understand why this smart, as it seemed, woman didn't believe him. Did she not feel the danger that her brother-in-law and, most likely, her own family was in? He pitied Polina.

"You're too young, my dear Polina. There is still much you don't understand, because there's still much you haven't seen," uttered Gerasimovsky, irritated. "Why are we even arguing whether or not you should believe me? All I know is that Leonid is in danger, and it's inevitably tonight. We still have time to warn him, hide him. And you, Polina, should trust me. After all, we're the same, aren't we? You are the daughter of Prince Vikhulev Igor Dmitrievich, and even though you are an illegitimate child, you were raised in his manor. I knew your father. I even knew your mother."

Silence fell.

"Polina, is that true?" Aleksey sounded anxious and troubled. "You told me you didn't know who your father was. You told me that you lived with Sophia at earl Verbitsky's manor, where your mother helped manage the manor."

"Yes, Aleksey, it's all true. But it wasn't earl Verbitsky. It was prince Vikhulev," Gerasimovsky said in a hard voice.

But Aleksey ignored him. He still indignantly gazed at his wife, failing to hide his curiosity and irritability.

"Tell me. Tell me, why you needed to lie about this. And what about Sophia, is she the prince's daughter? Who was her mother?"

Polina was sitting, staring at the floor. Her cheeks were burning and her palms were itching from her nervous tension. She was silent. The men gazed at her, awaiting a response. Aleksey was so worried that the chair on which he rested his hands began to tremble. Polina was still silent. Tears streamed down her burning cheeks, timid, then heavy. Her shoulders trembled from her mute crying. She couldn't say a word.

"Polina, my darling, don't cry. Of course, I believe you had a solid reason to hide your true origins, but we will discuss this later," Aleksey's voice was gentle, yet alarmed. "But tell me one thing. What about Lisa? Elisabeth Nikolaevna - my sister? How is Sophia related to you, through your mother or your father? This is very important for me."

Aleksey waited for a response.

"Polina, do you remember how I told you about my dear sister, Lisa, who married prince Vikhulev? We haven't seen her since 1912. Did you know her? Is she Sophia's mother?"

Polina still couldn't utter a single word. Her tears continued to stream down her face, and her shoulders trembled in phase with her rocking head. Finally, she forced herself to speak.

"Sophia is my sister. Elisabeth Nikolaevna died. She was very sick."

Aleksey looked at his wife fixedly. His eyes reflected his pain and torment.

"Polina, is she the daughter of your father or your mother? Who was her mother?"

"Aleksey, please, stop torturing me. I beg you. She is my sister, and my only relative from that life. We've been through so much with her." Polina's voice changed from quiet and afraid to loud and hysterical. "I don't want to talk about it. I can't. Leave me alone..."

Polina laid her back on the sofa and cried. The men exchanged gazes. They were both afraid for her, and confused. Ukhtomsky was the first one to come back to.

"Polina, my dear, my darling, it's alright. Calm down. I understand Sophia is your sister. We won't touch this subject again," Aleksey stood up from the sofa, and turned to Gerasimovsky. "Andrey, there is no time to spare. We have to hurry to Leonid and warn him. You, Polina, will stay here."

Leonid was surprised to see his brother and Gerasimovsky. First of all, he knew that Aleksey always spent his Sundays with Polina. Second of all, he would have never thought that Aleksey kept in touch with Andrey.

"Come in. Olga, dear, we have guests. Could you make some tea, please? To what do I owe the pleasure of your visit?" Leonid formally asked Gerasimovsky.

"Leonid, let's go into the other room, away from Olga and your daughter, so that nobody can hear us," offered Gerasimovsky, ignoring the flat tone of Leonid's voice.

Leonid threw a questioning look at his brother. Aleksey nodded, without uttering a word.

"Well, then, let's go into the study."

Leonid silently listened to his former friend. When Andrey finished talking, the oldest Ukhtomsky brother spoke to him in a rough voice.

"I don't fully understand you. What is your aim? Do you want to destroy me?"

Both Aleksey and Gerasimovsky looked at Leonid questioningly.

"Yesterday, I was interviewed by the State Protection Authority in the second department. I was questioned by Uglovaty, the deputy chief. He was asking me about my trip to the States, about my job at the institute, and what I do in my spare time."

"You went where?" Gerasimovsky was troubled. "Uglovaty is one of the most sophisticated prosecutors at the People's Commissariat for Internal Affairs. His velvet paws hide his sharp claws. Do you know who Uglovaty used to be before the revolution? He was the superintendent at prince Vikhulev manor. In those times, he was a cruel and sly person."

Silence fell. Leonid stared at Andrey uncomprehendingly. It took a few seconds for him to force a few words out.

"What are you trying to tell me?" asked Leonid.

"Nothing, really. But the way I see it, Uglovaty had a reason, and a good one at that, not to arrest you in his office. I doubt this will end peacefully, though. He granted you a small respite, but you will be arrested sooner or later."

Leonid gazed at Gerasimovsky with distrust. He remembered how respectful Uglovaty was with him during the interview. He cheerfully shook hands with Leonid, and even offered him tea and doughnuts. Uglovaty didn't seem to hate him, but he wasn't too cordial, either.

""Mister Ukhtomsky, it was a pleasure seeing you. Everything you told me was interesting. See you next time." Those were Uglovaty's last words," said Leonid in a dull voice. "His last words were "see you next time". Now I know what he meant."

Leonid practically collapsed onto his armchair. His gaze wandered around the room. His dark brown eyes suddenly became colorless, as if something washed the color off. His left cheek trembled as he tried to stop his nervous tick with his hands.

"Leonid, we came for you. You have to hide," Aleksey tried to relieve the tension in the atmosphere. "You have to leave for some time."

"No, no, I can't go anywhere. What about Olga and Lida? What will happen to them? What will they do without me? And I can't leave my work! We just started working on a new project, a very important project for the country. I am the chief engineer, and they can't do it without me." Leonid's voice was getting stronger, harder, and more convincing with every word.

"Aleksey, thank you for warning me. And Andrey, thank you. To be honest, I did not expect this from you. It's so nice to know that we are still friends."

"It's up to you," Andrey said to Leonid, just like in the old days. "Perhaps, you're right. We noblemen shouldn't be hiding like criminal. Especially you. You are known for your honesty and integrity."

Gerasimovsky went silent for a moment. He suddenly stood up, walked up to Leonid, held his shoulders and picked him up from the armchair. He looked into the eyes of the older Ukhtomsky brother, as if trying to pass him his thoughts and concerns from the depth of his soul.

"Leonid, you know that I am one of the most important and valued people at the Supreme Council of Natural Economy. I know exactly what goes on in the authorities, and I know under what criteria people are arrested. Do you think that the People's Commissariat for Internal Affairs aim to annihilate the public enemy? What an expression they came up with, Public Enemy. And how exactly do they characterize a person as a public enemy? Since when do they arrest and execute people for their honesty, integrity, intelligence and education? Why are you looking at me like this, Leonid? Trust me; I know what I'm saying."

Olga appeared in the doorway.

"Leonid, darling, the tea is getting cold. Why don't you all come sit at the table?"

"Yes, why don't we go and enjoy a cup of tea? But please, don't mention anything in front of Olga," he asked his uninvited guests.

In an hour, Leonid saw his guests to the door and, once again, confirmed his reluctance to hide.

"I don't believe that a person can be convicted, arrested, and executed for an uncommitted crime. I did nothing illegal and I have nothing to fear. That is all."

Chapter 12

In the beginning of February, the phone rang in Vladimir's apartment. Alexandra picked up.

"Hello, can I speak to Vladimir, please?" a young woman asked Alexandra in bad Russian.

"Vladimir isn't home now. Perhaps, I could pass a message on to him?" Alexandra smiled.

The young woman was silent over the phone. Alexandra could hear that two girls were discussing something in a foreign language. Then, another, more confident female voice continued in better Russian.

"You must be Vladimir's mother. My name is Jane, and my cousin is called Darya. We are calling from America. Could you please tell Vladimir that we are planning to come to Russia?"

Alexandra's heart paced and her mouth was dry. She was worried and speechless.

"Hello? Hello? Can you hear me?" the voice over the phone was persistent.

Alexandra braced herself and responded in a trembling voice. "Yes, Jane, I'm listening. When exactly are you going to come?"

Jane said that she, along with her cousin Darya, was planning to buy their tickets once they received their Russian visas, which would be no later than February 20th. They would call again to confirm their arrival date. Once she finished talking, Jane put the phone down.

Alexandra was standing by the table with the phone, frightened. She always associated America with danger. When her son won a contest in computer programming and was invited to be trained at Microsoft in America, Alexandra was troubled and anxious. She hoped that the events of the twenty years ago would never come up. America was a massive country, and the chances that Vladimir would meet that couple, which she met at the time, were insignificantly small. But deep inside, she was troubled. She could feel that these two girls weren't random people. One of them was called Darya. In Russian, Darya means "a present", "a gift", "a gift of destiny". In Russia, this name is usually given to the long-awaited daughters. Alexandra was shaking feverishly.

She closed her eyes, immediately picturing the old events, which she tried so hard to forget, but couldn't, and heard the interpreter's voice clear as day.

"Greetings, Alexandra Petrovna. We're here to see you."

A man and two women walked through the wide open door.

The woman walking in front of the couple was their interpreter, and she introduced Alexandra to her clients. They were a nice married couple from America, who had lived together for many years. It took Alexandra a long moment to realize why they came to the children's home, where she worked as a director at the time. Many foreign couples desired to adopt the children from her children's home. She felt that the poor Russian orphans will have an opportunity in wealthier countries and wealthier families who waited for and wanted these children so much. On the other hand, Alexandra couldn't understand why the Russian families couldn't love someone else's children just as much, and why orphans are considered unfavorable. She couldn't understand the absurd presumption that crimes are in orphans' genes. It saddened her that many talented orphans leave Russia, the country they were born in. Alexandra considered this a leak of talents and smart minds.

Alex and Melinda made an unusually good impression on Alexandra. She felt she could trust them. Besides, Alex was the descendant of a Russian prince. For the past ten years of marriage, Alex and Melinda wanted a child, but fate decreed otherwise, and they turned to adoption. The Americans admitted that this was not an easy decision. But now, they were sure that they made the right choice. They only had one demand. They wanted to adopt a girl under the age of one. Alex explained that they wanted to raise their child "from diapers". The conversation in Alexandra's office lasted two hours, until they decided to meet again the following day.

In the morning, the warm rain was drizzling, refreshing the young green tree leaves, moistening the blooming flowers on the ground. But by ten o'clock, the rain gave way to the sun, warm enough for everyone to put away their boots and raincoats, and put on their shirts and light shoes. Alexandra was cheerful on her way to work.

Finally, another child will live in a happy loving family, she thought. *I wonder what awaits her there. The Tommy couple seems like they're nice people and the child should be happy with them.*

When Alexandra walked into her office, she informed the chief doctor and the nurses in the baby unit of their guests. Melinda and Alex arrived right on time. Alexandra noticed how elegantly Melinda was dressed; she wore a beige pant suit, which emphasized her figure and matching beige shoes on a small heel. Alex wore a blazer of the same color and brown trousers. His shirt matched his trousers. The Americans looked elegant and festive. Alex held a big plastic bag.

"Hello, Mrs. Alexandra," said Alex in bad Russian. Then he switched to English. Their interpreter explained that they apologized for their bad Russian, and that they hired her for that reason. Alex passed his plastic bag with children's toys to Alexandra. She thanked him for the gift and invited them into the baby unit.

The big bright room had six small beds with the little children sleeping on them. All of them were dressed in the same white romper suits with little flowers adorning the cloth, and white loose jackets.

"Oh, how adorable! Alex, look how sweet they are!" Melinda was touched and delighted.

Carefully trying not to wake the children, the Americans walked up to each bed and stopped to admire the sleeping gems. The last bed, with a five-month old girl, stood by the window. She was enjoying her balmy sleep, making an adorable smacking sound with her little lips. Melinda and Alex admired her. Suddenly, a sunlight spot reflected by Melinda's silver brooch slid over the baby's face, causing her to open her little eyes. She glanced at Melinda and Alex, and smiled. The baby closed her eyes as she stretched before falling back asleep.

"Alex, Alex, did you see that? This is it! This is my adorable little girl. She smiled at me! It means she likes me!"

"Children often smile in their sleep," Alexandra said as she smiled at Melinda.

The adults quietly left the room on tiptoes.

"Alexandra Petrovna, the Tommy couple chose the adorable little girl in the last bed. Could you please tell them more about her?" the interpreter said in a businesslike manner, always glancing at her watch.

This irritated Alexandra. She was already shocked by the Americans' decision. According to the documents, the little girl was called Sveta, and she was valuable to her. It was Alexandra who brought the girl in last month...

On one of her business trips, Anastasia met Ivan. He was much younger than her and he wouldn't leave her alone. Anastasia couldn't understand what it was that he liked about her. Ivan came from a good family, and he had exceptional manners. His green eyes, always watching her, radiated warmth and inner purity. The age difference of ten years didn't stop him from flirting. At first, it was simple signs of attentions, like helping with a heavy bag, or helping to set up a tent on an expedition. Every morning, Anastasia would find a bouquet of wild flowers outside her tent. After coming back from an expedition, Ivan would always walk her home, not letting her carry the heavy bags and suitcase. He would leave her things by the elevator, mumble "goodbye", and run away. Ivan never asked to come in for a cup of tea or coffee. This made Anastasia think about how serious her relationship with Ivan was.

One time, Anastasia visited Alexandra.

"Alexandra, tell me, am I still attractive to men?"

Alexandra looked at her friend. She held Anastasia's head and kissed her forehead.

"Anastasia, you are an amazing person and beautiful woman. I know that one day you will find a man who will love you, and you will love him back. You deserve happiness. After all, behind your cold and firm front lies a gentle, vulnerable soul. The man who sees it will be a lucky man."

Anastasia's eyes watered. "I…think I found him," said Anastasia as she handed a piece of paper to her friend.

"What is this?"

"This is the first time in my whole life that someone dedicated a poem to me. I really want you to read it."

Alexandra unfolded the piece of paper.

Love cannot be expressed by words.
They are dry, like long dead ashes.
When will love come? Nobody knows.
And we cannot know how long it lasts.

I wonder, will love burn me whole in one blaze,
or will its light warm and soothe me?
Will it be a flickering candle, soft and quiet?
Yet… staring into the fire gives me no answer.

Yet in the dark of my doubt, there is a spark,
and an impetuous emotion runs amok with matches.
And you, so gentle, distant and bright,
are the reason my sun and stars burn, day and night.

Alexandra slowly folded the piece of paper and silently passed it back to Anastasia. She walked up to her happy friend and gently hugged her.

"I am so happy for you, honestly. The person who wrote this is not shallow. Who is he? How did you meet him?"

"About a year ago, a young scientist joined our university. His name is Ivan Andreevich Lobkovich. He is a lecturer at the geology faculty, and he defended his Candidate's dissertation. He began flirting with me ever since the first time we met. But you know, his courting was quite timid. I thought it would never go past the bouquets, carrying my bags and walking me home. Then, yesterday, I received this message. I don't know what to do."

"Oh my God, you're acting like a little girl," Alexandra laughed. "I think you need this. He seems intelligent, cultural, interesting, romantic, and it looks like he has serous intentions. As they say, you should seize the bull by its horns before someone else does."

Anastasia glanced at her friend, her eyes sad.

"He's ten years younger than me! I'm almost forty-five. At my age, people already have grandchildren!"

"And you will have a young man," Alexandra interrupted. "They do say "life begins at forty". Look at yourself. You're gorgeous, you don't have a single wrinkle, and your eyes are so bright. You'll leave any young woman in the dust. I recently read that English doctors—sexual pathologists—have concluded that a fifty year old woman can only be completely satisfied by a man between the ages of thirty and thirty-five. And you're only turning forty-five."

"You know exactly what to say, my friend," Anastasia giggled. "So you think I should get closer with Ivan?"

Alexandra hugged her friend and looked her in the eyes. "Anastasia, what about you, do you have any feelings for him? If your heart doesn't skip a bit when he looks at you, then you shouldn't torture the poor fellow. But if…"

"I love him, I love him so much. He's always on my mind, and it's not because he's young or handsome. No, it's because he has a pure, innocent soul. I'm attracted to him like a magnet…"

A month later, they were married. Anastasia bloomed. She was unrecognizable. She began to wear brighter colors and use makeup. Her appearance radiated the joy and happiness that she showered in. Anastasia was rejuvenated and she didn't look any older than her husband. Ivan and Alexandra represented such a harmonious couple, that nobody noticed their difference in age. Another month later, Anastasia noticed some changes in her body. The bras that she wore for many years were now smaller. Her breasts, which were getting heavier and heavier with every day, now ached from time to time. She had pains in the small of her back and her lower belly. The smell of the fresh coffee, which she loved so much in the mornings, made her nauseous. Even her taste preferences changed. Anastasia, who was convinced that she couldn't be pregnant, was perplexed. Firstly, it is highly unlikely for a woman her age to get pregnant. Secondly, she failed to get pregnant in her first two marriages. She could not believe that she was still able to become a mother.

At first, Anastasia was frightened.

"Alexandra, what should I do?" she asked for help the moment she realized she was pregnant. "I am too old to have my first child. At my age, women give birth to children with so many problems. All the medical magazines say that children born to mothers aged over forty are at a higher risk of having Down's syndrome. I don't want my child to have defects. I will never forgive myself if that happens. And I would be so embarrassed in front of Ivan. He will regret marrying me, an old woman who can't give birth to a healthy child."

Anastasia, who was always firm, began to cry.

"Anastasia, my darling, don't be silly," Alexandra began to soothe her friend. "Look at the bright side. Why do you think you didn't have children in your first two marriages?"

Anastasia glanced at Alexandra, perplexed.

"Because, my dear friend," Alexandra continued, "you didn't love your first two husbands. And so God decided that you didn't need children. But now, look at yourself. You changed so much. You're shining with joy and love. And it's adorable how you call your husband. Ivanko sounds Ukrainian. Are you partially Ukrainian or something?"

"I don't know, Alexandra, perhaps I am. It's just that Ivan sounds like a very serious name. Vanyushka sounds too simple, and it doesn't suit my husband. Ivanko, on the other hand, sounds proud, gentle and serious at the same time."

"See, now you're smiling. The child you're carrying now is the fruit of your love. And so he should be healthy, smart and happy."

Anastasia stopped going on expeditions. She was afraid of any complications which women her age often experience. Ivan also stopped going on business trips. They tried to spend their free time together. Every night, after dinner, Ivan would sit his wife down on their sofa and play his favorite vinyl record with Mozart's Symphony

№ 40. He was raised with classical music, and was taught to play piano. Mozart was his favorite composer. The Symphony № 40 stirred him with its melodiousness and lyricism. The melody appeased both of them. Anastasia and Ivan cuddled when they were listening to Mozart. It seemed that the wonderful sounds of the Symphony embraced the couple, raising them to the top of spiritual sensuality. Ivan often stood on one knee, kissing Anastasia's big belly.

"Where are you, my little girl? Daddy's waiting for you. Come out faster," he whispered.

"Why do you think it's going to be a girl? Maybe it's going to be a boy. Just imagine, a little Ivanko running around the room."

"No, no, no. It's going to be a little girl, and we'll call her Svetlana. It's such a beautiful name. It comes from the Russian word that means "light". She will be our little light when we're old. She will shine on us with her love and beauty."

"You're such a romantic, Ivanko."

They were happy. Only two people who are in love, and for whom nobody else exists, can be so happy. Anastasia often hugged and caressed Ivanko, saying, "I am so lucky to have you. I have spent so much time on everything but myself. I worked, wrote books, gave speeches on conferences… I thought that was my happiness. I had already buried the woman inside me and put a specialist at the pedestal. I was wrong, and I only realized this with you. A woman is happy with love, the love that is given to her by her man, and the love she gives to her man. A woman's happiness also lies in her children, which she conceives with her beloved man."

It was two weeks until the due date. Ivan's parents called in the evening, asking to pick them up from their country house. Ivan kissed his wife, and drove out of the city on his car. During the last days of her pregnancy, Anastasia didn't feel particularly well. Her kidney problems were beginning to show. She saw her husband to the door, and lay down for a little nap, but a faint knocking soon woke her up. A small black bird was hitting their bedroom window. Anastasia stood up and walked up to the window. Right in front of her, the bird, which looked like a crow, hit the window and fell to the ground. Shocked, Anastasia sat down. She had a nervous tremor. She looked at the clock.

It was half past midnight, and Ivan was still not home. She looked out the window. It was still light out. The night before, the long-awaited snow had finally fallen. The big fluffy snowflakes continued to whirl down to the ground. Anastasia glanced down. On the snowy ground by the birch tree was the black corpse of the bird. It was dead.

Anastasia felt uneasy. She was nervous and worried.

"I need to calm down. I need to relax," she was trying to convince herself. "Where in the world is Ivanko? He should be home by now. I need to call him."

She began to feverishly call the number of his parents' country house. There were long beeps. Nobody picked up the phone. She dialed her mother-in-law's cell phone. There was no answer. Anastasia went into the kitchen for a glass of water. And that was when the thought struck her mind. That bird was a sign.

"It was Ivanko trying to send me a message. He's trying to tell me something. No, he's asking me to protect him." Her growing feeling of doom refused to dissipate.

A sharp pain in her belly made her fall to the ground. Her waters broke. She was growing weaker. She crawled to the phone and called Alexandra.

Alexandra answered in a sleepy voice, "Hello, I'm listening."

"Alexandra, call the ambulance, I don't feel well…" whispered Anastasia.

With her last strength, she crawled to the main door, opened it for Alexandra, and lost consciousness.

"Finally, you're awake!" Anastasia heard a familiar voice.

Anastasia's eyes refused to open. Her whole body ached. She touched her belly. It wasn't the tight belly of a pregnant woman. Instead, it was a soft, flabby, empty belly. And it ached.

"What happened? Where is my baby?" Anastasia asked in a weak voice.

"Everything is alright, don't worry. You had a baby girl. She is a term infant, but she's very weak. She's sleeping now."

"I want to see her," whispered Alexandra with tears in her eyes. "What about Ivanko? Where is he? Has he already seen his baby daughter?"

Alexandra didn't reply. She walked away from her friend's bed, hiding her tears.

"Alexandra, say something. Where is Ivanko? Is he here?" Anastasia's voice was becoming more demanding and troubled. "Why aren't you saying anything? Where is my husband? Why isn't he here?" She was getting hysterical.

"Anastasia, my dear, please, don't. You're a strong woman. You'll get through this. Ivan and his parents were in a car crash. He lost control of his car. They hit a Kamaz. They were both travelling at maximum speed. Ivan and his parents died instantly, and the driver of the Kamaz is hospitalized."

Anastasia struggled to sit up, but she fell back onto her bed. Suddenly, she seemed so small, defenseless, and vulnerable.

"It's the bird. It's that bird that crashed into the window. It really was Ivanko. He was calling for help, and I didn't understand it, and the bird fell and crashed…"

Anastasia lay in her bed. Something unimaginable was going on with her. She trembled, and was covered in perspiration. Her face turned crimson red, her eyes blinked out of control, and the whole left side of the face was twisted. Her eye was swollen, her mouth was pulled to the left, and her left arm hung helplessly from the bed. Anastasia was trying to say something, but her tongue was out of control. She drooled… The nurse ran into the ward and froze in horror before running out into the hallway and screaming. The doctor, a woman around the age of fifty, ran inside. She was holding a syringe with some medicine. She glanced at Anastasia, shook her head and ran back out. Alexandra couldn't tear her eyes away from her friend. Anastasia's right eye was horrified while her left eye was closed by her lifeless eyelids. The poor woman raised her right arm and beckoned her to come and sit by her side. Alexandra leaned towards her and understood what she was trying to say.

"Take… care… of… Sveta…"

In a week, the baby girl was discharged from the hospital. Alexandra, her husband, and their children all came to pick her up. Anastasia was transferred to the neurology department. In the evening, the family had a council. The Zlotov family had one question to decide: What should they do with the girl? At the time, Alexander and Valery had three children—two girls and a boy. The girls were at school, while Vladimir was still in nursery. Vladimir wouldn't leave the girl. He caressed her little hands and touched her diapers to check if they were wet.

"Mummy, she's so cute. Can she stay with us? I want a little sister," Vladimir was shaking his mother's arm.

Valery loved children. He could never pass by a crying child on the streets. He would always stop, ask the child what was wrong and, if he could, he would help the child. If he couldn't, he always had some sweets in his pockets to cheer them up. Valery supported Vladimir.

"Seriously, Alexandra, why don't we keep Sveta?"

"What? Are you crazy? Anastasia is still alive, even if she is in hospital. When she is discharged, she will raise Sveta herself. But for now, Sveta will stay with us. She doesn't need much."

Anastasia was discharged within a month. There were no improvements, and her doctor refused to take care of her any longer.

"If a person doesn't want to receive treatment, no doctor can help her. And she doesn't want to be treated. She is in her own world, and she refuses to come out of it," announced Sergei Andreevich. He was Alexandra's schoolmate, and one of the best neurologists of the city. "Alexandra, take your friend home and only bring her back when she is ready to receive treatment."

Alexandra brought Anastasia home and hired a caretaker. Anastasia wasn't involved in anything. Sometimes a small spark of interest and joy would appear in her healthy eye. That was only when they would bring the baby to her. But she would get tired quickly and close her eyes again.

Four months passed. For Alexandra, these months were full of joy and expectations. She grew attached to the little girl, and she noticed that she often called Sveta her little daughter. Alexandra rejoiced at her first smile, first attempts to hold her head up, first attempts to hold a toy. She brought Sveta to Anastasia every day. Every day they were expecting to see improvements in Anastasia's health. But it was hopeless. The woman, who learned the greatest power of love and loss, refused to live. Even her daughter, the little creature which connected her to her beloved man, couldn't replace him. Anastasia was dying away. One night, when Alexandra visited her friend, Anastasia asked for a pen and a piece of paper. With a lot of effort, she wrote a few lines with her right hand, which she was losing control of.

Soon, I will leave this world and join Ivanko. Promise to care of my baby girl and raise her like your own.

Anastasia dropped the pen. She expressively glanced at the paper, then at her friend, and then back at the paper. With a gesture, she asked Alexandra to bring Sveta closer. She watched her daughter with her healthy eye, and tried to kiss her with her twisted lips. She cried.

The following day, Anastasia passed away.

"What do we do? What should we do?" Alexandra asked Valery after Anastasia's funeral. "You don't have a job, and I have a small salary. I can't launder money from the children's home like the others. I would never do that, no. We have barely enough money for food and your medicine. We have three children, and we have to put them on their feet. And we have to raise Sveta... I promised Nastya..."

"Alexandra, I have an idea," Valery suggests one night. "Why don't you put Sveta into your children's home? You're the director there, right? You'll be watching over her, and she'll be fed and dressed. When she gets older, we will be taking her home for the weekend. And once she finishes school, she can live with us."

"But what if I will have to leave my job? What if, God forbid, I'm transferred or fired?"

"Oh, if and what if the pigs had wings. Time will show. But for now, I think that this is the most optimum solution."

The next day, Alexandra put the girl into the children's home. A month later, the Americans came.

Giving Sveta away to the Americans was not an easy decision for Alexandra. She remembered her promise to Anastasia. Watching Melinda and Alex, Alexandra felt that Sveta would be happy with them, and they would love her like she was their own. She arranged for Sveta's documents to be handed to the Americans.

"I think I'm doing the right thing. She will have loving parents and be provided for. We love Sveta, too, but can I really support her and family? Vladimir is only five. The girls are small, too. Valery can't work, and his disability pension can't even cover his medicine. I promised Anastasia that Sveta will be loved and protected, and that is what will happen, even if it's not in my family. I know she will be happy with them. I will keep in touch with Alex and Melinda, so that I know everything about Sveta. I won't leave her. If Sveta ever needs my help, I will be there for her."

Alexandra reasoned with herself as she was signing the documents required for the Tommy couple to adopt Sveta.

The day came when Alex and Melinda came to pick Sveta up. They signed the documents. Both of them were glowing with an inner light, which is only inherent in loving parents who finally have their long-awaited child. In the director's cabinet, Alexandra was bidding her farewells. She gratefully shook the couple's hands, and wished them happiness and health. She was about to ask them to keep in touch with her when Alex politely interrupted.

"Mrs. Alexandra, thank you so much for your understanding and for our little baby girl. We will do everything we can to raise her happy and healthy. But there is something we would like to ask of you. In order to avoid any future misunderstandings, we would like to ask you not to call or write. Just forget about us and our little daughter. She can never know that she was adopted."

The American couple thanked Alexandra, and, as Melinda carefully and gently held her daughter to her chest, they left the children's home. Alexandra watched them walk away. She didn't fully understand what they said. She sank into her chair, mentally going through Alex's last words. When she finally realized what he had said, her eyes watered.

"What have I done? Oh my God, what have I done? How will I look my children in the eyes? I betrayed Anastasia's memory."

She laid her head on her desk. Her shoulders trembled. She couldn't feel the ground under her feet…

Chapter 13

"Mum, I have to go meet someone. I'll be back in about three hours," Vladimir kissed his mother and ran outside.

He was in a hurry. Nadya hated when someone was late for a meeting. Her days were planned minute-by-minute. She assigned two hours of her time, from two until four in the afternoon, to meet with Vladimir. They agreed to meet at Coffee Gamma, Nadya's favorite coffee-shop on Nevsky Prospekt. She didn't just come here to drink the magnificent coffee with cardamom cooked on hot sand, and to have her favorite dessert, Raspberry Entremets, which is made only in this café, on the Griboedov Channel. She also worked here. Nadya loved to sit at the table for two in the corner by the wall called Jazz. She would come at around three, turn her laptop on, make her usual order, and begin to work on her materials. The smell of fresh coffee stimulated her brain. It was at Coffee Gamma that her most interesting and asked-for articles were born. Nadya usually worked until eight or nine in the evening. She then turned her laptop off, ordered her last coffee for the night, and watched the crowds that would gather at the café by then. At nine, the jazz band began to play. People from all over Saint Petersburg would come to listen. Nadya immersed herself into her world of dreams when she listened to jazz.

Nadya was already thirty years old and she succeeded as a professional in her career. There was a high demand for her articles, and popular publications considered themselves lucky if they could get hold of her work. Nadya was a freelancer and she preferred to choose her own themes for the articles. She had a scent for sensational material. Her colleagues were amazed by how briskly, without hustling or getting nervous, she could find and wheedle information out of her sources and use it to write her articles, which were sold like hot cakes. You couldn't say that Nadya wasn't in like Flynn. Men loved her good looks, her bright mind and her ability to keep a conversation going. Some of them even proposed to her after a brief affair. But Nadya broke up with all her boyfriends. She was looking for *her* man. She was looking for someone who would make her complete. Her parents were a perfect example. They fell in love when they first saw each other at a bus stop, and they have been in love ever since. Nadya remembered how her parents did everything together. They would wake up together, run to the bathroom and wash up together, cook breakfast together, and run off to work together. All they had to do was look into each other's eyes and they would instantly know what the other wants. Her parents always laughed at that, joking that they would soon forget how to talk to each other. Nadya couldn't recall a single fight between her parents. Their eyes always sparkled with love, joy and tenderness.

By the age of thirty, Nadya had had three long relationships. The notion of length in Nadya's case is relative. Each of these relationships lasted just over a year and a half. At first, she would be attracted to her young man, and she loved bending them to her will, making them indulge her every whim, which ranged from simple presents to intimate nights. But then the usual relationship routine would begin, which quickly bored her, and that was when Nadya would abruptly end all communication without any explanations. Her ex-boyfriend would still follow her around, hoping that he would once again melt her heart. But none of them managed to wait for that moment.

"Perhaps I'm not made for love," she told her friend Alena. "At first, I burn up with desire, but I cool down really fast. You know, Alena, I'm tired of being single. I want to fall in love. I want to be in love, just like my parents are. When my dad passed away, my mum didn't want to live anymore. After all, they were practically never apart. Well, maybe just when my mum was giving birth to me. And even then, my dad never left the maternity ward. He gave presents to the whole medical staff so they wouldn't kick him out of the maternity home. Can you believe this? The head doctor gave him a doctor's smock, a stethoscope and some other medical accessories to make him look more like a doctor rather than a visitor. The head doctor admitted that she was committing a professional crime because this was the first time she saw such a connection between spouses. But I think I'll never experience such love."

"Nadya, don't despair. The day will come, and you will find your love. Trust me. Life is a fair thing. It punishes and rewards. But you never know when this will happen. Some people, like your parents, are lucky, and life gifts them with love in early adulthood. And others are less fortunate, and only find love after many tries. Others are even less fortunate, and they only find true love towards the end of their lives, and this often prolongs their life on this sinful planet. Love is a joy that must be deserved, and so life gifts it only to those who are worthy."

"Thank you. You know what to say."

When Nadya first saw Vladimir, she felt her heart beat faster. She stopped breathing for a split second. She never felt anything like this before.

She thought to herself, "This is it. I am "pogibosha aki obri". ("I am absolutely dead" in Old Slavonic.)

But she didn't show it. Nadya was anxious to help Vladimir research the Ukhtomsky family. She knew that a common interest could bring them closer together. However, the five year difference in age daunted her.

"At least it's not forty-five," Nadya told her friend. "After all, I look younger than what I really am, and people often think I'm twenty-five."

Nadya was sitting at the table at Coffee Gamma, waiting for Vladimir for seven minutes already. He literally ran through the doors and walked up to Nadya's table at a splitting pace, apologizing. Nadya laughed and offered him to sit down.

"No need to apologize, young man. It's alright. After all, you were late within the limits of the allowed academic minutes."

"Nadya, why are you so formal with me? I thought we were quite casual already."

"What? Oh I'm just joking with you. Let's be casual if you wish. I brought the results of the request I filed to the heraldic authorities."

"And?"

"Nothing. No one applied for the title of the Prince or Princess Ukhtomsky. So, I'm assuming that there's nothing there. I guess we're looking in the wrong direction. So what are you planning to do next, Vladimir?"

"I don't know. I guess I'll look for more documents and study them. Will you help me?" Vladimir's hopefully eyes looked straight into Nadya's.

Nadya hesitated for a moment. "Do I have a choice? I can't exactly abandon you, can I?"

Vladimir looked at Nadya gratefully. He took a small sip of coffee from a small cup, glancing at her again.

"Is there something you need to tell me? Your eyes look mysterious. Or am I wrong?"

"No, you're right, I do have something. Last night, I took another look at the things Anastasia left me. Her small casket was quite interesting and it has a little secret. Imagine this, it fell out of my hands, its bottom cracked, and I realized that it had a double bottom. Look what I found inside."

She handed two yellowed sheets of paper to Vladimir.

They were two letters, written in a messy man's handwriting. Both addressed to Polina Ukhtomsky. At the bottom of each letter, there was an illegible signature, and the name "Stepan Uglovaty" written in a woman's handwriting.

"This could be a lead!" exclaimed Vladimir. "We have to find this Stepan."

"Did the contents of the letter not surprise you?" Nadya wondered.

"No, not really, why?"

"Men are so inattentive. Let's take it step by step. In the first letter, a certain man, who seems quite illiterate, is threatening the prince's wife. In the second letter, he's begging her to give him back his daughter. What do we know? Firstly, Polina was Aleksey Ukhtomsky's wife, and we know this from the documents I gave you earlier. By the way, Vladimir, you still didn't tell me when Polina died."

"I looked through the documents and there was no information on Polina's death. To be honest, there was no information on her at all, other than the fact that she was married to Aleksey."

"Alright, let's continue. Secondly, the person addressing Polina is someone named Stepan Uglovaty. At first, he's demanding, but then he's begging her to give him his daughter back. This is where the questions arise. Who's the mother? On what grounds is he demanding the daughter? If Polina was the mother, I doubt Stepan would have the right to demand. Thirdly, did you notice that these letters are dated 1941? More questions arise. How old is the child, and why does Uglovaty suddenly need the child when the country is already at war? In short, these letters give more questions than answers. You're right. We have to look for Stepan Uglovaty and Polina Ukhtomsky."

"Nadya, I have two girls flying in from America tomorrow. Jane and Darya are the descendants of the Ukhtomsky princes. Jane speaks Russian quite well, and Darya only began to learn now. Can you do me a favor? Could you please host them? You know my mum, the word "America" only brings about arrhythmia and raises her blood pressure."

"Of course, Vladimir, you can take the girls to my apartment. If you want, we can meet them together."

"Thank you, Nadya. You're a savior. The plane lands at eleven in the afternoon. I'll pick you up at half past nine?"

Their meeting ended on this note. Vladimir said goodbye and left. Nadya stayed behind, using the excuse that she wanted to listen to some jazz. In her head, Nadya was replaying Vladimir's last words. She remembered how his voice changed when he mentioned the name of the second girl, Darya. His voice became soft, gentle and dreamy.

"I guess Darya is the girl that Vladimir is in love with," she said to herself. "Well, tomorrow we'll see how tough my competition is."

Nadya paid her bill and left the café. On her way home, she was thinking what to wear to the airport and how to behave when she meets the Americans.

The plane arrived right on time. When the girls entered the waiting lounge, they looked lost and nervous. Seeing Vladimir amongst the crowd cheered them up. Darya ran up to him, hugged him as she looked into his eyes. But she didn't kiss him.

What an interesting relationship. I think it's only the beginning, though, and there is nothing too serious, Nadya thought to herself as she watched Darya and Vladimir. *Not all is lost. She seems pretty and pure. Wait a minute… Who does she remind me of?*

Nadya's reasoning was interrupted by Vladimir, who was introducing the girls to each other. After having exchanged civilities, they walked to the car.

They arrived at Nadya's apartment by one o'clock. Nadya had outdone herself. The table was set in advance. All that was left to serve was the lamb from the ceramic thermo cooker. Darya kept noticing Nadya's stares, which made her uncomfortable. Finally, Darya couldn't handle it anymore.

"Why are you constantly staring at me? It makes me feel uncomfortable," she informed Nadya.

"I'm so sorry, Darya, but I just can't get this out of my head. You remind me of someone… Of… I remember! Give me a minute." Nadya stood up from the table and ran into the other room. In about five minutes, she came back, holding a photo album.

"Darya, take a look at this photograph. You really look like this woman, only much younger. This picture was taken when she was thirty."

Darya took the picture and began to study it. It was a picture of a woman of a Balzacian age dressed in a black sarafan and white blouse.

"Who is this woman?" Darya asked anxiously. Her voice trembled.

Chapter 14

The wave of repression between the years of 1930-1934 didn't involve the Ukhtomsky brothers' families. It was March 1939. The dirty sleet still covered the streets of Leningrad. The nights were cold. During the day, the sun rays couldn't break through the dense clouds. Leonid couldn't sleep. Lately, he was tormented by headaches. He was standing by the window in his bedroom, gazing outside. It was about five in the morning. The city was still fast asleep. A shaggy stray dog ran across the street and stopped by the bins. The noise from an approaching car scared it away from where the dog hoped to satisfy its hunger. The car stopped not far from Leonid's house. Three men came out. Leonid had a vague guess of who it might be. He jumped away from the window.

The doorbell rang.

"Leonid, who is it?" Olga asked worriedly. The sound of the doorbell woke her up.

"I don't know, Olga, but they seem persistent. I'll go check."

"No, Leonid, don't. I'm scared."

The ringing of the doorbell was replaced by the sound of someone kicking the door.

"I have to open it or they'll break the door."

"What took you so long? Were you hiding something? Search the apartment," said a short man in a leather coat and dirty cowhide boots. He barged into the Ukhtomsky apartment, followed by two militiamen.

"Mister Ukhtomsky Leonid Nikolayevich, you are suspected of conspiring against Stalin."

Without ceremony, the militiamen opened the cupboards, swiped things off the shelves and hangers, and threw things out of the drawers, ignoring Leonid's and Olga's reactions. They walked up to the library and began to furiously shake the books, one-by-one, throwing them on the floor. Just as unceremoniously, they walked into the bedroom, tore the bed sheets off, checked under the bed, and turned the chest drawer upside down.

"What are you doing? What are you looking for?" Olga was outraged.

"Don't worry, missy. We'll tell you when we find it."

"Mum, what's going on?" Lida was worried when she came out of her room. "Who are these people and what do they want?" She was frightened.

"Don't worry, my darling, I'm sure this is some kind of misunderstanding."

The militiamen began to search Lida's room. Her dresses, linen and toys, which she kept from childhood, all flew towards the floor. They found nothing. On his way out of Lida's room, one of the militiamen stepped on a teddy bear, which squeaked plaintively.

"What the hell was that?" yelped the militiaman.

When he realized where the sound came from, he kicked the teddy bear to the far corner of the room.

"We found nothing," the other militiaman reported to the man in the leather jacket.

"Ukhtomsky, you're under arrest. You will go with us," ordered the man in the leather jacket as he roughly pushed Leonid towards the door.

The door shut behind Leonid and the uninvited guests, leaving Olga and Lida screaming, "Leonid!" and "Father!" helplessly.

Uglovaty, who was the detective on the case of an attempt on Stalin's life, was sitting at the desk in the cabinet Leonid was sent to. A spark of hatred appeared in his narrow, swollen eyes. With his thick fingers, he picked up a pencil and sheet of paper as he stared at Leonid with a long, heavy, spiteful gaze.

"So, we meet again. Do you know Gerasimovsky?"

"Yes, I know Andrey Gerasimovsky."

"Very good," mumbled Uglovaty, as he jotted down Leonid's response. "What is your relationship to him?"

"We were friends when we were young, but now we're just acquaintances."

"Wonderful," Uglovaty mumbled again, noting everything down.

"And now, prince, tell me about the conspiracy that you plotted with Gerasimovsky to kill Stalin," Uglovaty yelled in a shrill voice.

Leonid looked at the detective uncomprehendingly.

"What are you staring at, you skunk? I know you, princes and earls. All you desire, all you dream of is to take our power down!"

Uglovaty's face and neck slowly turned from red to crimson, his eyes reddened with the flow of blood, and his arms trembled. He jumped up, raised his hand at Leonid, and struck him with a swinging blow. Leonid fell off the chair. His head ached. One of his top teeth fell out and he could taste the salty blood. His vision blurred. He tried to get up, but the sharp pain in his groin from the kick by Uglovaty's dirty boot caused Leonid to squirm on the floor.

"What are you doing?" Ukhtomsky heard someone's outraged voice.

He raised his head and saw a refined man come inside. The man walked up to Uglovaty and spoke to him through his teeth.

"Stop this arbitrariness, Stepan. Get a hold of yourself. You're not in the streets."

The man then turned to Leonid and helped him stand up. He apologized and introduced himself.

"My name is Nikolai Ivanovich Rozov. Leonid Nikolayevich, tell us about the workings of the anti-Soviet organization, which you are a member of."

"I'm afraid I don't understand what you're talking about," Leonid replied. It took him a lot of effort to move his lips.

"Well, you said you know Gerasimovsky quite well, right?"

"I already told you that we're only acquaintances. Yes, we were friends in the past, before the revolution. But now, we don't really keep in touch anymore."

"Very well. You don't really keep in touch. How often do you see each other?"

"The last time I saw Gerasimovsky was a few years ago."

"You're lying. Gerasimovsky claims that the two of you created an organization, the aim of which is to get rid of Stalin."

Leonid stared at Rozov, unable to believe what was going on.

"I don't understand. What organization are you talking about?"

"It's a shame that you don't want to tell us the truth, Leonid Nikolayevich, such a shame."

"Stepan, arrange for Gerasimovsky to be brought in," Rozov ordered. When Uglovaty walked outside, Rozov turned to Leonid. His stare was cold and cruel.

"Well, Leonid Nikolayevich, shall we wait for your friend? We'll see how you'll talk then."

In about ten minutes, Uglovaty walked back into the room. Behind him, Gerasimovsky was escorted, his hands tied. Leonid did not recognize him. Andrey's face was swollen from the beatings. There were bruises under his eyes, his right brow was slashed and bleeding, and his left eye was swollen. He could barely move his feet. Uglovaty pushed him and yelled, "Faster, you piece of filth. Or I'll make you run, if you want to."

"Stepan, quit shouting and just leave us alone. The three of us are going to have a nice talk," Rozov ordered.

"Andrey Mikhailovich, during the interrogation, you told us that you were the leader of an organization which aimed to eliminate Stalin, isn't that right?" Rozov subtly addressed Gerasimovsky.

Leonid looked at Andrey, shocked.

"Yes," Audrey's weak voice trembled.

Andrey glanced at Leonid with guilty eyes. His lips whispered something mutely. His eyes reflected his horror, fear, and despair. Leonid felt sorry for Andrey. The always arrogant, proud and independent Gerasimovsky now looked like an animal at bay who knows its end is near. His will was completely suppressed. Along with fear and horror, there was a hint of sheer indifference in his eyes.

"During the interrogation, you mentioned that Mister Ukhtomsky Leonid Nikolayevich was also a member of your organization. Is that right?"

"Yes," Andrey quietly confirmed.

"Andrey, what are you on about? What organization?" shouted Leonid. He leaned over to Gerasimovsky, trying to shake him up somehow.

"Sit down!" Rozov yelled at Leonid.

Andrey glanced at Leonid, scared, and uttered in his husky, hoarse voice, "Leonid, just agree with everything they say. It's better that way. They will still find a way to prove you're guilty, but first they'll destroy you like they did me. It's painful. And horrifying... It's degrading and humiliating. Look at me. They..."

"Shut up!" Rozov yelled once again. "Escort this one away," he ordered as he pointed at Gerasimovsky.

When Gerasimovsky was out of the cabinet, Rozov turned to Ukhtomsky.

"So, Leonid Nikolayevich, are you going to talk now?"

"About what?" Leonid asked calmly.

After the shock he experienced when he saw Gerasimovsky and listened to him, Ukhtomsky pulled himself together. He knew he was innocent. He lived an honest life during the Tsar's reign, and he still lived by the same principles after the revolution. Leonid was a patriot and he loved Russia. The interests of his country always preceded his own. Nobody could ever accuse him of betraying his Motherland.

"So I guess you're not going to talk."

Leonid sensed a threat in Rozov's voice.

Rozov walked up to the door and called for Uglovaty. Uglovaty slowly walked into the cabinet and stopped in front of Ukhtomsky.

"You may continue with the interrogation, Stepan. Just don't overdo it. You can report to me after you're done."

"Don't worry, Nikolai Ivanovich, I'll do my best," Uglovaty replied in an ingratiating tone. He turned to Ukhtomsky. "So, prince, shall we begin the interrogation?"

An evil smile appeared on Uglovaty's face. Leonid was surprised when Uglovaty addressed him not by his name or surname, but by his title. But when Leonid saw the spiteful, evil look on the detective's face, he understood. Uglovaty was emphasizing his own superiority of a former lout over a prince. Now, Uglovaty was the master of his own life. He, who was no one, had become someone.

"First question, what functions did you, skunk, carry out in your organization?"

"I don't understand what organization are you talking about?" Leonid looked the detective in the eyes.

Uglovaty knitted his brow, made a wry face, and crafted an evil smile. As he walked up to Ukhtomsky, he uttered ominously, "It's alright. Soon you'll tell me everything."

Leonid woke up, lying on a cold cement floor. With some effort, he opened his eyes. His whole body ached.

"Come to your senses, dearie?" Ukhtomsky heard someone's soft voice. "They were quite harsh with you. You have no whole spot on you."

Leonid's company was a white-haired man with cunning eyes.

"What have you done wrong? You don't look like a bad guy."

The old man helped Leonid get up and walk to the bunk bed. He kicked a dirty young man off the bed.

"I get it. You're under the 58th, right?"

"What's the 58th?" asked Leonid in a weak voice.

"Are you serious? Who is this guy?" An unshaven man with a pockmarked face and two knocked out front teeth joined in the conversation.

"Shush, nobody asked you to comment," the white-haired man interrupted. "You, darling, don't look like a criminal, so I guess you're arrested under a political case. And that is what Article 58 is about. There are many of you here."

Leonid looked around the prison cell. The two bunk beds took up most of the cell's space. On the left side of the door, in the corner, was a dirty close-stool. The weak sunlight entered the cell through a high guarded window. Besides the old man, the dirty man, and the pockmarked man, there were another four sitting on the beds.

They all gazed at Leonid but lacked interest. One of them, a middle-aged man in worn black woolen trousers and a Russian shirt, posed a question to Leonid in a nasal voice.

"So, cultured one, they've got you now, haven't they? Tomorrow, you'll disappear just like the others of your kind. We've already paid our tributes to five of them."

"Hey, Crooked, why are you scaring the man?" asked the old man. "Can't you see he still hasn't come to his senses?"

"He's not a man, anymore. He's just a piece of meat for them. They're going to thrush the life out of him," the man with a closely cropped head and brazen eyes joined in.

The old man looked at him and raised his voice. "Think before you speak." He then turned back to Leonid. "Tell us why you're here."

"I don't know. I honestly don't know anything," Ukhtomsky uttered quietly.

"Perhaps you spoke with someone obscene for the government? Somebody could have overheard it and reported you."

Leonid looked closely at the old man, who glanced back at the new prisoner with compassion.

"If you don't want to talk about it, you don't have to. We're not forcing you. You should get some rest."

Leonid rested his head on the dirty mattress and dozed off. He had nightmares.

"Wake up, dearie, you've had enough rest. I have some questions for you," the old man shook Leonid, trying to rouse him.

Ukhtomsky opened his eyes. The cell was pitch black, and Leonid realized it must have been late in the evening or even nighttime. Everyone but the old man was fast asleep.

"I'm leaving tomorrow. Is there anything you'd like me to hand over to anyone out there? Is there anyone you'd like me to contact for you?" the old man whispered softly into Leonid's ear.

Leonid glanced at him suspiciously. "Why, exactly, were *you* arrested?"

"It was nothing compared to you. I stole a wallet from a woman and some boy saw me. He yelled at the top of his voice. The red feathers were passing by at the time, and so they brought me in. While you were sleeping, I was being interrogated. Because I threw out the wallet, there are no clues, so there is no case. They weren't harsh with me. I'm old, after all. They're just kicking me out. If there is anyone you'd like me to contact for you, just tell me and I'll do it."

"I don't get it. Sir, you don't have any reason to help me."

"Everyone calls me Pakhomich, and you can call me that, too. You're prince Ukhtomsky, right?"

Surprised, Leonid looked at the old man.

"You had a sister, didn't you? Her name was Elisabeth Nikolaevna. She was a princess with the kindest soul. I served at the stables at Prince Vikhulev's manor. Uglovaty was the manor's superintendent. He was so ferocious, and he despised your sister. Elisabeth Nikolaevna loved justice. Once, she caught him red-handed at thievery, and he got what was coming for him."

"Oh my God," Leonid exclaimed quietly, "Lisa's still alive? Where is she? Tell me what you know."

"Oh no, dearie, you don't know anything, do you? Elisabeth Nikolaevna died in childbirth twenty-five years ago. But her daughter survived. The prince, her father, raised her alongside his first daughter, whom he had with one of his superintendents."

"Do you know anything about Elisabeth's daughter?"

"When the manor was burnt in 1918, she disappeared somewhere with her sister. Uglovaty was outraged and he wanted to torture the poor little girl, so as to have his revenge on the princess, even though she had already passed away."

"Pakhomich, can you at least tell me how the prince named his daughter?"

"Oh, sorry, I thought I told you. He called her Sophia, after his own mother. His first daughter was called Polina."

Leonid gasped. Thoughts rushed through his head at the speed of sound.

"Polina and Sophia. Polina is Aleksey's wife, and Sophia is her sister. I can't believe it. Sophia is Lisa's daughter and my little niece! No wonder I always felt close and affectionate to her."

A sharp pain struck through his head. His vision blurred and he lost consciousness.

"Hey, guards, call the doctor. Someone lost consciousness," Pakhomich yelled as he was hitting the door.

"Quiet down there, Pakhomich. Some of us want to sleep, you know," mumbled Crooked in a dissatisfied, sleepy voice. "If this foul enemy dies, then that was his fate. If he doesn't die, then tough luck, because a worse fate awaits him here."

"Shush, Crooked. You have to always remain human. He's not an enemy at all. He's just like everyone else, only cultured and a former prince."

The lock clanked, and the prison doctor entered the cell. When he saw Leonid, he froze for a moment, sighed and then silently examined the prisoner.

"His heart may not last until the morning. Guards, bring the stretchers and take him to the isolation ward."

In the morning, Leonid's heart stopped.

"He died! That skunk escaped our vengeance! What are we going to do, Stepan?" Rozov yelled in his cabinet. "We're not fulfilling our quota. They're not exactly going to give us a pat on our backs from up there."

"Nikolai Ivanovich, calm down. I have an idea. After all, I served their sister's husband, so I know the Ukhtomsky family quite well," Uglovaty tried to assure Rozov.

"Where are you going with this? Come on, don't keep me waiting. What's your idea?" Rozov sounded sarcastic.

"There is another Ukhtomsky brother, Aleksey. We can take that damned cultured skunk."

"Then what are you waiting for?" Rozov exclaimed joyfully.

Chapter 15

Late at night, the doorbell rang in Aleksey Ukhtomsky's apartment. Polina opened the door. Olga and Lida stood in the doorway, their faces tear-strained.

"Leonid. My Leonid died," Olga managed to mumble through strained weeping.

"What do you mean? How did he die?" Polina was shocked by the news.

Polina sat her guests down at the table. She made tea and put the biscuits, sweets, cups and saucers on the table. While she was setting the table, she sneakily glanced at Olga and Lida. Olga's cheeks were sunken, her eyes swollen with tears. She looked lost. She was fiddling with her handkerchief, bringing it to her eyes and nose from time to time. Lida tried to soothe her mother, but her own eyes were red and swollen from her sorrowful tears. Neither of them could speak clearly. Their sobbing was suffocating them.

"Olga, Lida, please don't cry. I can't understand what you're saying," Polina tried to get something out of them.

The doorbell rang.

"Aleksey, you came, finally. Olga and Lida are here. It's awful," Polina greeted her husband at the door.

"Why, what happened?"

"Leonid died."

"What do you mean? I saw him two days ago."

"Olga and Lida said something about an arrest and a search, but I can't really make out what they're saying."

Aleksey rushed into the kitchen. His sister-in-law and her daughter were sitting, hugging.

"Olga, what happened? Please try to calm down and speak clearly so we can understand."

When Olga explained what happened, Aleksey squeezed his head with his hands.

"Now I get it," he said in a flat voice. "Poor Leonid, my poor brother... Where is his body? We have to bury him," the youngest Ukhtomsky brother proclaimed anxiously.

"Uglovaty, the detective who is working on the case, refused to hand the body over. They will bury Leonid in some common graveyard. I didn't understand much of what he said." Olga managed to force a few words out.

"Did you say Uglovaty, Stepan Uglovaty?" Polina was shocked.

"Yes, Stepan Uglovaty. They didn't say his patronymic," Olga replied in a weak voice.

"Do you know him, Polina? Aleksey asked, surprised.

"Yes, I know him. He served at my father's manor. He's a very slippery and cruel person. He will make his way over corpses if he has to in order to get what he wants. Sophia and I were running from *him* in 1918."

Polina went silent. Aleksey walked up to his wife and hugged her.

"Tomorrow," he addressed all the girls in the room, "I will go to the authorities to see Uglovaty. I will demand Leonid's body. We have to bury him with dignity. Olga, Lida, don't worry, even though it's easier said than done. You lost a husband and a father, and I lost a brother. We all have someone to grieve for. But tears won't help. You don't have to come with me. Uglovaty and I are going to have a man-to-man talk."

The sound of the key turning in the main door interrupted Aleksey. The door opened and Sophia ran inside.

"Hello, everyone, I'm back!"

But when she saw Olga's and Lida's tear-stained faces, and Polina's and Aleksey's sorrowful looks, she stopped.

"What happened?"

Sophia was horrified by what she heard.

"Poor Leonid Nikolayevich. Who sways the people's destinies?! O Lord, why do you allow villains to decide the lives of honest and noble people?" Sophia exclaimed in a fit of temper. Then she added, quietly, "It's true what some say; Stalin is a great chemist. He can turn any distinguished statesman into shit, and vice versa."

"Quiet, Sophia, you can't say such things!" Polina interrupted, horrified. "You can be arrested for speaking like this."

Sophia raised her head in pride. "I don't exactly fear them. I've never done anything to hurt my country, while Uglovaty and his people are doing everything to destroy my people."

Aleksey looked at her with admiration, but decided to interrupt her.

"Sophia, such freedom of speech is punishable in our times. I don't want you displaying such freedom anywhere else."

"Thank you for your concerns, Aleksey. Although we're not talking about me now, I will take your wishes into account."

Sophia looked Aleksey in his eyes. She always looked him in the eyes when she talked to him.

Sophia was already twenty-six. She chose a career that she dreamed of ever since she was small. Sophia became a doctor and she was worked as a therapist in the local polyclinic. She loved her job she was fully dedicated to it. Her patients, especially the male half, loved her. Many desired her, asked her out on dates, and even proposed in letters. But Sophia's heart remained untouched. Her blue eyes, which glowed with intelligence and determination, were often sorrowful. Even when she smiled and laughed, her eyes remained sad. Many were amazed by this. It was what attracted them to her. Nevertheless, Sophia never revealed the reasons for her sorrow. She only loved one man, who never was and never would be hers. But she had too much pride and integrity to tell this to her one and only love. She loved him too much, and she loved her too much, to disappoint them.

"Aleksey, I don't think you should go to Uglovaty tomorrow," said Sophia quietly. "You might not come back. Leonid died without signing a single legal document. This means that their public enemy quota hasn't been fulfilled."

"What? What are you saying?" Polina was outraged.

"Polina, wait. Sophia, how do you know all this? How do you know about the quotas and public enemy?" Aleksey asked, surprised.

Sophia looked at him with sad eyes.

"Everyone knows. Sometimes I don't only treat the physical illnesses, you know. If you remember, I'm a doctor, and I spent half my workday visiting my patients at home. I've seen a lot of human pain," Sophia paused for a moment and then continued. "Every day, I face mothers and wives having heart attacks because their men were arrested under the suspicion of being the public enemy? I have to sit by their side, hear them out and soothe them."

Sophia trembled with indignation.

"Epicurus was right when he said that perturbation is a worse curse than physical pain. The body only suffers from the momentary pain of the present, whereas the soul is tormented by the pain of the past as well as the present. Tell me, what will be of our children once they will know the emotional pain of losing their innocent parents, who were mercilessly killed by their worthless, bitter enemies for uncommitted crimes? Who will they grow up to be? I see only two possible outcomes. They will either become obedient slaves, intimidated by power, or silent rebels, dreaming of a revolution."

"Sophia, be quiet!" Polina yelled. "You're endangering our lives by speaking like this."

"No, Sophia is right," Olga quietly took her side. "My poor Leonid, he never did anything bad! He stayed behind in Russia after the revolution because he couldn't imagine life without his motherland. He was an honest worker. He spent days on end at the institute, and then on the construction site of a tractor factory in Chelyabinsk. Leonid never complained about the disorder, and he never showed his dissatisfaction with life. His priority was the prosperity of Russia, rather than his own well-being. No, he's not Russia's enemy, he's not the public enemy!"

With every word, Olga's voice was getting firmer and louder.

"The public enemies are those who arrested and killed my Leonid," Olga paused for a moment. She raised her head, surveyed everyone in the kitchen with her dry gaze, and continued in a firm voice, "I'm afraid that our country will never be peaceful. We don't have faith in the people, or the faith in the fact that people, regardless of their flaws, are capable of good deeds. Having no faith in people means having no faith in peace. My God, where is this world going? What is going on with Russia and the Russian people?"

Olga went pale and reeled. Her daughter caught her.

"Mummy, what's wrong?"

"Nothing, Lida, don't worry. I'm just exhausted. I don't know how to live anymore, what to believe in… I have no reason to live."

Olga forced her last words through her tears.

Silence fell in the kitchen. Nobody uttered a word. They could hear a small child cry in the apartment next door. It was a six-year-old boy whose mother was trying to soothe him.

"Don't cry, Dima, or the bad guys will come and take you away from me. We will both be in big trouble then, won't we?" his mother tried to calm her little son down, loudly.

"Mummy, please don't let them take me away. I will always help you, and I won't cry," he sobbed and begged his mother.

The apartment next door was at peace. Everyone in the Ukhtomsky apartment was sick at heart.

"See, Aleksey? Even our neighbors" six-year-old son knows who these bad guys that take people away. He is already terrified of them. Later on, when he finds out that these bad guys are the Soviet Rule, he will begin to fear the power itself and he will become its obedient slave," said Sophia with confidence.

"I recently read what Berdyaev said. The revolutionaries worship the future, but live in the past," added Lida in a dull voice.

Lida was a year younger than Sophia, and she was teaching Russian and Literature at a local school. She was a tall, slim girl with small sapphire eyes, high cheekbones and a slightly big nose. Even though she was twenty-five, Lida didn't look like a fully-matured young woman. Books were her passion. She spent all her free time reading. Her parents were proud of her, yet disappointed at the same time. They were worried that Lida didn't have any admirers. None of the young men called her, walked her home or wrote letters to her. Lida always responded to her parents" questions jokingly, saying that when the time will come, her second half will seek her out.

"Berdyaev made an accurate observation on what the aims of the so-called revolutionaries are, didn't he?" Lida continued. Their aim is to create an absolutely equal society, and they always talk about it. But at the same time, they can't part with their slave pasts. It fuels their fear of the future. And their servile essence doesn't let them do good deeds. It pushes them on crimes. It pushes them to destroy everyone who's not a slave, everyone who's not like them."

The Ukhtomsky families sat in the kitchen for a long time. They drank not one, but many cups of tea, and ate all of Polina's supplies of biscuits and sweets. Polina was known to have a sweet tooth. The memories of her old life and the concerns for her current life were discussed and summed up. Olga and Lida left at about midnight. They were calmer, but their faces still reflected their torment and pain of losing a husband and a father. It was doubtful that a wife and a daughter would quickly get used to the fact that they would never see Leonid again. It was decided that Aleksey would go to the authorities in the morning and demand his brother's corpse, while the women would wait in Olga's apartment.

"Morning is wiser than the evening. Let's go to bed, my darlings," Aleksey hugged Polina, wished Sophia a good night, and went to sleep.

Sophia was lying on her sofa, her eyes wide open. She couldn't fall asleep. Her gaze stopped on a small black spot on the white ceiling. Without blinking, she stared at that spot which was becoming smaller and bigger, appearing and disappearing... She felt like she could see someone's face, twisted in a devilish smile. It was a rough, ugly and lascivious face. Disgusted, Sophia closed her eyes and fell asleep.

The loud piercing sound of the doorbell woke her up. She glanced at the clock. It was almost six in the morning. The doorbell rang again, this time long and impatient. Sophia jumped up from her sofa, threw on a robe and ran out of her room. In the hallway, she bumped into Aleksey, who was hurrying to the door in his underpants and shirt. They exchanged gazes, embarrassed. The doorbell rang for the third time. Someone's boots were kicking the door. Aleksey came back to and rushed towards the door.

"Sophia, go into your room. It's inappropriate for a young woman to be seen like this by strangers," Aleksey ordered Sophia in a rough voice.

She obeyed her brother-in-law, returning to her room.

Aleksey quickly opened the door. A fat, flabby man with an unpleasant face stood in the doorway, accompanied by two militiamen.

"Mister Ukhtomsky Aleksey Nikolayevich?" the man asked abruptly as he let himself into Aleksey's apartment.

"Yes, that's me," Aleksey responded calmly. "How may I help you?"

"How can you help us? You're going to come with us. You're under arrest," announced the man loudly as he smiled insidiously. His face was insolent.

"On what grounds am I being arrested? Could you please show me your credentials?" Ukhtomsky demanded calmly and politely.

The man nodded to the militiamen. They twisted Aleksey's arms.

"You want documents? Oh, I'll show you my documents alright."

Without concealing his rage, he punched Aleksey in the stomach with all his might. Caught off-guard, Aleksey bent forwards and fell to the ground. He was in pain.

"I like that pose more, prince," the man made an evil smile as he shoved his credentials in Aleksey's face.

At the same time, Sophia and Polina ran out of their bedrooms.

"Aleksey, what happened?" Polina shouted anxiously.

Sophia stood in her bedroom doorway and stared at the man, not blinking. Her eyes were filled with hate. She recognized him. It was Uglovaty. Now he looked even more insolent and loathsome.

"Go and bring him some clothes. NOW!" he yelled at Polina. "And you, women, go back to your rooms, or I will arrest you as well."

When the door shut behind Aleksey, Polina and Sophia held each other and fell to the floor, crying.

"Sophia, what are we going to do? What are we going to do?" Polina asked as she sobbed.

Sophia didn't say anything. She suppressed her tears. Only her eyes reflected her torment and pain.

"Don't worry, it will be alright. I won't let Aleksey die," announced Sophia confidently.

Polina looked at her sister, surprised.

"Are you sure? What do you have in mind?"

"I recognized him," Sophia said quietly. "It was Uglovaty. He didn't change a bit. He simply became more sickening. And trust me, I know what to do."

Chapter 16

Nadya liked Darya. Nadya liked her even when Darya would glance at Vladimir with love and Vladimir would respond with an affectionate smile. For some reason, Nadya didn't feel jealous or upset. It was weird. She was sure that she was in love with Vladimir. She dreamed of him at night, her heart paced when she saw him, and a content bliss passed through her body when Vladimir accidentally touched her, or when she purposely touched him. Nadya was quite alarmed by the fact that she didn't feel jealous. She couldn't understand why. And when she couldn't understand something, she did everything she could to get to the bottom of it.

Jane, on the other hand, was not in Nadya's good graces. Her undue familiarity and the fact that she set her cousin at naught irritated Nadya. Besides, Nadya instantly recognized a huntress in Jane, and she was a huntress herself. Nadya loved to win everyone over using her display, starting with her physical appearance and ending with the expression of her opinions. She instinctively felt Jane was exactly the same. Nadya didn't like it. She was afraid that she could lose to Jane, and Nadya hated losing. If she respected Darya and felt unusually calm towards her, all she felt for Jane was hostility and trouble. But because they were her guests, and Vladimir was there, too, Nadya had to be affable and hospitable.

"Vladimir, do I really look like this woman?" Darya inquired in her soft voice.

Vladimir took the photograph from Darya's hands and examined it. He took a long look at Darya, closely observing it, and smiled.

"Well, let's compare. We'll start with the eyes. You have blue eyes, but we can't tell what color the woman's eyes are because the photo is black and white. Now, the nose… Your noses look alike. In fact, your foreheads have the same form. They're high and point to your intelligence."

"Vladimir, stop joking around. I'm trying to be serious," laughed Darya.

Jane, who sat next to Darya, grabbed the photo from Vladimir and examined it.

"I think there *is* a resemblance. The noses and foreheads are the same, but I think your eyes are different. On the other hand, my forehead also resembles the woman's forehead," Jane summed up.

"All of us, humans, have something in common in our appearance. After all, we were all created from the same image and likeness," Nadya added. "If everyone lived by God's Ten Commandments, then we would all be absolutely the same. Our appearances reflect our souls. And seeing as every individual lives by his own principles, aims and targets, there are no two exact same people. But, Darya, I think you do look a lot like the woman on the photograph. It's not just the nose or the forehead. It's also the facial expression and the look in your eyes.

Darya took the photo from Jane and looked at it closely. She walked up to the mirror to look at her reflection, and then turned around to face her friends on the sofa.

"I want to know everything about this woman. Who was she?"

"In that case, I'd like to invite everyone to my place. My mum was friends with Anastasia, so she should be able to tell us something about her," Vladimir offered. "Why don't you rest tonight? After all, there's a huge time difference with America. And tomorrow, I'll come to pick you up at midday. We'll have lunch and discuss this."

Vladimir glanced at Darya, hoping she would approve of his offer. It seemed that Darya didn't hear anything. She continued to observe the photograph without stopping. Suddenly, tears streamed down her cheeks.

"Darya, what happened?" Vladimir was worried.

"I don't know," Darya replied quietly. "I don't get it. The more I look at the photograph, the closer I feel to the woman. It's like we're somehow connected."

"Don't be crazy," Jane interrupted. "You can't be connected. You were born and raised in the States. You're American, and she's Russian. Look, her eyes are horrified and melancholic."

"You're wrong, Jane," Nadya was upset by her guest's comment, which had a hint of quasi superiority over Anastasia.

"I don't think she's horrified. I can see her melancholy and sorrow, but not horror," added Darya.

"Girls, I can see that you're exhausted. I think you should rest," Vladimir carefully interrupted the growingly unpleasant discussion.

He walked up to Darya and faced her so that no one else could see his face.

He mouthed, "I love you. I really miss you."

Darya's face went crimson red. She didn't expect Vladimir to express his feelings in front of other people. Nevertheless, she smiled and nodded, while her left hand reached towards him. Vladimir seized the moment, pressed her hand towards his heart. Darya drew her hand back and instinctively fixed her hair. She turned back towards Jane and Nadya, and noticed that their hostess was fixedly looking at them, making her feel uncomfortable.

"Vladimir, thank you for being so caring. We really do need some rest. My head feels so heavy," Darya uttered, trying to be as calm as she could.

"Same here. We need to sleep. I can hardly keep my eyes open," Jane decided to throw in her two cents. "Nadya, can you please show us where we can rest our fatigued bodies?"

The girls slept until late in the evening. It was around ten when Darya opened her eyes. She got up from her bed and walked up to the window. The city was shining with neon lights. The cars were flying by and the pedestrians were rushing to places. Darya liked to observe the rushing crowds. She was trying to guess where everyone was headed. That middle-aged woman with a huge trunk in her hands was hurrying home, where her husband and their children awaited them. And that young couple holding hands was probably running to a nightclub. The girl was carrying a bundle with shoes. Darya's gaze stopped on an elderly couple. The woman was well-groomed, dressed in a light mink coat and elegant shoes with a high heel. Her loose chestnut brown hair was fashionably styled. Her husband, wearing a black cashmere overcoat with a red scarf, black fancy shoes and black woolen trousers, was holding her by his arm. The couple treaded carefully on the snowy pavement, afraid to slip and fall. Their journey wasn't long. A big silver car was waiting for them by the side of the pavement. The man helped his wife get inside, and then got in. The car's engine started and it drove away.

"I wonder where they're headed, dressed like that," thought Darya.

"Why are you staring out of the window?" Jane mumbled in her sleepy voice.

Darya turned around to see Jane stretch on the sofa, trying to wake up.

"Come here, Jane, look at the beautiful city. And the people. It's fascinating to watch them!"

Jane walked up to the window.

The phone rang, and Darya picked it up.

"Darya, it is Vladimir. Did you get some rest? I decided to show you what Saint Petersburg is like at night. So get ready, we'll be there in ten minutes to pick you two up," his voice was excited and anxious. "We're on our way!"

"That was Vladimir. He said he's on his way here, and he's not alone," announced Darya thoughtfully. "Come on, let's get dressed or we'll be late."

In exactly ten minutes, the doorbell rang and Jane rushed to open the door. Vladimir was standing at the entrance with a young man.

"Jane, meet my friend Kostya. We studied together. I think you two will find something in common." Vladimir sounded intrigued as he glanced at the two of them.

Jane and Kostya faced each other silently. Their eyes slowly changed from shocked, to strikingly attentive, then gentle and thoughtful.

"Guys, why are you standing as if you're rooted to the ground?" Vladimir asked.

Kostya came back to. He reached his hand out to Jane and introduced himself.

"Hi, my name is Kostya. You're so…so beautiful," he complimented shyly.

Jane suddenly seemed different. From a wild girl, she turned into a well-mannered lady.

"Hi, Kostya, please, come in. My name is Jane. Pardon my bad Russian. Thanks for the compliment, I'm so grateful. Do you want a coffee or anything? I'll go make some right now," her voice turned from rough to mellow.

Darya and Vladimir, who were all ready to go, stopped, perplexed, staring at Jane. She didn't seem to care about anyone or anything. She just continued to stare at Kostya, who also couldn't tear his eyes away from her.

"Jane, are you seriously planning to make coffee now? If you are, make some for us, as well. I'll help you," Darya smiled.

In the kitchen, the girls were alone again.

"What's up with you? You don't look like your usual self. You have some new strange manners," Darya observed.

"Did you see him? Did you see how handsome he is?" Jane was anxious.

"Kostya? Yes, he seems like a pleasant young man," Darya agreed calmly.

"No, he's not just pleasant. He's the most pleasant, the most handsome, the best…"

"So you think this is love at first sight? I would have never thought you would fall in love this way," Darya laughed.

Jane smiled and glanced at her cousin. "This is so wonderful! It's amazing!"

The coffee was served in small coffee cups which Darya found in Nadya's cupboard. She apologized for not being able to find bigger cups. Vladimir laughed and explained to Kostya that Americans drink coffee from much bigger cups.

"This coffee is luscious! Jane, you have gifted hands," Kostya complimented the young woman.

Jane thanked him and glanced at Darya, who nodded to her cousin and turned away. She decided not to tell Kostya that her cousin really can't make a decent cup of coffee. In fact, Jane couldn't and never liked doing anything around the house. Her only favorite activity was to go around bars and nightclubs. Darya gazed at Jane, who was tensely looking back at her.

Darya walked up to her and whispered, "Don't worry, my dear, I won't tell him. Win your prestige."

After the coffee, the boys offered the girls to go to the nearest nightclub, Phoenix, where Lady Waks was supposed to be working that night. Jane, the biggest entertainment fan, suggested staying at home, using the excuse that she was tired.

"What's wrong with you? Are you sick or something?" Vladimir inquired compassionately.

"Let's go, Jane. You'll keep me company. Please," Kostya begged. "It's rare for Lady Waks to work in this club, and we'd love to show you her skills."

Jane smiled. It felt nice that the young man was trying to make her join him.

"Who is Lady Waks?" she asked.

"Oh, she's very famous here. And trust me; she has a great future in show business. She is the best DJ in the city, as well as a talented promoter and producer. People say she is a person of all professions in today's show business. She's a very talented girl. You absolutely have to see and listen to her. I can guarantee you that you've never seen anything like this back in the States."

In an hour, the group was in Phoenix. The club was chock-full of young people. Even though it could only hold a maximum of two thousand people, it seemed like there were well over three thousand. Vladimir took his friends to the bar to have a few drinks. The bar also had the best view on the stage and the dance floor. While they were waiting for the famous DJ to come, the guys ordered beer for themselves and two glasses of white wine for the girls. Jane and Darya were excited about everything.

"Tell me, Jane, is this club like the ones back in America?" enquired Darya, who had never been to a nightclub before. She believed that nightclubs were a waste of precious time.

"American clubs are nothing compared to this. It's so different here. It's more spacious, more decorated, more impressive… The clubs I've been to in America are decorated and organized more simply. I really like it here," Jane shouted into Darya's ear.

"Lady Waks is about to come on stage. I just saw her get out of a car by the staff entrance," Kostya informed everyone.

While waiting for the DJ, they sat by the bar stand and sipped their drinks.

"Well, well, well. Who do we have here?" Nadya exclaimed cheerfully as she approached her friends.

"Hello again, what are you doing here?" Vladimir greeted her.

"I'm working. I have to interview Lady Waks, the upcoming star in show business."

"Really? You're going to talk to her? Can we come with you?" Kostya interrupted.

"I'm sorry, Nadya, I forgot to introduce you two. This is my friend Konstantin," Vladimir apologized.

Nadya quickly glanced at her new acquaintance. He didn't arouse any interest in her.

Too sugary, she thought to herself, but still invited them all to the interview with the DJ.

The night was a success. Lady Waks was up to the mark. Her virtuous music won the hearts of everyone in the club. Ten minutes before the show ended, Nadya, accompanied by her four friends, entered the DJ's room. The security was reluctant to let them all in, but Nadya's credentials in a red cover did its job.

When everyone left the club, it was early rather than late. It was almost sunrise. The guys saw the girls home and confirmed that Vladimir would pick them up at midday, just as they agreed earlier. Vladimir sneakily kissed Darya, while Jane held hands with Kostya for longer than what was considered appropriate. Nadya simply waved to everyone.

As always, Nadya analyzed the past day when she was in bed. This night, she had some revelations. Firstly, she noticed that Darya was reluctant to publicly display her affection to Vladimir, and shyly accepted Vladimir's courting. At the same time, Darya couldn't tear her eyes away from the young man. Her eyes gleamed with passionate love for Vladimir.

Either Darya was raised like a puritan and can't publicly express her intimate, passionate emotions, thought Nadya, *or her emotions aren't strong enough, and she can easily hide them, remaining indifferent.*

Secondly, the chemistry between Jane and Kostya couldn't escape Nadya's vigilant eyes. She was glad. At least Nadya had no competition from her side.

With these thoughts, Nadya immersed herself into sleep.

The next day, Alexandra was waiting for her guests, whom Vladimir was picking up. She was worried. The premonition of some upcoming news tormented her, whether they were good or bad. Lying on her comfortable sofa, under her checkered quilt, Alexandra was listening to her inner voice. No, she didn't feel sick at heart—her breathing was calm and cadent. But at the same time, she felt uneasy, like something was destined to happen. Lyuba, the housekeeper, served the table, fixed Alexandra's bed, and helped her tidy herself up. The sound of the key turning in the door made its way through the house.

"Mum, we're here. Meet my friends," Vladimir exclaimed cheerfully.

Alexandra sat up in her bed. A wide smiled filled her face.

"Come in, my dear, and invite the guests to the table. It's lunch time. Lyuba and I were waiting for you."

Vladimir introduced his mother to his friends. When the girls entered the room, they hesitated. They didn't expect to see Vladimir's mother lying motionlessly on the sofa. But Alexandra's warm welcome, her happy eyes and joyful smile worked magic on the girls" shyness. Jane and Darya thanked her for the invitation and sat at the table. Alexandra watched her guests closely. The girls seemed so different that she could hardly believe that they were so closely related. Darya radiated warmth, serenity and refinement. Jane, on the other hand, was wild, inadequate and worn out. Darya sat opposite Alexandra, which allowed Vladimir's mother to closely observe her. Alexandra was overwhelmed by how close she felt to Darya. Something about Darya's hand movements, the way she turned her head towards her interlocutor and even her manners in using cutlery were highly familiar to Alexandra. At first, she couldn't understand what this was. But after lunch, when her son asked her about Anastasia and the photograph that Darya was so interested in, Alexandra understood everything.

"Tell me, what Darya's surname is?" she asked.

Darya and Jane exchanged glances and responded together, "Tommy."

Alexandra closed her eyes and rested her head on the pillows.

"What's wrong, Mum? Are you tired?" Vladimir was worried.

After a moment of silence, she replied, "I'm sorry, dear, but I'm really tired. Is it alright if you don't ask me any questions? I need to get some rest."

An unexpected tear streamed down Alexandra's right cheek.

"Mum, can I bring you anything? Just tell me, if anything."

"No, Vladimir, darling, thank you. Just take care of your guests. I need some rest at the moment."

Darya gazed compassionately at the woman. She walked up to Alexandra and spoke in broken Russian. "Thank you so much for lunch. God bless you." She then leaned towards Alexandra and kissed her right cheek, which was still wet from her tear.

"Thank you, my dear. May the Lord watch over you," Alexandra uttered quietly. She closed her eyes, as more tears streamed down her cheeks.

Jane also thanked their hostess and headed towards the exit. Vladimir kissed his mother and said he wouldn't be back until the evening.

The three of them walked out.

Chapter 17

"Aleksey Ukhtomsky? Pleased to meet you. My name is Rozov, Nikolai Ivanovich Rozov. You don't look much like your brother. So, are you going to admit that you conspired to murder Stalin?" the senior detective sounded derisive, mocking and harsh.

"I have no idea what you're talking about," Aleksey responded calmly.

"That's exactly what your brother claimed. And your mutual friend, Gerasimovsky, also denied it, but then admitted that he planned to undermine the soviet power by killing Stalin. And where are they now, do you know? I can tell you. They're gone… They're not here anymore… But you are!" with every word, Rozov's voice became enraged and wrung-up.

He literally yelled his last words. Ukhtomsky's heart thumped with hatred, but he kept his cool. Not a single muscle twitched on his face. His eyes, staring at Rozov, were concentrated and attentive. It seemed like he didn't want to miss a single word that Rozov directed at him. The senior detective could not understand Aleksey's calm confidence. And this agitated him. Rozov wanted to punch Ukhtomsky, beat him up with his boots, and humiliate him. But he wanted to be remembered as a refined investigator, and so he decided to use the services of his friend, detective Uglovaty. Together, using the carrot-and-stick approach, they've cracked a number of public enemies.

"Well hello, prince. How are you?" Uglovaty mockingly asked the prince as he entered the study. "I still can't believe that you, just like your brother, love the soviet power so much that you actually want it to prosper."

"I love my country. I love Russia. I hope you love it, too," replied Aleksey.

Rozov and Uglovaty exchanged glances. They did not expect such an answer. Silence fell.

"Guards!" Rozov yelled. "Take the prisoner away."

When Ukhtomsky was escorted out of the study, Uglovaty stared at Rozov, bewildered.

"What just happened?" he asked his boss.

"Did you not realize? Use your brain. Do you love Russia?"

"Russia? Oh, Russia, Mother Russia! Of course I do."

"See? You didn't even realize what I was talking about at first. Ukhtomsky was talking about our motherland, Russia, where we were all born and raised. We, on the other hand, always talk about the Soviet power. Do you see the difference?" Rozov asked with a hint of sarcasm in his voice.

Uglovaty glanced at Rozov, puzzled.

"Of course I see it. It's so obvious. I understand you, Nikolai Ivanovich," he responded with an under plot.

"You don't understand. What *can* you understand? You only understand something when you can use it to your advantage," Rozov threw a glance at Stepan and went silent.

What a rascal. He'll make his way over corpses. Thinks he's a protector of the soviet power. Nikolai Ivanovich thought to himself. Then, out loud, he said, "Stepan, we have to remember that today Russia *is* the Soviet power. And anyone who dares to encroach upon the Soviet power is encroaching upon our motherland, Russia."

That evening, when Uglovaty was about leave, there was a knock on his door.

"Who is there?"

But nobody entered. Stepan stood up from his table and impressively walked towards the door. When he opened it, he could hardly believe whom he saw in the doorway. It was the young girl from Ukhtomsky's apartment.

"Please, come in. Take a seat. You want to talk to me, right?" Stepan uttered in a sickly-sweet voice.

"You didn't recognize me, did you? I recognized you the moment I saw you. You haven't changed a bit. You're still just as disgusting and insolent as before. Only, you became obese feeding on the public bread."

The young girl was enraged and indignant.

"Could it be? Mademoiselle Sophia? You have the same eyes and resolute voice as the princess!" Stepan was astonished.

"Good, you finally recognized me."

"Princess, to what do I owe the pleasure of your visit?" inquired the detective in a complaisant voice.

"Uglovaty, I didn't come here to exchange pleasantries. Tell me, where is Aleksey Ukhtomsky? Why did you arrest him?"

"Are you worried for your uncle? That's adorable," Stepan sounded repulsively sweet.

"Yes, I'm worried. Now answer my question," Sophia demanded roughly.

"He is a public enemy."

"A public enemy... Aleksey is a public enemy? Do you seriously think that Aleksey Ukhtomsky is a public enemy? What exactly did he do against the Russian people?" Sophia practically yelled in Uglovaty's face. "No, *he* is not the public enemy. *You* are the public enemy. You, and those like you, are destroying this country. You seized power like thieves and you're ruling the country, looking back, fearing everyone and everything," Sophia spoke fast and brusquely, staring into Uglovaty's eyes. "So tell me, why did you arrest Aleksey?"

Uglovaty sat opposite Sophia, staring back at her with his impudent, lascivious smile. His eyes glistened, and his body filled with fleshly desires.

"You want to know why I arrested him?" Stepan asked, his voice trembled with desire. "Nothing. We need five people to fulfill our quota, and report it to the higher authorities. Your uncle, Leonid

Nikolayevich, died without admitting his crimes, so it didn't count. So instead, we decided to arrest his brother."

"What a rascal." Sophia was outraged. "What will happen to him?"

"We'll take depositions from him, and then hold him in jail incommunicado." Uglovaty moved his chair closer and closer to the young girl. Sophia sensed the detective's stinking breath and saw his lustful eyes. She tried to ignore his claims.

"What do you mean, incommunicado?" she asked.

The detective stood up from his chair, moved towards the table and glanced at Sophia with greedy eyes.

"Ten years incommunicado..." he mumbled slowly, "What a perfect replacement for the other words... Ukhtomsky will be shot, executed. He's considered to be a public enemy, after all. He encroached upon the most sacred of all things. He encroached upon Stalin's life."

Sophia went pale. She gasped for air. Her vision blurred and she felt like she was going to faint.

"He'll be executed. Aleksey will be executed." words rushed through her mind. The news was killing her. "I can't let this happen. I won't. I have to think of something, but what?"

Sophia glanced at Uglovaty, standing opposite her, devouring her with his glistening eyes, mumbling something.

"So, princess, do we have a deal?"

This was all that Sophia heard. She stood in place, perplexed. The detective's words made no sense to her. Uglovaty slowly approached Sophia. He looked like a predator that sensed its splendid prey, and tried to keep hold of it. In a moment, this predator in human form, grabbed Sophia with its paws. His sweaty, sticky hands groped her flesh, pressing it against his rough body which stank with perspiration. His hands reached lower and lower until they grabbed and painfully squeezed her buttocks. With his loathsome hands, he lifted the hem of her skirt and reached for her hips and belly, until his fingers clasped her crotch. During all this time, Sophia stood stock-still.

The detective's smelly lips whispered into her ear, "If you want, I can let Ukhtomsky go, but first you'll have to put out, be mine. Only then will I do what you want. If you put out, I'll grant Ukhtomsky his freedom."

Sophia nodded, closed her eyes and decided to throw herself in the mercy of the lustful detective.

"Just let Aleksey go. Let him go," she said over and over again.

"Don't worry, I'll keep my word and let the prince go. Just give yourself to me," Uglovaty hissed into her ear with his lustful, trembling voice.

The detective picked up Sophia's weak-willed body. He pondered about where to fulfill his needs. Uglovaty lay her back down and began to feverishly rip her dress off. When she was lying nude and helpless in front of him, he roared like a wild animal, sensing a splendid upcoming satisfaction. He hustled to take his trousers off to expose his erect penis, ready to enter her womanhood. Sophia lay on her back apathetically. She felt the detective's sweaty body throw his weight on her, pressing her to the floor, and his penis penetrate her body. She yelped from the striking pain, bit her lip trying not to scream, and fell unconscious.

Sophia came back to when Uglovaty slapped her face.

"You woke up, princess? Good, I liked it. You've got a nice body. You were keeping your virginity for someone, weren't you? Yes, I deflowered you. Oh how sweet your flower was!" Uglovaty gleamed with pleasure.

"Let Aleksey go," Sophia demanded harshly.

"I will, as promised. Besides, I finally had my vengeance on your mother, who publically humiliated me. I had my vengeance by being the first man to have her daughter," he laughed, baring his yellow teeth. "Anyway, princess, you should head home. Aleksey will be free in the morning. Even though I'm a lout, I'll keep my word, don't worry."

As she exited the building, Sophia dragged herself along the road, shaking as if she was drunk. She was nauseous. Having walked around ten meters, she felt the need to hurl. Sophia squatted by some building, trying to calm down. Fortunately, it was late and the streets were empty. Nobody could stop her from talking to herself. In her head, she needed to sort out what had happened. The pain in her lower stomach would not go away. That was the only thing that comforted her.

"Tomorrow, Aleksey will be home. He'll be alive, and that's what's important. I'll survive this humiliation. I will."

Sophia cried. Her soft crying quickly grew into heavy sobbing. Slowly, she calmed down. She didn't feel like going home. She roamed the streets of Leningrad, trying not to think about the incident. She thought about Aleksey. Sophia remembered the first time she saw Aleksey when she was a small girl. She knew from that moment in the train that Aleksey would be her one and only love. But he fell in love with her sister. At first, Sophia was mad at Polina. She hated her. But with time, she got over the fact that Aleksey belonged to Polina. She still loved him and she never gave up hoping that Aleksey would reciprocate someday. She wanted to do something for Aleksey to make him change the way he looks at her. Sophia wanted Aleksey to look at her with grateful, admiring, loving eyes. That was why she did this. She wanted to save her one and only love from sure death. But nobody could know about this. Nobody could ever know the price she paid for Aleksey's freedom.

The sun was rising in the East. A new day was coming. Sophia plodded back home and climbed the stairs to her floor, and quietly opened the door of their apartment, trying not to make much noise. She made her way to her bedroom through the darkness. Undressing herself, she grabbed a towel and went into the bathroom. Sophia stood under the shower, washing her body with a sponge, gently at first, then furiously. She wanted to wash off all the dirt that stuck to her after being with Uglovaty. Tears welled up in her eyes. She wanted to scream from the pain and humiliation. A small one escaped. She hoped that the pouring water would cover up the sound. It took a few moments for Sophia to realize that someone was knocking on the bathroom door.

"Sophia, darling, what's wrong? Come on, open the door. Open the door!" Polina yelled.

Sophia came out of the bathroom, calm. She smiled at Polina and kissed her cheek.

"You weren't home all night long. Where were you? Who did you spend it with? Sophia, tell me. Don't be afraid. I can see something is troubling you." Polina was persistent.

"Polina, everything is alright. You're making an elephant out of a fly. I took care of everything, and now I really want to sleep. And, please, don't ask any questions."

The following morning, Uglovaty set Ukhtomsky free.

"You know, I'd be only happy to keep you under arrest. I hate your kin, I hate the Ukhtomsky kin. You all want to be respectable and honest. But yesterday, I finally got what I desired for many years. I finally felt good yesterday," Uglovaty's voice was dreamy and sickly sweet. "And that is why I'm letting you go. You're free. Here, take this pass."

Ukhtomsky grabbed the pass and silently left the room. In about five minutes, Rozov barged into the cabinet.

"Stepan, what do you think you're doing? Why the hell did you let Ukhtomsky go? Who will we use to fulfill our quota?" Nikolai Ivanovich yelled at his subordinate.

In the meantime, Uglovaty continued to sit in his chair, calmly and silently watching the senior detective.

"Stand up when your superiors are talking to you!" Rozov continued to yell.

"Calm down, Nikolai Ivanovich. There's no need to worry, I took care of it. I have a perfect candidate."

Rozov suspiciously glanced at Uglovaty and anxiously sat in the chair.

"Who is it?" he asked, worried.

"Just a moment, Nikolai Ivanovich, just a moment," Uglovaty smiled as he dialed a phone number. "He's here," he mumbled quickly.

In a few minutes, the chief of the militia entered the cabinet, followed by guards.

"Rozov, you're under arrest for participating in anti-Soviet activities."

"You reported *me?*" Rozov yelled.

Stepan smiled insidiously.

In a week, Uglovaty was promoted to senior detective.

Chapter 18

"Darya, Jane, these folders contain documents concerning the families of Leonid and Aleksey Ukhtomsky. Vladimir and I have collected them through various channels. Read them. Vladimir and I will help you translate them." Nadya handed four massive folders to the girls.

The cousins anxiously took them. They all sat at the oval table in the living room. With trembling hands, Darya opened the first folder titled "Ukhtomsky Aleksey Nikolayevich. Volume One". Leafing through the documents, the girls came upon Aleksey's death certificate. It mentioned that Aleksey Nikolayevich Ukhtomsky was sentenced to be shot as an agent of imperialism. The document was dated September 1944. Next to it was another document, certifying the death of Polina, Aleksey's wife. She was executed as an accomplice of an agent of imperialism.

"I don't get it. What do they mean, "Agent of imperialism"? He was executed? How could they do such a thing?" Darya couldn't find the words to express her indignation. The documents made no sense to her.

"Let's take a look at the other documents, Darya. Maybe something will come to light," offered Jane.

They studied the first folder until the dead of night, until Darya and Jane gave up.

"That's it. We're exhausted and we're dizzy. We have to rest and digest all the information."

The girls saw Vladimir to the door and began to prepare for sleep.

"Girls, do you know that Polina and Aleksey had a child? I just don't know who it was," Nadya mulled as she prepared the beds for Jane and Darya.

"A child? If the child survived, it means that Aleksey Ukhtomsky's family had its continuation. Perhaps his descendants survived," Darya mumbled hopefully.

She walked up to the window. The roads were almost empty. The city was sleeping. Darya glanced at her watch. It was half past three in the morning.

"Jane, why are you so silent? Are you sleeping already?"

"Nope, I'm thinking about Aleksey. I wonder if he was happy with his life. What did he value? What did he love? Whom did he choose as his wife? We only know that her name was Polina. But who was she, and why did Aleksey fall in love with her?"

"I doubt that we will find the actual answers to these questions. But if we read in between the lines of what is written in the documents, I think we can discover a whole lot of new things," Darya stated confidently.

The two cousins spent the next few days with Nadya and Vladimir, analyzing the contents of all four folders. Darya and Jane refused to go on tours, parties and nightclubs. They were so overwhelmed by the events described in the documents that they emotionally lived the lives with the protagonists of the folders—they cried, raged, marveled, suffered and were horrified. Gradually, the four of them drew a clear picture of the Ukhtomsky brothers" lives in their minds.

Sophia woke up late. She felt uneasy. Her whole body ached and her lower stomach hurt. Her nightmare haunted her. She dreamt of Uglovaty laughing in her face. His mouth made nasty sounds, which didn't make much sense at first, but gradually formed into words. *Are you sad, princess? Don't be. I made you happy, just like you made me. Hahahaha. I'm full of joy! What about you, my darling?*

Uglovaty's hands reached out towards Sophia and hugged her. She felt disgusted and yelled.

"Sophia? Sophia, what's wrong?" Sophia faintly heard Polina's voice through her sleep.

She opened her eyes. Polina kneeled by her sofa and shook her younger sister.

"Honey, you screamed. Did you have a bad dream?"

"Yeah, it was just a nightmare. But don't worry, it will pass. What time is it?" Sophia was anxious.

"It's almost midday."

"Is Aleksey back yet?"

"No."

Suddenly, the doorbell rang and the girls rushed to open the door. It was Aleksey.

Uglovaty actually kept his word, Sophia thought to herself as she smiled cheerfully at Aleksey, who was hugging Polina.

After a tumultuous welcome, they all walked into the kitchen where the breakfast Polina had made for Sophia was getting cold. Polina quickly put it away and set the table anew, arranging fresh plates, cutlery and wine glasses. Out of the cupboard, she took an old bottle of red dry wine, which she was saving for an occasion. She cut bread, cheese and sausages, and opened a few cans of fish. Aleksey opened the bottle of wine and poured it into the glasses.

"I love you both so much. Polina, my darling, you have no idea how much I missed you."

He went silent, as if he was thinking about something. The girls were silent, too. In a few moments, Aleksey continued.

"Sitting in my jail cell, I realized how short life is. When you think that your time is near, you begin to remember and analyze your whole life. I tried to decide whether I lived my life for nothing or not. I agree with Michel Montaigne. Do you remember how in his "Experiences", he wrote that life itself isn't good or evil? It's simply a container for good or evil, depending on what you make of it. I really hope, and still do, that my life has more good than evil, otherwise there is no point in living. I raise my glass for you, my darlings. I hope you fill your life with good deeds and not waste it for nothing. Paraphrasing Kafka's words, only those who truly understand life are unafraid of dying. Fear of death is merely the result of an unfulfilled life…"

Andrey lapsed into silence. He brusquely shook his head, trying to rid himself from unpleasant thoughts, and apologized.

"Polina, Sophia, pardon me for being so philosophical. I couldn't hold myself in. Let us drink for a joyful, fulfilled life."

"Aleksey, let's invite Olga and Lida for dinner," Polina offered quietly.

"Of course, my dear. But for now, I think we should go rest together."

They left the room. Sophia followed them with wistful eyes and began cleaning. She then went into her bedroom, sat on the sofa and took one of Dostoevsky's books. He was her favorite author. Whenever Sophia was feeling down, she always read Dostoevsky. His works took her into another world, where her troubles and fears were replaced by empathy for the protagonists. It was almost as if she was one of the protagonists. They made her think, look for solutions to problems, and even reflect on everything. Sophia was halfway through *"A Little Hero"*, a short tale, when she heard a knock on her door. It was Aleksey.

"Can I come in?" he asked.

Sophia blushed and invited him inside. Aleksey walked up to her, held her hands and said sincerely, "Thank you, Sophia."

Horrified, Sophia thought to herself, *Did Uglovaty tell him everything?*

"What are you thanking me for?" she asked anxiously.

"What do you mean what for? Thank you for supporting Polina. She told me how you cheered her up, assuring her that I'll be back. Even though Polina is much older than you, she's very vulnerable and sensitive. You're stronger in spirits. I'm glad that you're living with us." Sophia smiled without saying anything. Aleksey continued, "You know, Uglovaty was acting weird when he let me go. He looked so happy and satisfied. And he was talking insolently and presumptuously to me."

Sophia remained silent.

"I feel sorry for him," continued Ukhtomsky. "He's like a lone wolf, roaring at everyone, yet he fears them all. And he hides this fear behind his cruelty."

"Don't feel sorry for him, Aleksey. He's not worth it," Sophia uttered. "He was and still is a rascal. I don't want to talk about it." Her face twisted in agony. "I'm sorry, but I would like to be alone now."

Aleksey had something else he wanted to tell her, but her last words made him leave. When the door closed behind him, she sat on her sofa, covered her face with her hands and began to cry quietly.

Three weeks later, Sophia realized she was pregnant. At first, she was terrified. Her first thought was to have an abortion. The only thought that Uglovaty was the father of her future child disgusted her. She hated him more than anyone else.

"What shall I do? What shall I do?" she kept asking herself. "How can I possibly kill an innocent child? I am a doctor, and I swore the oath of Hippocrates. Even though the child hasn't been born yet, he's alive. He has feelings. No, I can't kill him," she reasoned feverishly.

"Yes, it's Uglovaty's child, but it's my child, too. There is no way I can kill it. Perhaps, this child will be my only comfort in this life. I can never love anyone else. But I'm a woman full of love and tenderness. And I will give all this love and tenderness to him, my child."

Sophia decided to keep the child.

Knowing that she had a new life growing inside of her changed Sophia. She became gentler and warmhearted and she shined with a soft inner light. Aleksey was the first to notice it. One evening at dinner, he noted that Sophia didn't look her usual self. She was more beautiful, womanly and proud.

"Sophia, what's going on? Are you in love?" Aleksey wondered.

She blushed, silently, as Aleksey continued to nag her.

"Come on. Tell us who the lucky man is. When will we meet him?"

Sophia stood up from her chair, thanked Polina for dinner, and excused herself from the table in a flat voice. She left to her room. Aleksey was shocked. This was not Sophia's usual behavior.

"Polina, maybe you can tell me what is wrong with your sister?"

Polina pondered. She also noticed a few changes in Sophia and thought that it was because her sister was in love. But Sophia's behavior at dinner confused her. Polina began to doubt her initial assumptions. A faint distant guess made her wonder.

"Aleksey, I'll go talk to her. I feel sick at heart."

Polina found her sister sitting on the sofa, reading a book.

"Sophia, darling, what are you reading?" she asked, hoping to gradually get Sophia to talk.

Sophia glanced at Polina and replied, almost interrupting, "I'm sorry, but I'm not in the mood now. Can you leave me, please?"

When Polina left, Sophia walked up to the window and looked outside. Spring was gaining strength. April in Leningrad was still cold, wet and chilly. But the sun rays broke through the clouds more often, awakening nature. On the trees, the swollen buds blossomed with small green leaves. More and more birds were coming back from their distant travels, and filled the city with their songs. Observing the waking trees under her windows and the windows of the house opposite, watching the pedestrians hurry to places, and watching the little bird build its nest on one of the maple tree's branches calmed Sophia. Her hand mechanically rested on her belly.

And I also have a new life. He's growing inside me. He's my continuation, she thought.

Sophia remembered Feuerbach's quote: Your most important duty in life is to make yourself happy. If you are happy, you'll make everyone else happy. A happy person can only see happy people around him.

She loved Feuerbach for the precision of his opinions.

I will be happy, and I will make my child happy. I'm strong. I can do this, she thought to herself.

These thoughts made her light at heart. She smiled, giggling, and began to quietly sing young Robert's song from "The Children of Captain Grant", which she watched at least ten times.

Three months later, Sophia's pregnancy was obvious. During dinner, she decided to announce it to her sister and Aleksey. To her surprise, they were delighted to hear the news.

"Sophia, my dear, I'm so happy! You have no idea just how happy I am!" Polina couldn't suppress her emotions. "You know, God can't give Aleksey and me a child. At first I've shed so many tears, but then I accepted it. And now, at last, a little child will be running in this apartment, laughing, messing around and playing. Life will finally be complete."

As Polina was saying this, she glanced at her husband, who was looking at her, smiling.

"But who's the father of the child?" Aleksey wondered. "Why don't you introduce us to him? And why aren't you getting married?"

Sophia lowered her head, feverishly thinking about her reply. Polina and Aleksey were impatiently looking at her, waiting.

"You don't know him. He's… He's…my colleague, a doctor from Novosibirsk. He was here on advanced training. That's where we met. He was so charming, gentle and attentive, that I couldn't resist," Sophia cried as she said these words.

All she could see was Uglovaty's blatant, mocking, laughing face. She covered her face.

"He… He has a family. He's married. He went back to Novosibirsk," Sophia's voice was firm. "I don't need him. I don't want to get married, anyway. I know I will never love anyone. Don't worry. I will raise my child by myself. I will raise him with love and make him happy."

Polina and Aleksey exchanged glances. In a few minutes, Polina broke the silence.

"Sophia, do you honestly think that we will leave you? We will never do that. This child will be ours, too. And trust me; he will be the happiest child in the world. Isn't that right, Aleksey?"

The remaining six months of Sophia's pregnancy passed quickly. She bloomed; the pregnancy adorned her. In the evenings, Polina and Sophia discussed how to decorate the baby's corner in Sophia's room, what to buy, and what to name the child.

"If it's a boy, I'd like to name him Michael. It means *"godlike"* in ancient Hebrew. It is not without reason that they say, *"Nomen omen"*. *"Your name shapes your destiny"*. This is why my son Michael will be a just, honest, kind person. This is how I'll raise him."

"Well, what if you have a baby girl? What will you call her?" Polina wondered, smiling.

Sophia gave it a moment's thought, going through girls' names in her head.

"You know, I never even thought about having a girl. I want a son. But if I do have a girl, I'd like to call her Anastasia, just like in our Russian tales. And she will be the most beautiful, smartest and kindest girl. This proud name will bring her love and happiness, I'm sure."

Olga and Lida became frequent guests in Aleksey's apartment. One dinner, Olga talked to Sophia.

"You know, Leonid Nikolayevich didn't treat you just like the sister of his brother's wife. You were something more to him."

Sophia glanced at Olga, shocked.

"I'm not sure what you're trying to say, Olga Petrovna," Sophia was slightly perplexed.

"I think you misunderstood me," Olga giggled. "It's just that Leonid always told me that he had deeper kindred feelings for you, like you were more closely related to him. You know that Aleksey and Leonid had a sister, whom they last saw at her wedding. Well, Leonid Nikolayevich always thought that you look like her."

Sophia tensed and glanced at Polina, discretely shaking her head. Sophia shrugged her shoulders and replied in a dry voice, which gave away her excess anxiety.

"Really? Well, there are many people who look like each other. I have the appearance of an average Russian woman, meaning I have something in common with the majority of women in Russia, especially here in Leningrad," Sophia's last words had a hint of sarcasm.

Polina and Lida silently watched the verbal duel. Lida couldn't conceal her interest. Polina was also sitting as if on pins, trying to keep herself from telling the truth. Olga smiled again and patted Sophia on her back.

"Don't worry, Sophia. It's just that Leonid Nikolayevich really loved his sister and he looked for her for so long, but never heard anything from her. You know what? Next time I'll bring Elizabeth's photo. She was slightly younger than you are now when it was taken. You'll see how much you look like her. Also, I think you might be interested in that picture. It depicts all the Ukhtomsky brothers with their wives and children."

"We've seen that photo. Aleksey has it, too," Polina replied.

Sophia was silent.

When the guests left, Polina asked her sister, "Please tell me why you're making me hide the truth? It's the same as lying, and you know I hate lying."

"Polina, please, not now. We will tell them everything, but not now. Trust me, it's better that way. We hid the truth for so many years. It would be awkward for it to come up now all of a sudden. Everything is so calm now. Let's keep it that way."

Sophia was worried. Her face was red and her eyes blinked involuntary. The kitchen towel, which she used to dry the plates, turned into a bulged lump.

"Let's make a deal, Polina. I will be the one to tell Olga and Aleksey the truth. I will tell them everything when I feel it's right."

"Do I have a choice? Agreed.... Although I think you're wrong. Anyway, we'll do it your way." Polina hugged her sister and kissed her forehead. "Don't worry. Everything will be alright. You'll tell them when the time is right. After all, it's your story, not mine."

"Polina! Polina! Help me!"

Polina was woken up by Sophia's alarmed voice.

She jumped out of her bed and glanced at the clock. It was half past four in the morning. She ran into her sister's room. Sophia was lying on the sofa, pale, holding on to her stomach.

"What's wrong? Where does it hurt?" Polina was bustling around her sister.

"Polina, please, call the ambulance," Sophia's voice was getting. She was sweating. "Polina, I... I..." She fell unconscious.

Polina practically sprinted to the telephone in the hallway and called the ambulance. She then phoned Olga, asking her to come over. She ran into the bathroom, grabbing the first towel she saw, wet it with cold water, and rushed back to Sophia, who was lying on the sofa, pale and sweating. Her breathing was irregular. Polina quickly began to dry her sister's face, arms and chest with the wet towel. She remembered about ammonia spirit in her medicine chest and dashed to get it. Feverishly, she poured a few drops onto a cotton wool, and passed it over Sophia's forehead, temples and under her nose. Her young sister shrugged and opened her eyes.

"Polina, something's wrong," she mumbled in a weak voice. "Did you call the ambulance?"

"Yes, honey. It's on its way. Let me wash you up. Just lie there and don't move."

"Polina, I'm scared," Sophia uttered with aspiration and fell unconscious again.

The ambulance arrived about fifteen minutes later. It was enough for the elderly doctor to simply glance at Sophia to order the paramedics to bring the stretchers.

"We're going to hospitalize her. I can't guarantee that everything will be alright. She has a hemorrhage!" exclaimed the doctor when the paramedics shifted Sophia from the bed onto the stretchers.

"The bed sheets are soaked with blood. How are you related to the patient?" the doctor asked Polina.

"Sisters. I'm her sister," she replied, hurriedly.

"Come with us. You can help. Why are you still standing there? Help us. Delay may mean death!" the doctor shouted to Polina.

The ambulance took them to the nearest maternity home. Polina waited in the admission room, arms crossed over her chest. "Time is passing so slowly… Lord, please help us! I'm begging you, help us! Please, don't let Sophia or the baby die!" she whispered.

It had been almost two hours since the ambulance brought them to the hospital and Sophia was rushed into surgery.

"Why isn't anyone coming? Something must have happened. I can feel it. Something happened…" Polina's inner fear began to take over. She sat on the chair, covered her face and cried quietly. Then she threw her head back, closed her eyes and immersed herself into her thoughts.

"Are you Sophia Khulev's sister? Excuse me, lady, are you Sophia Khulev's sister?" a nurse shook Polina's shoulder.

"What? What happened?" Polina came to. "Yes, Sophia's my sister. Is she alright? Is the baby alright?"

Without looking at Polina, the nurse responded, "Please go to the doctor's cabinet on the second floor. The doctor wants to talk to you."

The nurse hurried away. Polina's feet almost gave way; she lost control over them. With a lot of effort, she made it up the stairs to the second floor and into the doctor's cabinet. She caught her breath and quietly knocked on the door, but opened it without waiting for an answer. Behind a small desk sat a young man around thirty-five wearing a white doctor's smock and a hat, writing something. He raised his head and saw Polina enter the room.

"Who are you? What are you doing here?" he enquired brusquely.

"I was told that you're expecting me," she replied timidly.

"Aaaahh, you're Khulev's sister, aren't you?"

"Yes, yes, I'm her sister. Is Sophia alright? How's the baby?"

The doctor asked Polina to sit down while he walked up to the window. "The weather's changing, the sky is clouded. Look how dark it is. It's going to rain now," the doctor's voice was slow and quiet.

Without a rush, he closed the window and turned away to face Polina. She sat stiffly on the chair, afraid to move, and watched the doctor closely. The doctor slowly returned to his seat behind the desk, and, for some reason, shifted a few folders to the other side of the table as he gave Polina a long stare. He finally broke the silence.

"We did everything we could, trust me. But we couldn't save your sister. She died. But the baby is alive, albeit weak. It's a baby girl. She is being looked after. We will keep her under observation for a week, and then her father can pick her up."

The doctor gazed at Polina, trying to figure out whether she heard him or not. She watched him with wide, unblinking eyes. Her face turned into a mask. It was pale and not a single muscle twitched. Her fingers interlocked so tightly that the skin on her hands turned blue. Polina was sitting straight. Too straight. It seemed that she was petrified, unable to come to from her stupor. The doctor called for the nurse.

Suddenly, Polina stood and uttered in a trembling voice, "Thank you, but there's no need to call for the nurse. I understood everything. When... When can I pick my sister up?"

Chapter 19

Aleksey returned from his academic trip two days after Sophia's funeral. When he opened the door of his apartment, he was shocked by the silence. Usually he was greeted by his wife, followed by Sophia. But this time, no one.

"Polina, my dear, I'm back," Aleksey announced.

Silence.

"What in the world is going? What happened?"

He checked the kitchen and Polina's room. They were empty.

"Perhaps she went for a walk with Sophia," Ukhtomsky thought to himself.

A faint cry brought him back to reality. The cry was coming from Sophia's room. Aleksey rushed into the bedroom and saw his wife sitting on the sofa, hugging a pillow and crying into it.

"Polina, I'm back. Didn't you hear me? Where is Sophia?" Aleksey asked, perplexed.

When Polina saw her husband, her cries turned into sobbing. For the first time after hearing the news of her sister's death, she finally gave in to her tears.

Two weeks passed. During this time, Aleksey and Polina officially adopted Sophia's daughter. The father of one of Lida's students helped them throughout the adoption process as he was a lawyer. The little girl was still in the maternity home. She was born prematurely and was still very weak.

"Polina, we should clean Sophia's room and prepare it for baby's arrival," Olga said over the phone. "Lida and I can come over and help you, if you want."

"Thank you so much. I already thought about cleaning the room, but I can't get myself to clean out her things. It feels like she'll come back sometime soon... Sure, you can come tomorrow at lunch."

"Look, it's Sophia's little chest," uttered Lida, surprised, as she was dusting the bookcase.

"Show it to me, Lida." Polina walked up to her. "Yes, I's Sophia's chest. She inherited it from her mother," she mumbled thoughtfully and carefully opened it.

Three envelopes were lying on top inside the chest. Polina picked them up and took out a few old photos, along with an old emerald necklace, which seemed to arouse a lot of interest in Olga.

"It's Lisa on the photo. I remember how this photograph was taken before the wedding at the Ukhtomsky manor. And on this photograph, there's Lisa with her future husband, prince Vikhulev." Olga's voice was surprised and excited at the same time.

"Polina, what it is this supposed to mean? I even know this necklace. It was Aleksey's wedding present for Lisa. He ordered it especially for her from a famous jeweler in Saint Petersburg, but I can't remember his surname. Ah, I remembered, it was Khlebnikov. It's a unique necklace. There is no other necklace like that." Olga's voice trembled. "Polina, is that true? These things... this chest..."

"This was Sophia's chest and everything inside it was hers as well. I think it's time I told you the truth. Sophia wanted to tell you herself. She was waiting for the right moment... I guess the moment has come," Polina's voice was filled with sorrow. "Let's wait for Aleksey. He should be home from work soon."

Polina glanced at the envelopes. The first one read, "To my dear sister Polina", and it was written in Sophia's handwriting. The second envelope was for Aleksey, the third one for Olga.

"Olga, there's a letter for you from Sophia," she uttered quietly as she handed her the letter. "I think you should read it first, and perhaps it will make everything clearer."

Olga took the envelope with awe.

"Olga, do you mind if I go into my room to read Sophia's letter?" asked Polina. She was already heading to her room, opening the envelope on her way.

"No, no, of course you can go," Olga answered quickly. She sat on the sofa, ready to read Sophia's letter.

Polina worriedly opened the sheet of paper covered in Sophia's small handwriting.

Polina, my dear sister,

If you're reading this letter, it means that I'm already dead. I always knew that my mother's fate awaited me. And even though my baby, whom I carry underneath my heart, isn't a fruit of love, I couldn't bring myself to kill him and hence prolong my life. He is my blood and flesh. He is my continuation. If it's God's will to let me live, I will be the happiest and most loving mother in the world. If it's God's will…. But nobody knows what his will is. I haven't been feeling well these last days. I'm getting weaker day by day. Recently, I had a prophetic dream. I saw my mother. She looked just like her photos, young and beautiful in her bridal dress with the emerald necklace on her chest. She smiled and lured me towards her.

"It's so nice here, my dear. Don't be afraid. Soon we will be together again," she told me.

My mother lead me through a picturesque field with massive flowers that I've never seen before. Butterflies with huge wings hovered above us. A soft, warm light surrounded me. I felt so good. Now I'm not scared anymore. I don't fear death. I only fear for my child. Polina, I want you and Aleksey to be the parents of my child.

And now, the important part… I got pregnant from Uglovaty. It was the price I paid for Aleksey's freedom. This is my only excuse for being with that rascal. Please don't be mad at me. I had to do this, otherwise Aleksey would have died and you would have been a widow. Forgive me for everything, please. I love you both too much to watch you suffer.

One more thing… I wrote a letter to Aleksey, and I think you have the right to know about it… But I think Aleksey will tell you everything, anyway. I regret nothing. My life was short, but I was happy. Goodbye, my darling. You weren't just a sister to me; you were also my best friend. I hope you will become a loving mother for our child. Goodbye.

Tears streamed down Polina's cheeks, yet she didn't notice them. When she finished reading the letter, she closed her eyes and squeezed her temples until it hurt, trying to suppress the pain that was eating up her heart.

"Sophia, Sophia... What have you done? Thank you, my darling! Thank you so much! How did I not see it? Why did you never tell me about this? My poor little girl…"

She stood up and walked to the wardrobe, taking a handkerchief out to wipe the tears from her eyes. Her actions were all mechanical. With her treasured sheet of paper, she walked to the window and opened it. The cool autumn air filled the room. It refreshed her face, wiping her tears off. But they were replaced by new involuntary tears. Polina looked outside the window but couldn't see anything. It was getting dark. The rain clouds filled the sky. The trees were almost bare. The late autumn put itself on the map.

"What will I do without you? What? Tell me, Sophia," repeated Polina, barely able to move her lips.

A gust of wind almost ripped the letter out of her hands. She pressed it closer to her heart, crossing her arms on her chest, and sobbed. She sobbed loudly, unashamed of Olga and Lida who were in the other room, unashamed of the passers-by who looked up to locate the source of the loud sobs, which sounded like the cries of a wounded, abandoned animal. Another gust of wind, the sound of the slamming window, and the heavy rain brought Polina back to reality.

"Sophia, if you can hear me now, I promise to do everything I can to make your child the happiest person in the world. I will be a worthy mother, and I will tell your daughter about you when she grows up. She will know about you, Sophia. She will look up to you, your love, your dignity and your endurance."

After making the promise to her sister, Polina was at peace. She knew what she had to do. She owed Sophia a lot. And keeping this promise will be Polina's aim in life.

Someone rang the doorbell and Polina dashed to open the door. It was Aleksey.

"Polina, were you crying?" asked her husband caringly.

Olga and Lida came out of Sophia's room. Their faces were also filled with tears.

"What happened?" he asked, confused.

He glanced at Sophia's door and shook his head.

"Please excuse my callousness. I didn't mean to be like that."

There was an awkward silence. Polina broke it.

"It's dinnertime. How about we all sit down, eat and talk? Olga, Lida, why don't you come and help me set the table?"

In twenty minutes, everyone sat around the small kitchen table. During these twenty minutes, nobody uttered a single word. Nobody felt like talking. Each one of them was digesting the new information. Aleksey took a shower and changed for dinner.

"Oh, good job! Dinner looks delicious!" Aleksey exclaimed with admiration.

He was trying to cheer up his wife and his guests, who were silently waiting for him.

After dinner, which passed in complete silence, Polina handed Sophia's letter to Aleksey.

"Sophia wrote this. It's addressed to you," Polina said nervously. "She also wrote a letter to Olga and me. Each one of us has the right to decide if they want to tell the others about the content of their letter."

"I'm sorry, but I would like to read the letter in my room, alone," Ukhtomsky apologized as he hurried away, opening the letter.

"Polina, I think Aleksey has to know what Sophia wrote to me. It concerns the whole Ukhtomsky family. Please, hand him this letter. Of course, you also have the right to read it, although I'm sure you know everything already. Lida and I have to go now. It's late and you have a long day tomorrow. You're picking up your little girl tomorrow."

"Thank you for helping me. Come tomorrow for dinner if you can. I'll make a festive meal. After all, we will have a new member of the family join us!"

Polina hugged her guests and saw them to the door.

Aleksey sat by his desk on which he put Sophia's letter. His unseeing stare was fixed on one point. His temples ached. His hands, which rested on the table, were nervously fiddling with the tablecloth. Ukhtomsky walked up to the window and looked outside. It was dark. The bare trees were lit by the faint light from the stars and the moon, which appeared after a short drizzle. The streets were empty. Only the noise of the occasional car broke the peace and silence of the sleeping city. Aleksey massaged his temples, but the throbbing pain was persistent.

"How could I not see or feel that girl?" Aleksey asked himself.

All he could see in front of him were the lines of Sophia's letter.

Dear Aleksey,

We never talked heart-to-heart with you. I often wanted to sit by your side, bury my hand in your thick hair, turn your brave face towards me, gently kiss your eyes, and tell you about myself. No, not about the whimsical, obstinate, and, at times, rough and mean girl you saw every day. I wanted to tell you about the girl who turned into a tender, shy, loving woman under you invisible influence.

Aleksey closed his eyes. He saw a whole new side of Sophia as she revealed herself in the letter.

Aleksey, I'm not writing this letter to make you feel the same way I felt for you, or to make you feel pity for me. It just so happens that my end is near, and I don't want to leave this world leaving you in the dark. Of course, Polina would have told you everything later, but I would like to be the one to tell you first. I am guilty towards to you. I hope you forgive me someday... I really hope you do.

Aleksey put the letter aside and went back to massaging his temples, which ached mercilessly. The pain was never-ending. He settled back in his chair and closed his eyes. An abject tear rolled out of his eye, trying to make its way through the stubble that grew on his cheeks through the day. Aleksey swiped it away and opened his eyes. He took the letter back in hand and continued to read Sophia's small and messy handwritings, which is inherent in doctors.

I never got to meet my mother. She died when she was giving birth to me. But I know who she was and what kind of a person she was. My father raised me and taught me to love and respect her. I always felt her presence by my side, even though she wasn't physically there.

Here, the ink was washed out. Aleksey could see a trace of Sophia's tear on the letter. After, her handwriting became less confident and shakier. Between the two sentences, there was a significant gap, filled with messy periods. Aleksey was overcome with anxiety.

The door opened and Polina entered the room.

"Aleksey, have you finished the letter?" she asked, concerned.

Aleksey turned to his wife and waved his hand silently. Polina had something to say, but when she glanced at her husband, she changed her mind. She carefully closed the door and left to the kitchen on tiptoes. Aleksey continued reading the letter.

Aleksey, I have no idea how to express what I am feeling right now... And I don't know whether you will understand me. Do you remember the first time we met in the train? Ex ungue leonem. (We can recognize a lion by its claws - Latin). And it's true. The moment I first saw you, I was overwhelmed by your noble, brave face and your eyes, which radiated love and goodness. I was only thirteen years old, but the age difference of over twenty years meant nothing. You are the only man I ever loved. You are the reason I have lived. If a person can easily describe his love, then his love is weak. I can barely write these lines. I'm afraid I can't find the words worthy of my love for you. Please, forgive me for my miserable confession.

Aleksey settled back in his chair again. He could hardly breathe. Ukhtomsky unbuttoned the top of his shirt, hoping it would help. But he was wrong. He walked to the open window and gazed outside again as the fresh night breeze cooled his face and eased his breathing.

Aleksey sat back at his desk, and took the letter into his hands.

I fell in love with you before I found out who you were. I couldn't do anything with myself. For a long time, I tried to fight it, tried to drive away the gift of love. But then I realized that I simply have to carry on because the meaning of life is life itself. I realized how amazing it felt to wake up every morning, bump into you on your way to the bathroom, have breakfast and dinner with you... Even though you weren't mine, you were by my side, and we breathed the same air. It was my joy. It was fragile, but it was mine.

Do you remember Pablo Picasso? If the wings of the butterfly are to keep their sheen, you mustn't touch them? To keep the fragile joy I had living with you, I forbade Polina to tell you the truth about me. I think that was my biggest sin in this life... My mother was from the Ukhtomsky family. Yes, yes, Aleksey, it was your sister, Lisa, whom you and Leonid Nikolayevich were looking for all those years. When we first met in the train and you introduced yourself as Ukhtomsky, I squeezed Polina's hand, signaling her not to tell you anything. And the reason for that was my love for you.

Aleksey painfully squeezed his head. He remembered the feeling of warmth and closeness that he felt when he first met little Sophia in the train. He clearly remembered that his emotions were not aroused by her physical appearance, but by her faint resemblance to Lisa. And afterwards, Aleksey often felt that he had a deep connection with Sophia, the origins of which he didn't know. Yes, even Leonid felt a strange feeling of propinquity to Sophia.

"Oh my God, I was so blind! If only I paid more attention to Sophia, I would have seen this!"

Aleksey reeled from the anxiety and dissatisfaction. He remembered the day Gerasimovsky came to him, demanding to go to Leonid. Gerasimovsky said it, and Polina confirmed it; she lived with Sophia at prince Vikhulev's manor. Why didn't I make Polina and Sophia tell me about it?

Emaciated, Aleksey sank into the sofa. The pain pierced through his temples. His vision blurred. A small vein pulsed vigorously in his right temple, his forehead was covered in perspiration, and his face twisted in agony.

"Aleksey, what's wrong?" Polina worried. "You've been in here for so long. Are you feeling alright?"

Polina's voice was a faint echo in Aleksey's ears. With a lot of effort, he opened his eyes and said quite firmly, "I need to be alone. We can talk later, but for now I'd like you to leave. I'm sorry."

Polina looked at her husband with her tormented eyes and quietly left the room.

His life, from the moment he met Sophia and Polina, had passed before his eyes. All the years he spent with them, he was happy. Yes. He felt good and calm with his loving wife and the welcoming, attentive Sophia. Aleksey remembered the quote he read from a philosophy book: *The better our present it, the less we think about the past.*

"I was happy all these years, and so I forgot the problems of my past... Was I right to do so?"

Aleksey carefully folded the letter, stood up, put it on the desk and walked up to the window. When he opened it, the cold autumn wind broke into the room. The streets were quiet – no cars, no people. He glanced at the clock. It was half past three. Suddenly, a small sparrow sat on the pane of the neighboring window. As it shifted from one leg to another, it looked at Aleksey with its button-like eyes and tried to fly into the room. Having made a few weak movements, it brusquely turned around and flew away. It sat on a tree branch closest to the window. Aleksey forced a smile and closed the window. He was feverish. He wanted to lie down and escape reality.

You'll understand what I'm talking about when you will talk with Polina.

That phrase from the letter pestered him. He could barely keep his eyes open. As he was falling asleep, he mumbled like a curse, "I must talk with Polina tomorrow."

Polina peaked into the room. Her husband, still dressed in his everyday clothes, was sleeping on the sofa. She walked up to him, carefully put a pillow under his head, covered him with a quilt and gently kissed his forehead. Polina went inside Sophia's room and lay on her sister's sofa, still wearing her robe, and fell asleep under her quilt.

Chapter 20

It was around eight when Polina finally woke up. The apartment was silent. On her way to the bathroom, she noticed that the light was on in the kitchen. Her husband was standing by the open window, smoking. A saucer with a pile of cigarette buds was on the table.

"Aleksey, what are you doing? You don't smoke! Where did you get the cigarettes?" his wife's voice was highly disappointed.

Ukhtomsky slowly turned his head to face Polina. She was struck by his facial expression. His ever sparkling eyes were now dim, the corners of his lips were lowered, and a few tiny wrinkles filled his forehead. Aleksey looked like he gained a few years throughout the night. Polina walked up to her husband, took the cigarette out of his fingers and put it out. He did not resist. She sat him on the chair and obeyed him as if he had no will of his own. He seemed so apathetic. His lackluster eyes aimlessly skimmed the kitchen until they stopped at Polina's face. She began to vigorously shake him by his shoulders.

"Aleksey, Aleksey, what's wrong with you? Please, talk to me!"

Aleksey pushed his wife aside and asked, "Please, make some tea, Polina. Make it strong and add some mint. I don't want to eat anything, just tea." His voice was grey and remote.

Polina nodded, turned towards the stove and put the kettle on it. In one motion, she swiped the saucer with the buds, two empty cigarette packs and an opened one off the table. She swiftly threw everything into the dustbin and took it outside.

In the meantime, Aleksey waited for her on the chair, motionless. He only closed his eyes. His face was still tense and tormented.

In about three hours, Aleksey found Polina, who was giving the final touches to Sophia's room, to have everything ready for the baby's arrival.

"Polina, we need to talk."

Polina silently handed him the letter that Sophia addressed to her. "Read this. Then we can sit and talk. I know I have a lot to tell you."

Aleksey took the letter and retreated to the kitchen. What he read in Polina's letter shocked him. He pictured Uglovaty's complacent, blatant face. Uglovaty got what he desired. Aleksey didn't give much meaning to Uglovaty's words.

I finally got what I desired for many years. I finally felt good yesterday.

Now these words made sense. Horrible and terrible sense.

"Sophia, Sophia, what have you done?"

He squeezed his head so hard that his face and neck turned crimson read. Aleksey wanted to squeeze out the emotional pain that overwhelmed him. It was the compassionate pain he felt for the little girl who was more than a daughter or his wife's sister. And now, after reading the letter addressed to him, Sophia filled a place in his heart, which had been empty since the day they lost Lisa.

"I'll kill you, Uglovaty! I'll kill you! I swear to God, I will!" he yelled in a gust of rage.

Polina ran into the kitchen. She had never seen her husband like this. He stood by the window, his face resentful and enraged. His eyes were burning with hatred. Aleksey was tense, ready to explode any moment. Terrified of the image before her, Polina quietly left the room.

Over half an hour passed before she finally returned to the kitchen. Aleksey was sitting at the table, blindly staring at the wall opposite him. She approached her husband and carefully placed her hand on his shoulder.

"Honey, it's time to get dressed. We have to pick up the little girl in an hour."

He looked at his wife with remote eyes and retreated into the bedroom, swaying nervously on his way. In transit to the maternity home, Aleksey said quietly, "We'll adopt her. Tomorrow, we'll start preparing the documents. And we'll name her Sophia."

Polina quietly nodded her head.

Two weeks passed. The Ukhtomsky couple was happy. It was a new period in their lives. They were finally parents. They only had one argument. It came when they were registering the baby.

"I want to name her Sophia," Aleksey insisted firmly the day before the registration.

Polina hugged her husband and said calmly but insistently, "Aleksey, I perfectly understand. You want to name her in memory of your niece. It's very nice of you. But don't you remember how Sophia wanted to name her baby girl Anastasia? We can't go against her will, against her last wish."

They registered her as Anastasia, Anastasia Ukhtomsky. In the evening, Polina and Aleksey invited Lida and Olga for dinner. The Ukhtomsky family was welcoming its new member. When Anastasia was finally asleep and the agitated conversations about her ceased, Aleksey asked his wife, "Polina, I never questioned you about your and Sophia's life before we met. But now, when Olga and Lida are here, I would like you to tell us everything. It's important for all of us, and I'm sure it would be important for Sophia, too."

Everyone glanced at Polina attentively. The silence that filled the room was only interrupted by the cadent ticking of the second hand of the clock hanging in the kitchen. In a few moments, Polina finally braced herself and began the story of her old life, long ago, when she was still a girl.

"I don't even know where to begin. I'll just start with my own story. My mother died when I was ten years old. We lived in the distant rooms of Prince Vikhulev Igor Dmitrievich's enormous manor. He was my mother's distant relatives. After my mother's family went bankrupt, he let us live in his manor. My mother, who liked to be independent, worked as his housekeeper. It was only after her death that I found out Igor Dmitrievich was my father. He told me himself. To be honest, I treated him like a father my whole life. Ever since I was small, he spoiled me, played with me, and hired tutors."

"Wait, wait, wait. So Igor had a child before he and Lisa were married?" Olga interrupted. "Aleksey, did you know about this?"

Ukhtomsky shook his head.

"I wonder if poor Lisa knew…"

"I remember when Igor Dmitrievich—I never called him my father—brought Princess Lisa home for the first time. I ran outside to greet everyone. The prince introduced me as his foster child rather than his daughter. I think Elisabeth Nikolaevna knew nothing about it. Moreover, my mother always taught me to be humble and modest around the manor." Polina stopped to catch her breath and moisten her throat. Her nervousness was obvious.

"Elisabeth Nikolaevna was always cordial with me. When she was pregnant, she always said that if she would have a girl, she would like us to be friends. And as fate had it, I became close with her daughter." Polina's voice was filled with sorrow and tears filled her eyes. In a few seconds, she continued.

"Elisabeth Nikolaevna was an extremely demanding but just lady of the house. Almost everyone in the manor loved her. But there were a few who hated her, despised her. Once, she caught one of the workers stealing silverware. It was later discovered that the superintendent, Stepan, forced the workers to steal valuable items and pass them on to him. He had an accomplice in town to which he passed all the stolen items. And Uglovaty profited from that. Soon after, he wanted to flee from the manor. Princess Elisabeth's baby was due soon and this whole story upset her. She reported Stepan Uglovaty to the police. When he was being arrested and taken away, he swore to have his vengeance on her, no matter what. That same day, the princess had hemorrhages and fell unconscious. Sophia was born that night and… Elisabeth Nikolaevna passed away." Tears streamed down Polina's eyes.

She forced her last words through her sobs. Olga's and Lida's eyes were tear-filled, too. Aleksey jumped out of his chair and paced the room, mumbling, "Uglovaty, I'll make you pay for everything. You just wait. Your time will come, and I will kill you!"

"In the beginning of 1918," Polina continued, "Uglovaty returned to the manor where we all still lived. Unlike the neighboring manors, ours wasn't bankrupt, and most of our workers remained with us. Igor Dmitrievich respected them and they respected him, too. And then Uglovaty announced that the Bolsheviks let him out and he joined their party. They had sent him to confiscate our manor for the benefit of the working class. It was chaotic! Before, everyone hated him, and now they almost tore him apart. The prince defended him and he ran away. A few days later, Uglovaty came back with a group of soldiers with red bands on their sleeves and an order to arrest the owner of the house and kick everyone out of the manor. Our house was going to be passed to some council. I don't remember which one. Igor Dmitrievich ordered Sophia and me to hide in one of the remote rooms while he met the soldiers. Oh, why did he go?" Polina's voice sounded grieving, and then trembled from anger and hatred.

"Uglovaty approached prince Vikhulev and hit his face with all his might. Igor Dmitrievich lost his balance, fell down the stairs and hit his head on a stone. We heard Uglovaty scream. He was angry and he cursed Igor Dmitrievich for being able to escape punishment so easily. Out of the window, Sophia and I saw how they picked the prince up and carried him to the carriage. We never found out where he was taken, and we never heard anything about him ever since. Poor Sophia huddled in my arms. I hugged her and repeatedly whispered that she should be quiet. At first, she cried, and then she tore away from my embrace and ran towards the door. At the same moment, Uglovaty entered the house and Sophia ran right into him."

Polina's eyes watered. She looked at her family with stress and torment.

"I can't remember what happened next. How come there are such people on this planet?"

Aleksey hugged Polina. "Honey, I'm so sorry for making you remember I know it hurts, but you have to continue. You need this, too. I know how long you've been keeping this horrible secret. I always felt your hidden pain from your past. Please, my darling, tell us what happened next."

"When Uglovaty literally had his arms around Sophia, he squeezed her and took her outside with a predator's smile. She screamed and struggled to get away from him. She was only six years old. I tried to pull her out from that rascal's grasp, but I got a powerful kick in my stomach with his boot and fell unconscious."

Polina clenched her fists. She tensed and burst into sobbing. She continued her story in a sorrowful, tormented voice.

"I came back to my senses because I was very cold. When I opened my eyes, I felt someone's hand pressing over my mouth. It was Pakhomich, one of our workers. He ordered me to be quiet. I was terrified, but Pakhomich whispered that I shouldn't fear. When Uglovaty and the soldiers left, we exited the basement, where Pakhomich had hidden me. Sophia was nowhere to be found. I cried, calling for her. But Pakhomich, a kindly soul, told me what had happened after I fell unconscious."

She closed her eyes. Her hands trembled and she shivered, experiencing the pain of the events from her distant past.

"Uglovaty took Sophia, screaming and frightened, to a shed near the house where the workers kept various instruments and implements. When Uglovaty came with the soldiers, the workers hid. They knew how cruel Stepan was, and that he wouldn't be gentle or merciful to anyone in his way. He could easily order the soldiers to shoot anyone he saw as an obstacle. And trust me, they would listen to him."

Now, Polina's eyes burned with hatred. Her lips shivered indignantly, her face was crimson red. Her whole body was tense. Her audience gazed at her, worried. In a moment, Polina's face began to regain its natural color. The anger faded from her eyes and her body was more relaxed.

"I'm sorry, it's so tough to relive the horror from those days. If it wasn't for Pakhomich and his son, Uglovaty would have raped Sophia. His sixteen year old son broke into the shed through a small break. Uglovaty didn't see him; he was too busy getting ready for the shameful act. As he was taking off his trousers, the boy hit the back of Stepan's head with a shovel. Uglovaty collapsed to the floor, unconscious, with his loose trousers. Poor Sophia screamed and shrank into the corner. Pakhomich's son—I forgot his name—covered her mouth and took her from the shed. He picked her up and ran into the forest, holding her in her arms.

"When Uglovaty came to his senses, he was furious and outraged. He ordered the soldiers to search the house and the surroundings and bring back the "dirty-girl", as he called Sophia. But the soldiers refused to follow these orders, stating that they already did what they were initially ordered to do. Stepan was ferocious and banged on the windows. The senior soldier ordered to have him tied to calm him. Three soldiers stayed behind to guard the "Communist property", which used to be our manor. The workers were asked to leave. When the soldiers and Uglovaty left, Pakhomich sought out his son and Sophia. I waited for them behind the house so the soldiers wouldn't see me. In a few hours, I saw three people come out of the forest and ran towards them. It was Pakhomich, his son and Sophia. She trembled with fear and shock after what had happened. Her face was cut, and her arms and legs were covered with bruises from Uglovaty's strong hands."

Polina stopped and covered her eyes with the palms of her hands. She cried silently. Aleksey, Olga and Lida were in a nervous stupor.

"My God, poor Sophia. I can't even begin to imagine what she's been through!" Olga uttered.

Silence fell in the room.

Aleksey hugged his wife and said gently, "Polina, sweetie, it was all in the past. Now you're here, with us. You saved Sophia… But you two have a different surname. He was prince Vikhulev and you are Khulevs."

Polina calmed down. A timid smile adorned her face.

"When we fled the manor, I decided to change our surnames. Knowing Uglovaty, he would do anything to find us. Trust me. He often threatened to have his vengeance on the princess. That's why I decided to shorten our surname from Vikhulev to Khulev."

Amazed, Aleksey asked, ""And how did you manage to do that? I have one more question. Polina, I'm sorry, I know that bringing up these terrible memories is painful for you, but I'd also like to know where you and Sophia lived before you met me in the train."

Polina stood up, walked to the stove, lit it up and left the kettle to boil.

"Why don't we all have a cup of tea? My mouth is dry. Then I'll try to continue our story."

After the tea was finished and the doughnuts were eaten in utter silence, Polina was true to her word and continued.

"It was the end of April. The sun was gaining its lively, warming strength. Sophia and I were practically naked. We ended up on the streets in the same clothes that we wore at home: Light dresses and slippers. Pakhomich sent his son to fetch warm clothes for us from the manor while he stayed with us. In about an hour and a half, his son came back, but he had no clothes with him. All he had was the small chest that you, Lida, found in Sophia's bookcase. He barely got away from the soldiers who saw him break into the house. He grabbed the first thing he saw and took to his heels. He couldn't explain why he grabbed the chest per se. He said that he acted upon instinct. Pakhomich showed us how to get to the nearest city, and then disappeared with his son into the forest."

Polina was talking quieter and more measured. She stared blindly into emptiness. Her vision was blurred as she immersed herself deep into her memories.

"We walked for a long time across the green fields and birch groves, where we encountered a fox. It stared at us with hungry, unpleasant eyes. Terrified, Sophia pressed herself to me and cried. Her crying quickly grew into sobbing. It seemed that her emotions and horror were finally coming out. Gradually, she calmed down and collapsed on the wet ground, exhausted. I found a more-or-less dry spot under a huge birch tree, picked Sophia up, and sat under it while she slept in my arms. The sun rolled down towards the horizon. Soon the grove was in twilight. I could hardly tell the trees apart.

Sophia was still asleep, and I was afraid to wake her. Slowly, I fell asleep myself. I woke up when an elderly nun shook me, trying to rouse me. Figures out, if we had walked a bit more, we would have reached a monastery in Zvenigorod. The nun took us there, where we were given refuge. We lived there for just over a year, until it was closed down. All the residents of the monastery had to register with the Council of Zvenigorod. And that was when I changed mine and Sophia's surname to Khulev."

"What happened next?" Lida asked anxiously. "I would have never imagined that you and Sophia went through all this! Where did you live after the monastery?"

Polina gazed at everyone in the room. They were looking back at her with interest. She sighed and continued her story.

"In Zvenigorod, I was lucky enough to get a job as a proofreader in the local printing house. There was a lack of educated people. The director of the printing house was a very nice old man who worked there ever since Adam was a boy. He was amusing. He got on with everyone. Sophia and I were roaming the city, searching for a refuge. I found a newspaper by some building near a bridge. I picked it up and started reading it, just in case I could find an appropriate notice. Then, an old man ran out from the building and asked if I could read and write. Shocked, I nodded. He grabbed my arm and exclaimed, "Thank God! Then you'll be a proofreader in my printing house. I'll even show you how to type. The Bolsheviks have flooded us with work. There are leaflets and propaganda and all that. You and your sister can live with me. I have a big house and I'll find you a room."

"That's how I got a job and a place to live. I worked as a proofreader there until 1925. Sophia went to school there. Then the old man died, and his son inherited the house and kicked us out. One of the peasants became the head of the printing house and I, as a member of the enemy class, the bourgeoisie, was fired. So I decided to move to Moscow. Fortunately, I managed to save up some money. By the time I met you, Aleksey, Sophia and I had no money and no place to stay. I'm ashamed to say that Sophia begged for money at the October Station in Moscow. I will never forgive myself for this. Moscow wasn't our home."

Polina paused for a moment, thinking of what to say next. She decided to end her story. Her voice became more cheerful.

"In the end, I decided to move to Leningrad. I had a premonition that something good awaited us here. When Sophia and I met you, Aleksey, our lives changed for the best. We figuratively sat in the right train and got off at the right stop. I will be thanking destiny, God, foresight, or whatever you like, for the fact that Aleksey was sitting with us in that train."

Polina's face gleamed, her cheeks became pink and her eyes glistened. She shrugged her shoulders and took a deep breath, as if she was free from the weight of several years.

"Let's have some tea with pie. I know an amazing recipe, and it takes only half an hour to make the pie. I'll go make it now."

Chapter 21

The Tommy cousins had been in St. Petersburg for almost a week. They spent every day studying the new information Nadya and Alena found in the archives. One night, Nadya came back with an overfilled laptop bag. Her face expressed the kind of fire typical of creative people who are about to make a discovery.

"Darya, Jane, are you home?" The girl called everyone from the hall. "I found something, well, not something; I found a very important piece of the puzzle that was missing all this time!" Nadya's voice sounded impulsively intriguing.

The cousins rushed into the hall together, where Nadya was almost done taking off her coat. Their eyes were sparkling with excitement and surprise.

"Hurry up, Nadya, come on, let's go into the living room—no, the kitchen. Darya made tea with éclairs. We'll have a snack, first. We haven't had dinner yet because we've been waiting for you. And you'll tell us what you found while we're having tea, alright?" Jane uttered quickly.

"Sounds good. I'm starving as well." Nadya replied right away.

"I was at Mom's. You know my mom and Anastasia Huleva were friends, right? So my mom told me a lot and showed me a bunch of pictures and papers concerning their childhood and youth. It paints a very interesting picture." Nadya was eating and talking at the same time, as if she was afraid she didn't have enough time to tell everything.

"Stop talking so fast. You should swallow your food first because we can't understand everything you're saying," Jane remarked.

"Sorry, girls." Nadya smiled. "I'm starving and eager to tell you everything. These éclairs are really good. Where did you learn to make them, Darya? I thought they were a Russian dessert. Russian women love to make them for special occasions, and bakeries always have them, as well. I've loved them since I was a child."

Darya looked at Nadya in surprise and stated, laughing, "Well, first of all, éclairs were originally created by the French in the beginning of the nineteenth century. And when the "Boston Cooking School Cook Book" came out, which had the recipe for them, éclairs have conquered the entire world. That was second. Third, in the States, we call them Long Johns for their shape. Anyway, I'm happy you liked my éclairs. I love them." Darya finished her speech. "Nadya, can I ask you a question?"

"Go ahead. What do you want to know?"

"Why didn't you ask your mother earlier? You could have already done that a month ago when Vladimir was just beginning his investigation."

Nadya looked at her calmly and spoke quietly, but distinctively. "My mom is a very interesting person. She's protective of everything that has to do with the past. There are people that consider conversations about events of their past to be off-limits to everyone, especially if they weren't very fortunate. They try not to bring it up again, not to recall it; they're afraid it might be too hard for them. My mom is one of those people. I've come to her asking to tell me about Anastasia many times, to show me photos, documents she still has. But she would have her guard up every time."

"Alright, but how were you able to retrieve these documents and information, after all?" Darya asked, surprised.

"It's a long story, girls. But I think you'll be curious to learn a bit about my mom, as she was so involved in Anastasia's life."

"Come on, tell us now!" The Tommy cousins exclaimed.

The three went into the living room and made themselves comfortable around an oval table where Nadya began to unload papers and documents from her huge bag. Darya and Jane curiously watched her. Finally, Nadya spoke.

"So, I will show you the pictures and papers as I tell you the story. Are you ready?"

The girls nodded silently.

"My mom was born in the spring of 1941. She never knew her parents; she was a foundling. A child caregiver who worked at an orphanage found her at the gate when she was going to work. There were no documents on the baby, so they gave her the last name Naydenova ("a foundling"), and named her after the caregiver, Varvara. My mom lived at that orphanage until she graduated high school. The caregiver who'd found her treated her like her own, and sacrificed her own share of food to feed her. It was during the war, and people starved. She protected her from bullies. One time, she came into work with a girl who was the same age as my mother. Well, Anastasia was about half a year older. Yes, she brought Anastasia. That was in 1944. Anastasia was three and a half, and my mom was three years old. The nanny called over my mom and told her she brought her a lifetime friend. Anastasia and my mom were like sisters to each other. In a way, they even looked alike. Look, here's an old photo of the girls. This is my mom, and this is Anastasia. They're about ten years old in this one. They're hugging, just like two sisters." Nadya was looking at the photo with love in her eyes.

"Could you show it to me more closely?" Darya asked quietly.

She saw two girls wearing the same dresses, their light blonde hair braided and tied with bows. Their big blue eyes expressed happiness, concern, and curiosity all at the same time. Darya felt something familiar, something dear to her, as she stared into the eyes of the taller girl.

"Look, Jane, don't you feel like we've seen this girl somewhere?"

Jane took the photo out of her cousin's hand and laughed. "Yes, very much so. This girl reminds me of you when you were ten. Only your hair looked different. You preferred a single braid. She looks so much like you. It's amazing." Jane's voice grew more and more surprised.

"Nadya, this is already a second picture in which Anastasia possesses a striking resemblance to Darya. Doesn't that make you wonder?" Jane carefully looked at the hostess.

Nadya remained silent for a bit, and then spoke in a quiet, trembling voice that emitted a sense of concern. "Anastasia had a child, a daughter. However, I don't know what happened to her. My mom didn't keep contact with Anastasia for the last ten years of her life. For a very interesting reason. It also explains why mom didn't want to tell me anything. I brought a bunch of photos and documents from my mom, as well as what she's told me herself about how she and Anastasia were friends. Are you ready to listen?"

Darya and Jane nodded their heads excitedly. Sitting on a comfy, wide and soft sofa before the table, Nadya continued her story.

"When the girls were around fifteen or sixteen, Varvara, the nanny, invited them into her home. She lived in the same apartment that had earlier belonged to Alexey and Polina Ukhtomsky. As she walked in, Nastya was literally stunned. Everything there seemed familiar. She circled around the apartment in some sort of fog. Varvara watched her, silently wiping the tears that were running down her cheeks in two continuous rivulets.

"It all seems familiar to you, doesn't it, sweetie?" The nanny asked in a soft voice.

"Yes, Aunt Varvara. I feel like I've been here before," Nastya replied in a trembling voice.

"You have. More than that, you used to live here, my dear. This apartment belonged to your parents, Alexey Nikolayevich and Polina Igorevna Ukhtomsky."

"My parents? Did you know them, Aunt Varvara?" And why do I have a different last name? Why is it Huleva and not Ukhtomsky?" Anastasia asked Varvara with panic and impatience.

The woman didn't reply right away. She sat the girls down at an old table in the kitchen, offered them sweets she had bought God knows when, and had been saving for special occasions, put an old pot on the stove, took out cups from the cabinet, about as old as the pot, pulled out a small can of tea of unknown origin, threw a few pinches of the strange tea into the teapot, and poured boiling water inside.

She was doing everything in complete silence. The girls watched her, almost hypnotized by her smoothly moving hands. Only Nastya still had panic and concern in her eyes.

"Aunt Varvara, please, don't make me wait any longer. Tell me about my parents, who they were, and why you live in their apartment," Nastya spoke impatiently.

The caregiver got up, slowly walked into one of the bedrooms, and came back with a small box.

"Nastya, this box belonged to your mother. Her name was Sofia. She was Polina's sister, and, as it turned out, Alexey Nikolayevich's niece. Sofia died giving birth to you. Alexey and Polina adopted you. You had amazing parents. Beautiful on the outside as well as in. Open up the box, look inside. Polina asked me to keep it for you. We will talk after you do. We'll have a lot to talk about."

The girl gently accepted the box and went out to another room so she wasn't disturbed.

"Aunt Varvara, do you know anything about *me*?" Varvara asked worriedly with hope in her eyes.

The woman looked at her with sadness.

"No, my dear. I found you by the orphanage gate. You were only a few weeks old. I don't know how you didn't freeze to death. It was late fall. All I remember is that you were wrapped in a brown military blanket. It had a tag... Hold on. I saved it. Back then, I thought it might be useful in case the girl wanted to try and find her relatives. Where is it? What an old hag, completely forgot where I put it. Don't worry, it's alright. I'll find it. I sure will, honey."

The girl's eyes, having lit up with a spark of hope, turned sad and tearful.

"Shall we look together, Aunt Varvara?" She asked modestly.

The nanny looked at her with sorrow, and firmly said, "I will find it. Don't worry about it, my dear Varvara."

Anastasia entered a room that once served as both bedroom and living room to the Ukhtomskys. Visions flashed in front of her eyes, so distant and so familiar. They appeared before her like scenes on a movie screen. A little girl running into the room. She's still wearing her pajamas. The sun is barely coming up from the darkness of the passing night. The girl runs up to the bed and pulls her mother's hand resting on the blanket.

"Mommy, Mommy, I'm scared! I had a nightmare about a scary alligator. It wanted to swallow me!"

Her mother opens her eyes. Laughing, she lifts the girl up and gently lays her down in bed between her and her husband. They both hug their daughter, drifting away into early morning sleep.

Following that, there was another memory that worried Anastasia. A man in military uniform enters the room. The girl and her mother are sitting at the table, painting. They're laughing, poking each other's noses, cheeks, and hands with paint brushes. They are finishing up on their masterpieces when her father enters the room. He tries to smile to both of his girls, but his smile is forced. The woman immediately catches that. The girl runs up to her father, hugs his leg and asks, "Daddy, why are you dressed so angrily?"

The man laughs, picks up his daughter, kissing her.

"Why is it, Nastya, that you think I'm dressed angrily? You don't like my suit?"

"No I don't, it's all scary, dark. It's bad."

He and his wife's eyes meet, hers expressing fear and concern.

"Come on, sweetheart, it's just the uniform of a soldier, a man who defends his homeland. Your father is a defender. It is a very honorable title to carry as a man."

He lifted her up and kissed her.

Nastya rubbed her eyes that grew wet from tears. As she wiped the tears away, she saw a room filled with old furniture, and unwashed tulle on a big, dirty window. It was late fall. A small leaf, separated from its cradle, got caught up on its way to eternity in-between two window panes. It was getting dark, and the sky hidden behind storm clouds wouldn't let the beams of a setting sun shine through.

It's so sad and gloomy outside. It's the same mood that I'm in, Nastya thought.

She sat down on a worn out sofa and slowly opened the box. There was a stack of letters inside carefully tied together. Nastya took it out, and was about to break the thin pink ribbon that held the letters together, but she changed her mind. Thoughtful, the girl put the letters aside and, once again, looked at the box. There were photos, just a few of them. She gently took them out and began to study them. In the first picture, there was a young woman, a man who looked much older than her, and a little girl who looked like she was about three, who was sitting on the man's lap. The girl had her arm around her father's neck and was holding her mother's hand. The man was wearing a military uniform. The woman was wearing a well-fitted blue suit that looked like it was made before the war. The eyes of both didn't hold a hint of happiness. They expressed sadness and hopelessness. Only the girl stood out in the picture, like a bright spot. She was radiating happiness. Nastya flipped over the photo and saw a date written in chemical pencil faded over time, which read "October, 1943". She set the picture aside and began to study the others.

The next one was of a woman about twenty-five years old. She was looking at Nastya with her wide eyes that expressed curiosity and surprise. A beautiful, prominent forehead and light blonde hair slicked back into a ponytail. Her sensual mouth was almost slightly open in a smile. Her face exuded so much warmth that Nastya instinctively clutched it to her chest. Then, she quickly flipped it over, hoping to find a written description. But the back side was empty. Nastya set the picture aside, just like the previous one. The girl shifted her eyes to another photo. It amazed her. It was a very old picture. It had three men and two women in it dressed in pre-revolutionary clothing. The women were sitting on chairs, and the men stood behind them. Nastya stared into the faces of five strangers for a while.

"Such beautiful faces. So dignified and independent." She admiringly glanced at the picture once again, and put it back in the box.

Nastya saw an amazing emerald necklace at the bottom of the box. She took it out in awe; carefully studied it, tried it on, went up to a mirror, admired it for some time, and quickly put in back in the box. She then grabbed the photos she set aside, as well as the stack of letters, stood around for a while, and decidedly walked out into the kitchen.

The nanny and Varvara Naydenova were sitting at the table, talking quietly. As Nastya walked in, the woman raised her kind eyes that couldn't see that well anymore to the girl, and softly asked, "You have a lot of questions, don't you? I can tell by the look on your face."

Nastya sat down on a chair. Her head was buzzing from all the emotions she had just experienced.

"Yes, Aunt Varvara. I do have a lot of questions. May I take these letters and pictures with me? You can keep the box with the rest for now. I'll take it from you later. You know there's no safe place to keep it at the orphanage."

"Of course, my dear. You should read those letters. And then you can come by and we'll talk. I'll tell you everything I know, alright? For now, though, you have to go, or they will start to get worried and won't let you leave anymore. Here, take some bubliks in case you get hungry later."

The girls hugged their favorite nanny, kissed her and said goodbye. When they were already halfway back to the orphanage, Nastya, who was silent the whole time, suddenly exclaimed, I'm so stupid! I forgot to ask nanny about the pictures!" But after a little while, she said, "It's alright, I'll ask her next time." Then, she pulled her friend's sleeve and yelled, "Varvara, let's go or we'll be late for dinner and stay hungry all night. Those bubliks alone won't make us full."

The girls grabbed each other's hand and ran towards the orphanage building seen far in the distance.

About three weeks later, the girls were invited to visit their nanny for her sixtieth birthday. They were the only guests, which surprised them.

"Both my husband and my son died in the war. They weren't drafted together; my husband left in 1941, and my son was drafted two years later, in February, 1943. Yet they died in the same year, same month, and on the same day. Both reached Berlin. They had already declared victory by then. It was on May 10, 1945. They were walking down the same street. They were so happy to see each other they rushed into each other's arms. That's when a German bullet got them. There was a sniper still alive on the roof of one of the buildings, and he killed both with one shot. Their commanders wrote to me, informing me about it. That's what happened, my sweethearts."

The nanny's eyes became wet, and she wiped them with the hem of her apron. Then, she hugged the girls and said gently but firmly, "The only people I want to see at my birthday are those I love. My husband and son are always with me. And I love you both just like my own daughters. I don't need anyone else. Gather around the table. We'll celebrate."

The table was served with simple dishes. Boiled potatoes with fried onions, two small herrings, pickles and cucumbers, sour cabbage, boiled bologna sliced into thin, see-through circles, and a few slices of gray bread spread out on a small plate. There was compote made from dried apples and pears in the pitcher. To the girls, that looked like a royal feast. Having grown up in an orphanage, they had never really tried bologna. They'd had herring before, but very rarely. Tomatoes and cucumbers were also rare guests on their table. The nanny watched her two girls eagerly swallow bologna sandwiches and wash it down with compote, happy that God had sent them to her as a kind of gratitude for her husband and son. She would do anything for them.

"Girls, we have a lot of time tomorrow, you know. I convinced the supervisor and the head of the orphanage to let me keep you here until tomorrow night. Tomorrow is Sunday; you have no school. We'll talk then. I will answer your questions, Nastya, and tell you what I know."

She impulsively ruffled the girl's hair the way she used to do to her son.

"Thank you, Aunt Varvara," Both girls replied with their mouths full.

Nastya swallowed her food and asked, "Will you tell me all of it?"

"All I know, honey," The nanny returned, smiling.

"Aunt Varvara, tell me, who is this?" Nastya asked her first question, pointing at the photo of the young woman. The nanny took the photo in her hands, retrieved her glasses from an end table, and looked at the photo carefully.

"This is your mother, your birth mother, Sofia, who died during labor. She was beautiful. Dignified. You're just like her, Anastasia."

Nastya took the photo out of Nanny's hands and looked at it carefully again. This time, the look on the young woman's face seemed different. Instead of curiosity, Nastya saw warmth and tenderness in her eyes. The girl quietly drew the photo to her lips and kissed it.

"And is this a photo of me with my adoptive parents?" Nastya asked another question.

"Yes, this is Polina and Alexey Ukhtomsky, and you, still tiny. You are three years old in this one. It was taken after your father was drafted. See, he's wearing a military uniform."

The nanny lovingly gazed at the photo. She stroked the faces of Alexey and Polina.

This means my visions were a reality. The little girl was me, and the man and the woman were my parents, Nastya thought, and several tears slowly ran down her cheeks. She subconsciously wiped them away and turned to the nanny decidedly.

"Aunt Varvara, please tell me everything you know."

"Well, my sweet Nastya, I promised to tell you, so I will. You must know the truth about your parents, the truth that I know. Did you at least read the letters? There's a lot of information in them."

"Yes, I did," Nastya replied quietly. "I learned about some of the things that happened before I was born. But what happened after? Where did my parents go? What happened to them? This is what I want to know. What if they're alive? I will find them!" The girl's voice grew firmer and more insistent with every word.

Having gathered her thoughts, the nanny began her story in a calm voice.

"We were living in this very building, in the basement. My husband was a locksmith and I, as you know, worked as a caregiver at the orphanage. Your parents were very happy together, Nastya. When you came into this world, they really were, as they say, in seventh heaven. They didn't have children of their own. You were given your adoptive father's last name, Ukhtomsky. In October, 1943, Alexey Nikolayevich was drafted.

"Why wasn't he drafted right after the war broke out?" Varvara Naydenova interrupted Nanny.

The woman looked at her reproachfully and continued.

"Alexey Nikolayevich was reserved as a scientist, a geologist who was working on developing oil fields. As soon as the war broke out, he began to regularly leave applications for draft, but got denied each time. And finally, in October, 1943, his application got accepted. I remember the day he left for the front. The entire apartment block was seeing him off. Alexey Nikolayevich was a very friendly and kind person. He liked to drop in on us and chat with my husband, Vasily. He accepted dinner invitations, and helped out all the neighbors when they were in need. And Polina was the same way.

One night, Polina came to me, said she wanted to talk. She looked very strange. Her hair was a mess, her eyes were fearful, and her voice was trembling. I sat her down in the kitchen, offered her some carrot tea and asked what happened.

She replied, "Varvara, I feel like something bad is about to happen. Alexey has not been sending any letters. And Uglovaty won't leave me alone. He keeps threatening to take my daughter away. If something happens, I beg you, look after Nastya. Here's a box I'd like you to give to her when she grows up. And find out how to change her last name to mine: Huleva. Uglovaty came by again yesterday. He was drunk. He mentioned something about my time running out.

"Then, she started crying really hard. I never saw her in a bad mood, let alone crying. I thought something bad was really about to happen. She also asked me to move in with her, until either Alexey came back or she was reassured in her well-being again. Well, I had nothing else to do. I loved and respected that family so much. I moved in to this apartment the next day. And three days later, they came after Polina. I never saw her again."

"Yeaaah," Varvara Naydenova chimed in.

Anastasia was quiet. Only small tears ran down her face.

"Okay, Aunt Varvara, but why did you put Nastya in an orphanage? Wouldn't she be better off living here with you, instead?" Varvara asked.

The nanny looked at her girl reproachfully once again and shook her head.

"Just think about it, sweetheart. What do you think would happen if Uglovaty showed up at the door again? Polina said he was trying to take Nastya away any way he could. I still don't know why. And Polina didn't tell me. Long story short, the day she was taken, I put you, Nastya, in the orphanage. And on our way there, I kept telling you to always tell everyone that your last name was Huleva, and that both your mom and dad were drafted, and you were left alone. You do not know or remember anybody. Thank God, the head of the orphanage didn't try to dig deeper, and took you in right away."

"Who's Uglovaty?" Nastya asked cautiously.

"God knows. All I know is, your mother, Polina, was very frightened by him. He was working for the authorities. I saw him once when my neighbor was being taken away. He came himself. Arrogant with a beer belly and very unpleasant. He didn't have a family or a woman. Probably why he was so crazy. He hated Alexey Nikolayevich and Polina Igorevna. Still can't understand why."

The nanny looked at her favorite girls and quietly exclaimed, "You guys are falling asleep! You should go lie down. I set up a bed in the small room. Are you going to brush your teeth before bed, or what?"

"Or what, Aunt Varvara," Varvara said, yawning sleepily.

"I think I'll go brush my teeth and wash my face, still. I don't like going to bed grungy," Nastya said, doing so more for herself rather than to please anyone.

Thirty minutes later, everyone in the apartment fell asleep.

Chapter 22

"Thank you for all the valuable information, Nadya. Your mom did a good job. She has a good memory. She remembered everything!" Jane said, amazed.

Darya was quiet. She was staring somewhere into far distance. It looked like she was miles away. Nadya and Jane tried to make silly faces in front of her, flick their fingers and turn the lights on and off. Darya still acted like she wasn't there. Then, concerned about her cousin, Jane grabbed her shoulders and began to shake Darya. Finally, the girl spoke.

"Stop shaking me. You're both acting like idiots, yelling and messing around."

"Are you seeing this?" Jane said to Nadya. "Tell me, cousin, what's going on with you? Why weren't you responding at all?"

Darya gave both girls a slightly confused look. Then, she quickly shook her head, as if she was trying to break free from some kind of weight, and her eyes turned clear and looked inquiring. Jane couldn't let it go: "Darya, tell me, after all, where did you go in your head? You weren't here, were you?"

"Can you believe this, girls, I suddenly felt like I was Nastya. I was there in the distant past. I felt scared and confused. Nadya, your mom didn't keep in contact with Nastya during the last ten years of her life. Can anyone tell us what happened during that time? And also, Nadya, did your mom tell why the two people who were friends since early childhood and remained friends throughout their youth and adulthood suddenly broke all ties as they grew old?"

Nadya stayed silent for a bit, gathering her thoughts, and then slowly said, weighing every word, "Yes, I know why. And I have the papers concerning that. This is a very peculiar and one of a kind sort of reason, and a natural one at the same time. I don't know where to start. It's very delicate, you know?"

The girls looked at Nadya, unable to grasp what she meant. Silence set, during which one of the two girls gathered her thoughts and spirits, and the other two kept waiting for her to talk.

"Here are the documents according to which Alexey Ukhtomsky fought at the Baltic front. He served among reconnaissance troops as he knew German very well. And here's the document stating that Stepan Uglovaty served there, too. And he was a commissar, or, to be more precise, a political officer of the regiment that included Ukhtomsky's troops. Long story short, here's what happened in 1944. After studying the documents, Alena and I were able to figure out the overall story of what has happened.

Alexey Ukhtomsky met the new year's eve of 1944 in the entrenchments of the First Baltic Front. For almost a week, he and his group of scouts were trying to gather information about the German troops in Gorodok. Gorodok was a small town in Vitebsk region, which was a very well reinforced foothold of the Germans. Uktomsky's troops were ordered to gather information about the defenses of the town. Not only did the scouts retrieve the information, they also managed to take a PoW, a German officer who left the encampment to relieve himself. He turned out to be a very valuable asset. Alexey delivered him to the headquarters of the regiment, together with the documents he acquired. As Ukhtomsky was reporting to the commander of the regiment about the completion of his task, a man wearing a political officer's uniform entered the room.

"Alexey Nikolaevich, meet our new political officer, Stepan Mitrofanovich Uglovaty. As you know, Petr Vladimirovich died three days ago," The commander of the troops interrupted his report.

Uktomsky turned around, and his eyes met the cold eyes of Uglovaty. They stood in silence for five minutes or so, staring into each other's eyes, which expressed implacable hatred. The Commander broke the silence, confused.

"You know each other?"

"Met at some point before the war," casually replied Uglovaty.

Alexey didn't say a word, only turned to the Commander as a technicality. "Comrade Colonel, allow me to be dismissed."

"Hold on, Capitan. You haven't finished your report," The Commander said confusedly.

"I have already reported the basics. Here are the documents concerning the defenses. The "tongue", the captive officer, is waiting outside the door. He's being guarded by two of my scouts. Allow me to be dismissed, Comrade Colonel." Ukhtomsky looked at his commander firmly.

"Well, Alexey Nikolayevich, thank you for your service. A job well done. Our political officer and I will now take care of this information, and the "tongue". Go have some rest." The Commander came up to Ukhtomsky and appreciatively patted his shoulder.

The freezing cold freshened Alexey up as he left the commander's dugout. But his temples were throbbing, and he felt sharp pain in the back of his head. Ukhtomsky squeezed his head with his hands.

"What's wrong, Commander? Are you ill?" a concerned voice of one of his troops inquired.

He turned his head towards the voice and saw Ivaschenko, the most experienced scout among his troops. Ivaschenko was looking at his commander carefully.

"Comrade Captain, would you like me to escort you to the medical unit? You look very pale, and you're not walking straight. What if you're sick?" Ivaschenko insisted.

"Don't worry, Ivaschenko, everything's fine. Report to the troops that they can rest. We have to get some sleep. Haven't slept in almost three days." Ukhtomsky's voice was quiet and weak.

"Yes, Comrade Captain," Ivaschenko replied energetically and headed off to complete his task.

Alexey was sitting on a tree stump, seemingly resting, with his eyes closed, his arms resting on his lap, and his head slightly tilted forward. In actuality, he was feverishly pondering the situation.

"This is it, my time has come. Uglovaty is here. The war is going on. Bullets are flying. Any one of them can easily get through and hit this bastard in the heart."

Those thoughts made Alexey sweat. He unbuttoned the collar of his tunic, took off his hat and began to gasp for cold air as if he was suffocating. Then, he got up, walked for about twenty meters through the crispy snow, stopped, turned around, and walked back. He still had dull pain in the back of his head, and his temples were still throbbing.

"No, I'm not a murderer. Uglovaty must be aware of what he's getting punished for. I will be the judge and the executor in one. But when... When... I have to think it through... I have to decide." Ukhtomsky decidedly headed towards the commander's dugout, stopped in front of the door for a moment, and then opened it.

"Allow me to come in, Comrade Commander," Alexey spoke to the commander of the regiment.

"You're already here. What is it about, Alexey Nikolaevich? Did you fail to report something?"

Uglovaty was sitting at the table sullenly watching Ukhtomsky. He was experienced enough to tell that Uktomsky was pale and had bumps moving around his jaw, which gave out his tension and restlessness. Stepan immediately realized Ukhtomsky was plotting.

"I'm listening, Captain," The commander of the regiment assured, looking at Alexey carefully.

"Comrade Commander, allow me to show the positions of the regiment to comrade junior political officer. He's new here. He must be interested," Ukhtomsky uttered the first thing that came to mind.

I'll figure where to go from there, Alexey thought to himself.

Uglovaty, being a coward by nature, felt frightened. His plans didn't include being alone, one-on-one with Ukhtomsky. As soon as Alexey was done with his report and left, Stepan decided he would get rid of the prince as soon as he got the chance. But it had to look like an accident. A war is a war. An enemy bullet also crossed his mind. The colonel looked at Uglovaty questioningly, and the political officer responded immediately.

"Thank you, Captain, but I've already had the opportunity to take a look. You can go ahead and rest," Stepan replied with a hint of mockery in his voice.

Uktomsky's eyes sparked with rage as he glanced at Uglovaty, and he dismissed himself with the permission of the colonel.

The next day, Ukhtomsky was informed he was being summoned to the commander of the regiment.

"Captain Colonel, allow me to come in," Alexey asked as he opened the door into the Dugout.

"Come in, Alexey Nikolayevich. Would you like some tea?" The commander asked in a very informal manner. "Sit down, be my guest. I'd like to talk to you. Inform you of certain details. Do you mind?" he asked Ukhtomsky.

Alexey felt surprised. He had only known the commander of the regiment for a couple of months. When they were first introduced, Valery Georgiyevich, as was the commander's name, came off as overly cold and harsh. He demanded everyone carry out his orders precisely, didn't like it when anyone mumbled while talking to him, treated everyone equally despite their titles or achievements, and didn't approve of cronyism.

"Thank you, Comrade Commander, but I've already had my breakfast and tea," The Captain replied, slightly shy.

"Loosen up, Alexey Nikolayevich. I invited you to talk, not as a commander and his subordinate. Sit down. Here's a cup. Pour yourself some tea. Warm up. It will help you make a conversation." Ukhtomsky felt even more surprised, but he accepted the invitation. Valery Georgiyevich was attentively watching the captain, who carefully poured boiling water in a cup and then grabbed a few pinches of strong tea from a small metal kettle. When Alexey took his first sip, the colonel smiled.

He liked the captain. He felt he could count on him, that he was loyal. His face looked open and honest. His look was straight, firm, and confident. The new political officer was different. His eyes were always moving, his stare sullen, villainous, constantly angry with something. The first time he met the commander of the regiment, Uglovaty sneered and sarcastically asked, "Are you one of the former,

Colonel? I've checked your background. And I will be watching you. I don't buy that types like you have a sincere devotion to the Soviet government."

Valery Georgiyevich carefully looked into the eyes of the junior political officer, and replied with dignity, "It's your right, junior political officer, whether to trust people or not. As for me, I protect my homeland, not people like you."

"Right," Uglovaty mumbled.

"What do you think of our new junior political officer, Captain?" The commander asked straightforwardly. He didn't like to beat around the bush. Coming from an officer family, Valery Georgiyevich favored fast decision making. Alexey didn't expect that question, and looked at the commander in surprise.

"According to the statute, I am not to discuss the credentials of the political officer, Comrade Colonel."

The colonel carefully looked at the captain.

Did I really read it wrong? he thought.

"Sit down... We're the same, you and I. I am a former prince, and so are you. I was a young junker when the revolution came. Back then, I thought it would bring new opportunities. I was ready to serve my country, and the Bolsheviks couldn't stop me. The wellbeing of Russia and its people is what I value above all. I couldn't care less about men like Uglovaty. Trust me, I've seen enough of them during the five years in the camps. Perhaps their proletarian and peasant background will provide them with an easy path in life. All because of their stupidity and laziness. There are many of them. But they're not the majority. I could immediately see right through Uglovaty. He has a shallow and dishonest heart. He'll take any opportunity to get what he wants for free, and take advantage of someone. Stay away from him, Alexey Nikolayevich. I noticed your silent argument, the way you looked at each other. What is it that happened between you two?"

Alexey was listening to the commander with his head down. He wasn't sure how to act. On one hand, he trusted the colonel, and was tempted to tell him about his desire to get rid of Uglovaty. On the other hand, Ukhtomsky knew it was his problem, and nobody else's.

That's why it was up to him to solve it, and he didn't think he should include anyone else in it.

"Well, Alexey Nikolayevich, I'm waiting," The captain reminded him. "Don't be afraid. I've been watching you for quite a while. But it was only when I saw you next to Uglovaty that I realized why you were always so restless. You want revenge. I don't know why, but I'm sure you have a good reason. But I must warn you, Captain, the one who makes you angry is the one in control. With the way you feel now, Uglovaty has control over you. And you might just do something stupid. Killing him, which is exactly what you want, is the easiest thing to do."

Alexey was carefully listening to the Colonel, and made the decision to trust him completely. *After all, I need an ally. And there is no better candidate than the commander of the regiment.*

Captain poured boiled water into a cup, added some tea, and began to tell his story about Uglovaty, looking into the commander's extremely focused eyes.

"Indeed, a vile prick," Valery Georgiyevich uttered as soon as Alexey finished his story. "You know, captain, life is like chess. The one who's a few steps ahead wins. The commissar might be a prick, but he's not dumb. He will do anything to take advantage of this situation. Although, just like all pricks, Uglovaty is also a coward. I doubt he will choose a fair fight. He's probably thinking of "enemy" bullets, mines, and so on."

"Valery Georgiyevich, explain to me, why would you want to help me in this unkind, though justifiable act?" Ukhtomsky interrupted the Commander.

The Colonel looked at him carefully, moved the chair he was sitting on closer to Alexey, and quietly replied, "When I was in the camps, I knew a professor. He was a quiet, very intelligent and "dedicated to his work" scientist, who wasn't interested in anything but his studies of bugs and what not. He was a neighbor of someone like Uglovaty, a bastard of his kind, who apparently really wanted the professor's apartment. So he told on him. As a result, our country lost a good citizen, and the science community lost a brilliant man. He was executed as a public enemy."

The colonel stopped talking and closed his eyes. He had bumps moving around his jaw. Ukhtomsky was also silent. Alexey recalled the story of his brother, Leonid. A minute later, Valery Georgievich continued, "I don't believe men like Uglovaty have anything in common with the people of this country, or the Soviet government they swear by so much. They're nothing but worthless weight on the shoulders of this country. And we have to lift that weight. The sooner, the better. Otherwise it will collapse on all of us."

They heard a knock on the door, and it opened without permission with Uglovaty standing in the doorway. His first reaction was to leave, but then, his eyes sparked with hate and disgrace.

"Well, well, the princes are all gathered together. What are we plotting? Could it be against the Soviet power?"

Ukhtomsky turned pale from the hate and disgust he felt towards the political officer. He was ready to throw threats in his face, but the colonel spoke first.

"Ah, Comrade Political Officer, me and the captain were just discussing a possible operation into the enemy's hideout. We have to double check certain details." Valery Georgiyevich's enthusiastic voice slightly embarrassed Uglovaty, and he was forced to believe it.

"Alright then, go ahead and work on your operations. I'm going to go check up on the kitchen, see what's going on in there. I'll come by later," He said confusedly. Then he quietly added, more to himself rather than for their benefit, "I don't know anything about military business, anyway."

Having tricked Uglovaty, Valery Georgiyevich closed the door tight after making sure no one was anywhere around the dugout.

"Here's what, Captain. This conversation isn't over. And I beg you, Alexey Nikolayevich, do not try to do anything yet. You will end it for yourself and drag others down with you. We have to think this through, but we also can't take too long. Uglovaty is cunning, and he won't wait too long to take action, either." The colonel's voice sounded conspiratorially quiet. But to Ukhtomsky, each word seemed like a hammer blow to an anvil.

"As far as I know, Uglovaty didn't plan to end up at the front. He started quite a lot of activity concerning the exposure of so-called public enemies on the inside. No one could match him at that.

The colonel's voice grew louder with each word, with more and more obvious hints of hate and contempt. His face was burning up, and his hands clutched in fists. It took him some time to calm down.

"Forgive me, Captain. I haven't met anyone more villainous than our new political officer. I had an old friend working in the regiment headquarters. Just like me, he was arrested in 1939, and we were both sentenced to death. But the system was flawed, so they delayed it and instead sentenced us to camps. And then the war broke out. My friend Georgiy and I, being experienced military officers, were freed. I still don't know who to thank for my freedom. Anyway, Georgiy called me before Uglovaty's arrival and informed me of certain details about him."

At that moment, the door into the dugout opened and Uglovaty appeared in the doorway. He came in without permission, and offhandedly proceeded to the desk and sat on a chair.

"So, Colonel, did you go over your plans with Captain?" he asked Valery Georgiyevich with a smirk on his face.

The colonel turned pale from rage, and harshly replied, "If you, Junior Political Officer, don't know anything about military business, then get out. Don't disturb us while we're discussing this operation." He added more quietly, "Got a spy on my back. You damn useless weight."

Uglovaty didn't expect such a set down from the Colonel, and stood there completely lost. He was used to everyone catering to his will. Back in Leningrad, in his department, Stepan was the boss. He hated and couldn't understand these princes, these "lousy intelligentsia". Sometimes, he would intentionally beat up and insult the arrested "former", as he called Russian aristocrats and intelligentsia, in order to provoke them to utter an insult in the heat of rage. Many of them broke and begged for mercy. He despised them and didn't even consider them human, subjecting them to creative means of torture until their trial and sentence. Those that wouldn't break and give in intimidated Stepan, and he wanted to get rid of them as soon as possible. He couldn't break their spirit and will, and he couldn't understand that. He feared anything he couldn't understand. The colonel and Ukhtomsky were of the second kind. Standing around angry and indecisive for a few minutes, Uglovaty headed for the door, hissing, "You will pay for this. I... I will bury you."

As he closed the door behind him, Commander tiredly said, "Well, this feels better, doesn't it, Captain?"

Chapter 23

"What happened next?" Darya asked quietly. "Did Alexey Ukhtomsky get rid of Uglovaty?"

Nadya was sitting with her head down. Her vision was blurry. She was ruffling her hair, going from temples to forehead. Having relieved the tension she got from telling the story, the girl opened her eyes, raised her head up and said, "If you're curious to know, cousins, I'll continue the story. But first, let's have some tea or something. My throat is all dry. And maybe a snack."

Darya and Jane immediately warmed up a pot of tea and served the table with teacups, sugar, cream, and a bowl of candy and cookies.

"You might just hook us up on tea," Jane said, laughing. "In America, we just have coffee all day. Drinking tea never really became a part of our culture."

Nadya poured hot, freshly made tea in her cup, gladly noting, "Yet it's hard to find a drink out there as noble as good, strong tea. I'm having so much fun, as Americans say, when its life giving force flows through my veins, especially when it's freezing outside."

"And we believe Russians drink nothing but vodka when they want to warm up." Darya chimed in, laughing.

"Well, actually, yeah. Vodka is a noble beverage. Did you know, cousins, that vodka is really a nickname for "voda", which means "water" in Russian. And up until the nineteenth century, vodka meant an infusion of herbs and roots or berries in strong alcohol? So, I think vodka is a noble beverage that should be consumed with caution. Just for the record."

"So, shall we continue?" Nadya asked energetically as she quenched her thirst.

"Yes, tell us what happened next!" They replied impatiently.

Two days later, five people arrived from the headquarters: One colonel, a major general, a captain, and two soldiers. They went straight for the commander's dugout. An orderly tried to stop them, telling them the commander was resting.

"Don't you see who's standing in front of you?" the newly arrived colonel snapped at the orderly. "Step aside, soldier. I'm the one who gives out orders, and you're the one who takes them."

The orderly had nothing else to do but step aside from the door. But the door opened immediately, and the commander of the regiment came out.

"Hail, comrades," he addressed the newly arrived. "I'm listening. To what do I owe the pleasure?"

The badges on the uniforms of the major general and captain identifying them as political workers didn't escape Valery Georgievich's attention. The major general stepped very close to the commander and distinctively spoke, looking into his eyes carefully. "Let's go inside, Comrade Commander. We have to talk."

He then addressed the officer and the soldiers accompanying him in harsher and commanding manner.

"Stay on guard. Do not let anyone in."

Thirty minutes later, the three of the arrived together with Valery Georgievich came out of the dugout. His coat was unbuttoned, his tunic wasn't belted, and he wasn't wearing a hat. The Commander sorrowfully glanced at his loyal orderly, who stood behind the arrived soldiers with his mouth open in a gasp, and rushed towards the major general, captain, and the two soldiers.

"Comrade Colonel, Valery Georgievich!" He heard a familiar voice belonging to Ukhtomsky, who was running towards him.

"Stay back. Where do you think you're going?" major general harshly stopped him.

Alexey stopped. He realized everything then. The commander looked at his soldiers, who began to gather around the dugout. Their eyes expressed surprise and horror, and were silently questioning.

"How can we go on without you? What is this for? Why?"

Suddenly, Valery Georgievich's eyes met the eyes of Uglovaty, who was standing aside. His were the eyes of a hyena, cunning and cowardly, evil and smug simultaneously. Alexey watched the expression on the commander's face change, with bumps moving around his jaw, it turned purple, and his eyes darkened. Uktomsky followed Valery Georgievich's stare, and crossed eyes with Stepan, whose face expressed one thing clearly: "That one's finished. You're next."

Another Colonel took the Commander's place. He was a complete opposite of the former Commander. Hariton Evlampyevich Sapozhnikov, as was his name, had a face of a peasant: Harsh, grumpy, and unattractive. He had a disgusting habit of constantly rubbing under his nose with his right hand fingers, which made that area of his face perpetually bluish. Hariton Evlampyevich treated unit commanders in a rude manner. After the first few minutes of knowing each other, Ukhtomsky and the colonel felt a cautious hostility towards each other. As for Uglovaty, the new colonel treated him as if he was almost his crony."

Every day, Alexey thought of revenge. He understood his revenge had to be of a physical nature, permanent. But when? Uglovaty was almost never out by himself anymore. He was always beside his commander, who seemed to enjoy the loyalty of his junior political officer. The thought of revenge ate Alexey up from the inside. The close proximity of his target mixed with his inability to act drove the captain insane. He looked haggard and grey and his eyes gained an ill spark.

"What's wrong with you, Captain? Are you sure you're not sick?" the Colonel asked at one of the meetings. "You can't be sick now. You have a mission. Tomorrow, you have to break into a German hideout. The authority gave an order to obtain the information about the defenses of this encampment." The commander poked the map with his pointer. "It would be very useful if you took another "tongue" officer."

Then, the Colonel stopped. He carefully looked at Alexey, and then shifted his look onto Uglovaty, and a cunning spark lit up in his eyes, disappearing immediately after.

"You know what, Captain; comrade junior political officer will come with you. He's been inactive for some time. And another man in our unit won't hurt. He might just turn out useful."

Neither Ukhtomsky nor Uglovaty expected that kind of decision. They both tried to argue against it. Alexey insisted than any operation on the enemy territory requires skill and dexterity Stepan most likely didn't have. Uglovaty argued that his duties as a political officer included ensuring the soldiers' spirit and their devotion to communism. Hariton Evlampyevich listened to both carefully, and smirked, "That's what I'm talking about here. You, Stepan Mitrofanovich, are supposed to ensure the soldiers' spirit by setting a good example. As for the skills and dexterity, Alexey Nikolayevich, those qualities show when the time comes. So yeah, you're heading off tomorrow at sunrise. Go make you preparations."

At four in the morning, the entire scouting crew, together, with Uglovaty, who looked ridiculous in his camouflage, stepped out. They had been walking for about three hours. It was still dark. They decided to make a stop and rest for a little while. Fluffy snowflakes were falling down on the ground, already covered in deep white blanket of snow. The complete silence would make any movement easy to spot. Thirteen men got down into a small ravine near a frozen river. Uglovaty, who wasn't used to long periods of walking, could barely breathe, stretched out on the ground.

"Junior Comrade Political Officer!" he heard one of the scouts whispering.

"What is it?" Stepan asked, frightened.

"You shouldn't lie in the snow. You're all hot and sweaty. You'll get sick. You'll be coughing and sneezing, and the Germans will hear us."

Uglovaty sneered viciously and got up.

Uktomsky skillfully set up guards around the camp and ordered to split up dry rations for breakfast. They didn't make a fire, afraid of being spotted. They washed their breakfast down with clean snow. Nobody paid attention to Uglovaty. However, as he got up and headed for a walk, he was immediately stopped by one of the scouts.

"Comrade Junior Political Officer, don't go anywhere. You'll break the silence by walking through the crispy snow. If you have to relieve yourself, please go behind this bush."

Stepan was angry and scared at the same time. He wanted to yell, "How dare you speak to me this way!" But he was afraid. The scouts were too grim. Uglovaty also noticed that Ukhtomsky had absolute authority among the scouts.

As they reached their destination, they set up another encampment. They had a clear view of the entire reinforced base of the Germans. There was a field spreading from the edge of the forest on the opposite side of which there were concrete barricades, German tanks and other armored vehicles. They could easily see the soldiers scurrying about.

"We've got a great visual here. Onischenko, gather your men and head out there." Ukhtomsky gestured his hand towards the field. "Do as planned."

The men acted synergistically, quietly and calmly. Uglovaty cowardly looked at the tanks the distance. It was his first time in the enemy's territory, and he had mixed feelings about it. On one hand, Stepan knew that in order to gain some influence among the regiment troops which he had failed to do thus far, he had to participate in an operation. During the two weeks Uglovaty spent at the front line, he couldn't find a common ground with officers or soldiers. Mistakenly believing that his title alone would provide him honor and respect among the fighters, he was rude and arrogant towards them. As a result, no one except for Commander Hariton Evlampyevich treated Uglovaty in a good manner. On the other hand, junior political officer knew very well he didn't have the skill, the knowledge, or the physical shape he needed for such operations. That is why he was afraid. He was afraid to die.

The darkness before dawn cleared. Cold winter sun was beginning its everyday cycle. The forest was silent. Scouts, wearing white camouflage, blended in with the snow. They were waiting for any update from Onischenko's troops. Alexey was carefully watching the target from his binoculars. The atmosphere over the field appeared calm. The Germans were lazily walking back and forth. An officer appeared from a gray building, and a few soldiers stretched in a line in front of him. He waved his hand at them, and headed towards a lonely booth standing aside. Then, the silence set once again.

Uglovaty was lying in the snow about ten meters away from Ukhtomsky, feverishly squeezing a handgun in his hands. There was only one thing on his mind: *Soon, soon, time will come...*

The thought made him sweat. Stepan took off his camouflage and began to unbutton his jacket when Uktomsky distinctively said, "Comrade Junior Political Officer! Put your camouflage back on, lie down on the ground and don't move!" Then, he added, quieter, "Are you trying to catch a bullet?"

Uglovaty began to shake, either from fear that suddenly took over him or the hate that became his constant companion. He put his camouflage back on and lay on the ground with his face down.

"God damn! Gluhov, get over here!" Ukhtomsky commanded firmly.

A middle-aged man immediately crawled to him and carefully looked at the commander.

"Here, Ivan, look into the binoculars. What do you see?" Alexey asked, passing the binoculars to Gluhov.

"Comrade Captain, it looks like Onischenko got that officer out of the booth. There, he's dragging him on his back," Gluhov observed in a low voice, waving his hand towards the field. "Comrade Captain, the Germans have noticed. They're running around."

"That's right, Gluhov. Do you know your part in this?" Ukhtomsky looked at his subordinate.

"Yes, Comrade Captain. Allow me to begin."

Gluhov crawled away, but a moment later, his low, hoarse voice said, "Fedor, Petro, Kolka, follow me!"

A group of four moved out and crawled towards the field.

Four men stayed. Uglovaty was on the ground, afraid to move. He was being a coward. And his fear paralyzed his entire body. Stepan couldn't even utter a word. But inside, he was still jittery. Somewhere from the depths of his villainous soul came ideas unworthy of a man of his title.

"The Germans are acting. There's so many. They have cannons, tanks... And we have nothing."

Uglovaty sorrowfully and desperately looked at the handgun he was anxiously squeezing with his cold fingers. Evil thoughts were dancing in his head.

Why not? Maybe I should shoot the three that's left and get away. I can tell them we had a shootout with the Germans. Suddenly, Uglovaty heard his inner voice coo, *why don't you get up and do as you want? Do so, and break free. It will make you feel good. Do as you planned.*

Obeying his inner voice, Stepan leapt to his feet and began chaotically firing shots, one after another. Then he spun in place like a spinning top and rushed towards the field. The captain was first to get up.

"Where are you going? There are mines all over —"

But it was too late. They heard an explosion, and parts of Junior Political Officer's body scattered around meters away from it.

The scouting group returned to the regiment one day later. The task was complete. Everyone made it, except for Junior Political Officer Uglovaty. Only Onischenko and his man Kruglov, who was about eighteen years of age, caught German bullets. Onischenko was injured in his leg, and Kruglov wasn't so lucky. A bullet went through his hip. Both were taken to the medical unit.

After Ukhtomsky informed the commander about the proceedings and the results of the operation, the colonel asked, "Captain, please tell me about the death of Junior Political Officer Uglovaty. But please, tell it as it was. No sugarcoating and no lies. It is important to me."

Back in the forest, when Uglovaty got blown apart into pieces, Alexey decided he would be unbiased about his death in his report. That is why the captain clearly and honestly described Uglovaty's actions up until his death.

The colonel was quiet for a while after the captain finished reporting, then he suddenly added, "An honorless life deserves an honorless death."

"How do you mean, Captain Colonel?" Ukhtomsky was surprised.

Hariton Evlampyevich looked at him tiresomely. "Come on, Alexey Nikolayevich. You know everything. It was Uglovaty who reported

Valery Georgievich and got him arrested. And yesterday, the man was executed for so-called treason, and because of the ongoing war, there was no trial." The colonel tiredly sat down on a chair, the same chair that had belonged to the former commander Valery Georgievich just seven days ago.

"Take a seat, Captain. Have a rest," the colonel said to Alexey, who was stunned, unable to move.

He still couldn't grasp the meaning of the colonel's last words. He couldn't believe Valery Georgiyevich was gone.

"So, what I'm saying is, a true crime against people and against our country is arresting a field officer, a commander of the regiment, just before a scheduled attack. He is not the criminal. Uglovaty is."

Hariton Evlampyevich's voice grew stronger with each word, becoming firmer and more unsettled. He wrapped his hands around his head and uttered a sound that resembled a lion's roar.

"I don't and I never will understand the government's policy of murdering people, those who are devoted to their homeland, Captain, those who love their country to pieces, only because they're the way they are: Intelligent, thoughtful, different."

Ukhtomsky sat down on the chair he was offered. He didn't feel like saying anything. He felt like all the energy had been drained away.

"Uglovaty reported you, too, Captain. But I was able to intercept it. I intentionally kept him close, you know, so that he didn't do anything stupid. And he managed to do it, too. Just before you left for you operation, he gave me a letter asking me to send it to the headquarters. So I decided I would take it upon myself, have it on my consciousness, and open the letter. And thank God I did. Here is it, Alexey Nikolayevich. It's about you. Read it if you like, and if not, destroy it, burn it. This never happened. I never got anything."

The colonel stopped talking. He poured himself some water from a teapot and eagerly took a few gulps.

"I sent Uglovaty with you on purpose, you know. I thought... Ah well. Now, how do I describe his death in my report? Died as a brave man? I just can't bring myself to say that. Died as a coward? Can't do that, either. Fine, I'll write it as it is. Got blown up by a mine due to his own carelessness. What do you think, Captain?"

But Ukhtomsky couldn't hear him. He subconsciously squeezed the piece of paper he received in his hand, got up and walked towards the door, staggering. Commander didn't stop him or say anything, only looked his way understandingly. Gluhov was waiting for Ukhtomsky outside.

"Comrade Commander, allow me..."

Gluhov didn't finish his sentence, the way Alexey looked made him stop mid-sentence. The captain passed by his subordinate without any acknowledgement. Ukhtomsky went inside his dugout and, without removing his coat, sat down on a chair and unfolded the piece of paper covered in Uglovaty's handwriting. He quickly looked through the letter written in crooked handwriting, then crumbled it and threw it in his potbelly stove. The thought of revenge he had been preoccupied with all this time haunted him.

"The bastard escaped me, after all. He escaped my vengeance." Ukhtomky squeezed his head with his hands as hard as he could. Unable to exact revenge, he felt restless.

He suddenly remembered the colonel's words: *An honorless life deserves an honorless death.*

And then a famous quote by Hegel came to his mind, the one that suggested that "all accidents were unrecognized intentions".

That means Uglovaty's death, infamous and almost shameful, wasn't accidental, it was premeditated. And it was due to his own life choices. He chose a way of vice and betrayal, and he got punished for it with his shameful death. The thoughts were making Ukhtomsky anxious. He got up and began to walk back and forth in his cluttered dugout.

"Yes, everything that happens does so for a reason. Perhaps...no, definitely, my destiny shielded me from committing one of the worst sins in this world: Murder. God, I thank you for this salvation."

Alexey had always been religious. He never told anyone about it, as his conversations with God were always during the most difficult times of his life, in quiet, secluded places, and was only his. And it was then that Ukhtomsky felt in need of support more so than ever. The captain looked up, but saw nothing but planks of wood that served as a ceiling for his dugout. Then, he sat back down on his chair, closed his eyes, and tried to withdraw into himself, ignoring the sounds and noise around him. He spent three minutes in complete inner silence. Suddenly, Alexey remembered his fascination with Alexis de Tocqueville when he was young. His philosophical and political views had influenced young Ukhtomsky long before the revolution.

"Life isn't a gift, or a punishment, it's a purpose that we must accomplish and fulfill honorably." The quote by de Tocqueville made everything fall into place.

"Uglovaty got what he deserved, according to the law of nature. Usually, those who die take their sins with them, and their good deeds live on. The political officer hadn't done a single good deed in his entire life. That means his life was empty, and he won't be remembered by anything or anyone. Isn't that the worst thing that can happen to a person? I'm not guilty of his death. My consciousness is clear. I will live on. I have my country, my city, and my home."

Ukhtomsky's face lightened up, and he felt a heavy weight lifting from his shoulders. He went outside and began to joyfully breathe in freezing cold winter air. Soft snowflakes were swirling in the air, gently falling onto the ground covered in snow.

"Life is good!" Captain shouted.

Chapter 24

"Damn Uglovaty, served him well!" Darya said with indignation as Nadya was done telling her story. "How much misery had he brought upon people with all the terrible things he did?"

Nadya was sitting with her face red from tension. Her eyes were sparkling with tears.

"Nadya, what's wrong? Why are you crying?" Jane asked sympathetically.

Nadya got up and wiped the unwanted tear away. Turning back to the cousins, who looked at her with surprise, she said with a lilt of sadness in her voice, "No one can judge others before they judge themselves. We don't have the right to judge those who lived in the past. We can only have unbiased options about their actions. And those opinions will be subjective. We all know how to criticize, yet we can't see our own wrongdoings."

"I can't understand you right now, Nadya." Darya objected. "What, are you approving of Uglovaty? You? How can you, Nadya?" Darya helplessly banged her hand on the table, making herself gasp from pain. "I'm asking you to clarify the meaning of those words," Darya said to Nadya coldly.

The girl turned to her guest, standing very closely. Their eyes met. Darya saw something she would never have anticipated. Nadya's eyes expressed pain, so deep and so hopeless, Darya subconsciously hugged her arms around her.

"Nadya, I'm sorry. I didn't mean to open your old wounds, though I'm not sure what caused them. Nevertheless, I feel bad and sorry about my insistence and presumptuousness."

Jane, who was standing aside, looked at both girls with curiosity. "What's going on? What are you talking about?" She asked.

Nadya looked at Darya with gratitude. "One day, I will tell you both about what caused me to cry and what has been bothering me for a few days now since I've talked to my mom. But now, it's time to sleep. Look at the clock. The morning will soon come. We've been up for too long.

The next day, Darya got a call from her father.

"Darya, honey, how have you been? How is Jane?"

Darya briefly described their life in the far land of Russia.

"How is it going with Vladimir?" Alex's voice changed, giving out slight concern.

"It's good, Daddy. We see each other every day. I met his mom, by the way. She's an interesting woman. Did you know she can't walk?"

"She can't walk? That's sad." Alex seemed upset.

After some confusion, he announced in a more cheerful manner that he and Melinda were coming in a couple days.

"We really miss you, Darya. Your mom wouldn't let it go. She made me forget about everything and buy plane tickets. So, honey, you'll see us soon. We're flying through Amsterdam."

"Jane, Jane, my parents are coming!" Darya exclaimed happily.

Jane, who was making breakfast, wasn't overly enthusiastic about the news.

"God forbid, mine will come, too. My mom would immediately start to criticize Kostya. We'd start fighting a lot... Nothing good would come out of that."

Cousin, honey, you have to accept your family for who they are," Darya said to her with a smile. "I'm going to call Vladimir and share the news right now." Darya began to dial her sweetheart's number when Nadya came out of her room, ready for work.

"What news, Darya?" She asked. When Darya told her about the phone call, Nadya suggested everyone, including Vladimir and Konstantin, gather that night and discuss Darya's parents" arrival.

"Parents are important. We owe everything in this world to them and, first and foremost, our life. So, Darya, please give me the phone; I'll invite Vladimir over for tonight."

Confused, Darya passed the phone to Nadya, and the girl began talking to the young man with a smile and a look of superiority on her face.

Despite the fact that she trusted Darya, Nadya was always secretly competing with her for Vladimir. She wasn't going to let her guest have him. The girl tried to always be there when Darya and Vladimir were together. And she'd managed to do so thus far. During the two weeks the American girls had spent there, Vladimir never got a chance to be alone with Darya. Nadya was always following the cousins everywhere, justifying it with her feeling responsible for them. Once, Vladimir explicitly hinted that he wanted to be left alone with Darya.

"Nadya, I want to go to the movies with Darya tomorrow. Could you be so kind as to keep Jane company?"

"You want to go to the movies? Okay. I get it," She had replied.

The next day, on an early Sunday morning, during breakfast, she announced she'd gotten tickets to a premiere of a new movie "Bastards" by Alexander Atanesyan.

"This movie is about the war, cousins, the World War II in Russia. I think you'll be interested. You'll learn a lot. We'll invite Vladimir and Kostya, too. Do you mind?"

That night, Nadya invited everyone into her home to discuss the movie. Nadya knew she was ten years older than Darya, and five years older than Vladimir. However, she hoped he didn't just value looks and modesty in a woman, which men believe to be a sign of inner purity and innocence, but also intelligence, education, bravery, fast judgment and decision making. And it was hard to find someone who could measure up to her when it came to those qualities. She was capable of having an intelligent and daring conversation on any topic. Her low, velvety voice was mesmerizing. On top of all that, her looks, her face, especially her eyes, her body, which was so flexible were so appealing, many men had fallen in love with her irrevocably and often hopelessly. That night, Nadya looked her best. Dressed in a navy blue knitted dress that flattered her beautiful curves and her blue eyes, Nadya looked enthralling.

In a convincingly empathetic voice, she was expressing outrage about the decision of the Soviet government during the first year of war, according to which minor offenders were trialed as adults and got the same level of punishment. Because of that decision, underage criminals were lawfully and legally used at the front lines in practically hopeless operations. The movie they saw described one of those cases. The minor offenders were the "bastards", according to one of the characters. Nadya's voice sounded impulsive and hysterical. She was physically feeling the pain of the tragedy of those kids, even though they were experienced thieves and murderers. She was shaking from anger, and her righteous indignation was contagious.

Vladimir suddenly saw the girl in a different light. Nadya went from an overly self-assured and bordering on arrogant journalist to a sensitive, deeply empathetic, expressive girl. The young man recalled a quote he had read somewhere: "If a person feels pain that means he's alive. If a person feels someone else's pain, that means he's truly humane."

Vladimir was astonished by this discovery. He saw Nadya differently. She was a self-sufficient person with moral principles. Her spiritually enlightened face was so beautiful he couldn't take his eyes off of it. And something happened inside Vladimir. He felt like he was being pulled towards her by invisible strings, making him and her into one. The young man slowly and unwillingly turned his head to Darya.

She was sitting in an armchair to his side. He saw a few tears run down her face as she was holding her breath, carefully listening to Nadya. Vladimir focused on her simple dress and face; he felt compassion and tenderness towards her, the kind that you feel towards good friends rather than lovers. It was the kind of tenderness more typically expressed towards relatives rather than a romantic partner. Vladimir felt confused. He suddenly felt uncomfortable inside. He got up, excused himself, thanking everyone for the evening, and walked away while everyone following him with their eyes, puzzled.

Darya tried to get up and hold Vladimir back, but something stopped her. She only looked at him with sadness. Nadya, too, felt like going after Vladimir, but she changed her mind. The expression in his eyes as he was attentively watching the girl and listening to her heated rant about the film didn't escape her attention and female intuition. That's why she decided to give Vladimir some time to figure out the way he felt about both girls.

The night they found out about Darya's parents coming, all the kids gathered together at Nadya's. Nadya also invited Alena, who was helping out a lot in their search for information about the Ukhtomskys. Vladimir's sister—and Nadya's best friend—was happy to accept the invitation. More than that, she promised to bring over something new she discovered in the KGB archives, to which she had been trying to gain access for almost two weeks. Nadya suggested Darya's parents stay at her place.

"Your parents will be very welcome in my three-bedroom apartment. I'll let them have the master bedroom, and I'll sleep in the living room."

"No-no, Nadya, thank you very much, but I wouldn't want there to be any kind of bother. And my parents probably wouldn't go for that, either. They wouldn't like to inconvenience anyone. I'm sure Dad has already booked a room in a hotel," Darya quickly objected.

"Yes, I agree with my cousin. Alex and Melinda are modest and independent. And if they stayed here, they would be dependent on you. And they would hardly like that," Jane added.

"I suggest we meet Darya's parents and ask them what they prefer," Vladimir chimed in. "Thank you very much, Nadya, for your invitation. I honestly didn't expect such hospitality from you." The young man looked at the girl with gratitude and admiration. It was decided.

The group somehow naturally split into two. The first one, including Jane and Kostya, went out into the kitchen to make tea. Everyone else stayed in the living room. Darya made herself comfortable in the same armchair she always sat in. She hoped Vladimir would sit next to her, but he chose a spot on the couch next to his sister. Nadya was sitting at the table. The room went silent. No one was looking at anyone. That seemed surprising to Alena. She was used to her best friend always taking the initiative and never allowing anyone to stay quiet. And now, everyone was completely silent. She almost felt awkward.

"So, guys, why are we all quiet? Is someone an odd one out here? Could it be me?"

"What are you talking about? Of course not!" her brother immediately reassured her, and glanced at Nadya.

The girl was meaningfully looking at him, and her stare made him sweat and feel good at the same time. Darya was also looking at Vladimir, unable to understand what was going on with him. It was almost as if he'd been avoiding her for the past few days. She tried to talk to him several times, but he made excuses, said he was busy. She felt lost, insulted, and resentful at the same time. And she felt that this time, he also wasn't there with her. He was having a silent conversation with Nadya. And that conversation worried Darya. She got up, came up to the window, and unwanted tears appeared in her eyes.

It was dark outside. Light and fluffy snow was slowly falling down on the ground. Darya looked down. There, on the sidewalk near the building, a tiny dog was running around, white, just like the snow. It was barking and catching snowflakes with its tongue. Then it stopped, looked towards the front door, and wiggled its tail happily. A girl about thirteen, wearing a fluffy white coat, ran up to the dog and put it on a leash. The two went out for a walk, looking very similar. The scene somewhat calmed Darya. She decided to talk to Vladimir later, when they were alone. But when? Then, suddenly, Darya felt somebody's warm hand touching hers, which was resting on the windowsill. It was Vladimir.

"Are you sad? Do you miss your parents?" He asked gently.

The girl looked into the young man's eyes, which expressed warmth and tenderness.

"Yes, I really do miss my mom and dad. I never used to leave my parents' house for this long. And you know how close I am with them," Darya replied calmly.

"It will be alright, baby. Remember that," Vladimir assured quietly, and hugged her shoulders.

Nadya, who was almost certain she'd already won Vladimir over, felt confused. This whole time, she never took her eyes off the young man and watched his every move. As Vladimir gently held Darya, Nadya became tense, and her face turned red. That didn't escape Alena's attention.

"Okay, bestie, I see something's bothering you. The expression on your face tells me you're unhappy about something. Tell me, what is it?" Alena whispered into the girl's ear.

Nadya looked at her friend and asked, "You don't know anything? Your brother hasn't talked to you about anyone or anything recently?"

"You're driving me into a corner, hon. You know, in our family, only mom knows everything about everyone. And Vova has an especially trustful relationship with her. But I'm not going to pry here, so please don't ask me to."

Jane and Kostya came in carrying a tray with a teapot, cups, and bowls of sweets.

"I have a cake, too. I baked it myself. It's called County Ruins," Nadya suddenly remembered.

Jane looked at her in surprise. "When did you have time to do that?"

"Ah, it's easy, doesn't take much. Let me go get it."

A few minutes later, when Nadya came into the living room carrying a big plate of airy white balls held together by oily peanut butter cream, everyone clapped their hands.

"So, you're a chef, too," Vladimir said admiringly. His burning eyes were looking at Nadya. Alena noticed his look, as well Darya's nervousness, and the way Vladimir's compliment made Nadya's eyes sparkle.

Everyone gathered around the table.

"Guys, I wanted to inform you all of certain archive material. Yesterday, I spent the entire day studying it. It paints a very interesting picture." Alena spoke to everyone, as they took their first sip of tea and a bite of cake.

"This information has to do with you and your mom, bestie." Alena turned her head to Nadya.

Nadya blushed, left the table and came up to a window. A bullfinch sitting on a tree branch, all clenched, was looking at Nadya from its tree, which stood across the apartment building. The bullfinch closed its eyes, hid its head under the wing, and went quiet.

"Just like my mom, hiding her entire life, she herself didn't even know who she was trying to hide from."

Her parents" past was always hanging over her head. Nadya wiped off a tear that ran down her right cheek, patted her left eye, also wet from tears, with a napkin, and turned to her guests.

"Yes, it looks like it's time to tell everything. After all, my mom also had something to do with the Uktomskys. No, she wasn't a relative, but her story played a big role in the family's life. I just learned about that recently from my mother. She kept it in her heart and in her memory. She never told anyone except Anastasia. It looks like you got this information in the form of official documents, Alena. And this is something I was going to tell you later, cousins. But the time has come for you to learn everything, and maybe lift this weight off of my mother's shoulders, and now mine as well."

Alena walked up to her friend, hugged her, and said quietly, but clearly, "You're right, sweetie. It really is about your mom's parents. I understand it was hard for you to learn. I also couldn't fall asleep for a while, had to let it all sink in, and kept looking for reasons, excuses for his actions. So, do you want to tell them yourself, or will you give me this right?"

Nadya sat down on a chair by the table, poured herself some tea, took a sip, and said, "This is my family, and I will tell this story the way my mom told it."

Chapter 25

The nanny was able to find the military blanket that came with my mom when she was left at the orphanage gate, after all. It had a stamp on it, typical of military property. There was a combination of letters and numbers on the stamp. My mom imagined herself to be a daughter of a military officer who left for war. She really, really believed he would search for her, and take her back as the war was over. She also believed her mother left for the front, as well, together with her father. But the war ended, years passed, and no one was looking for her. She tried to search for her parents, going by the information on the stamp, but wherever she went, nobody was willing to help her.

Anastasia and my mom finished eighth grade of public school and began to live on their own. They enrolled in Pedagogical Institute of N. A. Nekrasov. They got a room in the dorm. And one day, someone knocked on that door. It was a woman dressed in a black sweatshirt, with her hair tucked away in a gray shawl and rough boots. She was holding a sack tied up as a backpack in her hands. Her face might have once been pretty, but at the time, you could almost say it looked awful, if it wasn't for her eyes. It was gray in color, and her nose looked swollen from either perpetual cold or physical abuse, and her chin was slightly crooked to the right. But her eyes, they were beautiful. Sky-blue, they expressed intelligence, intellectuality, kindness, and empathy at the same time.

"Hello, my name is Ekaterina Buynovsky," The woman announced. Her attentive eyes kept shifting from my mom's face to Anastasia's, and back. "Don't be afraid. Forgive me for the state I'm in. I understand I look horrific. But this is normal for those who come back from where I've been. Which one of you is Varvara? Wait, it's you." The woman pointed to my mother. "Allow me to come in and explain everything," She asked the girls, who were both stunned.

Anastasia and my mom invited the guest inside, and begged the commandant to let her take a shower in the dorm. As a payment, they had to clean every floor of the dorm for the next week. They offered the woman some tea with bubliks, and then listened to her story carefully.

Ekaterina came from a modest, noble family. She lived with her parents in an apartment on Nevsky Avenue. This apartment had belonged to Ekaterina's grandfather even before the revolution. But they were forced to give a few of their rooms to their new roommates, one of them being Stepan Mitrofanovich Uglovaty.

"Uglovaty?" The cousins exclaimed both at the same time.

Nadya didn't respond, only cast her head down and asked, "May I continue?"

"Yes, yes, of course," Darya replied, confused.

Ekaterina's suffering began as soon as Uglovaty moved in with them. He wouldn't leave her alone. He would stop her in the hall, trying to kiss her, or enter the bathroom as soon as he saw her go there. Ekaterina had to constantly fight for her innocence. To make matters worse, all his harassment took place in the absence of her parents and their second roommate. Uglovaty behaved strangely around them. He tried to come off as a great activist of the revolution. He liked to talk about the role of the working class in the development of the country, and the death of intelligentsia. With that, he demanded Ekaterina and her parents sat at the table in the kitchen while he walked back and forth, gesturing his hands in endless rants. He had a poor vocabulary, as he never read any books, and had a religious education. However, being naturally smart, Stepan was able to memorize key points from speeches and conversations he overheard at work, during meetings, and in public transportation, and mainly talked about that. One time,

Ekaterina's dad said something about his poor vocabulary and that he needed to read more. It made Uglovaty extremely angry. He grabbed the old man by his shirt, his face against his, and was about to hit my dad's nose with his head, but, apparently, changed his mind. He let him go and hissed, "Don't tell me what to do, pest."

Then, he abruptly turned around and walked out of the kitchen.

After that incident, it became practically impossible for Ekaterina's family to live in their own apartment. Uglovaty would go into their rooms wearing dirty boots without permission, sit at their table without invitation and demand they serve him. Ekaterina's mother had bad eyes. Uglovaty once tripped her by sticking his foot out while she was carrying a hot pot of tea, which was at his own request. She fell to the floor, and the boiling water burned her hand, which wouldn't heal for a while. And about three months after the day Ekaterina's dad had made that unfortunate remark, her parents were arrested. Katya never learned what happened to them. She went to the authorities, tried to dig up anything she could, but everyone just pointed at Uglovaty. They said it was up to him whether she would be allowed to schedule a meeting with her parents.

Once, Uglovaty came home tipsy. He didn't try to break into Ekaterina's room as usual. He was in a good mood. He locked himself in his room and began to sing loudly in his disgusting nasal voice, and then Katya heard him talk to himself.

"Good job, Stepan! You got what you wanted! Keep it up! That's alright, she will crawl to me herself, when she's carrying my baby. I know my semen is strong!" After that, his body collapsed onto the bed and he fell asleep. Ekaterina kept listening to the sounds coming from Uglovaty's room for a while, until she heard him snore. Only then was she able to calm down and go to sleep.

In the morning, Katya heard a knock on the door, which she'd begun to always keep locked.

"Hey, open up, I'm talking to you!" She heard Uglovaty's angry voice.

"What are you so loud about, Stepan?" Their roommate asked, who had just returned from his business trip. He was a middle-aged man. Working as an engineer, he frequently traveled across the country.

"Oh, you're back, Ivan. How was your trip?"

She heard Uglovaty walk away from the door. Ekaterina was hiding under the blanket, afraid to move. She was nineteen then, and on her first year of the pedagogical institute. She had classes in an hour and didn't want to leave her room, afraid to face Uglovaty. She heard the front door close, and thought the hated roommate finally left, as it was his time to go to work. She quickly got dressed, grabbed her bag with textbooks and notebooks, and quietly came out of the room. But as she was walking towards the door, someone grabbed her wrist.

"What, are you all ready for school, girl?" She heard Uglovaty's nasal voice. "How about you get naughty with me?"

He dragged her into his room, taking the coat off her on the way.

"Stepan Mitrofanovich, what are you doing?" Bitter tears ran down the innocent girl's cheeks.

She fought him as hard as she could, hit him with her schoolbag, screamed, hoping someone would hear her, tried to bend her body and escape her roommate's strong hands. But his hands really were unyielding, and they never let go of anything he wanted. Uglovaty dragged the girl into his room, threw her on the floor, locked the door with his key, and hid it. The poor girl tried to crawl away into a corner while he watched, his eyes sparkling with lust.

"Yesterday, an Ukhtomsky princess, a princess herself lusted after me, and I put it in her. Successfully, I hope. And today, I feel like taking you, a noble girl. You're mine now. I'm gonna do whatever I want to you."

He was talking while taking off his shirt, his pants, throwing them at the girl. He then jumped at her like a beast and began to rip her dress, tights, and slip until all she had on was underwear. Through it all, Katya was in some kind of fog. She was paralyzed with fear. She couldn't yell, talk, or move her hands or legs. The man picked her up and carried her to his bed, carelessly made with dirty sheets. As he laid Katya on his bed, Uglovaty looked at her for a while.

"You're beautiful. All this beauty now belongs to me." He uttered a diabolical laugh.

He began to torture Ekaterina. Tying her arms and legs to the bed to stop her from fighting, ripping off the clothes left on her, and taking off his own, he lay down on top of her with his heavy body, and started to suck her lips. It looked as if a devil in a man's body was trying to drain the entire poor girl's life out of her. After the kiss, Uglovaty began to fondle her beautiful flesh. He squeezed her small breasts with his hands, causing agonizing pain. But Katya didn't make a sound, only her lips began to bleed as she was biting them. Stepan's hands kept going lower. As they reached the girl's stomach, they started to squeeze it like it was flour. Then his hands went even lower. Ekaterina didn't utter a sound, paralyzed with fear. Suddenly, his thick, springy penis entered the girl, and sharp pain in the bottom of her stomach sobered her up, causing her to scream. The rapist immediately covered her mouth with his hand. Katya didn't stop screaming. She kept biting Uglovaty's fingers and crying. A strong hit to her jaw knocked her unconscious.

She woke up later that night. Her arms and legs, tied to the bed, felt numb. She was naked, covered up with a brown military blanket. A weak ceiling lamp was lighting the room. Her rapist was sitting by the table, looking straight at her. In his eyes, Katya saw her unfortunate fate.

"Well, noble girl, you're going to live here, in this room, from now on. This is your permanent home. Do you understand?" Uglovaty said with an evil smirk. "When I'm home, you'll be in bed, the way you are now, to always satisfy my needs."

His eyes, once again, sparkled with lust.

"While I'm at work, you'll be here, cuffed to this bed with these handcuffs." He mockingly shook the handcuffs before her face. "I will feed you food from our cafeteria. It's not bad, by the way."

Katya screamed, but Uglovaty hit her in the face again. Her head moved to the left and sharp pain in her chin knocked her out. Uglovaty felt worried. He went into the kitchen and grabbed the first pot he could find, filled it up with cold water, and poured it all over the girl's face. Katya began to move. Slowly opened her eyes, she felt dull pain in her jaw. Then she heard Uglovaty's diabolical laugh.

"I like you this way, too. Though, your jaw is crooked. My hands are strong. You have to get used to it, noble girl. Open your mouth one more time, and you're dead. Remember, you are now mine, and mine only. Now, let's have some more fun."

Ekaterina became his slave. Uglovaty would take her outside once a week, always holding her hand, and he wrapped a shawl around her head, which made her mouth very tightly shut. And each time, he reminded her of his threat to kill her if she screamed. At home, she was subjected to emotional and physical abuse. They lived alone in the apartment. Uglovaty used his connections to make Ivan, their roommate, move out of the apartment to the opposite side of the city. He also visited her institute. Introducing himself as her husband, he announced that she was moving out of town to take care of his elderly parents.

Nobody ever visited their apartment. Katya lost a lot of weight, she suffered from constant headaches, and her dislocated jaw healed back crooked, deforming her once beautiful face. She often thought of death. In her thoughts, she addressed God and her parents. She had awful pains during her periods. Uglovaty, who hadn't been with a woman for many years due to his love for self-pleasure, which he had been engaging in since adolescence, almost went crazy. He would rape the girl all night long. And in the morning, he would happily leave for work, previously handcuffing Katya to his bed.

A few months had passed. One night, Katya threw up after the dinner Uglovaty brought her from the cafeteria. She thought she had food poisoning. But the next day, she felt nauseated before every meal, and threw up each time she ate. Katya was scared. Uglovaty was happy.

"Finally, you got pregnant from me, noble girl. I was about to get worried I wasn't potent enough. Good for you, Stepan!"

Since that day, Uglovaty treated Ekaterina slightly better. He didn't torture her at night anymore, and brought her fruit and sweets. He began to come from work earlier and immediately took her outside for a walk.

"You two, you and the baby, need some fresh air and exercise," Uglovaty said with an evil smirk.

Her due date came soon enough. During her entire pregnancy, Katya never saw a doctor. Only once, when she caught a cold and was feverish, Uglovaty brought some old woman who stayed with them for a few days, and treated Katya with herbal infusions and incantations. And it helped. In a couple of days, Katya's body temperature dropped, and she began to recover. The old woman did everything in complete silence, as if she couldn't talk. She tried not to make eye contact with the girl. On the fourth day, she finally looked at Ekaterina with kindness and compassion, and said, "That's it, girl, you won't need any more of my help. I will go now." Ekaterina wanted to say something to the healer, but the woman said, "Be quiet. I don't know you, and I've never seen you."

After some silence, she said: "Good luck, girl. Doesn't seem like you've had any so far."

She quickly turned around and left.

It was a warm May afternoon. Uglovaty was at work. Katya got up and got dressed. She couldn't close her robe anymore. She belted it with a rope and went into the kitchen. Her belly was so big, she could barely move her legs due to lack of special exercise pregnant women require. Suddenly, a sharp pain in her stomach caused her to sit down. Her water broke. Katya was scared. She grabbed a towel hanging on the headboard of her bed, stuck it between her legs and crawled on her knees towards the wall that separated her apartment from the neighbor. Ekaterina began to knock on the wall as hard as she could, and then knock on the radiator. In about fifteen minutes, she heard a doorbell. She cried out. Gathering her strength, she got up and rushed to the door. She heard a woman's voice from the other side telling her to open the door.

"I can't, I'm locked in from the outside. I don't have the key. Help! My water broke! Help!"

"We have to break down the door. Kolka, get a hammer and a saw, and bring uncle Petya from apartment 11," a bossy female voice ordered.

Then, the same voice spoke to her in a softer manner. "Don't worry, we'll help you!"

To Kolka, she yelled, "And call the ambulance!"

Three hours later, Ekaterina was in a hospital bed in the postnatal care. She gave birth to a girl, an extremely weak baby. As Katya was lying in bed while her daughter was being taken care of, her doctor, a woman with a strict face who was about fifty, walked in.

"Why weren't you taking care of yourself, or your baby, Mommy? Your girl is very weak. You must not have had a very good diet."

The doctor wanted to say something else, but stopped. Ekaterina suddenly broke out in tears. Throughout the whole time she was a prisoner, she didn't cry once. It's as if her heart had turned to stone, and couldn't feel anything. Katya didn't even recognize the baby she had in her as her own. She hated it. But now, as Katya gave birth to her child, she felt it was a part of her, though it came from someone she hated, and she was able to grasp the whole tragedy of her and her baby's life. Bitter tears ran down her cheeks. She didn't bother wiping them off. She kept sniffling, crying, sobbing. The doctor sat next to the young woman, wiped her face with a handkerchief, and spoke quietly and soulfully in a maternal manner.

"Tell me, Katya, tell me everything. It looks like life's been hard on you. You're my last patient for today. I have time."

"That bastard!" The doctor exclaimed in outrage as Ekaterina finished her story. "I won't let it slide. I'll report him."

"No, no, you can't! He will kill me! He's a horrible man. Nothing is sacred to him. I beg you!" Katya was frightened. She turned pale, shaking from a nervous chill that ran through her body. The doctor looked at Ekaterina with empathy.

"I'll give you some sedative. You'll have some rest. I check up on your daughter and come back. Don't worry, it will be alright."

The young woman trusted the doctor, and after taking the sedative, Katya, for the first time in many months, was able to go to sleep in peace."

Uglovaty rushed to the hospital that night. Ekaterina didn't recognize him. He had a huge bouquet of lilacs in his hands, a box of "Red October" chocolates and a bottle of wine in a grocery bag. Stepan was smiling, and appeared to be in a great mood.

"Katya, you did well. You gave me a daughter. I have to say, thank you. I'm happy," Uglovaty said with a hint of pride in his voice.

Then, he added quieter, in a low and harsh voice, "I hope you didn't tell anyone about our little secret. Watch yourself!"

Katya curled up in a ball in her bed, fear in her eyes that grew wet from tears.

This was how the doctor saw her as she quietly entered the room, overhearing Uglovaty's last words.

"Hello, you must be Ekaterina's husband?" The doctor casually asked Stepan, looked at Katya, who gave her a look of gratitude, and winked at the girl.

Stepan, who wasn't expecting to see or hear from anyone, shuddered and turned his head towards the voice. The look on his face went from harsh to kind and obsequious.

"Hello, thank you for...my wife, and my daughter. This is for you," Uglovaty said, handing a bag of treats to the doctor.

"No, no, there's no need for this, comrade Uglovaty. You'd better keep it and celebrate the new addition to your family as your wife and daughter check out," The doctor replied with a smile, but firmly. "Now, let me just see how Ekaterina is doing. Give us some privacy, please."

Three days later, when Ekaterina was ready to check out of the hospital, the doctor came in with her baby in her arms.

"You're starting a new life, Katya. You're a mom now. Your girl is adorable. Remember, she is a part of you. Cherish her. I think it will all work out for you." The doctor's voice sounded maternally protective. "And one more thing, Katya. Forgive me, but I reported Uglovaty to the authorities, after all. They promised to take their measures."

Ekaterina felt her heart start to race.

"What have you done? My life is over."

"Don't worry, girl. You'll be alright. Remember that."

But Ekaterina didn't respond. She quickly headed for the door. The doctor followed her. Uglovaty was holding a bouquet of flowers waiting for her by the entrance. He handed it to the doctor and said with an evil smile, "Thank you, comrade doctor, for everything, all your help, advice, and your trouble."

His smile made the doctor uncomfortable. She quickly thanked him for the flowers and went back inside.

"Let me take the baby, Katya." Uglovaty said to the young mother.

Three weeks had passed after Ekaterina returned home from the hospital. She was slowly getting better. Uglovaty was alarmingly polite with her. He often brought home the food she needed for her recovery diet, spent time with the baby, picked her up, held her in his arms and played with her. One thing was bothering Katya. His voice was always villainous, and his eyes expressed hatred. One day, as she was about to hold her baby, she heard a doorbell ring. She opened the door and saw three men dressed as civilians.

"Citizen Ekaterina Vladislavovna Buynovsky?" One of them asked.

"Yes," She replied, confused.

"Come with us."

Katya began backing up. She picked up her baby and started to circle around the room.

"You can't. I have to breastfeed her. She's too young."

One of the men came up to her, took the baby out of her arms, and put it back in the crib.

"She'll be taken care of. Let's go," he said quickly and grabbed her arms.

She screamed. The second man came up to her, his face very close to hers, and spoke with a rotten breath. "Shut up you sellout bitch."

She was arrested as a daughter of traitors. After physical abuse and torture, Katya, exhausted and in chains, was dragged out of an NKVD basement and thrown into a vehicle filled with other convicts. Somebody cradled her head and laid it on their lap. Katya felt a soft and gentle hand pull her hair back.

"Katya, is that you?" She heard the familiar but weak voice of her doctor.

"The bastard got you, too! Forgive me, my darling. I thought I was doing the right thing, I was doing justice. The monster had to be punished. And this is what happens..."

The doctor, a strong woman who hadn't cried before, even after losing her husband and son when they were arrested and executed three years ago, began to cry. She cried from resentment and hopelessness.

Ekaterina spent fifteen years in the camps. After she was freed, she began to search for her daughter. The apartment she used to live in and was later trapped in by Uglovaty now belonged to someone else. They knew nothing about its previous owners. Upon leaving the building in despair, Ekaterina ran into a neighbor who'd helped her out before. As a rule, neighbors used to know everything about one another. She was the one to tell Ekaterina that Uglovaty had put her daughter in an orphanage, and that he wasn't alive anymore. After that, it was quite simple to find her daughter.

"And I named you after my mom, Vasilisa. But Varvara is a beautiful name, too, very dignified." The woman finished her story and reached out to Varvara, trying to stroke her hair.

"So, it turns out that your mom is Uglovaty's daughter. But Anastasia is Uglovaty's daughter, too!" Jane exclaimed in surprise.

"Yes, girls, it's true that my mom and Anastasia were more than just friends; they were sisters. At least Anastasia was raised in a real family until she was three, even though they weren't her birth parents. Alexey and Polina were her true parents, the only parents she knew."

"So, what happened next?" Vladimir asked Nadya quietly.

Nadya gave him a long look, quivered her head, and continued.

"Ekaterina Buynovsky and my mom took a while to get used to each other. Varvara found it hard to let go of her belief that her parents weren't war heroes, that her father died shamefully, and was a scoundrel his entire life. She was prejudiced against Ekaterina. Varvara blamed her for everything, for her father not being a war hero, for her having to grow up without a family, and for spending a big part of her life in the camps. Varvara felt no pity or compassion towards her mother. She didn't feel anything. Katya naturally belonged to the group of intelligentsia that valued spirituality above all. Her parents taught her dignity, kindness, decency, honesty, and perceptiveness. Ekaterina didn't resent her daughter for the estrangement. She understood she couldn't possibly expect a different outcome.

The girl never knew her own parents, and got used to only relying on herself. Let her get used to knowing I exist, that I'm alive, and there for her, Katya thought. *Eventually, her heart will melt and accept me as her mother.*

Ekaterina was able to soon return to her institute, graduated in two years, and began to work as a math teacher at a school. She first moved in with her former neighbor, who lost her husband in the war. Her son, Kolka, who'd become a geologist by then, was almost never home. Efrosinya, as was the neighbor's name, gladly took Ekaterina in. After some time, Ekaterina received a studio apartment from the City Board of Education.

Varvara graduated from her institute and worked as a kindergarten teacher. Anastasia took her education even further. Geology seemed to appeal to her. She enrolled in a university. The contact between the two friends began to break slowly. They used to see each other once a week and share their news and struggles. Once a week turned into once a month. Later, they began to only occasionally give each other a call.

Ekaterina made efforts to grow closer with Varvara. She often came by the kindergarten, waiting on her daughter. But Varvara, naturally upbeat and sociable, would always put her guard up as soon as she saw Katya. Her daughter wouldn't acknowledge her mother's presence, passing by her with a straight face. Katya decided to turn to Anastasia for help. On a Sunday afternoon, when Nastya had just returned home from a research expedition and was resting on her couch reading a book, she heard a doorbell. It was Ekaterina. Anastasia hadn't seen the woman since the memorable day they met. Ekaterina looked like a different person. Her permanent deformity, caused by Uglovaty, no longer made her look unattractive. Her skin looked fresh and pampered, and her eyes were radiating with inner strength. Ekaterina excused herself for having come uninvited and asked Anastasia for a minute of her time. They had a long and serious conversation. The girl promised Ekaterina that she would talk to Varvara.

"Ekaterina Vladislavovna, do you remember the first time you told me your story, you mentioned an Ukhtomsky princess?" Anastasia asked her guest. "Could you please tell me her name?"

Katya carefully looked at the girl, closed her eyes, and cast her head down. In a few seconds, which seemed like an eternity to Nastya, the guest finally spoke, slowly and quietly.

"The princess' name was Sofia. Uglovaty would often mention her name, bragging about how she had willingly given herself to him."

Anastasia turned pale from those words.

"What's wrong, Nastya!?" Ekaterina asked her.

The girl told her guest about her life before the orphanage, as she heard from the nanny. Ekaterina came up to Nastya, put her hands around her head, with her deep, expressive eyes staring into the soul of the girl, and confidently said, "Don't think any lower of Sofia. She was a great woman. I know this story. I heard it from Lidya, Sofia's cousin. I met her in the camps."

Anastasia looked at Katya in surprise.

"I have an aunt? I thought I was alone in the world," The girl said with a hint of happiness.

"Unfortunately, Lidya died in the camps. It was an accident. But she had a daughter, Anna. Though, I'm not sure where she is now."

Ekaterina paused for a little bit, seeing Nastya's eyes grow moist with tears.

"So what did Lida tell you about Sofia?" The girl asked slowly in a quiet voice. Katya suggested they have some more tea. After the tea was served, the woman began her story about Sofia up until her early death. By the time she finished, Nastya's face was wet with tears.

Chapter 26

The living room was quiet. Everyone had their eyes on the silent Nadezhda. Her face grew red, eyes full of tears. She was fiddling a handkerchief in her hands, the one she always had with her. She found it hard to speak. Nadya knew that what she had to talk about next would be unpleasant to her mother, and therefore, to herself. How can she possibly tell the friends sitting there waiting for her story about how her mother had treated the person who gave her the gift of life.

Varvara never forgave her mother.

Once upon a time, the phone went off in Anastasia's apartment, waking her up. She instinctively looked at the clock. It was half past three a.m.

"Anastasia, is that you?" A female voice asked in a bothered but willful manner.

"Yes... It is me. And who are you?" Nastya replied, surprised.

"This is hospital calling. I'm the paramedic who delivered Ekaterina Vladislavovna Buynovskaya here. She gave us your phone number."

"What has happened to her?"

"She had an extensive myocardial stroke. She's in a very bad condition. You should be here."

Katya was in ICU, which is normally off limits to any visitors. But they made an exception for Anastasia. The chief medical officer of the hospital turned out to be a mother of a boy whom Ekaterina taught math. Katya attempted to smile as she saw Nastya. She barely managed.

Pale, with purple and lifeless lips, but bright blue, lively eyes, and light fuzzy hair spread across the pillow, Katya looked like an angel ready to be consumed into darkness. Her eyes gestured Nastya to move closer and, trying hard to open her mouth, she spoke.

"Nastya, in my desk, in my apartment, there's a notebook with a red cover." The woman went silent, and closed her eyes. It took her an enormous amount of strength to make out each single word. "It's my diary... Take it..." Suddenly her words turned into meaningless wheezing.

"Doctor, doctor, nurse!" Nastya screamed. But it was too late.

Nastya was allowed to make a phone call from the nurse's office of the cardiology department. She was dialing Varvara's home number. Her temples throbbed, her hands were shaking, and tears slowly ran down her cheeks. She heard a beep, and then Varvara's sleepy and annoyed voice.

"Yeah... Who the hell is calling, won't let me sleep?"

"Varvara, it's me, Nastya. I'm calling from a hospital. Your mom... has just passed away."

There was silence on the other end of the line.

"Varvara, can you hear me?" Nastya asked, worried.

"I can hear. I'm thinking." The emotion in Varvara's voice was unclear. "Which hospital? I'll be there."

An hour later, Varvara arrived at the hospital.

"What happened to her? What did she die from?" Varvara asked her friend impassively, trying to avoid the word "mother". Nastya told her about the phone call from the hospital, and Ekaterina's last words.

"You were what, her friend? Why would she give the doctor your phone number all of a sudden? Didn't she have other friends that suited her more?" Varvara said to Nastya with a hint of sarcasm.

Anastasia didn't respond.

Anastasia was the one to organize Ekaterina's funeral. She received help from the school where Katya worked, as well as from the Education Department which had a lot of respect for Ekaterina Vladislavovna Buyskaya, for her just character and her compassion towards children. Varvara didn't take part in it, but attended the memorial dinner held at Nastya's apartment.

"Stay. We need to talk," Nastya said to her friend who was about to leave. "I have to tell you, Varvara, I never understood, and never will understand your attitude towards your mother. Ekaterina Vladislavovna was a very kind, decent, endlessly loving... Endlessly loving you person. Until her last days, she hoped you would finally accept her. She was so worried about you. She didn't have anyone but you. And you...never gave her a chance." Anastasia couldn't finish, as Varvara bluntly interrupted her.

"Enough, enough telling me about her love for me. She betrayed me. She turned out to be weak. She couldn't fight this so-called father, Uglovaty. Why didn't she escape, call the neighbors for help? Why was she such a loyal slave to him? I hate it." Varvara's voice started to sound hysterical. Her face turned bright red, and her eyes sparkled with tears. She felt a feverish chill, forcing her to sit down on a couch.

Anastasia came up to the girl and handed her the notebook with a red cover.

"Here, take it, read it. It's your mother's diary. She's had it since she was young. She wrote about all that happened. Her thoughts, her concerns. She even kept it in prison, the camps. If they'd found the diary then, she would have been shot. She knew that, yet she still sat down every day in a secluded place and wrote. Ekaterina kept this diary for her daughter. Afraid of not making it till the day you two meet, she talked about herself here so you knew who she was. And you.."

Anastasia looked at Varvara accusingly.

"You know, honey, if you run away from something just because you don't like it, you won't like where you end up, either. These are not my words. It's John Wyndham's, in "The Chrysalids". And it's true. All these years, you kept running away from your mother, only because you decided she betrayed you. You did not like that. As a result, you ended up at her deathbed, losing the chance to ever talk to her, a chance at being close with the dearest person you had in the world... Read her diary. It will open your eyes about this brave, courageous woman, your mother."

Anastasia watched Varvara. The girl was sitting on the couch, clutching the notebook to her chest. Bitter tears fell from her saddened eyes, gathering in thin rivulets and running down her cheeks. They seeped through the pages of the notebook, scribbled in Ekaterina's tiny handwriting.

"Thank you, Nastya. I'll be on my way, if that's alright."

Varvara got up from the couch and walked to the door, gently holding the diary.

Nadezhda decided not to tell her friends about any of that.

"Let it be on my mother's conscience. She has already punished herself by cutting all ties with Anastasia after Ekaterina's funeral. My mother was ashamed. And she couldn't think of anything to do other than to stop being friends with Nastya, her only friend, and, as it turned out, her sister, in whom she, however, saw perpetual reproach."

Nadezhda looked at her friends who were staring at her with curiosity, and slowly spoke, attempting to draw a bottom line. "My mother struggled to get over Ekaterina's death. She became withdrawn and stopped seeing Nastya. My mom decided she would cross out of her life everything that had happened before the day Ekaterina died. She wanted a clean slate."

"So, what? Did it help her? Helped her build a normal and peaceful life that made her happy?" Darya interrupted.

"I don't know how happy my mom is. Or rather, how happy she feels," Nadya said slowly, weighing each word. "One thing I know for sure, romance in her life has been completely non-existent for fifteen years, ever since Daddy died. But there are so many sides to happiness. It isn't just about romantic relationships."

Nadya looked straight at Vladimir, who couldn't take his eyes off her beautiful face.

"And what is happiness to you? When can one consider themselves happy?" He asked.

"You're asking a weird question, Volodya. It's been asked too much by too many."

"Not necessarily, dear," Alena spoke. "For example, my husband and I still can't come to the same conclusion. When I complain to him, for instance, about the fact that we don't have one thing or another, that I'm poor, unhappy, and have to do everything with my bare hands, that my days are full of chores and responsibilities and he spends all day sitting in his office, bringing home so little, and when he's home he sits on the couch in front of the TV, he tells me how happiness is not a careless and happy life, it's a state of mind. How's that for a definition of happiness?" Alena looked at everyone questioningly and continued. "To be honest, I agree with him that happiness isn't about material things. For, as Heraclitus said, we would have to call bulls happy when they find peas for food."

Vladimir interrupted Alena, laughing, "My sis is a philosopher! How do you know Heraclitus so well?"

It was Alena and Nadezhda's turn to smile. Nadezhda came up to Vladimir, who was resting in an armchair, ruffled his hair with her fingers and playfully said, "Everyone who studies to be a journalist, my friend, studies ancient philosophers, including Herclitus of Ephesus. As to my understanding of the word "happiness", I will back up Alena and point out something once said by Foma Akvinskiy." She looked at Vladimir pointedly, "I will say that happiness cannot come from wealth, as you have to suffer to obtain all that wealth. Happiness really isn't a material substance. Neither physical strength nor money make people happy, but being truthful and wise does. Democritus said so, and I completely agree."

"So, according to that, if you feel like you're right about everything, and wise enough to figure out all life's challenges, you're happy and always will be?" Darya joined the conversation.

She didn't like the way Nadya acted around Vladimir. She could tell they already had an invisible, but strong connection between them. It hurt her. She saw Nadezhda trying to win over her beloved with her sharp intelligence, and perhaps she already has. The way the young man looked at her rival did not escape Darya's attention. She, just as well, studied ancient philosophers at her university, and studied diligently. Darya decided to take matters into her own hands, and show that she was no less smart and educated than Nadezhda.

"Oh, unhappiness! It is a crutch of happiness. Oh, happiness! It holds unhappiness within it. Who knows their limits?" She quoted the Chinese philosopher Lao-Tzu.

"What do you mean by that?" Asked Vladimir, surprised.

Darya smiled slightly at the young man. "It's just, everything is relative. And so is happiness. People are only as happy as they allow themselves to be. As Dale Carnegie said, happiness doesn't depend on the environment around us. It depends on the inside."

Vladimir looked at the girl ecstatically. He was glad she wasn't left out of this conversation, and he felt closer to Darya's thoughts than Nadezhda's overly smart arguments.

"I completely agree, Darya," Vladimir said as he came up to the girl and held her hands. "My mom, with whom I like to talk and debate different issues with, once quoted a line from one of Robert Rozhdestvensky's poems, which I remembered by its depth. I will try to recall it, as accurately as I can. "Happiness varies in size, from a tiny dot to Mount Kazbek, depending on the person." Indeed, each person defines happiness in their own way. One can be endlessly happy being with someone they love. Another sees his happiness in great career choices and achievements. Someone else doesn't even think of whether he's happy or not because, according to Bulgakov, happiness is like being healthy; if you have it, you don't notice it."

"This is an interesting discussion," Jane joined in. "I love what I'm hearing. I don't think anyone can give an accurate definition of happiness because it's so subjective. All I know is that it can't stay the same, as both inner and outer environments change for all people. Their goals, their purposes, feelings, views. I'm wondering if Alexei Ukhtomsky was happy."

Everyone stared at Jane with surprise. The sudden turn in their conversation stunned them.

"Why are you looking at me like that? I really want to know. After all, he's been through so much suffering and grief. How did his life end? "

The room went silent. Alena quietly got up from her chair and walked towards the hall where she had left her purse. She pulled out a folder of papers from the purse, and went back into the room.

"I wanted to show you these documents later, after I worked through them. I received them this morning. It's about Alexei and Polina Ukhtomsky."

Alena put the folder on the table, slowly untied its straps, and began to take out sheets of paper, one by one. The sheets had turned yellow; some marked "Top Secret" with huge seals made with blue putty, faded over time. Everyone trembled with anticipation, watching Alena's hasteless hand movements. The room was so quiet they could hear a kitten purring in the neighboring apartment.

"Where are you getting them from, sis?" Vladimir asked Alena worriedly.

"Don't forget, Vladimir, I'm a professional in my field. I've been doing journalistic research for a long time, and I have a great deal of connections everywhere, including the corresponding authorities. And then, there's the decision by the government dated February, 20, 1995, which approved the Regulations concerning declassification and extension of classification of archival documents of the USSR. So, according to this regulation, the documents concerning the Ukhtomsky case was declassified, allowing me to obtain them with the help of my friend with the KGB.

Everyone in the room leaned over the papers. Darya and Jane joined everyone in their impulse, trying to read anything they could make out. Alas, due to their poor knowledge of the Russian language, they couldn't understand a word. They stepped away from the table and sat down on the couch. Darya watched Vladimir. He was standing next to Nadya. Their heads almost touching one another. Darya saw that both of them sensed the physical intimacy of that moment, as they entwined their hands, with light shivers running through their bodies. Vladimir and Nadezhda slightly backed away from the table, looked into each other's eyes and smiled. The two then turned around and leaned over the table, covered with papers once again.

Darya's face flushed from her attempt to suppress tears. She got up and went to the kitchen to quench the thirst that suddenly took her over.

"No, we can't do it like this. I say we organize the papers in chronological order, study them, and figure out the big picture." Alena sounded indignant.

"I agree." Nadezhda added. "There aren't that many papers. We would probably only need around one and a half hours."

"I'm all for it," said Vladimir.

"Darya and I will prepare something to eat. We're not going to understand any of those documents, anyway." Jane got off the couch and walked to the kitchen.

It was decided. Alena organized the papers in chronological order, split them into three stacks and handed two of them to Nadya and Vladimir, keeping one for herself. They spread around the apartment and absorbed into studying the documents.

Two hours later, everybody gathered at the table in the living room, served by Darya and Jane. They swallowed their tea and sandwiches in utter silence. Their faces expressed deep concentration and seriousness.

"I think all of us who got to study the documents by now have an idea of what the last years of the younger Ukhtomsky were like," Alena said. "Let's not waste any time and start telling the story. I go first, then Vladimir, then Nadya."

For Alexei Ukhtomsky, the war ended in 1944. As he left the front line and arrived home, his wife wasn't there. Alexei came down to talk to the neighbor, Varvara, who kept in contact with Polina. Upon seeing the neighbor, Varvara threw her hands up in the air and cried, "Oh dear God, you came back, you're alive. We're grieving! Your Polina was taken. It's been a month since the authorities took her. They came at night, in a black "voronka" and took her away. I put your daughter at the orphanage where I myself work. Don't worry, I looked after her. I will bring her to you tomorrow, if you like."

Alexei stood there, listening to the kind woman, and couldn't comprehend a thing. He still couldn't grasp the meaning of those words.

"Polina knew they would come for her. A woman's heart always senses these things. So she gave me the keys to your apartment. She said that if she wasn't around, I would have the keys to give to you if you came back. And there you are. Here, take it."

Varvara handed Alexei the keys. Ukhtomsky accepted the keys and went to his apartment, prostrate. Carefully removing the sealed strip of tape, he opened the door and went inside. The place was a complete mess. The furniture was upturned, chairs flipped upside down, the contents of desk drawers and dressers scattered on the floor. Ukhtomsky stood in the middle of it all, and anger started to boil down inside him. He cried. His cry sounded inhuman, more like that of a wounded animal. Fifteen minutes passed and he fell to the floor, powerless, and bitter tears came running down to the floor, dirty and covered in papers and clothes. Twenty minutes later, he tried to pull himself together. Alexei washed up. He wasn't hungry. He started cleaning up. Before he went to bed, he decided he would bring his daughter, Nastya, back from the orphanage the next day. And then they will search for Polina together. Thank God, Uglovaty wasn't there. No one to cause more vileness. Feeling relief after making the decision, he fell asleep.

A loud knock on the door woke him up. Barely able to lift his head, Alexei looked at the clock. It was half past 4 a.m. The knocking continued, this time accompanied by a loud voice demanding to open the door. Reeling from fatigue, more mental than physical, Ukhtomsky went to open the door. He saw three men in military uniform carrying guns.

"Citizen Ukhtomsky Alexei Nikolayevich?"

"Yes."

"Get dressed. Come with us," Said the oldest of the three.

Alexei didn't ask any questions. He went back into the bedroom, got dressed and silently walked out.

Been here before.. he thought grimly.

An officer searched his pockets and, finding nothing, commanded, "Come with me."

Downstairs, near the entrance, there was a "voronok" waiting. Pushing Alexei to the middle of the back seat, soldiers took seats on both sides.

"Go!" The officer in the front seat commanded the driver. Ukhtomsky was put in the same department of NKVD and the same office where he had once met Uglovaty.

"Take a seat, Ukhtomsky," Said the Colonel of the KGB who was sitting behind a huge desk. Alexei sat. The Colonel looked at him silently and speculatively for about five minutes. He loved this trick. Few could resist his heavy stare. They would start to get nervous and wiggle around in their chair, and the Colonel was pleased to see fear get hold of them. But Alexei stared back. His eyes were straight and fearless. The Colonel was first to break the eye contact, and that angered him. He got up and went up to the window outside, where vile wind, typical of late fall, was swaying bare tree branches that viciously hit the glass. After about a minute, the Colonel turned around and came up to Alexei. His heavy stare once again met the straight eyes of Ukhtomsky.

"Do you have a brother named Alexander?" the Colonel asked.

Alexei didn't reply right away. He was stunned by this unexpected question.

"Yeah, I had an older brother named Alexander. He left Russia in 1918, and I haven't heard from him since. I don't think he's alive anymore."

"Why do you think that?" the Colonel asked in an insinuating tone.

"Me and my middle brother, Leonid, tried to search for him. But we couldn't find any information about him."

"Didn't look hard enough!" the Colonel's reaction was inappropriately loud. "Your brother is alive, safe and sound, living in the States. We got a letter from him."

Alexei couldn't believe what he was hearing. The information made him happy and afraid at the same time.

"Where's the letter? Can I read it?" he asked worriedly.

"You can, later. Right now, we need to know how you passed on the information about the movement of our first front line Baltic troops to the Germans."

Alexei choked at those words. He looked at the Colonel, trying to make sense of the question.

"Are you out of your mind, Colonel? I am a commander of reconnaissance"

The Colonel interrupted him. "You were, in fact, a commander of reconnaissance. So where's your army now, commander? I'll tell you where. It's in the ground. And you're alive. You're the only one left alive. Why?"

"We ran into an ambush. I was injured, I lost my consciousness. I woke up in the arms of a medic. Field operatives have already addressed this issue. I spent one and a half months in the hospital with a mine shard stuck in my chest," Alexey's voice grew angrier with every word. "Have you ever been to the front lines? How can you, a rear rat, talk about what happened at the front lines?"

Enraged, he wanted to say something else, but a heavy blow to the jaw knocked him out of his chair. He fell to the floor, unconscious.

Alexei woke up in a medical unit, supervised by a doctor standing beside him. His entire body hurt, especially his chest. It was hard to breathe. He saw tiny dark spots flashing in his eyes. Ukhtomsky tried to say something, but there were no words coming out.

"Easy, easy, lie down. You can't get excited right now. The Colonel is about to arrive, I'll report you woke up," he heard the doctor say. "You should drink more liquids." The doctor cradled his head and offered him a glass of water. In ten minutes or so, the Colonel entered the room.

"You're awake? Why'd you turn out to be such a weakling? Alright, we don't kick men when they're down. Once you come back to your senses we'll talk and see what we've got to do with you. Although, we already know the answer." the Colonel said coldly and mockingly, then turned around and walked out.

One week later, Alexei was able to get up and walk. When he was escorted to the same office, he immediately asked the Colonel two questions: "Where is my wife?" and "Where is my brother's letter?"

The Colonel looked at Ukhtomsky carefully with his heavy, fish-like eyes, slowly pulled out a cigarette and, just as slowly, lit it with a match. He was silent. To Alexei, those few minutes of silence felt like eternity.

"So, you want to know where your wife is?" The Colonel answered with a question. "Do you know what they do to traitors in times of war? They shoot them." His voice sounded vicious. "Your wife, Polina Ukhtomsky, was shot as a spy working for the Americans. The same awaits you." Alexei didn't hear his last words.

There was one thought hanging and throbbing in his head: *Polina is gone. I will never see her again.* He felt sick. With a painful buzz in his head, sharp twinge in his chest, his eyes clouded with darkness.

"What, scared?" the Colonel misunderstood Ukhtomsky's reaction. "What did you expect, reading your brother's happy letters from the

States, and then going around telling people about the better life they live in a capitalist country? No, that's not going to happen. You were arrested as an American spy. Yeah, yeah. America is our ally in this war, but nevertheless, our ideological enemy. And everyone connected with it in any way is an accomplice of American imperialism, and thus a traitor to the cause of socialism."

The Colonel then called for backup, and Ukhtomsky, barely able to walk, was taken away. A week later, he was executed in the prison yard without trial or investigation.

"And what about the letter? What did it say?" Darya asked worriedly, tears in her eyes." The letter was included with the Alexey Ukhtomsky case. Here it is. Unfortunately, I didn't manage to read it in time, it's written in such narrow handwriting."

"Let's read it together," Nadezhda suggested, presenting a small sheet of paper turned yellow with time with text written in blue ink. Gently holding the letter, Nadezhda started to read slowly and with deliberation, carefully studying the lines, some of them blurred out.

722 Welmore Ave
Everett 98201
June 5, 1943

Dear Leonid and Alexei,
Forgive me for not making any contact earlier. There are many reasons for that. Having left Russia, we had to travel across Europe for quite a while before we were finally lucky enough to board the ship sailing from Le Havre to the US. We were accepted well. Following verification, we received a place to stay and an allowance until we were able to get a job. After traveling across the state, we finally settled down in West Washington. The weather reminds us of that in St. Petersburg. I got a job as an engineer working for Boeing, Lena is a housewife, Georgy graduated from the University of Washington and received a bachelor's degree in law. He's been married for a while and has a son he named after our father, Nikolai. I'm sending this letter hoping you will receive it happy and healthy. Elena and I often recall our house and our family. We miss you so much. I hope Olga and Lidochka are healthy as well. Alexei, you must be married with children by now. I would really love

to get to know your other half and your kids. I'm sending this letter now, as the relationship between our countries warmed up, and we've come to be allies in this terrifying war of Hitler Germany against everyone else. Oh, and I almost forgot. Our last name is no longer Ukhtomsky, it is now Tomi. We had to change our last names. I must say goodbye. I wish you kindness and health.

Your loving brother,
Alexander

"This is my great-grandfather's letter. I never knew anything about him," Darya said, crying.

Jane hugged her. "Our great-grandfather, Darya. I remember him from the family photo of the Ukhtomsky."

"Darya, I gave my word to your father that I will find out what happened to his great-grandfather's brothers. Now we know everything. What a tragic life" Vladimir's voice was quiet but confident.

"Your parents are coming tomorrow. We have something to tell them."

Chapter 27

The flight from Amsterdam arrived on time. Alex and Melinda were met by an entire "delegation". Darya was very worried. She missed her parents, only realizing that now, as the reunion was so near. Jane was calm, but the idea of her aunt and uncle coming didn't make her happy. She was certain her parents would follow them sooner or later.

Vladimir was looking forward to Darya's parents' visit. He felt good about himself and the fact that he kept his word he had given to Alex before they had left the US. Kostya, who followed Jane everywhere, was also among everyone who came to welcome the visitors. Darya was first to spot Alex and Melinda.

"Mom, Dad! Over here!" she screamed, running towards them.

After everyone met and said hello, they went to the hotel, as insisted by Alex. However, Vladimir invited everyone over that night.

Alexandra awaited her guests with anticipation and nervousness. A sixth sense told her this was no ordinary visit. She made preparations extremely diligently. Alexanda asked her loyal Liubasha to prepare her evening gown, and a modest pendant her husband gave her for her fiftieth birthday anniversary. Together, they set up a dinner menu.

"Most importantly, the menu has to be simple yet sophisticated at the same time," Alexandra told her assistant over and over.

At seven o'clock that evening, the doorbell rang. The first guests to appear were Alena with her husband and kids, and Nadezhda.

"Mom, why are you so pale? Are you not well?" Alena asked sympathetically.

"Oh, everything's fine, my daughter. I'm just worried. I don't feel very calm. Maybe I haven't had guests in a while," Alexandra replied in a slightly nervous tone.

"Maybe. Okay, Mom, what can Nadya and I help with right now?" Alena asked.

"Ask Liubasha. She's both my chef and my evening organizer," Alexandra answered more calmly and even a bit jokingly. About twenty minutes later, the doorbell rang once again. Alena rushed to the door. It was the entire crew of the same people that had come to the airport, as well as Darya's parents.

"Please, come in," Alena invited everyone. "Come on, Vladimir, welcome everyone. Don't just stand there."

Alena rushed back into the room where Alexandra was, lying on plumped up pillows on the couch, all dressed up.

"Mommy, mommy, all guests have arrived!" Alena exclaimed happily, and suddenly stopped. Her mother was staring through her at the doorway. Her eyes darkened from tension, and her face expressed pain. Alena got scared. "Mom, are you feeling well? How is your pressure? Do you want me to call an ambulance?"

Alexandra slowly shifted her eyes onto her daughter.

"No, dear. Everything's fine. It's just because of all the hassle and preparations. Go bring the guests in here, let me say hello. Then you can help me move to the table."

Alena looked at her mother's face one more time. She looked well again, her eyes turning sky blue and her cheeks blushing. As they entered the room, Alex and Melinda saw a woman all dressed up with her hair beautifully done, lying on a couch and looking at them with tension.

"Good evening, Ms. Alexandra," Said Alex. He was looking at Alexandra and the expression on his face gradually went from friendly and smiling to surprised and frightened. Melinda's reaction was momentarily stalled.

"Hello, Ms. Alexandra. We're glad to see you." She slowly came up to the couch and kissed Alexandra's cheek, shaking her hand at the same time.

"Thank you," Alexandra said quietly, shaking Melinda's hand.

Alena, Vladimir, Darya, and Jane didn't notice a thing. They were too busy with the table.

"Alena, please help me," Alexandra worriedly called for her daughter.

Ten minutes later, everyone took their seat at the table. Alex, Melinda, and Alexandra were slightly confused, but didn't give out the fact that they knew each other. Dinner was quite relaxed, and they conversed until late night. Alex and Melinda, tired from their trip, decided to call it. Jane and Vladimir went to walk them. Everyone agreed to meet at Alexandra's again the next day. Vladimir and Nadezhda wanted the Tomi to learn about what they knew of Alex's great-grandfather's brothers and their families.

"Did you recognize Alexandra as the head of the orphanage we adopted Darya from?" Alex asked Melinda nervously as they were going to bed.

"Yes, honey, I did. She recognized us, too. Did you see how tense she was as we entered the room? What do we do? Darya is in love with Vladimir. And I think he loves her back. We have to talk to her," Melinda answered calmly and confidently.

It was amazing how that night, as always, she was able to talk Alex down and make him more certain, giving him faith in tomorrow.

It was a notably clear morning. But Alex and Melinda didn't get enough sleep. There was quite a big time difference. Not to mention, Alex dreamed of Alexandra, that she tried to take his daughter away from him, saying, "She's mine, my daughter. You took her from me. And her name isn't Darya. It's Svetochka. She's Svetochka."

His dream repeated several times that night. Alex tossed and turned, cried out, moaned. Melinda had to calm him down, and even lull him by the time morning came. They felt tired the next day. Alex told his wife about his dream the next morning.

"I wonder, what do you think it means?" he asked Melinda.

Melinda thought for a moment, then smiled and said, "You're like an old lady, trying to read into your dreams. It doesn't mean anything. Let's call our daughter and see her, take a walk in the city. I missed Darya so much."

Darya was ahead of her parents. Before Melinda could get to the phone, it started to ring. They agreed to meet an hour later at the entrance to the hotel. At ten o'clock, the Tomi went downstairs into the hall, where four young people—Darya with Volodya and Jane with Kostya—awaited them.

"Mom, Dad, you look terrible. Maybe we shouldn't go anywhere. You could rest in your room. I bet you didn't get any sleep. There, you have blue circles under your eyes, Mom."

Melinda felt embarrassed; she looked into the mirror in the hall, and answered with a smile, "It's all right, Darya. In order to adjust to the time difference, we have to rest for almost two weeks. According to doctors, it takes twenty four hours to adjust to every hour of the time difference. And we can't do that, right Alex? We didn't come here to sleep and rest, we want to talk and learn."

"Your mother's right." Alex came up to Darya and tenderly embraced her. "So, tell us, what do you have in for us today? Where are you taking us? What are we going to see?"

"I suggested, and everyone agreed, that we should start with the Hermitage, Uncle. I know you were always interested in art and sculptures. Do you remember when you visited us in San Diego, I was probably like ten, and you literally dragged my parents to the Timken Museum of Art? You also said you could admire "St. Bartholomew" by Rembrandt for hours. My Dad was so surprised. He couldn't understand your passion for art. I later decided to go and see "St. Bartholomew" myself. I was very impressed, you know."

Alex smiled, listening to his niece.

"That's right. Alex, Melinda, we want to show you the Hermitage first. Although, if you want to see all of it, giving each exhibit at least a minute of your time, it would take you at least eight years," Vladimir noted, laughing. They decided to visit the Hermitage.

By around six o'clock in the afternoon, they were at the bar cafe on the first floor of the museum. Each ordered a cappuccino and a "kartoshka" cake, Vladimir and Kostya's favorite since they were kids. Alex and Melinda's eyes were sparkling. They hadn't had so much fun spending time together in a long time. The atmosphere of the paintings and sculptures was so strong, they absorbed it completely. They kept talking about everything they'd seen.

"Cuis testiculos habes, habeas cardia et cerebellum," Alex said quietly.

"What was that, Dad? What did you say?" Darya asked, unable to understand.

"I was saying, those paintings drew my attention so much, they took over my heart and my soul. Thank you, guys. It was my dream to visit the Hermitage, see its paintings and sculptures with my own eyes. Yes, Mindy?"

Melinda was sitting next to her husband, her eyes filled with tears.

"Mom, why are you crying?" her daughter asked, worried.

"Everything's alright, my dear. These are tears of joy. I missed you very much. I'm truly happy right now." Melinda hugged her arms around Darya and kissed her.

Vladimir, smiling and watching these people that had become so dear to him, quietly said, "Please, forgive me, but we must leave. Remember that get-together were supposed to have at my place?"

Alex's eyes, expressing happiness and excitement this whole time, suddenly looked worried and frightened. Even the color of his eyes changed, becoming dull and grey.

Until late at night, Vladimir first, and then Nadezhda, were telling Alex and Melinda about the fate of Leonid and Alexei Ukhtomsky, showing documents, photographs that came with the cases, started against them by NKVD. Alex and Melinda were speechless the entire time. Their eyes were fixed upon the table, and they didn't look at anyone. When the clock mounted to the wall struck twelve o'clock, Melinda slowly looked up. Pain apparent in her eyes, she glanced at everyone sitting at the table and spoke in a quiet voice, faltering slightly.

"We have to rest. Let's continue tomorrow. Alex and I.." She looked at her husband, who hadn't yet lifted his stare off the table. Alex felt embarrassed by the tears filling his eyes. "It's very hard. Darya, Vladimir, please take us back to the hotel."

Melinda got up and walked towards the door. Alex followed his wife without saying a word. The entire ride back to the hotel was in complete silence. Alex, overwhelmed by what he had learned, couldn't utter a word. It was as if he would lose that connection with the Ukhtomsky princes if he spoke, the bond that he felt he established. Melinda was silent because Alex was. Having lived side by side with him for the past thirty years, knew what was going on inside of him. Darya, knowing his father well, didn't talk for the same reason. Vladimir found it uncomfortable to break Darya's parents' silence due to his deep respect for them.

Tired emotionally more so than physically, the Tomi couple couldn't fall asleep. They were lying awake with their eyes open, rehashing in their heads all they had learned about the Ukhtomsky that day.

"I wonder if there's a descendant of Leonid and Alexei Ukhtomsky out there, somewhere?" Melinda asked quietly, looking at her husband. Alex turned his head towards his wife.

"Yeah, yeah. You're right. We have to find that out tomorrow. If they're alive, we have to meet them." Alex's voice suddenly grew strong again, and his eyes regained that sky-blue color.

He got up in his bed and leaned against the headboard, becoming taller. The thought of possibly meeting the descendants of his family living here, in Russia, gave him strength.

"Mindy, you're so amazing. Now, let's go to sleep, honey."

Half an hour later, the two were calmly breathing, submerged into deep sleep.

Alexandra was unable to regain peace for several days. She saw the people that fate had brought her together with twenty years ago, whom she wanted to keep in contact with more than with anyone else, but couldn't due to their decision. After the Tomi had taken her Svetochka with them twenty years ago, forbidding all contact with her of any kind, Alexandra fell sick for a long time. She didn't know that they changed the girl's name, calling her Darya. In her thoughts, she always addressed her as Svetochka, and later Svetlanka. As time went by she accepted her loss, but the pain never went away.

When Vladimir introduced Darya to Alexandra, she felt something dear, something close about the girl. But her conscious didn't catch that feeling. Alexandra treated Darya as her son's girlfriend, although she wasn't happy about their relationship. Mainly because Darya was an American.

Sooner or later, all secrets are revealed, Alexandra thought as the guests left. *I can't allow their connection to deepen, it must not happen.*

As soon as her son returned, she called for him.

"Mom, you're still up?" Vladimir asked, surprised. "It's almost two a.m. Is something bothering you?"

"Sit down, Volodyushka. I have to talk to you."

"Can we talk tomorrow, Mom? I'm tired. I want to go to sleep."

"No, my son, we have to talk now. Not tomorrow." Alexandra's voice was trembling from anxiety.

"Alright, Mom. Let's talk. Just don't worry, you can't worry, you know that!" her son replied fast as he saw Alexandra shaking from uneasiness.

She looked at her son for a while, stroking his hair, then held his hands and in a heartfelt was spoke the words she'd been preparing all day.

"My son, I love you very much, and I respect your choices, whatever they are, but right now I'm not asking, but demanding that you change your attitude towards Darya. She cannot be your girlfriend, and cannot ever be your wife."

Upon uttering those words, Alexandra took a deep breath and looked straight into Vladimir's eyes. Vladimir looked at his mother, confused. She, his mother, whom he always told everything, shared everything with, who, as he thought, understood him better than anyone else, was asking the impossible of him.

"But why, Mom, why would you say that? I don't want to hear you, I can't hear you. You never told me anything..." Vladimir looked at Alexandra questioningly.

She didn't reply. He then turned around abruptly and left his mother's bedroom.

Neither Alexandra nor Vladimir could sleep that night. Vladimir stood by his window until three in the morning, watching fuzzy snowflakes land on tree branches, the sidewalk, the road, covering them with a soft white blanket, which, in the morning, would turn dirty from people walking and cars driving over it. Somewhat calmed down by the view, he lay down in his bed, thinking he'd better get some sleep. A new day will come and everything will fall into place. Alexandra, on the other hand, was lying in her bed, eyes closed, with pictures of the past flashing in front of her over and over, which she decided to share with everyone, and first of all with the Tomi couple, Darya, and Vladimir.

Chapter 28

"Mindy, honey, wake up." Alex tenderly kissed his wife, ruffling her short but gorgeous hair.

"What happened, honey?" Melinda asked, frightened, immediately upon opening her eyes.

Alex laughed. "Nothing happened, except that a new day started quite a while ago."

"What time is it, then?"

"It's almost nine, my sun."

Melinda smiled, feeling shyness from her husband's sudden affection.

"As Socrates said, there's a sun in every one of us, we just have help it shine," Melinda said softly, holding her husband. "You, my sweetheart, let me shine throughout our entire life together, for which I am endlessly grateful to you."

"And I am grateful to you and to God for bringing us together, and making us one." Alex said quietly, holding his wife tightly and kissing her.

At half past ten, they left their room, smiling and hugging each other.

"You're late, parents. We were waiting for you for like half an hour," Darya began to complain, but suddenly stopped. "Mom, Dad, what is it with you? You're all shining and look twenty years younger."

"Twenty? Yeah, right!" Melinda objected, squeezing Alex's hand, which didn't escape the young people's attention. Alex gently wrapped his arms around his wife, kissing her temple, and asked, "So, where are we going today, kids?"

"We could go see the suburbs, Pavlovsk or Peterhof," Kostya suggested.

"No, no, there's nothing to do there in the wintertime," Vladimir joined the conversation. "We'll show it to you during spring or summer. Alex, Melinda, I hope you can visit us more often from now on?"

He looked at Darya's parents questioningly. Alex didn't reply. The question caught him off guard.

"Yes, yes, I think we do have a few reasons to come more often." Melinda saved him.

"That's why I suggest we visit St. Isaac's Cathedral today," Vladimir continued. "First, it is probably the most brilliant example of Russian church architecture. Second, it is the fourth largest dome structure in the world, following St. Peter's Basilica in Rome, St. Paul's in London and St. Mary's in Florence. Third, we can go up to the colonnade of the Cathedral, and at the height of almost forty meters, overlook the entire city. So, how do you like my plan?"

St. Isaac's Cathedral made an indelible impression on everyone. Alex, who was very keen on history, tried to attentively study every sculpture and group of sculptures in all four facades of the Cathedral, including niches and doors. Every now and then, he would let out a long sigh of admiration. At around four in the afternoon, they left the Cathedral.

"I'm hungry, I'm thirsty!" Jane whined capriciously.

Everyone looked at her with slight reproach, unable to grasp how one could possibly crave anything of material nature after visiting St. Isaac's Cathedral. Nevertheless, they agreed to look for an "eating and drinking" place somewhere nearby.

"There's a business center not too far from here. It's called "Galley Yard." They have a great restaurant there. They serve good coffee, muffins, cakes, and pretty decent meals as well," Kostya suggested eagerly. Everyone enthusiastically followed him.

"I will also say that "Galley Yard" is located inside a building built in 1861, although, since the recent renovation, the spirit of the past is somewhat gone. Still, it's a very interesting place. I think you, Alex, would be very curious to see it." Kostya kept walking and talking fast.

The restaurant really did turn out to be cozy. They ordered coffee—black, cappuccino, latte, as well as marzipan buns. On top of that, the kids ordered two pizzas, the traditional "Margarita" and "Four Cheeses", and split a piece for everyone. The restaurant was playing quiet, "faceless" music that didn't interfere with conversation.

"I like how they're restoring cathedrals and churches destroyed during the soviet times," Alex said, starting a new topic. "This is the evidence of spirituality being reborn in this country."

"Russian people have always been spiritual," Kostya objected.

Alex looked at him, smiling, and suggested, "You're mixing up spirituality and soulfulness, young man. They're not nearly the same."

Kostya looked at Alex in surprise. "What do you mean? Is there really a difference between spirituality and soulfulness? I always considered those definitions to be quite closely related."

"You're wrong, Kostya," Vladimir chimed in. "Those definitions come from different words. You see, soulfulness comes from the word "soul", and spirituality comes from "spirit". If we try to pick it apart further, "spirit" literally means "Cherub's kindness", in other words, it's "kindness that comes from the highest angelic rank, Cherub."

"True, Volodya," Alex picked up. "It means that spirituality is a category of a higher order than soulfulness. Because "spirit" is a part of you that is related to God. And "soul" is a non-materialistic component of your personality, its inner world."

"I completely agree with you, honey." Melinda joined the conversation, smiling. "Soul determines a person's inner world, their social behavior, influences their view of the world. That is why, I believe, soulfulness can be defined as empathy, kindness, willingness to help others, love, honesty."

"Would a spiritual person necessarily be soulful, too?" Darya asked everybody. For a moment, everyone went silent.

"That's an interesting question, daughter." Alex looked at Darya, amazed and impressed. He liked having this discussion, and he liked the fact that no one remained indifferent to the topic of such an important and high moral value.

"The way I see it, a spiritual person is not necessarily soulful." Jane's voice was slightly thoughtful and hasteless. "But a soulful person has got to always be spiritual."

"Not necessarily so," Vladimir said. "It depends on the degree of spirituality and the degree of soulfulness."

"Sounds quite complicated, my friend. Please, clarify," Kostya mockingly asked him.

Vladimir was quiet for a while, as if he was trying to remember something, or gather his thoughts. Everyone looked at him, intrigued.

"Satan, too, was spiritual, but we can hardly call him soulful. If a man, while trying to be spiritual, begins to lose his soulfully human nature, he is no longer a man of God. He is now closer to Satan. Russian writers wrote about this quite well. For example, Vladimir Sergeyevich Solovyov and his "Tale of the Antichrist". It's very interesting, I recommend you read it. And how about "Demon" by Lermontov?"

"I agree with Vladimir!" Alex said excitedly. Let's say that, according to the Bible, God granted Adam soul, and only then did the first man become a living soul. With that, initially, a man's soul is his personality, it's intelligent and free, has power and will. And it's the soul that creates spirit. Spirituality is something that is developed by a man throughout his entire life. Unfortunately, people often waste the energy of their soul on the wrong things. They don't use it for the good, or for love, but for cruelty, greed, malignancy. As a result, their soul becomes smaller, and their spirit grows bitter. We don't say people like that have a wicked soul, we say they have an evil spirit."

"How about monks?" Darya asked thoughtfully. "They are, in fact, people of high spirit. Their spirit reigns over their soul. Being extremely spiritual, they're very soulful people as well."

"This is one of the examples of soulfulness and spirituality living together in harmony, daughter, with the spirituality prevailing. In the cases Vladimir and dad talked about, the soul itself fully subdued and was absorbed into the evil spirit it created."

"This is, of course, a very interesting debate, my friends, but we've got to go. We have a lot to do today, don't you agree?" Vladimir spoke to everyone. They nodded.

At exactly seven o'clock, everyone once again gathered at Alexandra's apartment. The hostess had been mentally preparing for the visit. She knew she would have to reveal a lot. And her story could very well be unpleasant to some of the listeners. As the company consisting of Vladimir, Darya, Jane, Alex, Melinda and Nadezhda took their seats around the big dining table served with tea; they all looked to their hostess.

Alexandra slowly looked at everyone with worry and sadness in her eyes, pausing as she met the gazes of Melinda and Alex. Silently asking their permission, she received a slight nod from Alex.

"Today, I want to tell you about my friend, about Anastasia."

"But Mom, we already know Anastasia was Sofia's daughter and was raised by Alexei and Polina Ukhtomsky," Her son interrupted her.

"I'm already having a hard time talking about this, son, please don't interrupt. It's not nice. It's disrespectful to me."

"Forgive me, Mom," Vladimir said quietly, confused.

Patting her son's hand as he was sitting next to her, she started, "Today, I will tell you about Anastasia's personal life, about how she lived here until she died.

"We were friends, and more than just friends." Tears appeared in her eyes. Wiping them off with a handkerchief, the hostess told about Anastasia's last love, her pregnancy, childbearing, and death. About how she took in Svetochka, her friend's daughter, and they had to put her in an orphanage where Alexandra worked.

.Alexandra did not look at anyone during her story. Her eyes were fixed on the wall across the room from the couch. It seemed like, just for her, the wall played pictures of her friend's past she had been such a large part of. When she began to talk about the couple from the US visiting the orphanage, Alex and Melinda both suddenly got up to everyone's surprise.

"Perhaps you should rest, Alexandra," Alex spoke.

She looked at him for a while, and then closed her eyes for about thirty seconds and, opening them once again, said, "No. I must tell all of it. The children must know. This is in your interest, as well. I know your life has been full of perpetual worries for the past twenty years." Alexandra spoke every word extremely clearly.

The Tomi couple stood a little while longer before taking to their seats.

"Alright, Alexandra. Continue," Melinda whispered, holding her husband's hand.

"No, it can't be!" Darya screamed with tears in her eyes when Alexandra finished her story. "Mom, Dad, you're my real parents! It's true!"

"Yes, daughter, you are our dearest, favorite, most beloved girl," Melinda said reassuringly. "It doesn't matter who gave birth to you, it only matters who raised you, who stood by your bed when you were sick, who helped you make your first steps on this earth, who was and is always there." Melinda was hugging her Darya and kissing her eyes and cheeks, wet from tears.

"This means that I'm Anastasia's daughter, and an Ukhtomsky by blood, a real Ukhtomsky," Darya roused.

Alex came up to his daughter, put his hands around her head and held her tight.

"I always felt like you were a God's gift to us, Darya. Even then, twenty years ago, when Mom and I saw you lying there in your tiny bed, smiling, we knew you were ours, our dear girl. *Our* daughter."

Alex unwillingly shed tears that slowly ran down his cheeks. He didn't try to wipe them away. The three stood, holding each other close, as if they were one.

"So, it turned out I'd cradled my future bride in a crib!" Vladimir said, amazed in his surprise. "I felt an invisible connection between us the moment we met. I remember that day, when Michael introduced us. I thought to myself that I felt like I'd seen that button nose, those bright blue eyes somewhere. I have no words. I don't know what to say. "

Vladimir came up to Darya and hugged her tenderly. He then turned to Alex and Melinda confidently, and shook their hands in gratitude. Nadezhda was sitting aside, nervous. She felt that Vladimir distanced himself from her once again. She slowly, grudgingly got up from her chair, walked up to Vladimir who stood next to Darya. "So you're now a bride and a groom? Congratulations." She then walked towards the door just as slowly. Somewhere, deep inside, she heard a quiet voice whisper, *Not all is lost. He will be yours. Don't rush it.*

Nadezhda turned around to see Vladimir one more time, and her eyes suddenly stopped on Alexandra.

Alexandra was lying on plumped up pillows with her eyes closed, but her face expressing suffering. The corners of her mouth crawled down, her eyelids twitched, and her hands were fumbling with a handkerchief she never parted with. It was an old but perfectly clean handkerchief that used to belong to her husband. She suddenly turned pale. Opening her eyes, frozen in sadness, she commanded, "This can't happen! It cannot!"

"What can't happen, Mom?" Vladimir asked, surprised.

"You will not marry Darya. She can't be your wife." Alexandra was almost screaming.

"But, why? For what reason? You don't like her? Isn't she your beloved and lost Svetochka, who you've been crying over this whole time? You don't want us to be happy?"

Alexandra looked at her son, then Darya, with her eyes burning. Tears suddenly ran down her face, but the woman didn't wipe them off. She began talking fast, grabbing both their hands. She then fell back onto the pillows, exhausted, shutting her eyes.

"My mom has to rest. She's tired." Alexandra heard her son's worried voice.

She opened her eyes. "No, my son, don't leave. I'm alright. Let me just rest for a bit. My guests can have some tea, meanwhile. Nadya, heat it up. It's all cold." The woman spoke in a tired voice.

Alexandra was lying on her couch watching her guests. She had a weird feeling. On one hand, the woman was happy. The weight of the secret she had had to keep for all those years had finally been lifted off her shoulders, and Svetochka, who was now Darya, was there, near. She looked so much like her mother. Her eyes, nose, smile. Alexandra unwillingly smiled looking at Darya. But her son just had to fall in love with her, meeting her miles and miles away in the United States. On the other hand, Alexandra felt worried. She was anxious about what she had yet to tell. Seeing Vladimir look at Darya with such love and tenderness, she was afraid her son wouldn't understand her, and would distance himself from her.

About forty minutes later, after everyone had tea with sweets, cookies and the cake "Fairytale" Nadezhda had brought with her, Alexandra asked everyone to gather around her and listen to another story about the Ukhtomsky family.

Chapter 29

"I had a brother, his name was Yevgeny," Alexandra began.

"Wait, Mom, why don't I know anything about my uncle?" Vladimir asked her, stunned.

"You're interrupting me again, son," Alexandra told him reproachfully.

She began to talk slowly and with deliberation once again.

"Yevgeny died a long time ago, before Volodya was born. Yevgeny worked as a second secretary of the Kalinin district committee of the party. Unfortunately, my brother was a narcissist by nature. He only loved himself and his own desires. The way he viewed people was based on their usefulness to him. That's why he didn't really have any friends. When it came to women, however, he was very favorable, and would chase every skirt. As a rule, he expressed his affection to single women, so he wouldn't get in trouble. Poor things thought they'd finally found a dream man capable of protecting them from their troubles, and gave themselves to him completely, physically and mentally. My brother ruined many lives. The ones he dumped were cursing him. That's probably why he got so sick and died early.

"During the last two years, he had a secretary named Anna Tomina, who was about forty years old. She was calm and quite educated, not a beauty. However, the men that stopped by my brother's office always noticed her. They had mixed feelings about her. They didn't see a female, they saw a woman with a capital "W", the kind of woman they bow to, write poetry about, and admire. Despite all that, Anna was lonely. No one knew anything about her private life. She was always dressed fashionably, but professionally. She braided her blonde hair into two braids, and miraculously put them together in a hairdo. She wore little makeup, only black mascara on her lashes and light pink lipstick. When I saw her for the first time, her noble manners amazed me. Anna spoke beautiful literary Russian with no slang. I liked her a lot. I thought Zhenya should marry a girl like that. And he still keeps messing around. It" was time to settle down.

"One time, in May, Zhenya called me. It was a Sunday afternoon. My husband and I, Valera, were cleaning the windows. It was warm. I remember we kept laughing and joking around, and Alena and Tanyushka brought us buckets of water and crumbled newspapers. We could barely hear the phone ring, thankfully, Alena was close to it. I couldn't recognize my brother's voice. Always so confident, clear and willful, his voice suddenly turned hoarse, colorless, and sounded anguished. That's when I found out Zhenya had a disease everyone in the world is afraid of. He was diagnosed with throat cancer, inoperable stage.

"My brother could barely make out his words, "Sashenka, I lived as I pleased. I did a lot of bad things, but a lot of good things, too. Forgive the sinner." And then I heard short beeps.

"I rushed to his house, but it was too late. He decided he didn't want to be a burden to anyone, so he shot himself in the head. There were a lot of people at his funeral. When most were gone, and I was leaving, I saw Anna, dressed in a black suit and wearing a hat with a veil, come up to the grave, place a big bouquet of red roses on it, and quietly begin to cry. At first I wanted to come up and talk to her, cheer her up. But something stopped me. I decided I would call her in a week. But I wasn't able to do that. She quit her job and moved out of the apartment she rented. It was like she disappeared.

"And by the end of February, Anna suddenly calls and asks permission to visit. I set the table, as our Russian tradition dictates, and sit down, waiting for her. At around nine, the doorbell rang. It was Anna. My God, did she change. She was pregnant and on her ninth month. But that wasn't it. Her face... Her face was covered in tiny wrinkles. Her bright blue eyes still shined through, but they expressed exhaustion and indifference. She was, as always, dressed nicely, wearing a beautiful, wide black and white checkered coat and a white knitted hat, barely holding up her gorgeous hair, which was tucked away in a very unsophisticated way. She was wearing black leather boots, holding a big purse with paper folders sticking out.

""Excuse me, Alexandra Petrovna. May I come in?" She asked quietly. She took off her coat, walked into this very room, and sat on the closest chair by the table. Anna still looked good. Pregnancy hadn't ruined her figure, but there was something inside her that was broken. I could feel it, that she was unhappy. Anna refused to eat, saying it was due to morning sickness, and only asked for a glass of water, which she drank in one go.

"Alexandra Petrovna, I'm carrying your brother's baby in my belly. We loved each other, though we tried to hide our love. It is frowned upon to have a relationship with your secretary. Zhenya wanted a son. But he died before he even learned I was pregnant. The baby is due very soon. But I'm afraid I won't make it. I have bad kidneys. The doctors demanded I get an abortion, but I decided to keep our baby in the memory of Zhenya. Please, if something happens to me, take care of the boy. I know it's going to be a boy.

"She then handed me two folders of papers, saying, "These folders contain information about my parents. You can study it. It's not a mystery anymore. Especially since you will be the boy's aunt. He has to know who his mother was. I beg you, if I don't make it, please tell my son about his father and me." Anna slowly got up and walked towards the door.

Alexandra went quiet and closed her eyes. The room was completely silent. Volodya was first to break the silence.

"Who's Anna, Mom? Why are you telling us about your brother and her?" Vladimir's voice was giving in, trembling.

Alexandra opened her eyes, took her son's left hand and softly said, "When the right time comes, Volodya. May I continue?"

Everybody nodded their heads yes.

"When Anna left, I began to study the documents she gave me. I spent several weeks trying to put all the pieces together and get a clear picture of what her and her parents" lives were like.

After Leonidas death, Olga was sick for a while. Losing the only man she loved deeply and devotedly made her very fragile. She gradually began to lose interest in life. Lida, their daughter, continued to work at a school, teaching Russian language and literature. Once, she was invited to an evening dedicated to the work of Ernest Hemingway. Lidya, who naturally wasn't outgoing, was very nervous while getting ready for the evening. For a while, she couldn't decide what to wear: A light and flirty dress her mother recently gave her, hoping her daughter would someday go on a date, or a strict business suit she was so used to. She decided on a navy blue suit which she completed with an artificial pearl necklace. Having said a prayer in her head, Lidya entered the building that held the gathering.

There were a lot of people. There was only ten minutes left until the start. The girl stood aside from a group of young men enthusiastically discussing something. She tried to make out what they were saying, and realized it was in English. Curious, Lidya subconsciously approached the company. Knowing three languages since she was a child—French, German and English, taught to her by her parents—Lida understood that they were talking about one of the latest novels by Hemingway, "To Have and Have Not". Normally following all the latest literary publications, not only had she not read the novel, she'd never even heard of it. Intrigued, Lidya stood next to a tall blonde man wearing a beautiful worsted suit of blue steel color with a matching blue shirt and blue tie showing underneath. The girl accidentally touched his hand, which was followed by the young man's immediate reaction.

"Excuse me, miss. What can I do to help?"

His grayish eyes were looking at Lidya with curiosity. She was caught off guard, felt her face turn red, and said in a trembling voice, "Thank you, I'm fine. Sorry to stop you from listening to the discussion."

The young man expressed surprise.

"Are you American? I've never seen you before."

Lida blushed again and explained to the young man who she was, and what she was doing there.

They met. David Stewart, for so his name was, worked at the Institute Leonid once worked at, as well. David came with a group of American specialists sent from a bureau of Cannes. He was stunned to learn that Lidia's last name was Ukhtomsky. David remembered Leonid, who'd visited their bureau. He had just started working at the time, having graduated a university. David was lucky, as there weren't that many specialists in his field, so he was the center of all communications with the delegation from the Soviet Russia. David immediately singled Leonid out of the entire crew. He felt like the man was very morally decent. David told Lidya all about that, and she listened to him with tears in her eyes. She immediately invited David over without any hesitation.

"My mom will be so happy to see you! Ever since my father's death, she hasn't been well."

Hesitant for a little while, David accepted the girl's invitation, especially because he liked her a lot.

David's appearance really did make Olga happy. The young man became a frequent guest of the Ukhtomsky family. Each time he came over, Olga asked him to, once again, tell the story of how he and Leonid had met. She would set the table for him and serve all kinds of food and drinks. Normally, the young man had nothing but tea with sweets and cookies. Olga would sit across him, her hands resting on the table, and ask, "Please, David, tell me about the time you met my husband."

That was followed by a long story. Olga would listen to the guest attentively, sometimes shutting her eyes for a while, picturing the events of the story. She then went into her bedroom and closed the door. She would return about ten minutes later with a photo portrait of Leonid. She put it on the table. "Here, dear Leonid, were having David over. You know him."

Quiet tears ran down her cheeks, but she didn't notice it, and continued to talk to the portrait.

A month after he had met Lidya, David proposed. His business trip was coming to an end, and he soon had to return to the States. David could no longer imagine his life without Lidya. He dreamed of coming home together with the girl he loved.

On a Sunday night of September, 1940, a small group gathered in Leonid Ukhtomsky's apartment. Other than David, Lidya, and Olga, there were also two of David's friends from America who worked with him, as well as their girlfriends they met in Russia. They were celebrating the engagement of the two. It was extremely fun and interesting. They told lots of jokes, made plans for the future, and dreamed of the new life over in the far land of America with their other halves.

Olga was sitting at the table and contemplating her daughter, feeling happy for her. Then she quietly went into her room. Olga sat on the bed, took her husband's photo in her hands and began her nightly conversation with him.

"So, dear Leonid, our daughter will soon fly away to a land far, far away. She found a man from over the ocean and fell in love with him. God bless, I hope it works out for them, so her life can be peaceful and full of happiness. Who is he, you ask?" Olga gently stroked the photo. "You know him. He's a good young man. He deserves our daughter. Everything will work out for them. It has to."

She kissed the photo tenderly and clutched it to her chest. "I'm feeling tired, honey. I'd like to rest." Olga lay down on the bed, still holding her husband's picture, closed her eyes and fell asleep.

By twelve, everyone was gone. David also wanted to leave, but Lida stopped him.

"Stay, David. Please..."

Her burning eyes were looking straight at him.

"But what about your mom?" David asked quietly, holding her in his arms.

"She's asleep. I just checked."

David nodded silently. "Alright, my dear, I'll stay. Soon, were going to be husband and wife, anyway." Holding each other tightly, they went to Lidia's room. In the morning, when the sun was still beginning its daily journey, David and Lida were standing by the window, embracing each other. Her head was resting on his shoulder.

"I would stay this way forever with you, my love", the girl whispered, "I'm so happy right now. I couldn't even imagine it could ever be this good! Thank you, and thank God I've met you."

The young man didn't reply, only hugged her even tighter and passionately kissed her lips. They stood there for twenty more minutes or so, adoring the early sunrise.

"I have to go, honey," David said quietly and gently. "It would be awkward if your mom saw me here at this hour. I will go... I'll see you tonight."

Before leaving, David held her close, wrapped her hands around her head, and looked into her bright blue eyes for a while. He then gave her a long kiss, first tender, and then wildly passionate.

"Alright, sweetheart, I will go," David said decidedly. He turned around and walked down the stairs.

Lida stood by the door for a while, listening to his steps, then went back inside and quietly closed the door. She had yet to learn that their first night of love would be their last.

After David was gone, Lida still stood in the hall for a while. She didn't have the strength to go back into the room where they had spent the night together. Without David, her favorite room now felt empty and cold. Lida went to the kitchen to fix breakfast. It was ready by seven. Any other time, she would be done in fifteen minutes. But now, every move she made was slow and hindered, so it took her about an hour. Lida was making breakfast completely thoughtlessly. Her mind was somewhere else. She was thinking of him.

"Oh, daughter, you already made breakfast! Good morning, my girl." Lida heard Olga's voice as the woman came into the kitchen.

"Good morning, Mommy. You look great!" Lidya replied, walking up to her mother and hugging her.

"Yes, Lida, I slept very well. I haven't slept that deeply in a long time. So, where's David? I thought he was going to sleep over."

Lida blushed and didn't reply for a while, thinking whether she should tell her mother that David had stayed over. She then decided it was better to be honest.

"Nothing gets past you, Mom." Lida answered with a half-smile on her face. "Yes, he spent the night."

"But where did he sleep, Lida? And why did he leave so early, even before breakfast?" Olga asked in a strict voice.

Her daughter felt nervous. Because of her deep love for her mother, Lida was also afraid of her. She had a warmer relationship with her father. But Olga raised her daughter with discipline, the way her mother had once raised her. After some hesitation, Lida admitted, after all, that David and she had spent the night together.

"We love each other, Mom. You know that. And soon we will be husband and wife. And I don't see anything bad about what we... What we..."

The girls voice was trembling, her face covered with red blotches, and her eyes were filled with tears. Olga came closer to her daughter, hugged her and whispered into her ear, "Thank God you have found love, my daughter. I'm happy for you, and I give you my blessing. I think dad would support me right now."

Lida grew wings when she was going to work. She only had three classes that day. She was getting ready to be off by twelve, then window shop for wedding dress fabric, and then to see David. After teaching her last class, the girl went into the teacher's room to put back a class journal. The teacher's office was empty. Putting the journal back in its place, the girl was about to leave when she heard a powerful male voice.

"Are you Lidya Leonidovna Ukhtomsky?" A man asked, appearing from the principal's office.

The girl turned to him.

"Yes, that is me. And who are you? Whose parent are you?"

The man scoffed, then came up to Lidya and pointed at a chair, telling her to sit down.

"A parent? Nah, sweetheart, I came here for you. I've got to talk to you. And then, we'll see," The man said with sarcasm.

The girl sat down, putting her bag with students" notebooks sticking out on another chair, and looked at the man who was watching her every move. He handed her an identification card, which stated that he worked for NKVD. A cold chill ran through Lidia's back. Her knees gave in, shaking. She forced herself to calm down and looked straight into the man's eyes.

"I'm listening." She spoke clearly in an unfamiliar voice.

"No, I'm about to listen to you," The man replied harshly.

Then there came a lot of questions. It seemed like the authorities knew about every day she spent with David. She turned red after the question, "So, how were you in an imperialist's bed? Any good?"

It made Lidya flip out. She got up, moved closer towards the man, and shouted in his face. "How dare you! What kind of people are you? No, you're not even people. You don't even fear God. The devil, yes, the devil is who you serve." She began to shake, and sat back on the chair, powerless.

"You believe in God, scum! Comparing us to the devil! You're a lowlife that messed with an imperialist, our enemy!" The man grabbed her hand and hissed into her ear, "Get up, vermin. You're coming with me. You will rot in the dungeon until your lover gets sent back home."

Lida backed away from the man, her eyes sparkling with hate.

"What? What did you say?" Her voice was trembling.

"Get up. let's go, you American whore!" The man said wrathfully.

Olga was waiting for Lida for dinner. As an old custom goes, she set the table with a white, crispy fresh cloth, and put down two large plates with a knife and a spoon near each. She stood around for a while before adding a third plate and silverware.

Lida will probably come with David, Olga thought. She brought a bread box from the kitchen, covered up with a white embroidered towel.

"I will serve the hot dishes as they arrive, otherwise they will get cold." Olga sat down in a comfortable armchair in the living room, previously grabbing a tome by Chekhov.

Olga loved to read his books, especially the stories, so short but so spot on in their mocking of the flaws of Russian reality. The tome contained the less popular stories by Anton Pavlovich. She opened the book and read the title "American Way". Olga had read that story about three times. It was so interesting that she was going to read it again. It was about a man who wanted to marry, and posted an ad describing himself and the qualities his potential wife would have to possess. When she reached the words "...she must be able to sing, dance, read, write, boil, fry, pamper, bake, borrow money for her husband, dress with taste and on her own money, and be fully obedient. She can't be able to buzz, hiss, squeak, scream, bite, roar, break dishes, or give flirty looks to our friends....." Olga laughed loudly and contagiously. "Good job, Anton Pavlovich! I love Chekhov!" she declared out loud, still laughing, and then looked at the clock.

I was already around ten p.m. She came up to the window, thinking that Lida and David might be standing by the entrance. The street was empty. There was only a neighbor from an apartment across who went out to walk her poodle. The poodle was running around on the sidewalk, happy to finally get a chance to move. The sky was shadowed with clouds, and it was already dark outside. The street was lit mainly by the light coming from the apartment building windows. The bulb inside the street light across the building was broken.

"I'm starting to feel sad. Where is Lida? Is she really still out in the city with David?" Olga thought.

Suddenly, the doorbell rang.

"Finally!" Olga lightened up and rushed to open the door.

She saw Irina, a girlfriend of one of the David's friends, who had recently come over.

"Hello, Olga Vladimirovna. May I come in? I have to talk to you."

Olga looked at the uninvited guest, nodded her head towards the hall and invited her to sit on the couch by the wall.

"I'm listening, Irina," Olga said in a voice that expressed concern.

Irina sat down on the couch, unable to find a comfortable spot for a while, getting up and sitting back down, sliding all the way back, and then moving to the edge of the seat. Finally, having found the right position, the girl looked at Olga, who was carefully watching her.

"Olga Vladimirovna, your Lida won't come home today," Irina said in a trembling voice.

The girl was moving around in her seat, trying to find a tactful way to break the horrendous news concerning the woman's daughter. Finally, she gathered her thoughts and uttered, "Lida has been arrested. I saw her leave with a man from NKVD. It was around one o'clock in the afternoon. My brother works for the authorities. He warned me, told me to leave Roddy, my Roddy. You know him. He's a friend of David's. All foreigners are being monitored at all times. So are those who know them. David was deported today. Thank God he got off easy. Lida was arrested for her relationship with him. My brother says it's unlikely they let her go..."

Irina was still talking, but Olga could no longer hear her. Her eyes got clouded and she lost consciousness.

Lida found out about her mom's death of a heart attack from a note passed on to her by the prison guard who brought food to her cell.

"Lida, Please accept our deepest condolences. You mother, Olga Vladimirovna, passed away at the hospital when they were unable to bring her back to consciousness on October 1st, 1940.

"I and K."

The handwriting was unfamiliar and crooked. It looked like it was written by a man. The first thing that came into Irina's head was to knock on the cell's door to find out who the author of the note was. She then realized she couldn't do that, as it would endanger several people that cared about her.

She didn't comprehend the meaning of the note right away. She began to read it over and over.

"Mom, Mommy!!! How..." Something was throbbing in her head. Her mind didn't want to believe the words on the paper. Suddenly, she felt weakness and tightness in her throat, and saw dots moving in front of her eyes. She could barely get to her bunk.

A week later, she was in a camp located in Arkhangelsk region, in Vorkuta village, Komi Republic of ASSR. She was convicted under the act 58 as an international bourgeoisie agent. No proper investigation took place. Her relationship with an American, David Stewart, was the main argument of prosecution. It turned out to be sufficient enough to sentence her to ten years in one of the most horrendous camps of Gulag.

Like all women in the camp, Lidya worked as a lumberjack. That morning, when she once again grabbed an ax and made several sweeping hits to a tree, a sharp pain in her stomach pierced her. She lost consciousness. She woke up in a hospital. An elderly nurse who was a live-in at the hospital was sitting beside her.

"You're up, sweetheart? Let me call for a doctor."

The doctor came in. She was a large, harsh-looking woman with manly hands. She had a weird name – Doroteya Aristarkhovna.

"Alright, Ukhtomsky, you're pregnant, on your tenth week. What do you want to do?" she asked impersonally.

Lida looked at Doroteya Aristarkhovna, confused.

"That's impossible," She whispered.

"What's impossible? Have you slept with a man? I know you have. You weren't a virgin when you got here. Anything's possible!" The doctor abruptly objected.

But as she looked at the pale and confused Ukhtomsky, the woman held Lida's hand in hers, which were surprisingly soft and warm.

"Don't be afraid. We'll do whatever you want to do. Was it unexpected? It was your first and only time, am I right?"

Lida nodded her head.

"I understand. Well, was it at least with a man you loved, or God knows who?

A weak smile appeared on Lida's face, a barely visible spark of happiness twinkled in her eyes, and she suddenly lightened up, with a fire of love shining through her, the kind of fire that turns any woman into a queen.

"Alright, girl, I'll help you out." Doroteya Aristarkhovna said confidently, seeing the amazing change in Lidya. "You'll stay here for a little while, gather your strength. Then I'll try to transfer you to the kitchen."

The doctor kept her word. Lida stayed at the hospital for another week. During this time, Doroteya Aristarkhovna did all she could to help Ukhtomsky regain her health. She gave her carrot tea, vitamin injections that she kept for herself in her home cabinet in case she wasn't feeling well, and demanded that Lida slept more. She made sure Lida was transferred to work in the kitchen. In order to make that happen, she had to give herself to the head of the camp, which had been lusting after her for a long time.

"It won't kill me, and the girl will be saved," the doctor decided, agreeing to be with the colonel. "At least one way to redeem myself before... Before."

Doroteya Aristarkhovna quietly began to cry. Pictures of the past, dating two years back, appeared in front of her eyes again. Back then, her daughter, Masha, who had just turned eighteen, came to her and happily announced she was pregnant with a baby of a man she loved. This man turned out to be about ten years older than Masha. When he came to ask for Doroteya's blessing, she denied him, threatening to report him for sexual relations with a minor. Doroteya Aristarkhovna grabbed Masha's hand and dragged her to the hospital to get her an abortion. During the procedure, the girl suffered a bleeding that could not be stopped. She passed away two days later from blood loss. Lida somehow reminded her of Masha. Doroteya Aristarkhovna hoped that helping Lida would at least somewhat help her redeem herself before her daughter.

On Lida's due date, she gave birth to a daughter. Doroteya Aristarkhovna was delivering the baby. The girl was born weak. Again, the doctor had to make a deal with the head of the camp so that Ukhtomsky could stay at the hospital with her baby for another week. Lida was endlessly happy. Whenever she looked at her daughter, every little bit of her reminded her of David, her mom, and her father.

"What do you want to name the girl?" Doroteya Aristarkhovna asked her the next day.

"Anya. That was the name of my grandmother, the one mom told me so much about. I decided a long time ago, if I ever had a daughter, I would name Anya."

"That's a beautiful, royal sounding name. God give her happiness," The doctor said.

Chapter 30

A week after childbearing, Lida returned to the barrack. They wouldn't let her take the girl with her. Doroteya Aristarkhovna promised to take care of her. Lida continued to work in the kitchen. Her work included cleaning pots, cooking utensils, mopping floors in the kitchen and the dining room, cleaning the space around the dining room, and also assisting the chef. By the time she returned to the barrack, everyone was already asleep, and she got up while everyone was still sleeping. She was still visiting the hospital for two more weeks, where the doctor looked after her daughter. Lida breastfed her, unable to take her eyes off her tiny pink face, trying to memorize it as much as she could. After feeding the baby, she held her tightly, breathing in that dear and sweet baby smell. She stayed that way until the nurse came to take her daughter. Two weeks later, she was called into the office of the head of the camp.

"Ukhtomsky, enough slacking in the kitchen. You're going back to the logging camp tomorrow."

"But I have to feed my daughter. I won't make it in time. It's too far away." Lida's voice was trembling with concern.

"You won't have to hurry anywhere. Your daughter was put in the orphanage. Go work. Getting way too lazy. Get out! Guard, get her out of here!" By the end of his speech, the colonel was shouting.

Lida rushed to the hospital. She pushed the door wide open, screamed, "Doroteya Aristarhovna, where's Anya, where's my daughter?" and then stopped.

Doroteya Aristarkhovna was sitting on a wobbling chair in the middle of the room. Her head was down and her shoulders were twitching. She was holding a diaper made out of old overused sheets. The doctor looked up at Lidya with eyes full of tears.

"Forgive me, my girl, forgive me. The orphanage committee came early this morning. They took our Anya. They took her away," Doroteya Aristarkhovna quietly said in a broken voice.

"Where did they take her? Did they tell her which orphanage they took her to?" Lida screamed.

The doctor got up from her chair, came up to Lidya, hugged her shoulders and spoke in a quivering voice. "Stay strong, my girl. You will most likely never see you daughter again. The system is built so that the children born from public enemies are taken away and put into orphanages, given new first and last names, so that their parents, having survived the camps, can't ever find them and have their bad influence on them."

Lida pushed Doroteya Aristarkhovna away.

"I don't believe you... I will find Anya. I will find her, whatever it takes!"

Deep in the middle of the night, when everyone in the barrack was asleep, one of the convicts heard a loud cry that sounded like a howl suppressed by a pillow. She got up and began to walk in between the bunks towards the noise. She saw Lida close to the front door, lying on a lower bunk bed with her face pushed into the pillow. She was weeping. The convict sat on her bed and put her hand on her back.

"Don't do this to yourself."

Lida turned around and yelled, "No, you don't understand, you don't know! I will never, ever see my daughter. You can't understand what I'm going through."

"I understand you completely. I have a daughter, too. She was taken away when she was three weeks old. I also don't know where she is now. But I believe I will find her, and we will reunite."

Lida looked at the convict again.

"Katya, you have a daughter?"

"Yes, Lida, I have a little daughter. I named her Vasilisa, after my mom. Although, I do not know what first and last name she goes by now. But that's not too bad. You know how they say, the one who looks always finds. I will look for her? First, I will search by my last name, Buynovskaya. And if that doesn't work, I'll think of something. Remember, Lida, there are some good people in this world. Someone will help you. You just have to be strong and have faith, have faith in yourself."

Since that night, Lida and Katya became friends. They supported each other as much as they could, and shared their dreams of finding their children and living happily. But... One day, something irreversible happened. Lida was still working at the logging camp. She was in her ninth year of imprisonment. She was standing next to a tree she had just got done chopping. Lida stepped three meters away from it and stopped. She was thinking about her daughter, picturing how she would find her, and they would live happily, reunited. She couldn't even hear her partner yell, "Watch out! Move, now!" A huge pine was falling down to the ground at an accelerating speed. It crushed Lida's young body.

When Lida was retrieved from under the tree, she was dead, her face having been disfigured, turned into a mess. She was buried the next day at the camp's cemetery in a nameless grave. Katya Buynovskaya visited the fresh grave that night, squatted beside it and whispered very quickly, "Rest in peace, Lidya. I will take care of your girl. I give you my word. I will find her. I will tell her about you and her father."

She then quickly got up and walked away.

Another six years passed. The end of Ekaterina's sentence was near. About a month before her release, Katya decided to talk to the doctor.

"Doroteya Aristarkhovna, I know you helped Lidya and her daughter. I will be freed soon. I want to find Anya. Could you tell what orphanage she was taken to?"

The doctor looked at the convict with sadness in her eyes. Weighing every word, she said, "Katya, I doubt you will be able to keep your promise to Lidya. I don't know anything. The girl could be found in any orphanage of our vast homeland. Her "parents" field will most likely be empty. Besides, Anya will soon turn fifteen, which means she might not even be at an orphanage anymore. She could be anywhere. I'm not sure how you're going to search for her."

Doroteya Aristarkhovna looked at Katya with sorrow. The girl wrapped her hands around her head in desperation and screamed. Her scream wasn't loud, but trembling and hopeless. She could no longer control her voice. It turned hoarse, and after a few minutes there was no wheezing. Her mouth remained open, but was silent. Katya lay down on the floor, powerless. Her hands were fumbling with her hair. A minute later, she got up and turned to the doctor.

"No, it can't be completely impossible to find any information about the kids that were taken away from their parents. It can't be, right?"

Doroteya Aristarkhovna was looking at the woman inconsolably. Suddenly, her eyes livened up, her lips spread into a slight smile, and she lightened up.

"Katya, yes, yes, you're right. The system doesn't ever just throw anything away. It stores everything like a good and diligent housewife, putting everything away in drawers, anything that could be useful later. There are certain authorities responsible for this; in this case, it's ARP of NKVD of USSR. Just an advice, though – don't go there yourself, and don't ask questions. They won't give you—a repressed public enemy—any information."

"Thank you so much, dear Doroteya Aristarkhovna, thank you for your advice, and your concern."

Alexandra took a deep breath, and then breathed out. Everyone in the room locked their eyes on her, waiting for continuation.

"Vladimir, my son, please bring me some water, my throat is all dry."

After drinking the water, Alexandra glanced at everyone and the story continued.

After she left the camps, Katya's main goal was to find the two girls, her Vasilisa, and Anya, the daughter of Lida Ukhtomsky. At first, she tried to search for them by mailing letters to the NKVD authorities. But they were always met with indifference and contempt. Once, she was even told that there is no such thing as "former" public enemies, and that no one is going to grant them any information about their bastards.

She turned to her former neighbor, Efrosinya, for help, and the old woman began to flood household administration management of NKVD with letters. The search yielded results. Ekaterina found her daughter, whose name was now Varvara instead of Vasilisa. She found Lida's daughter, too, who went by the last name Tomina.

Anna grew up to be a beautiful, elegant girl, but she was quiet and lacked initiative. She lived in her own world she created for herself. Perhaps that was the right thing to do. In orphanages, you can only survive by either turning into a jerk, getting everything you want by force, or withdrawing into yourself, blocking everything that happens around you. The girl read a lot and lived in the dreams the books provided her.

Ekaterina didn't fish for the young girl's friendship. She told her about her mother, and having realized the girl wasn't going to take the wrong turn in life, watched over her from afar. From time to time, she would visit Anya's neighbors, and through questions, gradually learned the daughter of her friend from the camp. As for Anya, ever since she'd been self-aware, which started when she was four, and got punished by her orphanage caregiver for reading under the blanket, promised herself she would find her parents.

"You, traitor brat, are you going to obey your supervisor or not? I'm asking you! Just look at this American bastard!" The caregiver said loudly, grabbing the girl by her scruff. Anya remembered those words for the rest of her life. Back then, being a four-year-old baby exposed to the cruelty of the adult world, she decided to withdraw from that world and into herself… And find her parents, no matter what. That decision helped her survive in the orphanage, and become a self-sufficient, but, unfortunately, an anti-social person. After finishing school, Anya gladly left the walls of the orphanage and embraced adult life. This transition wasn't painful to her. She was used to relying only on herself.

Anya finished a course of typing lessons, securing a job at the typing bureau of the faculty of history at the Moscow State University (MGU). Being quite well-read and having books as her only friends, the girl noticed every spelling and syntactic error. As Anya typed out the works of professors of the faculty, she changed their style, perfecting it. After of month of working there, she became the star of the typing bureau.

"This Tomina will soon take away all of our jobs. There will be no place here for us. Where did they even find someone like her, so literate?" Anya once overheard a bathroom conversation between her co-workers.

"You know what, Marusya? We should dig up some information, so that... You know."

"No problem. I have a friend in the authorities. All I have to do is ask. She'll give me a complete lowdown on this know-it-all."

"Alright, let's go, or we'll get in trouble."

When she heard the door close, Anya left her bathroom stall.

A month later, she was fired. The reasoning was strange. The order read, "Anna Tomina is to be fired due to her losing the trust of administration." That kind of reason made Anya laugh. She thought about going to the authorities to prove that such argument didn't apply to her, as she was certain it only applied to workers that directly handled items of monetary or trade value. However, after giving it some thought, Anya realized that as a public enemy, she will not be able to get back her job, anyway. Her co-workers wouldn't let that happen, as it was them who filed the complaint. The girl decided to work at home. She hung fliers around in all the faculty buildings of MGU. A good reputation will follow you around just like a bad one. Those who'd previously had their works typed by her began to recommend her to their friends and co-workers. Indeed, she was getting tons of orders.

One day, a young man visited the apartment where Anya lived and worked. He was dressed in the latest fashion: Neat, handsome and pleasant. Having opened the door, Anya felt embarrassed and asked, "How may I help you?"

"Hello, Anna. Don't be shy. Vladimir Ivanovich Khmelev recommended you to me. Do you remember if he bought your services often?" The young man said quickly, looking straight into the girl's eyes.

After some hesitation, Anya let him in.

"Allow me to introduce myself, Anna. I'm Mikhail Alexandrovich Dronin. Or just Mikhail," the young man stated. "I need your help. Vladimir Ivanovich spoke highly of your work. He assured me you are a fast and literate typist."

"He's exaggerating," Anya said shyly. "I'm on the same level as many typists out there, believe me."

Mikhail smiled. He liked the girl, and the way she talked about herself, modest, but dignified.

"I understand. But please, can you help me type out my manuscript? I'm a historian, and I have recently finished a work that took me ten years to complete. It is very important to me."

"Mikhail, do you know why I was fired from the typing bureau? They expressed a lack of trust, do you understand? A lack of trust..I won't work on anything big. I'm more into term and degree papers that can have such a vague meaning. Well, you get what I mean." Anya looked at the man challengingly.

"You seem fit for me, Anna. I trust you. Besides, I will pay you well." Mikhail moved closer to the girl and put his hands on her shoulders. "You are a beautiful girl, and a great person. Your kind, bright eyes give that out right away."

Anya felt embarrassed. She took the man's hands off of her shoulders, moved a couple meters away from Mikhail, and looked at him. Her big blue eyes were looking into his, and he felt like she was looking into his heart. It started beating faster, and his large, manly body felt an embrace of warmth that went through it. Mikhail closed his eyes, no longer able to resist her stare.

"Fine, I'll take the manuscript. Show it to me." Dronin heard Anya's quiet, businesslike voice.

Mikhail lightened up, and began to retrieve paper folders from his big black suitcase.

"Let's go to my room. It will be more comfortable there," Anya suggested, smiling. While the girl was studying the manuscript, determining the complexity of the handwriting, Dronin was visually examining the room. It was almost "Spartan", very minimalistic. A small desk with a typewriter stood by the window with open curtains.

The bed was by the wall to the left of the door, tucked with a blue linen bedspread. A two-door dresser was to the right. That was all of it, other than the chairs, one by the desk and one by the bed.

"I'm sorry, I didn't offer you to take a seat," Anya suddenly realized. "Actually, everything's clear. You have good, clear handwriting. I will start typing your work tomorrow. Today, I have to finish two more term papers."

Anya looked at each folder, trying to estimate how long it would take, and slowly said, "Your work should be ready in a couple of weeks. Leave your number in case I have questions."

The next day, Anya heard a doorbell ring once again. It was Mikhail. He had a small bouquet of violets in one hand, which were extremely hard to find in October, and a bag of groceries in another.

"Hello, Anna. I'm sorry I came uninvited," Dronin babbled shyly.

Anya was looking at him sternly, frowning, though she felt happy inside. Nobody had ever taken care of her before. She didn't know how to behave in that situation.

If I invite him in, he'll think I'm too compliant, and if I ask him to leave, Mikhail might feel offended and never come back again.

Anya stood before Mikhail, undecided. He took the initiative.

"Don't worry, I won't bother you. I'll just set the table with what I brought here, and you can eat. Look how skinny you are," he observed gently.

The girl finally smiled and invited him in.

An hour later, Mikhail and Anna were sitting in the kitchen, where Mikhail served a few tasty dishes. There was bologna and salami sliced in thin circles, boiled eggs and potatoes covered in green onions, and sour cabbage with onions smeared in fragrant vegetable oil. For dessert, there was a small biscuit cake with roses made out of frosting.

"Thank you for all this, Mikhail, but you really didn't have to," she said shyly.

Mikhail looked at Anya. His eyes expressed surprise, confusion, and tenderness. He didn't quite get the girl, but he was attracted to her. Anya made Dronin want to protect her, take care of her, admire and worship her all at the same time, attracting him physically, as well. He fantasized about kissing her eyes, hair, and especially her lips.

"Anya, please eat. I will keep you company. You will rest for a bit. We'll talk." Those last words came out very quiet.

Anya and Mikhail spent the rest of the day together. While Anya worked, he sat on the chair by the bed in her room, reading. Then he daydreamed, looking at her back, then thought about work, then daydreamed again, thinking of Anya. By seven o'clock, Anya stopped typing, got up from her chair, stretched a little, and smiled.

"Mikhail, I'm almost done with your first chapter."

"Why are you going so fast, dear Anya?" Mikhail replied jokingly, and suddenly stopped.

The girl gave him a cold look that made him uncomfortable. Once again, she made him feel timid.

This girl is special. I have to find a way to approach her. She's proud and independent. The thought suddenly flashed in Mikhail's head. He then spoke the words that melted the ice in Anya's heart.

"Dear Anya, please let me call you that. Don't be offended, I'm not trying to be overly bold. I just associate you with a blue flower, tender and beautiful, but requiring attention and care. I'm sorry if I accidentally offended you somehow."

To Anna, those words sounded like a confession of love. She lost herself for a moment, and turned to the window. The raindrops falling down from the sky were tiny and cold. A small bird landed on the windowsill, seemingly winking at her. It cheered Anya up. She laughed, turned to Mikhail and said, "You can call me that, if you like. Although, I have to confess, nobody ever addressed me that way, even when I was a child."

A friendly romance developed between them. The kind of romance when one thinks of the other as a friend, and the other, having fallen in love, but afraid to confess their love, also acts like a friend. One time, Anya, having never told anyone about her parents, told Mikhail. She asked him for advice on how to find information on them. Anya told him everything she had learned from Buynovskaya, but those were only words. She wanted to find documents confirming everything Katya had told her.

"Dear Anya, I think I can help you. Thank God it's not 1937 or 1952. It's already 1967." He talked anxiously. "I work with the latest historical events. I've been wanting to study Stalin's repression for a long time. Your parents will be the first subjects of my study!" He continued ecstatically.

As Anya was looking at the historian, her look went from warm and tender to cold and distanced.

"My parents will be the subject of your study? My mom and dad, their life and their love will be a subject of study! Do you even listen to yourself?" The girl reacted indignantly.

Mikhail looked at Anya, confused.

"Yes, a subject of study. There are such terms as a subject, an object, a method of study. It's a quite popular terminology used in scientific studies."

Anya covered her face with her hands and began to cry.

"Dear Anya, what's wrong? Did I upset you? Please, tell me so I can understand." Dronin held the girl close.

She was sobbing on his shoulder, and Mikhail didn't feel pity, but a desire, a desire to be with her all the time. To protect her. Dronin put his large hands on her face, passionately kissing her. She didn't stop him. He took her into his arms and carried her to bed carefully, like she was his most precious treasure. He lay her down on her bed, and used the checkered plaid that rested by the headboard to cover her up. Did he physically desire her? He did, extremely. But Dronin was too afraid to lose that string of trust he felt when he was holding Anya. She was lying there, so vulnerable and trustful, that Mikhail was afraid to touch her. He sat on the chair beside her, took her hands and gently kissed her fingers.

The next morning, to the neighbor's surprise, Anya's apartment was quiet, unlike the usual noise coming from the typewriter. Mikhail was lying in her bed with his eyes open. His body was numb from an uncomfortable position, but Dronin was afraid to move. Anya was sleeping, her head resting on his shoulder. Mikhail looked at the clock. The small arrow was pointing towards seven, and the big one towards twelve. He had a meeting planned at nine. Carefully, trying not to wake Anya up, Dronin attempted to get out of bed. The girl opened her eyes. The first thing she felt was fear. She quickly got up in her bed, covering herself with the blanket, and mumbled words of apology.

She felt ashamed of herself, of the weakness she had expressed the night before. But it wasn't unpleasant to her. Inside, Anya felt glad. She could still feel the warmth of his hands stroking her body, his soft and tender lips kissing her head to toes. Anya felt happiness and embarrassment simultaneously. Mikhail smiled, held the girl close to his naked chest, and whispered, "Thank you, dear Anya, thank you for this happiness."

He suddenly recalled a line by Stendal, which he immediately quoted. "Don't be ashamed, sweetheart. Shame is the mother of the most beautiful passion of a human heart – love. I love you very, very much."

Anya wrapped her arms around Mikhail's neck, clinging to his powerful chest, and began to kiss his eyes, cheeks, and lips.

"I love you, I love you," Her lips whispered.

Two weeks later, Mikhail handed her a folder with documents.

"Anya, this folder contains documents I managed to get from the authorities. I promised I would retrieve it for you, and I did. I'll be honest with you, what I did is dangerous and could get both you and me in trouble, and especially my childhood friend who agreed to help me. But I'm happy I could be of use." Watching Anya carefully with saddened eyes, he pulled her close to him, kissed her and began to quietly whisper, "The issue of your mother's rehabilitation has not yet been raised. She is still considered a public enemy. We can start the case, if you want. I have connections in the public prosecutor's office."

Anya was shaking, the nervous chill wouldn't let go of her body. She began to circle around the room to calm down. Mikhail was watching the girl carefully. Anya stopped, came up to Dronin, hugged him, kissed him on the lips and whispered into his ear as quietly as he had.

"Thank you for help, my sweet Mikhail. I will never forget this. Let me just take a look at these documents, make copies of them, and then you can take everything back. Because if we apply for a rehabilitation, the papers have to go back, don't they?"

Anya and Mikhail studied the documents together for a few days. The girl made copies of some of them with her typewriter.

They saw each other every day. Their love grew stronger. Anya's heart was gradually melting. She became softer, more open and cheerful. She smiled more.

"Let us get married, sweet Anya," Michael proposed to her one night. "I can't imagine my life without you. You are all I have. My father died at the front line, and my mother died during evacuation. I don't have anyone left, only you, honey."

"I don't have anyone, either," Anya replied quietly. "I think there is God, after all. Otherwise, how do you explain this happiness that we have found with each other?"

They decided to apply at the registry office the next day. At exactly two o'clock in the afternoon, Anya was waiting by the office. Half an hour had passed and there was still no sign of Mikhail. It wasn't like him to be late. Anya began to worry. She was walking back and forth, compulsively checking her watch. After another thirty minutes, she decided to show up at his work.

"Which Dronin are you looking for? Mikhail?" The secretary answered with a question.

"Yes, yes, I need to see Mikhail Dronin. Where is he?" Anya yelled.

"Lower your voice, please. No need to yell, my hearing is just fine." The secretary replied. "He's not here. He doesn't work here anymore."

"What do you mean? He said he was a docent at this university." Anya was talking fast and anxiously.

The secretary left her desk and walked towards a door, gesturing Anya to follow her. They went through a long hallway. One floor down, they walked down another hallway until they reached a door that was locked, and it appeared as if it had not been used for a while.

"Listen to me, Mikhail Dronin quit yesterday and went away. Far away," The secretary whispered.

"What do you mean he left? We were supposed to..." Anya couldn't finish her sentence. Her eyes filled with tears, her chest felt tight. She couldn't breathe and passed out.

Anya came to at a hospital. A nurse was sitting beside her, gently stroking her hand.

"Be strong, honey. You're still young. You'll be alright."

"What happened? Why am I at a hospital?" Anya asked in a fragile voice.

"Hold on, sweetheart, let me tell the doctor you're awake." The nurse left the room.

Anya felt terrible. She felt her body under the blanket, discovering she was wearing nothing but a patient gown. There were some kind of oilcloths and sheets tucked under the pelvis area of her body. She felt she was leaking something sticky.

"Blood. It's blood. What's happening to me?" Anya started to panic.

A young and attractive female doctor came in.

"Hello. How are you feeling?"

"Where am I? What's happening to me?" Anya asked worriedly.

The doctor sat down on the chair by Anya's bed, took her arm and began to measure her blood pressure. Then, she pulled the blanket off Anya and felt her belly.

"Let's see... Good, your pressure is normal. Your belly is soft. We'll check you out in a couple of days. But we'll look after you for now," The doctor spoke impersonally.

Anya grew mad.

"Will you ever tell me what happened or why I'm here?" She said in an angry but weak voice.

"No need to worry. An ambulance brought you here. You were nine weeks pregnant. I'm not sure what caused you to faint, but you got hit pretty hard, suffering a bleed. We were unable to save the baby. "

Anya couldn't believe what she was hearing.

"I was pregnant?" To herself, she thought, *It's his, Mikhail's baby... But the baby's gone... So is Mikhail... He left me, left me all alone.*

Everything inside her clenched and she turned to withdraw into herself.

"From this point on, I don't need anyone. And no one needs me. I'm all by myself. I don't need anyone," Anya kept repeating over and over.

It had been almost twenty years. Anya was thirty-six. She lived detached from the world. She didn't have a family or a loved one. Throughout those years, she was unable to trust anyone else. Even though she had plenty of admirers. Anya spent her nights reading or sewing. About fifteen years ago, she had finished sewing classes. Back then, Anya decided to change her life, upgrading from Cinderella to princess. It was impossible to find nice clothes to buy. She didn't have any connections in the trade market, so she had to dress herself. With the extremely good taste she had, she was creating masterpieces. She worked as a secretary at the Academy of Sciences. Always dressed fashionably, she stood out from other women due to her elegance, modesty and superiority at the same time. She was a legend to both men and women of the academy. Both felt intimidated by her, tried to befriend her, loved and hated her . When an academician, Ezhi Ivanovich Polonsky, began to notice her, his wife, who also worked there, showed Anya the door. Polonsky recommended Anya to his neighbor who was a second secretary of the party committee, Yevgeny Petrovich Zlotov.

At first, Anya and her new boss maintained a good relationship. Evgeny considered Anya overly cold and arrogant, though he appreciated her professional qualities since day one. As for Anna, Evgeny Petrovich reminded her of a male peacock parading his tail feathers each time he noticed a female. She couldn't stand men like that. She considered them foolish studs. Following her first day at the party committee, after having had dinner, Anya didn't grab the novel "Three Comrades" by Erich Maria Remarque she had just started, even though she found it interesting. Nor did she touch her sewing machine with an unfinished dress lying beside it. Anya took out an envelope, slightly turned yellow over time from a box sitting on her dresser. Gently holding it in her hands, she sat down in an armchair, turned on a lamp and began to read.

"Hello, my only love, my dear Anya. I understand there's no forgiveness for me for betraying our dream. There is no excuse... Nevertheless, I'm writing this letter, hoping that you, my sweetheart, will understand and forgive me. The day we decided to get married, I was already far gone. The plane took me to Vladivostok overnight. You wonder why? The day before that, by late night, my good friend from KGB paid me a visit. He informed me of the possibility of my arrest due to the theft of the known documents from the archive. The

friend who helped me in this ordeal had to repay with his freedom. I was in for the same. I don't know where exactly they got the lead on me, but I have a few guesses. Although you probably won't care much for that. That is why I informed the head of the department about my leave, and the personal reasoning behind it. He turned out to be a very attentive and honest man, so he advised me to go to the Far East, where there was high demand for people like me, and other specialties, in universities. Without giving it much thought, I packed and left for the airport. Thank God there were still tickets for the flight to Vladivostok. My entire trip there, it pained me that I didn't tell you or take you with me. Please, try to understand that I acted out of fear, not only for me, but for you. As you know, there was no mention of you in those documents. That is why I decided not to tell you anything, hoping you will not be a part of this ordeal. I don't know how long I'm going to live. Unfortunately, my entire family isn't known to have a long life expectancy. All I know is that you will always remain my only love. Forgive me. I am already punished by being unable to see you or hear from you. Goodbye, my love. Your Mikhail."

Anya received this letter fifteen years ago. It was passed to her by a man who didn't reveal his name. He came to her door, said hello, excused himself, gave her the envelope, and walked down the stairs. After reading the letter, Anya wept for a long time. She fell ill, didn't want to eat, drink, or do anything else. On the third day, Anya was scared she would fall into a deep depression, the kind that people cannot escape for years. She forced herself to get up, go to the bathroom, take a shower and make sandwiches and tea. Then, she read the letter one more time. She felt like going to Vladivostok to find Mikhail, but her inner voice told her it would be a mistake. Anya always listened to her gut. She put the letter in a box, placing the box inside her dresser. "That's it. Enough. I will live with dignity," Anna decided.

That was the first time in fifteen years that she had taken out the letter. Surprisingly, it made a different impression on her this time. As she was reading it, she didn't feel like it was her reading her dear

Mikhail's letter, but rather like she was a stranger reading some other man's letter to some other woman.

Indeed, time is a great healer... Anna thought to herself.

The following morning, Anna came to work wearing a sophisticated navy blue suite she had sewed according to the latest fashion trends. She braided her blonde hair into two braids, and put them together in a crown-like hairdo. She was wearing elegant black shoes on small heels. By the time Evgeny Petrovich walked into reception, she was already at work. Anna was watering plants, a habit she'd had since her previous job.

She didn't notice her boss come in, and he stopped to admire his secretary's grace. Anna turned her head and their eyes met. *What a beautiful woman, Evgeny thought. So much grace in her. She's so different from everyone else.*

Anna thought he had sad eyes. *He looks more pathetic than attractive.*

Anna said hello and he responded. He sat down in his chair, daydreaming. He was thinking of her. For the first time in his life, he didn't feel physical desire, but a desire to take care of her, worship her. The feeling was new to him, and he didn't know what to do with it. Anna, on the other hand, scoffed, returning to her desk and working.

A week passed by. The relationship between Evgeny and Anna remained strictly professional. But Evgeny caught himself wanting to come into work earlier and leave much later than usual. He literally flew to work every day, excited to see and hear Anna. He wasn't interested in any other woman. More than that, he suddenly realized how poor and shallow his relationships with women had been until then. He'd never felt anything but a physical desire. None of his many lovers left a trace in his heart. As soon as Evgeny got bored of a woman he was seeing, he'd buy her off by getting her a new apartment, paying for her vacation, providing her with a good job opportunity, etc. Once, Anna accidentally overheard her boss's phone conversation with his friend as the door into his office was cracked open.

"No, Nikolay. I'm not coming. This is it, I'm done with that. Note that frequent trips to sauna are bad for your health. I don't need them.

No, don't try to convince me. Tell your girls they won't be seeing me anymore."

It appeared as if Evgeny's friend was making a five-minute speech, after which Evgeny replied, "I've already found the one I'm looking for. She's so close, yet I don't know how to approach her."

The overheard conversation made Anna see Evgeny in a different light. She began to notice the looks he was giving her, how overly polite he was when talking to her. Once, one of the women at work pointed out that Evgeny Petrovich would scold anyone except Anna.

"Anya, I think he's in love with you," she had hypothesized.

Anna smiled in response. Gradually, her attitude towards Evgeny began to change, becoming warmer and friendlier, to say the least.

Six months later, Evgeny confessed his love. Anna, shy at first, reciprocated his feelings. They were discreet about their relationship. Their love wasn't fueled by madness and passion, typical of young love. Their love was much deeper, richer, and had much more to it, which made it a lot more valuable. They gave themselves to one another completely. They cherished each day as if it were their last. When Evgeny found out he had cancer, he immediately made a decision he thought was the only right thing to do.

"I love Anya too much to cause her any kind of trouble in life. I don't want her to see me dying. I don't want her to change my diapers and curse me for it. I don't want to be a burden to her. She's still a young and beautiful woman. She deserves love. I will only be a bother. Let Anya remember me healthy and strong."

Evgeny came up to his desk, opened one of the drawers with a key, took out a branded pistol he had received as a gift from a general when he was young, found a pack of bullets, and loaded the gun. He picked up the phone to call her sister, Alexandra, to say goodbye. Then, he got up, sat back in his chair, drew the pistol to his head, and pulled the trigger.

Alexandra went quiet. Everyone was silent.

"And what about Anna? What about her baby?" Vladimir broke the silence.

Alexandra's tired eyes looked at her son, and she spoke in a hoarse voice: "It's late. Let's continue tomorrow. I'm very tired. And you have to rest, as well."

It was decided. By midnight, Liubasha closed the front door after their last guest.

Chapter 31

"Andrew and Michael are coming tomorrow. We'll have to meet them," Alex said as they left Alexandra's house.

"Uncle is coming?" Darya was surprised.

"Yes, honey, Daddy called him and asked him to come. You don't know, but ten years ago or so, Andrew tried to find his great-grandfather's brothers himself. But he couldn't."

"And what about Mom? Is she coming, too?" Jane asked, slightly annoyed.

"No, your mom didn't want to come. She said it gets too cold in Russia during winter. She prefers warmer climates." Alex replied, smiling.

"That's good. But why is Michael coming?" Jane asked another question.

"I called him and asked him to," Darya admitted quietly.

"You? Why's that?" Her sister was surprised.

"Well, I thought he'd want to be here with us." Darya said shyly.

Vladimir didn't say a word, only looked at the girl perplexedly. They decided to meet Andrew and Michael in the company of Darya, Vladimir, and Jane. Nadya asked if she could come, too. She still had hopes for Vladimir to reciprocate her feelings.

The flight was a bit late. The kids were waiting at a small restaurant inside the airport. They ordered coffee and chocolate croissants and sat down at a small table all together. Darya suddenly got up and stepped away towards the window overlooking the airfield. Vladimir followed her. Nadya wanted to join them, but Jane stopped her.

"You should leave them alone. I'm sure they have a lot to talk about."

Nadya looked at her new friend with anger.

"I see the way you look at Vladimir. Do you like him?" Jane asked Nadya quietly.

"Yes, I do."

"Then don't rush it. It will all work out," Jane said with a cunning smile.

"I don't understand... What do you mean? You know something?" Nadya sounded impatient.

"I just know the way Darya was raised. Give it time. Let's drink our coffee while its hot."

Nadya wanted to ask another question, but Darya grabbed her cup and shook her head, refusing to say anything else.

Darya was standing by the wide window, watching a plane, which was preparing to take off. There was almost no snow outside. It was still visible at the distance, grey from dirt, almost all cleaned up by winter service vehicles. The sky was gray from storm clouds, ready to unleash either rain or snow. The weather forecast predicted wet snow. Darya was sad and happy at the same time.

"What's the matter, Darya? Are you not feeling well?" She heard Vladimir's concerned voice.

"No, everything's fine. I've learned so much for the past few days... It will take a while to sink in."

"Tell me, Darya, why did you ask Michael to come?" The young man asked in a trembling voice.

Her bright eyes looked into the worried eyes of Vladimir, and she slowly answered: "He's my friend. Ever since I remember myself, he was always near, witnessing all my joy and all my sadness. And now, as I've learned so much about myself, I want to share it with Michael. Why, are you upset with me?"

Vladimir felt he was losing connection with Darya. He was scared. He instinctively grabbed Darya's hand and began to whisper, "And how about me? Aren't I important to you? Aren't I your friend? Do you really need anyone else, other than me? I... I..."

He let go of Darya's hand and turned away. Darya grabbed his elbow, trying to turn him back to her.

"Why do you talk like that, Vladimir? You know how I feel about you. Each time I think about you, I feel so much warmth, so much tenderness in my heart. You're important to me, you're like family. I value you, and I love you. I love you as someone dear and close to me. Don't think badly of Michael. He's your friend, too, isn't he?"

Vladimir looked into her eyes. He saw warmth, tenderness, empathy, but he didn't see love, the kind that a man and a woman share. Vladimir couldn't understand Darya, and that made him uncomfortable.

"The plane landed. They just announced it. Let's go meet them, Darya." The young man's voice sounded hollow. The two stepped away from the window and walked towards the restaurant where Jane and Nadya were waiting.

Darya was first to spot the guests. She waved her hands and yelled, "Michael, over here!"

Those words cut through Vladimir's heart like a knife. She didn't call over Uncle Andrew, but Michael, he noted somewhat angrily.

Nevertheless, Vladimir was glad to see his American friend.

Michael has nothing to do with his. He's not the one making the choice, Darya is, Vladimir thought to himself with sadness, looking at Darya, who was radiant with happiness.

Michael ran towards his friends, stopped in front of Darya, held her hands, looked into her joyful eyes, and gently hugged her.

"Hey."

He then came up to Vladimir and raised his hand.

"What's up, Vladimir. I was starting to miss you, pal."

Vladimir heartily shook Michael's hand, feeling that through all this, he'd missed him, too. Nadya watched as the friends reunited, and, having the observational skills of a professional journalist, she knew the relationship between the two young men and the girl was a bit complicated, and Darya was the reason.

Jane was excited to see her father. Andrew and she were always on good terms.

"Daddy, you'll learn so much about the Ukhtomsky family today, about your family! Are you excited? Tell me, are you?" Darya was pumped up.

Andrew wasn't just excited. He was happy.

"Daddy, Michael, meet Nadya. She's our new friend. She helped us a lot. Hell, if it wasn't for her, we probably wouldn't have learned all this." Jane hugged Nadya's shoulders, introducing her to the newly arrived.

Nadya was blushing. Jane's words were flattering.

"Thank you, honey; although, I wasn't the only one leading the investigation. Alena, Volodya's sister, Volodya, Alexandra Petrovna, Vladimir's mother, we all did it." Nadya felt overwhelmed, taken over by the "journalist" in her. She suddenly realized it, and apologized for being overly chatty.

"You're all tired. You should rest. Let's go," She concluded, embarrassed.

That night Alexanda Petrovna was expecting her guests once again. She had to finish her story about Anna. She was nervous, eager to start, and a bit scared. She'd been waiting for that day because it would finally lift the weight of a secret off her shoulders, the secret she willingly and illegally had taken upon herself. The secret had always weighed her down, especially for the past year, as her health worsened dramatically. Alexandra asked Liubasha to make dinner for ten. That's how many people she was expecting that day. As usual, at seven o'clock exactly, Alena and Nadya arrived. Everybody else was there about five minutes later. Vladimir introduced Andrew and Michael to his mom.

"Vladimir looks a lot like you," Andrew noted.

Alexandra looked at her son with love in her eyes, and didn't reply. She invited her guests to the table set for dinner. Liubasha worked hard. As Alexandra requested, she made traditional Russian dishes. There were aspic, fish pie, cabbage coulibiac, and poppy seed cake and tea for dessert.

"My God! I have never tried any of this," Melinda exclaimed. "Delicious!" She concluded satisfactorily.

"Yes, honey, this is Russian cuisine. Alexandra, thank you for your attention and hospitality," Alex said with gratitude.

After dinner, as usual, everyone took seats around Alexandra, who was resting on her couch.

Alexandra looked over her guests with attention, let out a deep sigh, and continued the story she'd started earlier.

"On the day of Anna's estimated due date, I went to visit her, going by the address she gave me. But she wasn't home. Her neighbor said the ambulance had come for her the night before. I was working as a doctor on Lavrov street at the time. It didn't take me much to find out what hospital Anna was taken to. It was maternity hospital number five. Anya gave birth to a son. Anna died during labor. Her kidneys stopped working. I knew Anna didn't have anyone but me. That's why I made a deal with the chief physician of the hospital for the boy to stay there for a week, as he required medical attention. During that week, Valera and I went through with the adoption. And this is how we got another child, whom we named Vladimir."

Alexandra went quiet. She took Vladimir's hand, kissed it, and whispered, "Forgive me, my son. Forgive me."

She closed her eyes and fell back onto her pillow, silent, ignoring the tears slowly running down her face.

Vladimir looked at his mother, stunned, unable to comprehend what he had just heard. The room was so quiet they could hear a mother cradle her baby in the neighboring apartment.

Vladimir was shocked. His vision was clouded, and through the clouds he saw the face of his mother, drowning in quiet tears. He felt completely lost. Pictures of his childhood suddenly flashed before his eyes. His mom was always, always there. Just the feeling of her touch, her warm hands touching the endless cuts and scrapes he got from fighting other boys, falling down the swing or other events of his childhood, immediately eased the pain, reminding him of the presence of someone dear, someone who loved him. Alexandra might have not given life to him, but she gave him love, care, and understanding. Vladimir was overtaken by a strong feeling of warmth and tenderness, and held his mother in his arms.

"Mommy, my dear Mommy. Thank you for always being there for me. You are the only mother I have. Perhaps Alexandra would have been a good mother, too, but nobody in the world has a mother like you. You are my dearest, my most beloved." Vladimir was kissing Alexandra's tearful eyes, and her shaky hands. "What is there to forgive, Mom? You wished kindness and happiness for me. And you gave it to me. I grew up in a good and loving family, my mom and dad were the greatest parents in the world. I always felt your love."

Subtle tears appeared in Vladimir's eyes. He quickly wiped them off, excused himself and went out to the kitchen. Immediately, two girls got up from their seats–Darya and Nadya. They looked at each other. The eyes of both of them expressed suffering and empathy. They stared at each other for a few seconds. Nadya stepped down. She sat back in her chair, recalling Jane's words at the airport. Darya went after Vladimir.

The young man stood by the window. His eyes were closed, his face looked tense, and his palms were tapping on the windowsill.

"I know how hard it is for you right now, Vladimir," He heard Darya say, who quietly approached him and stood next to him.

She put her hands on his shoulder and gently kissed him, not on his lips, but his eyes instead.

"You have an amazing mother. Kind, loving, strong. You're a lot like her."

"Thank you, Darya." Vladimir tried to hug her.

"You know, it's weird how we turned out to be related. Your birth mother, Anna, and my biological mother, Anastasia, were related, maybe they weren't sisters, or even cousins, but they were related. They had the same blood, the blood of the Ukhtomskys. And we represent them, as well." Darya smiled and backed away from Vladimir. "I think the way you feel about me is the same way I feel about you... It's the kind of love between two blood relatives. Do you understand?" Darya was carefully looking at Vladimir.

"You're telling me that, as Kipling wrote, we be of one blood, ye and I?" Vladimir sneered with sadness and painfully looked at Darya.

"Let's go, Vladimir. They're waiting for us," she said quietly, pulling his sleeve.

The room was still silent when they came back in. No one had anything to say; the news they'd heard was too overwhelming. Alex was first to break the silence.

"Life is an interesting thing. You never know what it has in for you. The older I get, the more surprises I get from life. Our family's story is quite a twist. Right now, as amazing as it sounds, the two last generations of the Ukhtomskys are here, in this room. For all those years, my great-grandfather, and then my father, Andrew's brother, tried to find at least some information about the remaining Ukhtomskys in Russia, and couldn't find anything. And now, in just two months, this is what we get. Thank you, dear God, for this kindness."

Alex clasped his hands together as if he was praying, and closed his eyes, smiling. Everyone also smiled at his speech.

"God gives us a chance, but we make things happen," Nadya said, laughing. "If it wasn't for Alena and her professional perceptiveness, we wouldn't be here now."

"Dear Nadya, we're not underestimating what you've done for us. We're endlessly grateful to you." Melinda joined the conversation. "In fact, I'm amazed at how you were able to gather all this information in such a short period of time after all these years."

"I swear, I'm starting to agree with Denis Fonvizin, who once said life was merciful. It tries to bring together similar minds with similar views and character," Alena added with delight. "And, let me add, those of the same blood. We're all related here. Vladimir, my brother, is also Darya's relative. Nadya, my friend, is Darya's sister. What an amazing twist of fate."

When everyone was having lunch at the hotel the next day, including Alex with Melinda and Andrew with Michael, they were excitedly talking about everything they'd learned while being there.

"What an amazing country Russia is. Plentiful, but cold. What amazing people Russians are. Did you notice those eyes that Alexandra, Alena, Nadya, and Vladimir have?" Michael's voice sounded a bit too dramatic. "Their eyes, the look, it somehow resembles the look of Orthodox saints painted in icons, so sad, melancholically staring into the distance, the future. Only Russians have that. I don't know why.

Maybe because Russia has always had strong Orthodox roots, those that even communists weren't able to defy."

Alex was looking at Michael with surprise.

"Since when are you interested in Russian culture, Michael?" He asked the young man.

"Since the time I found out Darya was Russian. I love her so much. I want to be closer to her and learn more about her."

"Yes, but Darya, just like me and Andrew, grew up in the US and was raised the American way. There's not much left in us that's Russian, unfortunately. My mom is American, and has Swedish roots. My dad is, of course, pure Russian. My grandfather told me that his father, Alexander Ukhtomsky, upon migrating to the US with his family, told his son to keep the line of the family pure Russian. Back then, Russians in the States supported each other. My grandmother was a born Trubetsky princess. And my father fell in love with the neighbor, Ingrid, who became his wife. Although, mom died early.

Andrew felt sad listening to this conversation. It is then, in Russia, that he realized how much he and his daughter missed out on culturally. Before, he'd never thought of himself as a descendant of a Russian prince, a Russian. He did teach his daughter how to speak Russian, and spoke to her in Russian at home, but that was about it. He never read any Russian books, and never encouraged Jane to do so. She never read any of Dostoevsky, Tolstoy, Pushkin, Lermontov, Gogol, or Nekrasov. She never knew the troubles of Anna Karenina, Tatyana Larina, Sonya Marmeladova... Andrew blamed himself for that.

Before they could finish breakfast, he suddenly heard his daughter's voice.

"Hi Daddy. Bon appetite! "

Jane was standing behind him, and her warm arms wrapped around his neck. Andrew was both happy and surprised. Jane wasn't naturally sentimental, gentle, or proper. He turned around and kissed his daughter, and she didn't back away the way she used to, but smiled and whispered, "I love you, Dad."

Those words brought tears to Andrew's eyes. Darya and Nadya showed up next. The girls were talking about something.

"Don't you understand, Darya, that that will be very hard to do. As a rule, they were never buried in individual graves," Nadya tried to explain loudly.

She had a habit of raising her voice when arguing.

"But we have to try, Nadya. We have to!" Darya replied firmly and distinctively.

"What are you arguing about, sweetie?" Melinda gently asked her daughter.

"Mom, I suggested we find the burial sites of the Ukhtomsky princes and their descendants and honor them, but Nadya keeps saying it's too difficult to do."

Alex and Andrew immediately got up. They were excited.

"Yes, yes! That would be fantastic!" Alex exclaimed. "We owe it to them. We owe it to our family."

Andrew only nodded, agreeing with his brother.

"I'll back you up on that." Everyone heard Vladimir's excited voice. "I know what to do. Alena and I spoke yesterday. She promised to help. Let's wait for her. She should be here any minute."

Everyone agreed.

Vladimir decided to approach Darya, and was already walking towards her as he saw Michael also traveling in the same direction. Darya was looking at Michael. Her face lit up with a happy smile.

"Hey, how'd you sleep? Are you alright?" Michael asked, gently hugging her.

Vladimir saw the girl snuggle to Michael's chest, and an unpleasant feeling overtook him. He was about to turn around and get away, go somewhere to put himself together, but Darya's gentle voice stopped him.

"Hello, Vladimir. Let's talk while we wait for Alena."

She then said something to Michael quietly and walked towards Vladimir.

"Let's stand aside. I have something to tell you. And it's very important." Darya's voice was slightly hollow and tense.

"Alright, let's take a seat at that table over there, order some coffee, I haven't had any yet. And then we'll talk." Vladimir replied worriedly.

When they sat down and ordered a cup of American coffee each, Darya began to talk.

"Vladimir, I thought about us a lot, about how I feel about you. Back in the US, when you left, I missed you so much I was going crazy. One day, I dreamed about you, reading some sort of papers in your room late at night. And now I think I really saw you there. I was certain it was my love for you that helped me see you and sense you then. But what kind of love? I thought it was the kind of love between a man and a woman. I wanted to be with you. So I came here."

Darya stopped talking, trying to catch a breath. She was talking fast, afraid she would miss something.

"So what happened then? What changed, Darya?" Vladimir asked the girl in a raised voice that sounded painful.

She was silently looking at Vladimir, and he couldn't decode her look. He couldn't understand the point of it. Darya said quietly: "I don't know. Being here, in Russia, with you, I realized, that what I feel isn't love. Yes, I love you, but it's a different kind of love. How do I explain... I think I had this crush on you that fueled me as fire, spun my head like champagne, and drew me to you. You left, and I indulged in this feeling. And it made me come here. And when I did, I saw you... in a different light, although not right away, but gradually. Do you understand... There are many sides to love. It unites all three kinds of attraction - spiritual, intellectual, and physical."

Vladimir was about to say something to Darya, taking her hand. But she quite abruptly pulled her hand away and asked: "Please, don't interrupt me. It's hard as it is laying all this out. But we have to figure out our relationship. I want to be honest with you, and not lead you on... May I continue?"

Vladimir didn't reply, only nodded with his head down.

"So, now, I know for sure, that I love you, but there are only two kinds of attraction that I feel, the spiritual one, the one that creates the most loyal, most sincere friendship, and the intellectual one, the one that creates deep respect. But there is no third kind of attraction, the one that creates physical desire and passion. That's why my love for you is a sisterly love. Vladimir, I will be the most loving and devoted sister to you. ...So there it is!"

Darya took a deep breath, and then breathed out, looking at Vladimir.

Vladimir sat with his head down. He didn't want Darya to see his stare, painfully lost and unsatisfied. A few seconds later, he spoke in a trembling voice: "I understand... Yes, Darya, I get you... Tell me, what about Michael... How do you feel about Michael? I'm sorry for asking this. But I'd like to know..."

Vladimir raised his head and looked at Darya questioningly.

"You really want to know that? Alright. It's also important to me that I tell you about that, for you to understand me completely. As you know, Michael and I have been friends since we were kids. I can't remember a time when we were apart. I ... I always thought of him as not only my friend, but a brother. And he called me, and still does, his sister. Mom once told me Michael was in love with me. But I didn't read too much into that. So I came here. These two weeks were the first lengthy period of time I spent away from him, without seeing or talking to him. I realized I missed him, both physically and emotionally. And now I know, Michael is the only one who makes me feel peaceful, makes me feel good. I understand him, I feel secure around him, I feel cozy, I feel free. You know, Vladimir, there were many times I doubted you, and was jealous of Nadya, and the girls at that night club, remember? Love isn't like that. Doubt and jealousy are the qualities typical of a simple crush, when there's still no trust between the two. This is my firm opinion. With Michael, I don't have to pretend, I am myself, and I don't try to be better or worse for him to like me..."

"What are you guys talking about here?" Darya heard Michael's soft voice.

She got up from her chair, followed by Vladimir. She stood next to Michael, took his hand, and said distinctively, but gently: "Well, I was just telling Vladimir that I love you, and I want to spend the rest of my life with you."

Michael turned red in surprise, then turned pale, squeezed the girl's hand so much it hurt her, making her scream, then let go of her hand, put his hands on her face and began to tenderly kiss her eyes, cheeks, and lips.

"Thank you, thank you. I've been waiting for your confession for so long. I lost all hope. You know I've loved you for a long time, my sweet Darya, and every day, my love is stronger, more mature... I want to spend the rest of my life with you, too."

Darya clung to Michael's chest. He held her as if she was the most precious treasure in the world. Vladimir felt like a third wheel, and stepped away from his friends. He was hurt, but Michael remained his friend.

"I am that guy. I have to stand down. It's alright. Time will pass, and I know Darya and I will be good friends and siblings." Vladimir decided, and walked towards everyone else who were watching the scene of confession in awe.

Jane was talking to her father when everyone heard a pleasant male voice say, "Hello there."

Andrew noticed a happy spark in his daughter's eyes, and her entire face lit up, blushing. The reason for her excitement was a tall young man dressed nicely, who couldn't take his eyes off Jane.

"Daddy, meet Kostya. He's Vladimir's friend, and...a good friend of mine." She was full of excitement.

Andrew liked the kid.

"Daddy, do you mind if Kostya keeps us company during our trips?" Jane asked.

"Of course not. Join us, young man. Many places await us." A big and kind smile spread across his face.

"Hello, everyone." Alena's voice came from afar as she entered the cafe. She was holding a large folder of papers in her hands. "Did Vladimir tell you I used to do research on locating burial sites of Ukhtomsky Princes?" Alena asked everyone. "Well, this folder contains documents regarding that. Unfortunately, there are no burial sites of Alexei and Leonid Ukhtomskiy, or Polina Ukhtomskaya. They died in the dungeons of NKVD, and back then, they often buried bodies in the courtyard with no tombstones or any identification sings. They just dug up holes, dumped the bodies of those shot or deceased, and buried them."

"That's awful!" Melinda whispered.

"That is why I suggest you lay flowers near the building that used to serve as NKVD ground, where they passed away, or in its courtyard. Sofia and Olga, however, were buried at the same cemetery, Bogoslovskoye, and their graves are not too far from one another. Anastasia's grave is on Kazanskoye cemetery."

Alena's voice sounded impersonal and practical, completely irrelevant to the atmosphere of the room, with everyone expressing empathy and pain on their faces.

They decided they would visit the NKVD building that day, Anastasia's grave the day after, and Bogoslovskoye cemetery the day after that. Meanwhile, they would purchase plane tickets to Vorkuta, receive all the papers needed, and five days later travel to the north of Russia to honor the memory of Anna.

Two weeks later, Alex with Melinda, Darya with Michael and Jane were going to leave. Everyone came to say goodbye. Vladimir, Nedejda, Alena, Kostya, and even Alexandra, radiant in her wheelchair, accompanied by her loyal Liubasha. They went to a restaurant while waiting on their flight. Vladimir approached Darya.

"Darya, thank you for everything..."

The girl put her hand on his shoulder. "Don't, my brother. I understand everything. You are my favorite and...my only brother. It will be alright. Trust me."

He looked at Darya with gratitude and hugged his arms around her. "I love you. Be good."

"Daddy, please, just don't worry." Jane's voice sounded slightly anxious.

"What do mean?"

Jane and Kostya were standing together, holding hands.

"Andrew, I love your daughter very much," Kostya spoke slowly, but firmly.

"Daddy, I love Kostya very much, too," Jane uttered quickly.

Andrew stood in front of the two young people, not knowing what to tell them. He liked Kostya. Just the fact that he was Vladimir's friend meant a lot. Kostya was a serious young man, educated, kind, and smart. Darya changed, thanks to him. She became softer, friendlier. She looked radiant just standing next to him.

"Daddy, I decided I'm going to stay here, in Russia. I am Russian... Half- Russian, but still." Jane seemed anxious and was talking fast. It was clearly a tough decision for her.

Andrew's smile faded from his face. His face grew dark and his eyes saddened. He grabbed the back of his chair. Andrew would never expect such a decision from his eccentric daughter.

"Andrew, don't worry. Your Jane is a very smart, very decisive girl, with a firm character. I will always be with her, I won't let anything happen to her. Trust me." Kostya's voice was persuasive, and Andrew felt shaken up.

He looked at his daughter, who was hopeful and waiting for her father's decision. Memories of his daughter's childhood, adolescence, and early youth flashed before his eyes. She's grown up so much during these weeks here, in Russia. This country makes her better, and now she's found a deserving young man. Back home, in the States, she didn't even have any close friends. Her nights out at clubs, smoking weed every now and then, absence, or maybe lack of desire or inability to find a decent partner, made Jane's behavior intolerable. She was rude, frivolous, mean. But what if it helped her deal with her vulnerable and tender heart? And here, she doesn't pretend, she is herself. She feels good here. After all, this ball we call Earth isn't all that big.

Andrew held his daughter, kissed her and asked: "So what am I going to tell mom?"

Jane smiled widely: "Thank you Daddy. Tell Mom I love her very much, and I will miss you and her."

Andrew looked into Kostya's eyes with seriousness and spoke imperatively: "Take care of her, Kostya. I trust you, and I believe in you. You're worth each other. I hope to expect a wedding invitation soon."

Young man shook Andrew's hand energetically and gave him a hug: "Yes, yes. Of course. Thank you. I won't let you down. Jane is my first, and I'm sure, last love. I will take care of her."

"I feel so enriched. I've got a second wind. It's like destiny gave me a new life," Alexanda told his son with tears of joy in her eyes, "Vladimir, you told me, there's a chance I can have the operation?"

"Mom, you agree? But you were against it!" Vladimir exclaimed.

"I must be healthy, my son. I still need to go to America for Darya's wedding. Even just to see Alex and Melinda. And how about Jane and Kostya's wedding? And then you will get married. I have to take care of my grandchildren." Alexandra sounded convinced and excited.

Nadezhda smiled as she watched. She always loved Alexandra Petrovna. Nadya also felt an unusual surge of energy, and a voice inside her whispered: "It's time to act. It will all work out for you."

She smiled to her inner voice and approached Vladimir decisively. "Vladimir, when are you going to the States?"

"My vacation ends in two weeks. I've already ordered the tickets." The young man's voice was slightly dreamful.

"I'm going with you too." Nadezhda said decidedly.

Vladimir looked at the girl questioningly.

"I convinced my agency to send me on a business trip to the States to make a series of reports and articles about the lives of Russians in America. Besides, we have to find your grandfather, David Stewart, don't we?"

Оглавление